MY SISTER'S BABY

LOUISE GUY

Boldwood

First published in Great Britain in 2024 by Boldwood Books Ltd.

Copyright © Louise Guy, 2024

Cover Design by Becky Glibbery

Cover Illustration: Shutterstock / iStock

A CIP catalogue record for this book is available from the British Library.

Paperback ISBN 978-1-83533-132-3

Large Print ISBN 978-1-83533-128-6

Hardback ISBN 978-1-83533-127-9

Ebook ISBN 978-1-83533-125-5

Kindle ISBN 978-1-83533-126-2

Audio CD ISBN 978-1-83533-133-0

MP3 CD ISBN 978-1-83533-130-9

Digital audio download ISBN 978-1-83533-124-8

Boldwood Books Ltd
23 Bowerdean Street
London SW6 3TN
www.boldwoodbooks.com

In loving memory of Brian Guy
20/10/1964 – 25/07/2023,
and to the selfless organ donor who gifted Brian an additional 15 years and
25 days.

1

It's all my fault. Toni's words played over in Olivia Montgomery's mind as the aircraft turned and lined up, ready for its final approach to Melbourne airport. 'She's not coping', Toni had said, her voice shaky when they'd spoken earlier that morning. 'Liv, I don't know what to do.'

Liv had been enjoying a slice of homemade orange and almond cake with her eighty-seven-year-old neighbour, Barb, when her older sister had called. She'd instantly sprung into action after hearing the panic in Toni's voice. 'Mum's lost it, Liv. She's drugged up to the eyeballs and not getting out of bed. The house is a wreck, and Mandy looks and smells like she hasn't showered in weeks. I'm so sorry. It's all my fault.'

Toni hadn't needed to say any more. Liv had apologised to Barb, hurried back to her apartment to pack a bag and, just a few short hours later, raced down the main south-facing runway at Sydney airport en route to Melbourne. She had no idea why Toni thought the situation at their childhood home was her fault, but she imagined she was soon to find out.

Once the plane came to a stop at the gate, Liv took her bag from the overhead locker, glad to be able to bypass the wait at the baggage claim, and within a few minutes, slid into the back of a taxi. She sent Toni a text to let her know she'd arrived and would meet her at their mother's Forest Hill home.

Nerves rumbled in the pit of her stomach. Her quick, take-action approach had seemed appropriate as she was doing it, but now the reality of being here, knowing she needed to deal with whatever she was about to walk in on, had her feeling apprehensive.

Forty-five minutes later, the taxi pulled up outside the aging brick house. The front garden was overgrown and a line of black plastic garbage bags were piled on top of each other next to the green wheelie bin. Liv paid the driver, scooped up her bag from the passenger seat and pushed open the door. It looked like there was going to be more to do here than sorting out her mother and Mandy. She had a feeling that if her father could see his neglected garden, he'd be doing backflips in his grave right about now.

* * *

Toni pulled up in front of her mother's house just as a yellow taxi drew away from the kerb. She gave a gentle push on her Lexus's horn and waved when Liv turned to look. Her sister was standing, bag in hand, staring at the garden. Toni could only imagine what was going through her mind.

In the six weeks since their father's funeral, the garden had gone to rack and ruin. So had the inside of the house. It had been unexpected when she'd visited her mother earlier that morning to discover how badly everything had been let go. The guilt that had sat with her since her discovery continued to nag at her. She should have been visiting regularly, but she'd found it too difficult to step inside the family home knowing their father was gone. And then there was their younger sister, Mandy, who, as much as Toni knew she shouldn't, she'd always struggled with. Even to her own ears, they were weak excuses.

The reality was that she'd hardly been able to get out of bed herself, and it had nothing to do with her father's passing or her intellectually challenged younger sister. She blinked away tears. She *would not* allow herself to go there.

She pushed open the car door and hurried across to where Liv stood waiting for her. Liv dropped her bag, opened her arms and Toni gratefully stepped into them.

'How are you?' Liv asked as they pulled away.

Toni smiled. It was like Liv to know she'd be falling apart and be concerned. 'I'm okay. Feeling guilty that I didn't know this was going on.'

'Neither did I,' Liv said.

'Yes, but you live eight hundred kilometres away, whereas I live thirty minutes up the road. I've got no excuse.' None that she was planning to burden Liv with.

'Come on.' Liv placed a hand on Toni's back and guided her towards the front walkway. 'Let's go inside. You don't need to have an excuse. We're all grieving and trying to cope. Mum and Mandy aren't your sole responsibility.'

Toni sighed. 'I'd like to believe you. But we both know it's not true. Dad would be pretty upset with me.'

'If it's any consolation, I'm pretty upset with *him*. Who enters a triathlon at sixty-seven, for goodness' sake? He should have at least had a physical first. They would have seen he had heart issues if he had and stopped him from competing. All he achieved was adding himself to the stats that most triathlon deaths happen during the swim leg. Now, let's head inside and see what we're dealing with.'

* * *

Liv couldn't help but wrinkle her nose as they let themselves in through the front door. They'd knocked, but neither their mother nor Mandy appeared.

'Gah, what's that smell?' She covered her nose with her hand and did her best to breathe through her mouth. 'It's like something died in here.'

'It smelt a lot worse earlier,' Toni said. 'There were literally piles of food rubbish on the kitchen bench and by the bin.'

'You're kidding? That doesn't sound like Mum.'

'From what I could get out of Mandy, I don't think Mum's left her bedroom for weeks, so Mandy's been in charge of the kitchen. The fridge, freezer and cupboards are almost empty. But in typical Mandy style, she has no concept of how to clean up after herself. The entire house is a mess,' she added. 'I don't think the bathrooms have been cleaned since Dad died.'

'Mandy?' Liv called in the direction of the staircase. 'Are you home?'

'She'll be in her room watching *Titanic* or Netflix,' Toni said, 'and Mum's probably asleep.'

Liv nodded and made her way towards the stairs. The energy in the house in no way resembled the family home they'd grown up in. She could understand Toni's reluctance to visit, knowing their father's pervasive presence wouldn't be there, but she had to admit, she was horrified by the complete and utter chaos the house was in. Her mother was usually obsessive when it came to cleanliness. Could she really not have come downstairs for weeks? Was Mandy feeding her?

She reached the landing and followed the hallway to her mother's room. She knocked gently before pushing the door open. The smell wasn't so bad in here. The window was wide open, and her mother's tiny frame was curled up underneath the bed covers, an open bottle of pills next to her on the bedside table.

'Mum?'

The shape in the bed didn't move. Liv walked over to the bedside table and picked up the bottle. Temazepam: prescription sleeping pills.

She shook her mother gently by the shoulder. It took a few goes, but eventually Sara opened her eyes.

'Liv?'

Liv nodded and reached down to hug her mother. 'Toni rang me. She's worried about you.'

'Toni? I haven't seen her in weeks.'

'She was here this morning,' Liv said. She hesitated, then continued. 'Mum, the place is a pigsty. It reeks of rotten food downstairs and there's rubbish everywhere. When did you last leave your room?'

Sara pulled the covers up to her chin. 'What's the point? I want to go to sleep and never wake up.'

Liv picked up the bottle of pills and shook it. It was about a third empty. 'Really? Should I be getting rid of these?'

Her mother sighed. 'I would never do that to you girls. Mandy needs me. I know that, but I'm exhausted and devastated.' A tear escaped the corner of her eye. 'It's hard, Liv. Really hard. Your dad always made it easier. He took everything in his stride. Said we'd been blessed with our lives. That Mandy was a miracle, and we should be thankful.'

Toni cleared her throat from the doorway. 'Hi, Mum.'

Sara groaned and pulled the covers over her head. 'Your father would want to kill me right now. Such an insensitive comment. I'm sorry.'

Toni crossed the room and sat on the corner of her mother's bed. 'There's no need to apologise. Yes, I want a baby. I'm desperate to be pregnant, but I doubt I'd cope with a Mandy. And,' she added, 'I know I'm not supposed to say this, but it's true; Mandy's hard work.'

Sara pulled the covers off her face. 'How did your dad make it look so easy?'

Liv laughed. 'Because he gave instructions on how we should do things and then he'd go and enjoy a beer in his man cave. That's how. You let him get away with far too much. And he didn't make it look all *that* easy. He was the one who suggested you put her on the waiting list at that independent living place. It wasn't you who did that.'

'From what Dad told me,' Toni said, 'you didn't even want her moving into independent living.'

'She's not ready,' Sara said. 'The mess you say is downstairs proves that.'

'She'll learn once she's there,' Toni said. 'Anyway, right now, that's not our biggest concern. You are. We need to get you off the pills and back into the land of the living.'

'Yes.' Liv held out her hand. 'Let's start with a shower and fresh clothes. I'll strip the bed while you're doing that and then we'll open a bottle of wine and have a chat.'

'Livvy!'

The three women turned to the door where Mandy stood, her hair sticky and matted in places, her white t-shirt smeared with something orange and a brown smudge covering most of her left cheek.

Sara blinked as she took in her youngest daughter's appearance and pulled herself up to sitting. 'Okay, I'll go and shower. If anything's going to get me moving, it's seeing that. Child protection will be knocking on the door any minute.'

Liv laughed. 'Mandy's thirty. I'm not sure she's child protection's responsibility any more.'

'Maybe not, but you're both right. It's time to put a stop to this.'

Mandy walked towards Liv, her arms outstretched as Sara slipped out of bed and made her way into the ensuite.

Liv almost gagged as she accepted Mandy's hug, glad she'd brought a few changes of clothes as her current outfit would need to go straight into the wash.

'You smell like a fertiliser factory in a heatwave,' Toni said, squeezing her nose with her fingers. Liv met her gaze over Mandy's head, a smile playing on her lips as tears glistened in Toni's eyes. It had been one of their father's famous descriptions and right at this moment, as much as Toni's comment made her smile, his loss hit her harder than she'd ever imagined.

2

It took two hours, but Toni could only marvel at Liv's organisational skills as they sat outside in the late-afternoon sunshine with a glass of wine in hand.

'Thank you,' she said while it was just the two of them. Sara had gone inside with Mandy to help her find a copy of her favourite *Titanic* special edition DVD. Liv had offered to help, but Sara had refused, insisting she and Toni had done too much already.

'No problem,' Liv responded now. 'I'm glad you called me, as something needs to change. Mum's looking good right at this second, but I'm guessing the moment we leave, it will all go downhill again.'

After shooing both their mother and Mandy to have showers and change their clothes, Liv had handed Toni a shopping list and sent her off to the supermarket while she tackled the cleaning. By the time Toni returned laden with shopping bags, Liv had tidied each room and changed the bed linen, leaving them the jobs of wiping the surfaces, vacuuming, and cleaning the bathrooms. She'd instructed Mandy to clean her room and had placed her mother outside in a comfortable chair with a strong cup of tea and a magazine. 'You relax, and we'll chat once everything's back to how it should be.'

'The garden's next,' Liv said as Toni sipped her wine. 'I'll get up early tomorrow and mow the lawn and do the edges. Do you think your lovely husband would come and give me a hand?'

Toni shook her head. 'Joel's not back until Monday. He's in London. The airline has him rostered on quite a lot this month. I'll come back and help, though.'

Liv nodded, and her forehead creased, as it did when she was thinking. 'I have to go back to Sydney on Monday, so I can't do a whole lot more to help here. I have a client booked for a portrait shoot on Tuesday.'

'You've done heaps already,' Toni said. 'I really appreciate you coming down. I don't know why I'm so useless when it comes to Mum and Mandy. If it was a work project, I'd have no problem at all.' And it was true. Toni oversaw a team of twelve, had secured many of her advertising agency's top clients and was respected in the industry by her peers. But when it came to family life, just the thought of it turned her legs to jelly and made her want to run a mile.

Liv reached across and squeezed Toni's hand. 'Don't beat yourself up about it.' She gave a little laugh. 'It's easy for me to turn up here for forty-eight hours, clean up and disappear as quickly. I left Melbourne the minute I finished uni and could get away from here and I've never regretted it.'

Toni's eyes widened. 'You always said it was where the opportunities for your photography were. That the national parks and beaches provided the backdrops Melbourne couldn't compete with.'

'That's what Dad wanted to hear. If I'd said I wanted to get away from watching Mum put Mandy first all the time, I wouldn't have been too popular.'

Toni gave a wry laugh. 'No, you'd have been put in the bad sister category with me.'

'What bad sister category?'

The two women swivelled in their seats as their mother approached the outdoor setting.

'Oh nothing,' Liv said. 'Chatting about old times.' She held up the bottle of wine. 'Should you be drinking this with all the pills you've been taking?'

Sara shrugged, pulled out a chair from the table and sat. 'Probably not, but I'll have half a glass.' She sighed. 'I really am sorry you both walked into this chaos. I'll pull myself together, I promise.'

'It's understandable, Mum,' Liv said. 'Looking after Mandy, on top of grieving for Dad, can't be easy. Actually... now I think about it, why don't I take her back to Sydney with me for a few weeks and give you some time to yourself?'

Tears slid down Sara's cheeks. 'You'd do that?'

Guilt stabbed at Toni. There was no way she'd be offering to take Mandy for a night, let alone a few weeks. Liv, however, was always more tolerant of their sister and more understanding. She wished she could rise above her childhood hurts and be the same.

'I will, on one condition.'

'Anything,' Sara said. 'In all honesty, I'd do anything right now to have some time to myself.'

Toni stared at her mother. She couldn't recall a time in her life that her mother had suggested she needed a break from Mandy or the family, and she couldn't remember a time that she'd had one. Was it because of the death of their father, or was it something she'd been considering for a long time?

'I want you to check in with Toni and me every day. A call to each of us, Zoom or FaceTime, so we can see what you look like and check that you're out of bed and not a zombie on pills.'

'I'll drop in,' Toni said.

'Not every day,' Sara said. 'I can't ask you to do that. You work such long hours.'

'Every few days then. We're worried about you, Mum. I think you need to see a counsellor or psychologist. Someone who deals with grief.'

Sara put her wine glass down. 'I appreciate it. I really do. But I'll be fine. I just need a break.'

'You need more than that,' Liv said. 'Before he died, you know Dad wanted Mandy to move into independent living. He said he'd submitted an application and Mandy was on the waiting list at that place, Wattle something?'

Sara nodded. 'Wattle House. It's in Camberwell. Your dad was keen for her to move out, but the idea of abandoning her like that has never sat right with me.'

'Abandoning her?' Liv said. 'It's not like you'd never see her again.'

Sara sighed. 'I know, but I'd hate for Mandy to think she wasn't wanted, wasn't loved.'

Liv reached for her mother's hand and squeezed it. 'Mum, do you think this is your own hurt clouding your judgement?'

Toni stared at her sister. Liv was so much more intuitive than she was. She'd never have considered her mother being adopted as something that might impact her decisions around Mandy.

'Probably,' Sara admitted. 'As you know, my mother dumped me on a doorstep after I was born and never made contact. It's hard to shake that feeling of not being wanted.'

Liv nodded. 'The difference with Mandy is she *is* wanted. We'll all make sure she knows how loved she is. She won't be questioning who her family are or whether she's loved.'

'While that may all be true,' Sara said, 'I'm still not sure she's ready.'

'Mum,' Toni adopted her gentlest tone, 'she's never going to be ready. If she moves in there, she'll learn *how* to become independent. Then you can visit her and have her home for dinner every now and then but not be tied down by her.'

Sara bristled. 'I've never considered myself tied down.'

'I didn't mean to upset you. But she's thirty. You and Dad had plans to do your own thing once we were all adults, didn't you? To move on to the next stage of life and enjoy yourselves? Instead, it's like you're stuck in a time warp where you're still doing all the things for Mandy you used to do when she was a kid.' Heat flooded Toni's cheeks. As gentle as she was trying to be, even she could hear the bitterness tainting her words.

'How about I try and get her doing a few more things on her own in Sydney,' Liv said, 'and that way, it won't be such an upheaval. I'll ring Wattle House on Monday and see where she is on the waiting list. I think it's time, Mum. Don't forget, one of the reasons Dad wanted her to go now was so that if something happened to the two of you, she wouldn't be dealing with a huge change at the same time and have to adapt to independent living without you around. This way, you'll still be here to support her and the change won't be as confronting. And while I'm happy to have her for a few weeks, I think I speak for both Toni and myself when I say that if something happened to you, I couldn't put my hand up to look after Mandy full time.'

Toni nodded in agreement. It was a relief to know she wasn't alone in her feelings towards their younger sister.

Sara took a small sip from her glass and sighed. 'I know you're right, as was your father. It's a big step for both of us. When we tried to discuss it with Mandy before, she went crazy. Crying and screaming and then sat on her bed with that damned doll of hers saying "no" over and over again.'

Toni covered her mouth and did her best to turn her laughter into a cough. It was the first time she'd heard her mother describe the doll in the way Toni herself thought of it. That *damned doll* had been with Mandy for as long as she could remember, and as kids, they always had to make room for Baby, as it had been named. Baby sat at the dinner table, in the back seat of the car and everywhere Mandy went. Her mother had always told them to go along with it and Toni had to admit she'd been tempted to throw Baby in the rubbish bin on more than one occasion. She'd hated that the doll seemed to get more attention from her parents than she did.

'I'll talk to Mandy about Wattle House,' Liv said, breaking into Toni's thoughts. 'We'll talk about it in Sydney. Don't worry. I'll make sure she's excited about it.'

Sara put her wine glass down and stood. 'I should go and tell her about Sydney so she can prepare for the journey and being in a new place.'

Liv placed her hand on her mother's arm. 'No, stay and enjoy your wine and talk to us. Stop putting her first all the time, Mum. She's an adult, not a little kid any more. We can tell her tomorrow. I'll take her out for a few hours and have a fun time with her. She'll still have twenty-four hours to get used to the idea and pack before we need to leave on Monday.'

Sara hesitated. 'She's the equivalent of about a twelve-year-old, Liv. Intellectually, she's not an adult, and you know how much she hates surprises. It's better to give her as much warning as possible.'

'Twenty-four hours' notice is hardly a surprise,' Liv said. 'And anyway, both Toni and I were independent by the time we were twelve. We made our own school lunches, caught the bus to school and walked to basketball practice in the afternoons.'

Sara sat down slowly. 'Okay, maybe she's even younger than that then. I don't know, eight?'

'Give her a chance, Mum,' Liv said. 'I think with some instruction, she's capable of a lot more than you give her credit for.'

Toni stared at her sister. Liv had openly admitted that she'd left Melbourne to get away from Mandy, and now she was suggesting her problems weren't actually too bad.

Liv caught her gaze and gave a tiny shrug and a slight nod in the direction of their mother. Guilt resurfaced in Toni. Liv was doing this for their mother. She was going to put up with Mandy and her difficulties to give Sara a break. It was a completely selfless act which added another layer to Toni's guilt. Usually, she'd be the first to jump to help someone but when it came to Mandy, she couldn't make herself do it.

Other than the first few months of Mandy's life, when her parents had brought the new baby home and both Liv and Toni had been fascinated with their sister's development, she'd resented her. It wasn't Mandy's fault of course; contracting meningitis at three months had resulted in a lengthy hospital stay and brain damage which caused long-term intellectual disability. When her parents returned home from the hospital with Mandy, Toni had been so excited to see them and to spend time with her baby sister, but her parents had kept Mandy away from her and Liv, saying she couldn't afford to get ill again. They then seemed to spend every minute talking about, and worrying about, Mandy.

Toni would never forget the day when she'd come home excited from school with an invitation to Alexa Jacobson's eighth birthday party. Alexa was the most popular girl in the third grade and had only invited four girls to a horse-riding day and sleep over, and Toni was one of them. She'd proudly put the invitation on the fridge only to be devastated the night before the party to overhear her parents talking. 'We'll have to tell Toni she can't go,' her father had said. 'This weekend is too important for us and Mandy. It's an opportunity to meet other families and develop a support network. We're lucky to be being given so much help; we can't say no to it.'

'Do you think it's essential Toni comes?' her mother had asked.

'We all need to be there,' her father replied, 'to show that we're a family and we're here to support Mandy.'

What about me? Toni had wanted to cry out. *What about supporting me?*

'I think she'll be pretty upset.'

'Honestly, Sara, that's the least of our concerns. This is all so overwhelming, and I don't have the capacity to care about Toni's feelings right now. There'll be other parties, parties that Mandy will never get to enjoy.'

It was at that point that Toni's resentment started, and with each year that passed, and she found Mandy being prioritised over her, it increased. Sometimes it was related to finances when due to Mandy's expenses, the family couldn't afford extras for her and Liv, but if she was honest, it was the amount of attention Mandy was given that hurt the most. Now that Toni was an adult, she could see the situation from an objective point of view, but as much as her rational mind knew that Mandy had required more attention from her parents and more financial assistance than either Liv or herself, it didn't make it any easier when you'd been made to feel less important all of your life. It was ironic to have heard her mother admitting that her own experience with abandonment was affecting her decisions with Mandy, yet she'd never realised how abandoned Toni had felt throughout her childhood. Mandy had become a living reminder of the happy childhood she and Liv were deprived of and she couldn't imagine ever being able to view her sister without the shadow of that painful past.

3

Toni and Liv found themselves alone in the family room later that night once their mother had gone to bed and Mandy had disappeared to watch *Titanic* in her room. Her mother had hardly touched the pasta Toni made.

'You're going to need to watch her,' Liv said, nursing a cup of chamomile tea. 'Make sure when you drop in to see her that she's eating. She's fading away.'

Toni nodded. 'Hopefully, getting Mandy out of her hair will make a difference. Are you sure you're up to having her?'

'She'll be fine.'

Toni raised an eyebrow. 'Really? What about work? You can't leave her at home by herself all day.'

Liv nodded. 'That thought crossed my mind after I made the suggestion. She does stay home alone sometimes though, doesn't she?'

'I think so, but I'm not sure how she'd be in a strange place. I guess she'll watch *Titanic* on loop. What is it with that movie and her? I never understood the obsession.'

'Jack.'

'Who's Jack?'

'You know, the main character played by Leonardo DiCaprio. Mandy always loved him. Said he was the brother she always wanted.'

'Really? She wanted a brother?'

Liv stared at her. 'You never heard her say how she would have preferred a brother to two sisters?'

'She said that?'

Liv nodded. 'As much as she annoyed us growing up, I guess it wasn't a one-way deal. Mandy was very aware of the fact that we weren't exactly delighted with how much time and attention she took up.'

Toni fell silent. She knew how unsupportive she'd been of Mandy over their lifetime, she just hadn't realised that Mandy had felt the impact of her behaviour.

'Anyway,' Liv continued. 'You're right that I can't leave her at home every day. She can come with me to some jobs, and maybe my neighbour, Barb, will be able to keep an eye on her on the days that she can't. Barb gets lonely, so she might enjoy the company.'

Toni nodded. 'Hopefully she's not too much for her.'

'Fingers crossed. But there's no need for you to worry about it. I'll work it out.'

Toni forced a smile. She wasn't sure she was worried so much as feeling guilty.

'I know that look,' Liv added. 'None of this is your fault.'

'I think it is,' Toni said. 'Karma's playing a dirty trick on me.'

'Karma?'

Toni nodded and gripped her tea cup tighter. She hadn't planned to tell Liv, but she owed her an explanation.

'Ton?'

Toni's eyes filled with tears as she forced herself to meet Liv's gaze.

'You're scaring me. Is it you and Joel?'

Toni shook her head, her hand instinctively moving to rest on her stomach. Liv's eyes followed her hand and understanding flooded her face.

'Oh Ton, not again?'

Toni nodded. 'Three weeks after the funeral. It's part of the reason I haven't come around here. I've hardly been able to function.'

Liv moved next to her on the couch and put an arm around her sister. 'I'm so sorry.'

Toni closed her eyes as her head rested on Liv's shoulder. While she'd always had issues to deal with when it came to Mandy, with Liv, it was the exact opposite. She was the one person she knew she could call at any time, with any problem, and she'd always have her back. As they'd grown older, it was as if Liv was the big sister, not Toni. Right now, the comfort Liv provided was exactly what she needed. Joel's absence had been badly timed. While he'd been home when it happened, and for the two weeks that followed, she was pretty sure going back to work and flying to the other side of the world was his way of coping. She knew her mood swings and despair were hard for him to deal with.

Liv pulled back gently. 'Why would you think losing the baby was karma?'

Toni took a deep breath and moved away from Liv. 'Because of something I said to Dad.'

'Dad? He knew?'

Toni nodded. 'I'm not sure whether I should tell you this or not, but Dad helped Joel and me pay for the IVF treatments, and I promised to let him know as soon as I was pregnant.'

'Did Mum know?'

'No. Dad didn't want her getting excited and then being disappointed if the treatment didn't work. It was also a lot of money, and I think he wanted to keep that to himself. It was our secret. I found out a few days before the triathlon that I was pregnant, and I told him.' She smiled at the memory. 'He was so excited. He kept going on about how he'd be the best grandfather and that he had his fingers crossed it might be a boy, even though he'd love a girl just as much.'

'Okay, so what did you say that caused karma to take the baby from you?'

'When I told Dad, he could hardly sit still. He said that having a family was the best thing he'd ever done. That having three daughters was a blessing and to think that he would become a grandfather was amazing.'

'That sounds like Dad.'

A tear rolled down Toni's cheek. 'I said, "What about Mandy? Surely, you'd want to change that?" He shook his head and said he'd learned more from Mandy than from any of us. That she'd taught him tolerance, patience and understanding and that he wouldn't change anything about her.' Liv appeared to be holding her breath, waiting to hear what Toni said next. Toni wiped her eyes. 'I didn't say this out loud, but my immediate thought was *I'd kill myself before having a daughter like Mandy.*'

Liv gasped.

'See,' Toni said. 'I told you it was bad.'

'But you didn't say it,' Liv said, 'so the words didn't hurt anyone.'

'No, I didn't say it out loud, but I meant it, Liv, I really meant it.' Her cheeks heated. 'I'm not sure I'd actually kill myself, but I wouldn't want to raise a baby like Mandy. We saw how hard it was when we were kids. If I had a Mandy, then I couldn't have any more children. I couldn't do that to them.' She squeezed her eyes shut and did her best to stop the cascade of tears that were threatening to fall. She opened them and met Liv's gaze. 'That's why I said it was karma. My thoughts are terrible, un-Christian, and awful and I've been punished for them. As I should be.'

Liv squeezed her sister's arm. 'I don't think it works like that, and as we aren't religious, the un-Christian bit probably doesn't mean much. What did the doctor say? Did they give you an explanation?'

Ton rolled her eyes. 'It was likely caused by a *random genetic abnormality.* That's all they ever say.' She gave a wry laugh. 'Listen to me. I'm an expert in the one thing no one wants to be an expert in.'

'You don't think...' Liv hesitated; it was something she'd wondered with each miscarriage Toni had had, but never dared to voice.

'Think what?'

'I'm almost scared to say it,' Liv admitted. 'But do you think donating your kidney impacted your fertility?'

Toni snorted. 'Of course not, why would you even think that?'

'It was a pretty major operation and you're functioning with one kidney.'

'So are you.'

'Yes, but I'm not trying to get pregnant and have no plans to ever try. You know how I feel about babies and kids. I adore them at a distance and will love any nephews or nieces, of course.'

'It won't be the issue, Liv. They told us that at the time, remember?'

'Did they? I have no recollection.'

'You were coping with a lot, so I'm not surprised.' Toni would never forget receiving the phone call from her mother saying Liv had been involved in a high-impact car accident. Her best friend had been driving and was killed instantly, and for Liv, the compression of being jammed between the front dashboard and the seat had caused acute kidney failure. Toni had been devastated to see her sister so distraught, trying to come to terms not only with the loss of her friend, but at the same time dealing with an uncertain future. Toni would have done anything to trade places with Liv, but as that wasn't an option, she did the next best thing and offered her kidney.

'Test me,' she'd insisted after both of their parents had proven not to be a match. 'That way, we can just get on with it. I don't need it, do I?'

The doctors had assured her that no, she could live a perfectly normal life with one kidney, including having children if she chose, and that's all the information she'd needed. In all honesty, even if there had been major risks, she would have gone ahead. She couldn't imagine her life without Liv in it. Her sister was the person she'd turned to since they were young children. It didn't matter how big or how trivial her problem might be, she knew Liv would listen and provide advice or comfort if she could. She'd been tested, and within two weeks of the confirmation of a positive match, had undergone major surgery.

'There were no predicted issues around fertility,' Toni continued now. 'There could have been complications later in the pregnancy around pre-eclampsia and gestational diabetes, but both would have been monitored and treated if I ever got that far.' Tears filled her eyes. 'But in six positive pregnancies, I've never moved past twelve weeks.'

Liv put an arm around her shoulder and drew her to her. 'I'm sorry, Ton, really, I am. I wish there was something I could do to help.'

'Maybe you should have a baby for me.' The words left Toni's lips before she could stop them.

Liv pulled back. 'What?'

Toni sighed. 'Don't worry. I'd never actually ask that of you. I'm getting desperate, that's all. I'm getting too old to try again, and I think Joel's had enough. He was talking about fostering kids, but I don't want to do that.'

'Why not?'

Toni couldn't help but notice the relief on Liv's face when she assumed

Toni had been joking about having a baby for her. The thing was, she wasn't really joking. If Liv had looked less horrified and discussed it as an option, she would have liked to explore it. It wasn't unheard of, using a sister's egg and her uterus to grow your baby. But it was a huge ask and not one that Toni could see herself pushing. The most likely scenario would be Liv saying no and it driving a wedge between them.

'Fostering's not for me,' Toni said. 'It's a bit like the Mandy scenario and me saying I don't want it. A lot of kids in foster care have been through a hard time. They've seen and experienced things they shouldn't have and are damaged. I don't want to deal with any of that, and I know how awful it sounds, but I don't.' She hesitated before dropping her head into her hands. 'What's wrong with me? The words come out of my mouth and as much as I don't want them to be true, or be from me, they are. I just couldn't do it.'

'Even if you have your own baby, it probably won't be perfect,' Liv said gently. 'He or she will have their own personality and probably push your buttons as they grow older. And you can't guarantee they'll be 100 per cent healthy.'

'I know all of that, and it's obviously a risk I'd take if I could carry a pregnancy through to term. If there's something wrong with the baby, then I'd deal with it, but I don't want to take on a kid that already has problems.' She sighed. 'See, and karma is punishing me for thinking like that too. I bet other people aren't this awful and selfish.'

Liv squeezed her arm. 'You're being honest, and I'm sure you're not the only person to think like that. Given a choice, I'm sure most people would wish for a healthy baby. Raising a kid is a huge responsibility without adding complications. You've been unlucky, nothing more, and I'm sorry.'

Toni forced a smile, hoping with all her heart that Liv was right. That she was unlucky rather than being punished.

* * *

Monday morning arrived quickly, and after saying farewell to their mother and having her promise she'd remain in daily contact, Toni had driven Liv and an excited Mandy to the airport.

Liv couldn't help but notice Toni making an extra effort with Mandy that morning, which she was grateful for as the weekend had revealed more than Liv had anticipated, and she found herself deep in thought. After their discussion about the miscarriage and Toni's fears about raising an intellectually challenged child, Liv had lain in bed on both Saturday and Sunday nights thinking about their childhoods. It hadn't been easy with Mandy around, but Liv hadn't understood how affected Toni had been. While Liv had been quick to move out of home to distance herself from the Mandy factor, she hadn't resented Mandy to the extent Toni had. Mandy was who she was. While childlike and different from her and Toni, she was loving and sweet most of the time. She had her quirky behaviours and at times, obsessions, but overall she lived a simple life. At most, Liv had pitied her at times, because she didn't have what Liv considered a normal life and probably never would. But that morning, Toni had engaged Mandy in conversation about Sydney and had even hugged her and told her she'd miss her when they said their goodbyes.

Mandy's eyes filled with tears when she waved goodbye as Toni drove away from the drop-off zone. 'Toni's going to miss me,' she'd said with childlike wonder in her voice before turning to Liv. 'Do you think she loves me?'

'Definitely,' Liv had said. Although she had to admit, Toni's words had surprised her too. She imagined that opening up to Liv about her guilt over her awful thoughts about Mandy was the catalyst for her effort. 'Toni's going through a tough time, so occasionally she might seem a bit uninterested. She and Joel are desperate to have a baby.'

'Then they should,' Mandy said, slipping the backpack off her back and taking her doll from it. She held the old, worn-looking doll up for Liv. 'I have Baby, and they should get one too. Baby is no trouble.'

Liv smiled. 'It's a little more complicated. Toni doesn't seem to be able to get pregnant, and they want a baby that breathes and eats and cries and grows. A little different from your lovely Baby. It makes Toni sad at times that she can't have one.'

Mandy nodded. 'I would be sad without Baby. Poor Toni.' Mandy looked downcast for about ten seconds, but then her eyes lit up as they walked into the airport terminal, and Toni's issues were replaced with the adventure unfolding before her.

Now, as the plane pushed away from the gate, Liv closed her eyes and leaned back in her seat. She wasn't sure why her mother had been worried about Mandy needing to adjust to the idea of travelling back to Sydney with her. She'd taken Mandy out for lunch and a visit to St Kilda the previous day to tell her the news, and she'd been nothing but excited. 'I can't wait, Livvy. I've never been to Sydney. And I think Mum might get mad with me if I stay at home with her.'

'She wouldn't be mad, Mandy. Mum only ever wants the best for you. You know that. She's just struggling since Dad died. It's hard on her.'

'And me too,' Mandy said, the excitement she'd shown only moments earlier fading. 'I miss him every day.'

Liv had reached across the table and squeezed her hand. 'We all do, Hon.'

The trip had left Liv both physically and mentally exhausted. It might have been a flying visit, but the house had been returned to an acceptable level of cleanliness, and the garden was looking neater after they'd spent a few hours pulling weeds, cutting back plants and mowing the lawns. Toni promised she'd get Joel to come around once a fortnight and see if anything needed attention in the garden. She'd also promised Liv she'd drop in on a regular basis and check that their mother was coping and would organise a referral for Sara to see a psychologist. Now, as the plane taxied down the runway and Mandy let out an excited squeal, she wondered what she'd let herself in for. It was a nice idea to give her mother a break, but in reality, Mandy was demanding and, at times, became annoying. And on top of that, Liv had received an unexpected shock the previous day. One she wasn't ready to deal with yet. She'd get back to Sydney and think through her options before making any decisions.

'Liv?'

Liv groaned as Mandy elbowed her in the ribs. She opened her eyes as she rubbed her side. 'Be careful, okay?'

'Will I come to work with you in Sydney? I can't stay at home alone.'

'We'll work something out.'

'I need to know now, or I can't go to Sydney.'

The plane turned onto its departure runway and the engines revved. Whether Mandy thought she could go to Sydney or not, she no longer had a say in the matter. However, Liv saw the fear in her sister's eyes and knew she needed to put her at ease. 'If we can't find anyone to stay with you during the day, then yes, you'll come to work with me.'

Mandy's fear was replaced with a beautiful, beaming smile. 'I can be your assistant.'

Liv returned her smile. She wasn't sure how taking Mandy to work would play out. Mandy's patience levels were short, which didn't bode well for photography. As Mandy turned back to look out of the window and the plane hurtled down the runway, Liv sank back into her seat and re-closed her eyes. Only a few months earlier she'd made the trip to Melbourne to celebrate her father's sixty-seventh birthday. It had been a lovely weekend. Everyone was happy. Their father spoke non-stop about his upcoming triathlon, her mother had been planning a holiday to Tasmania and Toni had looked happy and smug. Liv remembered how she'd declined champagne and opted for water, saying she was on a health kick. Liv understood now that she must have been in the process of the IVF round.

How, in such a short space of time, could her father be dead, her mother a mess and Toni devastated after another miscarriage? And now, here she was on her way back to Sydney with the reason she left Melbourne in the first place sitting next to her. Mandy gripped Liv's hand as the plane rose from the runway into the sky. Liv squeezed it back. It might only be for a few weeks, but this would be an adventure for both of them.

4

Only for a few weeks. Liv stared at her computer screen, willing Toni to appear as she thought back to the trip to Melbourne. It was crazy to think that the few weeks she'd expected Mandy would stay had somehow morphed into three months. But the arrangement had worked surprisingly well. Mandy was loving her change of lifestyle and their mother had embraced having her own space for the first time since starting a family. She'd hesitated when Liv told her Mandy wanted to stay longer but hadn't demanded she return either. A place at Wattle House would be available in two months, and it made sense that Mandy stayed with Liv until then.

But now, as she waited for Toni to join her on the FaceTime call, she pushed Mandy from her mind. She had more concerning issues to deal with. She had been up half the night deciding how she was going to broach this subject with Toni. She hoped Toni would see it as it was meant: a gift. Because she'd been looking for the perfect gift to give her sister for the past fifteen years. But nothing had ever seemed enough to express her gratitude for what Toni had done. Nothing until now.

She took a deep breath. If this wasn't so messed up, she'd be excited rather than apprehensive as to how her sister was going to respond to her... to her what? Announcement? Suggestion? No, it was a question, really, wasn't it? An opportunity? The ultimate payback for what Toni had done for her. She'd given Liv the gift of life through organ donation and now Liv hoped to gift her life in a whole other form. It was a secret she'd kept for several months now, but it was time to make plans and to see how Toni was going to react.

She tapped her fingernails on the desk, nerves rattling in her stomach as she waited for Toni to join the call. She glanced at the retro clock on the wall of her Sydney apartment. Ten past eight. It didn't surprise her; Toni was never late to work appointments but never on time for family.

She forced a smile as her sister appeared on the screen, red-faced and sweating.

'Sorry,' she grinned as she wiped her forehead with the back of her hand.

Liv couldn't remember her sister greeting her with anything but 'sorry'. She guessed when you were always late, you were obliged to apologise rather than say hi.

'I was out running,' Toni continued. 'Lost track of time.' She gave a little laugh. 'Not that that's a huge surprise. How are you? And how's Mandy? I honestly can't believe you've had her stay for so long. She must be driving you mad. I don't think Mum expected you to have her for more than a few weeks.'

'She's fine,' Liv said. 'In her bedroom immersed in the world of *Titanic*.'

'Figures,' Toni said and laughed.

'She drives me mad at times but the change has been good for her. You'd hardly recognise her.'

'What's changed?'

'What do you mean?'

'You said I'd hardly recognise Mandy, so what's changed?'

'Oh, she's more independent, I guess.'

'Mum mentioned that. She thinks you're a miracle worker.'

'I think it's more Barb, my neighbour, than me. She's taught her all kinds of skills, but it's nice to see the changes. Mum's probably being eaten away by guilt as we speak. I'm surprised she hasn't turned up here to check on Mandy. But it's not for much longer. The room at Wattle House is available from the end of October. The person who's going to be most affected by her returning to Melbourne is Barb. They spend every day together.'

Mandy would knock on Barb's door around nine and pull it shut behind her on the way out at five. It gave Liv peace of mind knowing neither of them was home alone. The fact that they watched television all day and gorged themselves on whatever cake or slice Barb had Mandy help her make wasn't relevant. Mandy had certainly ballooned in size since she arrived in Sydney but they were both happy and therefore, so was Liv.

'Is that a good idea?' Toni asked. 'Her spending all day with one person?'

'Why wouldn't it be?'

'Because she won't have that when she moves into the support house.'

'That's the whole point, isn't it? That she'll be surrounded by the other residents so they can support each other,' Liv said. 'A support house has people to support you. Look, let's not talk about Mandy. She's not why I wanted to speak to you.'

'Are you okay? You're acting weird and you look like you're about to vomit.' Toni's eyes widened. 'It's not your kidney, is it?'

Liv's heart swelled with love for her sister. Toni was such a bundle of contradictions. While she'd wished Mandy didn't exist when they were children and did her best to avoid her now, she loved Liv with a fierce passion and would do anything for her. She'd protected her in the playground against bullies, she'd punched Ben Diamond in the nose when he'd stood Liv up for what should have been her first date when she was fourteen, and at nineteen, when Liv had suffered kidney failure, Toni immediately offered to become a donor.

Liv shook her head as Toni waited for her response. 'No, it's not about my kidney.' She forced the smile back to her lips and took another deep breath. She could do this. The worst scenario was Toni might say no, and then she'd have to think through other options.

'Liv?'

Liv's attention turned to the computer screen where Toni was waiting for her to speak. After making her decision to approach Toni, she'd spent weeks trying to work out the best way to present the opportunity and even now, she wasn't sure whether she was doing the right thing. As soon as she uttered the magic words, Toni was likely to fall to bits.

Toni wiped the sweat from her forehead, distracting Liv and causing her to wonder where she might have run to. Knowing Toni, she'd probably run down to the Yarra River, into Southbank and back to South Yarra.

'Come on, Liv, fill me in. Is it Mandy? Are you sure you're happy she's still with you? No one expected you to have her for this long.'

Liv took a deep breath. 'When I was in Melbourne the weekend you called me to say Mum wasn't coping, you made a comment that's been playing on my mind ever since.'

Toni's eyes narrowed.

'It was about me having a baby for you.'

'You're actually thinking about it?'

The hope in Toni's voice caused Liv to grimace. 'Kind of, but not how you imagine.'

Disappointment clouded Toni's features.

Liv took another deep breath. She'd gone over in her mind a million times how best to tell Toni and still hadn't worked out exactly what to say.

'I'm pregnant.'

She blurted out the words before she could give any further thought to how she would deliver the news.

Toni's mouth dropped open. 'What? How? Is that even possible?'

If it had been anyone else, Liv might have laughed, but she knew what Toni meant and she knew that right at this second, her sister's look of surprise was hiding her devastation. 'Yes, it's possible. As you pointed out yourself when we were at Mum's, kidney transplant doesn't impact fertility.'

'I know that. I meant I didn't realise you were seeing anyone. Congratulations, I guess.' The dismay in Toni's tone contrasted directly with her words.

'I'm sorry,' Liv said. 'It wasn't planned.'

Toni stared down the screen at her, a flurry of emotions crossing her face. 'You don't have to apologise,' she said, although Liv knew that she did. 'As I said, I didn't know you were even seeing anyone.'

'I'm not.'

Toni narrowed her eyes. 'Does Mum know?'

Liv shook her head. 'No, I'm only telling you for now. There's more to it than just me being pregnant.'

The uncertainty on Toni's face was impossible to miss. If the circum-

stances were reversed and Liv had been trying to get pregnant unsuccessfully for eight years, she'd wonder why her sister thought she'd want to be
the first to hear the news.

'More? What is it? Twins? Triplets?'

Liv chose to ignore the bitterness in Toni's tone. Thank goodness it
wasn't. One baby was bad enough. 'It's just one.' She took a deep breath. 'I
can't do this, Ton. I'd like to gift him or her to you.'

Toni snorted, her hand flying up to cover her mouth. She stared at Liv
for a long moment before speaking. 'Is this a joke? Because it's not a very
good one.'

Liv shook her head. 'I can't have a baby. I've never wanted one for a
start, but who knows how long I'll be around? I'll probably need a second
kidney some time down the track, and that's only if I'm fortunate enough to
get one. I'll be lucky to get twenty years out of this one, and I've had it for
nearly fifteen already.'

'But you said it's working fine.'

'Yes, for now, but that's not the point. Regardless of my kidney, I *really*
don't want a baby.'

'Yes, you do. You just need to get your head around the idea. You'll be a
wonderful mum.'

Liv smiled. 'You're a great sister. Always there to support me, even at my
lowest times. But we both know I'd be a terrible mum. I'm selfish and
career driven, and most of all, I don't want a kid. Never have, never will. I've
never even understood why anyone would want one, to be honest.'

Toni's lips twitched as she did her best to suppress a smile. 'Well, okay,
but there'd still definitely be worse mums than you are out there. And if
you come back to Melbourne, I could help. Mum would too. You'd probably
love a baby if it was your own. That's what heaps of people who never
wanted kids say. It's different when it's yours.'

Liv shook her head. 'I know everybody says that and you're right, I probably
would love it, and I'm sure I'd adapt to the whole idea if I had to, but it's just not
something I have any desire to do. I love being able to travel and do what I want
when I want. This will sound terrible, but we were so tied down when we were
kids to Mandy's routine and everything needing to be done for her that it made
me selfish. I want my life to be about me and not revolve around someone else.

Not even a baby. I can handle a few weeks, or even a few months, but not a life-time commitment.' She shuddered. 'It's not for me. But there's no pressure either; if it's not something you and Joel want to do then I'll look into adoption.'

Toni was silent for a moment, then spoke. 'How far along are you?'

Liv stood, running her hands over the bump cocooned in her favourite oversized cable-knit jumper. 'Seven months.'

Toni's mouth dropped open again. 'Seven months? How come no one knows? Mandy must have told Mum. Surely, she's noticed? And anyway, I saw you in Melbourne a few months ago when you took Mandy back with you. You didn't look pregnant then.'

'I was thickening up,' Liv said. 'Ironically, it was when I was in Melbourne that weekend that I realised it was a possibility and a test confirmed it when I got back to Sydney. And as for Mandy, she's been sworn to secrecy. You know how much she loves secrets.'

Toni nodded, suddenly going quiet.

'I know it's a lot to put on you,' Liv said. 'And I'm sorry it's taken me so long to tell you. I didn't realise I was pregnant until I was four months. I'm one of those women we've always laughed at. *How could you not know you're pregnant?*'

'How could you *not know*?'

Heat filled Liv's cheeks. 'My periods have been all over the place since I first got them when I was thirteen, so I wasn't concerned. In fact, I wondered if I was hitting menopause early as I was putting on weight. But then I've had the added stress of Dad dying and worrying about Mum, so I've been comfort eating and feeling tired. I put it all down to that. I didn't get any other symptoms. At least I found out before I actually gave birth. I wasn't one of *those* women. You know, the ones who go to the toilet and come back out with a newborn. Look, I know I should have told you sooner. I've picked up the phone so many times, but the timing was never right. I worried it was too soon.' She gave a small laugh. 'I seriously considered waiting until the baby was born but decided that was going too far.'

'Why would you wait that long?'

'Ton, after all the disappointments you and Joel have had, I wanted to make sure the baby was healthy and would carry to term. Telling you too soon and then something going wrong would have been devastating. It's as safe as it can be now and I'm really hoping you're ready to become a mum. What do you think? Will you at least think about it?'

Toni shook her head slowly. 'I don't know, Liv.' Then it was clear from her face something else occurred to her. 'Oh God. What if you changed your mind a few months or a year or two down the track? I'm not sure I could handle that.'

'I'd never make this offer if I thought there was any way that would happen. I'm no good with responsibility. I have my life mapped out and it doesn't include children. I'll happily take on the role of doting aunt if you let me, but even that will be more than enough.'

'You've had Mandy with you for nearly three months now. It was only supposed to be for a few weeks. That's quite a responsibility.'

'It's a few months, not a lifetime, and it has an end date. And looking after my thirty-year-old sister is hardly the same as dealing with a newborn or a toddler,' Liv said.

'Mum described Mandy as an immature twelve-year-old.'

'Still not the same as a newborn, and she'll be moving into the support house in Melbourne soon. I only brought her up here because Mum wasn't coping, you know that. Look, think about it. There's no rush to make a decision. You obviously need to talk to Joel.'

Toni nodded. 'I do, but I have to decide whether it's what I want too.'

'I thought being a mum was something you'd do anything for? I've felt so useless up until now, Ton. Standing on the side lines, watching the heartache you've experienced with each pregnancy and IVF attempt. Finally, I can do something to help.'

Toni's face softened at Liv's admission. 'What about the father? Won't he want to share custody?'

'I've no idea who he is,' Liv said. It was true, she didn't. 'I'm not proud of this, but I had a very wild night at the time I got pregnant.'

'Wild night?'

Liv nodded. 'Gina was visiting from Perth at New Year. There was a party and far too much booze, and while it was out of character, I had a one-night stand that night with a backpacker. He was gone in the morning.

I have no idea how to contact him. I'm embarrassed to say I'm not even sure of his name.'

'I'm not sure these are key selling points, Liv. A baby conceived at a drunken New Year's party with no information about the father or his background.'

'I know it's not ideal, but while this baby might not be yours biologically, this baby does still share DNA with you. What do you think? Are you interested at all?'

'Of course, but I need to think about it. Give me a few days and I'll come back to you.' Toni hesitated, the worry on her face changing briefly to a small smile. 'And Liv, thank you. This is the most amazing offer anyone could ever make to me. I wish I was there and could give you a big hug.'

Liv blew her a kiss. 'Me too.'

They ended the call, and Liv could only imagine what was going through her sister's mind. She exhaled, realising how much nervous energy she was harbouring. She'd do anything to give Toni her dream, even if it meant manipulating the truth in the process.

5

Toni sat staring at the computer screen for a long time after Liv disappeared. Did that really happen? Her sister was pregnant and was offering her the baby? She shook her head, muttering to herself. It was like something out of a soap opera. An unbelievable one at that.

'You okay?'

Toni turned at the sound of Joel's deep voice. He smiled from the doorway of her home office; his dark hair was wet from the shower and his eyes tired from jet lag. He held up a mug. 'Peppermint tea?'

Toni smiled. 'Thanks, although tonight, I could probably use a real drink.'

Joel frowned, his eyes crinkling at the corners. 'That's unlike you. Everything okay?'

Toni shook her head. 'I was speaking with Liv.' She stood and took the cup he held out. 'Let's go into the lounge, and I'll tell you what she said.'

A few minutes later, they sat in the cosy lounge area of the apartment; an apartment that was definitely not child friendly. They'd always imagined moving to the suburbs and a house if Toni had fallen pregnant and carried to term, but it hadn't been relevant, and the South Yarra apartment was close to Toni's work and an easy commute to the airport for Joel.

Joel's eyes clouded with anger as Toni briefed him on her conversation with her sister. He shook his head, stood, and started pacing in the small space.

Toni silently willed him to speak but knew it was best to wait until he was ready.

An age passed before he finally opened his mouth. 'Was Liv drunk? Or are we pawns in some sick game she's playing?' He pushed his hand through his hair. 'Even as I say that it sounds wrong. Liv doesn't usually play games.'

'It's not a game,' Toni said. 'She's seven months pregnant and isn't keeping the baby. The baby can come to us, or it will go to another family, and we'll never see him or her. I saw her stomach. She's pregnant. Heavily pregnant.'

Joel stopped next to the drinks cabinet and poured a large whisky. 'You're right. Tea's not going to cut it.' He held it up to Toni, who nodded. He poured a second drink and took one over to her. He shook his head again. 'You really believe she's pregnant?'

Toni nodded. 'In typical flaky Liv style, she didn't realise until she was four months along, and she has no idea how to contact the father. He was a backpacker she met at a drunken New Year's party.'

'Should we worry about the genetics then? Drunk mum, and who knows what for the dad?'

'Liv hardly even drinks more than a glass,' Toni said, coming to her sister's defence. 'It was New Year; most people go a bit too far. And she's gorgeous and smart, so the baby will probably inherit those traits.'

Joel's brows furrowed as they did when he was deep in thought. 'She's really offering us her baby? A real live baby?'

Toni nodded again.

Joel took a deep breath and remained silent for some time. Eventually he smiled. 'This is crazy. We could be parents in – what – two months?' He sat back beside her and placed a hand on her knee. 'What do you think we should do?'

Toni lapsed into silence. She'd gone through six unsuccessful IVF cycles, each resulting in a positive pregnancy and each resulting in a miscarriage. She would not allow herself to get excited. 'I don't know,' she said finally. 'There'd be lots of things to think through. The baby wouldn't biologically be ours.'

'That doesn't worry me so much, you know that. I was always keen to adopt, but I know the biological link is important to you, which is why we persisted with IVF. And the baby would have a biological link to you, at least.'

'What if we fell in love with the baby, and a year or two down the track, Liv changed her mind and wanted it back?'

'We'd have to adopt it legally so she couldn't,' Joel said.

'Yes, but she's my sister. How would that work? It's not like some random person you're never going to see again. I'd lose my sister if we had to fight to keep her baby.'

'I guess that would be a risk we'd have to take. I'd want to speak to her to understand whether that was likely. I'm pretty good at reading people. Her pregnancy hormones might have her making crazy decisions. She might need to get a psych evaluation to ensure she's thinking clearly.'

'You're seriously thinking about this, aren't you?' Toni said.

Joel nodded. 'It's our dream, babe. It always has been. We imagined a huge family with our own kids, and I guess that probably won't happen. But I'd give anything to be a dad. Even to one kid. You know that. Does she know what sex the baby is?'

'I didn't even think to ask. Would it matter?'

Joel shook his head. 'Not at all.' He put an arm around her shoulders. 'I'd love a daughter so I can be her protector but a son would be wonderful too. However, I might have to study up on sports if it's a boy. It's not really my strong suit. Hopefully, he'll be into aviation?'

Toni laughed. 'If his dad's a pilot, I think that'd be a given, boy or girl.'

Joel grinned. '*His dad*. I like the sound of that.' He shook his head again. 'This is unbelievable. Do you think Liv would talk to us again tonight?'

'I'm sure she would, but I'd rather give it a day or two. Come up with all the questions we can think of and not rush into a decision. She's not going to give the baby to anyone else until we've decided.'

'Good idea.' Joel threw back the rest of his drink and stood to refill it. 'I think I need another one of these. This is a shock. A good shock, but a shock.'

Toni smiled as her husband did a happy dance on the way to the drinks cabinet. He'd done it before. Six times, in fact. Six positive pregnancy tests that all ended in miscarriage. It appeared she would need a miracle to carry a baby to term. Maybe this was her miracle? A ripple of excitement raced through her and she forced herself to quash it. Until a baby was placed in her arms, she wouldn't believe it was going to happen.

* * *

Mandy hugged Liv the moment she finished the call with Toni. She'd never tell Liv but she'd been eavesdropping. Liv had thought she was watching *Titanic*, but it had finished before her FaceTime call. She wanted to hear what Liv said to Toni.

Mandy knew a lot more than Liv realised, and she loved that Liv was trusting her with the secret. She loved her sister so much. Liv always looked out for her, not like her mum, who had wanted to put her in *that place*. Since living in Sydney, she'd come to understand it was her dad's fault. He was the one who came up with the idea to get rid of her, to a house that was full of old, nearly dead people. It would be horrible and she and Baby were going to refuse to go.

When her father died, she thought her mother would forget the idea, but then Mum didn't get out of bed, and things got hard. They'd been running out of food and the house smelled. Her best friend, Izzy, had been on holiday for six whole weeks too; otherwise, she would have come to help Mandy, but she'd been on a yacht in New Zealand with no phone reception so hadn't even been able to chat. It was lucky that Liv had come to rescue her. To think that she and Baby had gone on a plane and were now living a glamorous Sydney lifestyle. An apartment with views of the water, spending time with Liv's lovely neighbour, Barbara – or Barb as she insisted Mandy call her – and lots of outings. She'd pushed all thoughts of the support house out of her mind. She would live with Liv forever.

The best thing about Sydney though, was she had *secrets*. So many secrets. She squeezed Liv tighter as she thought of her lunch today with

Barb. Liv thought they'd been watching Netflix over at Barb's. She knew nothing about their outing to Darling Harbour, their lunch at Pancakes on the Rocks, or the ferry ride back across the bay. And neither Mandy nor Barb would tell her. *What she doesn't know can't hurt her, and what my grandson doesn't know won't hurt him,* Barb had said the first day they'd gone for lunch, and then the zoo and the following days when they'd enjoyed outings to Bondi Beach, the opera house, the botanical gardens and a trillion other places Mandy couldn't keep track of. She was having the best holiday ever.

She told Izzy each night when they FaceTimed about her outings with Barb, so it wasn't a total secret. Izzy loved hearing the stories and would tell Mandy how the animals were at the shelter where Izzy was employed as a kennel technician and Mandy loved to volunteer. Izzy and the animals were the main things Mandy missed. But the secret outings made up for it.

And then there was the other secret. The baby secret. It was bigger than any secret she'd ever had to keep. She hadn't told Izzy, and while the pregnancy couldn't be hidden from Barb, she was careful not to say too much about it. And now Liv had told Toni, maybe she'd be allowed to tell Izzy too. It was on the tip of her tongue to ask Liv, but then she changed her mind. She was thirty. She was an adult and there were some decisions she should be allowed to make for herself.

Liv pulled back from the hug and smiled at Mandy. 'How was *Titanic*?'

'Same ending,' Mandy said, disappointment flooding through her as she was transported back to the end of the movie that she knew backwards. She was convinced if she'd watched it enough times, the ending would be updated and Jack would live but it hadn't happened yet.

'And how are you?'

'Hungry.'

Liv laughed. 'Same ending then. Come on, let's see whether there's any of that ice cream left and talk about the weekend and what you'd like to do. We haven't been to the zoo yet. Would you like to go there or to the aquarium perhaps?'

'Aquarium,' Mandy replied. The zoo had been fun with Barb but she didn't want to go again. 'Can Barb come?'

Liv frowned. 'I'm not sure if she'd be up for all the walking. You can ask her if you like.'

'She'll be fine,' Mandy said. She was tempted to tell Liv how far Barb had walked earlier that day, but she stopped herself. She didn't want Liv to get angry and stop her outings. No, she was good at secrets. Liv had asked her to keep the baby secret and Barb had asked her to keep their outings secret. She wouldn't let either of them down.

Two days after the life-changing conversation with Liv, Toni had found herself staring at the computer screen for fifteen minutes before her sister was due to join the call with Joel and her. They'd spent hours discussing the pros and cons of adopting Liv's baby and had devised a list of questions. Now the moment had come to talk to her.

A hand rested on her shoulder, jolting her from her thoughts.

'You ready?' Joel sat down at the desk beside her.

'No. Are you?'

Joel gave a little laugh and shook his head. 'I'm excited, though. Have you got the list of questions?'

Toni nodded, pointing to the printed list on the desk beside her, as the video screen came to life.

'Hey, guys.' Mandy's doll, Baby, was being waved in front of the camera. A giggle erupted from the screen, and Mandy's face replaced Baby's.

'Toni!'

Toni forced a smile. The camera was so close to Mandy that she could practically see up her nostrils. 'Hey, Mandy. You need to move back a bit from the camera. You're too close.'

Mandy moved a fraction so that her cheeks and mouth were visible and giggled again. 'Liv doesn't know I'm on the call. She told me I had to wait until she was here.' She looked over her shoulder as if checking to see where her sister was.

'Really?' Joel asked. 'Why's that?'

'We have secrets,' Mandy said, looking over her shoulder again. She lowered her voice, her face now fully visible. 'Big secrets.'

Joel glanced at Toni and raised a questioning eyebrow. Toni shrugged. Knowing Mandy, she could be referring to anything. 'Are you enjoying Sydney?'

Mandy nodded. 'I spend my days with Barb, who lives across the hall and then I see Liv in the evenings. It's much better than living in Melbourne. I'd like to stay here.'

Toni nodded. She was aware that Mandy was dreading the move to Wattle House once she returned home from Sydney. 'Have you been anywhere nice?'

Mandy frowned and pursed her lips together and gave a little shake of her head. 'No. During the day, I go to Barb's apartment, and we watch *Titanic*.'

'Every day?' Joel asked.

Mandy hesitated before nodding.

'Even the weekends?'

'No. At weekends, Liv and I do something. We've been to Darling Harbour and Bondi and even to the mountains. You know, the coloured ones.'

'The Blue Mountains,' Liv's voice travelled from somewhere in the apartment. 'Mandy, I told you to wait for me.'

Mandy's eyes widened; she waved at the screen and disappeared.

Joel laughed. 'Nothing's changed with Mandy.'

Liv's protruding stomach appeared, stretching the sweatshirt she wore, causing Toni's heart to contract. She almost had to pinch herself. This was real. Liv was pregnant.

Liv sat and adjusted the camera so her face filled the screen. 'Sorry. I asked her to wait but she obviously had other ideas.' Her smile was tentative as she looked from Toni to Joel. 'I'm assuming you have lots of questions?' Liv frowned. 'Hold on a minute. I'd prefer Mandy doesn't hear this conversation. I want to check that she's in her room with headphones on.'

She stood and disappeared from the computer screen for a few minutes before returning. 'All good, she's listening to an audiobook. I don't want to tell her anything until the details of what will happen to the baby are finalised.' She took a deep breath. 'Okay, shoot. What are your questions?'

'Are you certain this is what you want to do?' Joel asked.

'Absolutely, without a doubt,' Liv replied. 'A baby isn't something I've ever wanted in my life, and I doubt I ever will.'

'My biggest concern is that you're going to change your mind,' Toni said, 'and I'm not sure what we'd do then. You're my sister. It would ruin our relationship.'

'I'm not really sure what I can say to convince you that I know what I want,' Liv said. 'It won't ruin our relationship. If anything, I hope it strengthens it. You did something amazing for me fifteen years ago and this is my turn to do something amazing for you. The difference is you did something completely selfless when you gave me a kidney. Whereas to be honest, I'm doing something entirely selfish.'

'Selfish?' Joel said. 'How do you figure that?'

'If you'd asked me to have a baby for you,' Liv said, 'I would have said no. Pregnancy and everything that goes with it is not something I would have done for anyone voluntarily. This happened by accident, so it's hardly a selfless act of kindness to give you a child.'

Joel nodded. 'It's still an amazing gift. Hypothetically, let's say we agreed to go ahead,' he said. 'How does it work? Would you want us to be at the birth?'

The lines in Liv's forehead furrowed as she considered this. 'I'm open to it, although I'm not sure I'd want you up, well, you know, not up that end, Joel.'

Toni laughed as her husband's face flushed bright red.

'Don't worry,' he said, 'I have no intention of being up *that end*. I would like to hold the baby soon after the birth, though, so we can bond quickly.'

'Sounds perfect,' Liv said. 'I'd suggest you come up a week before the baby's due. That way, when it all happens, you'll be there.'

Toni squeezed Joel's knee. 'I think we're getting a bit ahead of ourselves. We've got a list of things to discuss before we get to this stage.'

Liv folded her arms and leaned back in her chair. 'Okay, fire away.'

'How would it work legally?'

'You and Joel would adopt the baby. I've looked into it, and it all has to be done properly with a lawyer and the Supreme Court signing off on the paperwork. Inter-family adoptions are quite common but generally are for older children, not newborns. For the older children, you must have had a relationship with them for two years before you can adopt. Our case is obviously different, and I'll have the lawyer confirm exactly how it would work. The paperwork is really a formality. The baby would be yours from the moment it's born.'

'What if you change your mind?' Joel said. 'If we can't officially adopt the baby for two years, you might take it back during that time.'

'I'm not sure it will be two years,' Liv said, 'but whether it's two hours, two weeks or two years, I have no intention of asking for the baby back. Don't worry, I'm of sound mind and haven't made this decision lightly.' Her face softened. 'I know what you guys have been through and there's no way I'd do anything to make that even harder for you.' She patted her stomach. 'This baby is yours if you want her.'

Toni blinked back unexpected tears. 'It's a girl?'

'My gut feeling says it is, and Mandy keeps referring to the bump as her, but we could be wrong.'

Joel's arm snaked around Toni's shoulders and he pulled her close. 'A girl would be amazing.' His voice was raw with emotion. 'What involvement would you want in her life, Liv?'

'As much as an aunt who lives in another state would expect. Nothing more. Once she's out in the world, she's yours. I'll be thrilled to hear how she's doing and see you all when I come down for family events and Christmas.' She laughed. 'I'm not even promising I'll babysit. I'm not cut out for spending more than an hour or two around little kids. You know that, Ton. Remember when the neighbours asked me to babysit when I was seventeen? I lasted less than ten minutes before calling Mum to take over. You can try and convince me otherwise, but we both know it's true.'

Toni nodded. It was true, but that niggle that Liv would change her mind once the baby was here wouldn't leave her. Maybe that's how she needed to approach the situation: believing that Liv would change her mind. If she didn't let herself get too excited or attached before that happened, then she'd be okay. Perhaps this was something she had to do for Liv. At least if it was her and Joel, they would give the baby back, but if it was another couple and formal adoption papers had been signed, then that wouldn't be possible.

'What do you think?' Liv said.

Joel's eyes flashed with excitement as he and Toni shared a look. He squeezed her hand. 'I know what I want to say.'

Toni took a deep breath. 'How about we say yes, on one condition: if you change your mind within the first month of the baby being born, then we give her back?'

'Hold on,' Joel said, the excitement draining from his eyes. 'I'm not sure I would handle that.'

'It won't happen,' Liv said, 'so you don't need to worry. But if it makes Toni more comfortable, then I'll agree to that. Although,' and she laughed, 'if you take her and change *your* mind, I do not want her back. She becomes your problem. Deal?'

Joel laughed. 'Deal.' He turned to Toni. 'Can you even imagine that? That after everything we've been through, we'd want to give her back?'

Toni shook her head. As much as she wanted to hold her emotions at arm's length until they knew for sure Liv wouldn't change her mind, an overwhelming sense of protectiveness was settling over her.

'What about Mum?' Toni asked. 'What do we tell her?'

'The truth,' Liv said. 'I'd planned to tell her but wanted to know your feelings first. This will make it a lot easier than telling her she'll never get to meet her grandchild as she's being given up for adoption.' Liv's mouth contorted into a sly smile. 'I wasn't going to ask you for any payment for this *kind act* I'm doing for you, but I've changed my mind.'

Toni glanced at Joel. His look of disbelief mirrored her own. Neither of them would have ever expected Liv to ask for money.

'Payment will be in the form of you telling Mum,' Liv continued, 'so I don't have to. I'm not sure I want to hear a lecture about how irresponsible I am.'

Toni let out a relieved laugh. That was more like Liv.

'We'll have her over for dinner this weekend,' Joel said. 'I'll ply her with champagne and tell her the news.'

'I'm not sure you'll even get a lecture,' Toni said. 'You're doing something incredibly selfless.'

'I think that depends on your perspective. Mum, being adopted herself, mightn't see it the same way. Now, I'd better wrap this up. I promised Mandy I'd help her make some brownies tonight.'

Toni stared at her sister one last time. 'You're 100 per cent sure about this?'

'One hundred and ten. This pregnancy is for a reason, Ton: so you guys can become parents.'

Toni nodded, overwhelmed by emotion once again.

They said their goodbyes and ended the call, leaving Toni and Joel sitting in contemplative silence.

'I think we're having a baby,' Joel finally said. He shook his head, his eyes flitting around the room. 'Should we move?'

'What?' Joel's words broke Toni out of her thoughts. 'How do you go from that conversation to thinking we should move?'

Joel stood. 'We always said if we had a family, we'd need to move somewhere bigger.'

Toni shook her head slowly. 'Let's let the baby arrive first and then worry about that. She'll be fine here initially. Assuming all goes to plan, we could give some thought to moving somewhere closer to where we want her to go to school.'

'School? She's not even born yet.'

'I know,' Toni said, 'but it starts now. Waiting lists for day care, kinder and school. Daley at work is always going on about how hard it is to get a place.'

'Day care? I thought you wanted to be a full-time mum. That was always the plan when we were trying. You'd stop working until the baby went to school.'

That had been the plan, but at this moment, the whole thing was surreal and Toni couldn't imagine giving up work. 'I love my job,' she said. 'I'm not sure how it would work with a baby, but I'm not ready to give it up yet. I'm pretty sure I'd be entitled to take maternity leave. I think it's the same for adoption as it is when you give birth.' She frowned. 'Although I'm not sure how that will work as I can't imagine the paperwork for the adoption will go through quickly. I'd have to talk to human resources. Worst case, I'd be taking leave without pay which isn't ideal. But let's not rush to make any decisions on anything that's not essential. This whole thing is unexpected. I don't think I'm capable of thinking clearly right now.'

'You know what is essential?' Joel said. 'A name.'

Toni smiled. 'It is. Let's make a list.'

7

Liv's hand shook as she ended the call with Toni and Joel. She just hoped her explanation of the legal side of things sounded convincing. The reality was when she'd investigated the legalities, everything seemed too hard. She was sure there must be a better way to go about it, but she hadn't worked out what that was yet. She sighed. Maybe she should have gone with her initial instinct and organised a termination. Although the pregnancy was too far along for a termination to be an option, and with Toni's history of miscarriages, she knew it wasn't really her place to make that decision. It was a human life and she had no right to play God. However, it could be argued that she was doing exactly that. Regardless, she'd opened a can of worms that was growing more complicated by the day.

'Livvy?' Mandy called to her from her bedroom door. 'Are you okay? Is everything okay with Baby?'

Mandy had taken to calling the actual baby 'Baby', which was incredibly confusing, especially when she was holding her doll, as she was now.

'Everything's good, Hon. Now can you come and sit with me? I want to explain a few things about the baby and what's going to happen after he or she is born.'

'She,' Mandy said, smiling as she came to sit opposite Liv. She held up the doll. 'Same as Baby. They will be sisters.'

'Cousins,' Liv said.

Mandy frowned. 'Why don't *we* have cousins?'

'Because neither Mum nor Dad had brothers or sisters. That's why. If Mum had had a sister who'd had a child, then that child would have been our cousin. Mum would have been an aunt, and we would have been cousins.'

'Like I'll be an aunt to Baby?'

'Exactly,' Liv said and laughed. 'But she can't have the same name as your Baby when she's born, so you'll need to get used to the new baby being called by a different name. So, I want to make sure you understand what will happen after the real baby comes.' Now that Toni had said yes, she wanted to make sure there'd be no confusion for Mandy after the birth.

Tears ran down Mandy's cheeks as she listened to Liv confirming that the baby would go to live with Toni and Joel, and they would be its mummy and daddy. 'But why can't you keep the baby, Livvy? That way, I'd see more of her.'

'Hon, you'll be going back to Melbourne soon. Your room's ready at Wattle House in a few weeks, which is great news. It means you'll be close to Toni and Joel and the new baby and can help.'

Mandy shook her head. 'Toni won't let me. She hates me.'

'No, she doesn't.' Liv hoped she came across as believable. It was only since the trip to Melbourne a few months earlier that she'd seen that Mandy was aware of the full extent of Toni's animosity towards her. Although Toni had been nicer to Mandy the day they'd left, there was no guarantee that would continue. 'I'll talk to her about including you. After all, you'll be the baby's aunt, and she'll need your love too.'

Fat tears rolled down Mandy's cheeks. 'I want to stay here with you. I don't want to go into a home. It will be full of dead people.'

'What?'

'Like respite. The people in the house will be dead, or they'll make funny noises.'

Liv's heart contracted at Mandy's words. How had none of them picked up that this was the reason she didn't want to live at Wattle House? She thought it was the same as the aged care facility her parents had sent Mandy to for respite. They'd been unable to find anywhere that catered for younger people and neither Liv nor Toni had been able to look after Mandy when they'd gone on a three-week holiday. It had been unfortunate on Mandy's stay that an elderly lady she'd been sitting with at dinner had fallen face forward into her mashed potatoes. It appeared she'd been dead for quite some time before anybody had noticed. 'I thought she was like Toni,' Mandy had said when they'd asked her if she'd noticed anything strange about the woman. 'You know, pretending I don't exist. I asked her polite questions, but she didn't say anything and then she dropped dead in her potatoes.' The phrase *dropped dead in her potatoes* was joked about for many months after, but Mandy had refused to eat potatoes, and she'd refused to go back to respite. *They kill you with potatoes.*

'It's not the same place,' Liv said now. 'Look at this.' She patted the kitchen chair next to her, indicating for Mandy to move around the table and join her and typed *Wattle House Independent Living* into the search bar of her computer. 'I thought Mum and Dad showed you this when they were first talking about Wattle House?'

Mandy clung tightly to Baby. 'I closed my eyes and refused to look,' she said proudly. 'Dad said I'd learn lots of things about how to live, including how to cook the best pasta... and potatoes!'

Liv turned to Mandy. 'Dad said that? About the potatoes?'

Mandy nodded, and Liv shook her head. Her father had been clueless at times.

'Okay, but there will be no need to cook potatoes unless you choose to and—'

'Never,' Mandy said before Liv had a chance to continue. 'They're deadly.'

It was on the tip of Liv's tongue to ask Mandy what she thought McDonald's fries were made from, but she decided it was best not to upset her further.

'Okay, so no potatoes, but look at this. The house is lovely. It has a colourful garden and is modern inside, and the people are around your age that live there.'

'Thirty?'

Liv nodded. 'They could be anywhere from twenty-five to forty according to this.'

Mandy's eyes widened. 'They won't be old or dead?'

'No. The whole point is to get you living with people your age. And because they might face some challenges like you, you can help each other. Who knows, you might meet some great people.'

'A boyfriend?'

Liv bit the inside of her cheek. That was something she did not want to promise. 'Possibly, although hopefully in the house, it will be friends as it can become tricky with boyfriends.'

'Because they'll want to do...' Mandy lowered her voice, 'boyfriend things?'

The wicked look on Mandy's face was a little disconcerting. Yes, she was thirty, but Liv always thought of her as a child, so to have the sexual knowledge and interest it appeared Mandy had, and had had since she was a teenager, seemed wrong. Liv realised she'd need to talk to their mother about birth control. The support house might open a world for Mandy that none of them had anticipated.

'Possibly. Anyway, let's have a look at some more photos on the website. It shows people eating together and laughing. There are also photos of the rooms. You might have an ensuite like I do here.'

They scrolled through the photos and Mandy stopped on one which looked like family members visiting one of the residents. 'Do you think Toni will do this?' Mandy pointed to the baby one of the people in the photos was holding. 'Will she bring Baby to visit?'

Liv knew she shouldn't be answering on Toni's behalf, but right now, anything to make the move look sweeter for Mandy was necessary. 'I'll make her promise she will. And we'll see if you can visit her at her and Joel's home. I'm sure Mum will pick you up and take you to visit the baby. Toni might even let you babysit one day.'

Mandy beamed with delight. 'Imagine that. Baby, all to myself. I'll be careful.'

'I know you will, Mandy.' Liv didn't add that she meant babysitting when their mother was there too. They could deal with that and Mandy's reaction when it was relevant.

Liv was relieved when half an hour later, Mandy happily went back to her bedroom, although she realised she hadn't had a chance to tell her the plans for the birth of the baby: that it wouldn't be in a hospital. That she was going to book a doula to do the last few weeks of prenatal care and that the baby would be born at home. She thought back to Toni's question about how the legal side of things would work. She hadn't worked out all the details, but she was beginning to think there might be a way to just simply bypass the system. She wasn't planning to share this with Toni and Joel – they were law-abiding citizens – and on this occasion, Liv decided they'd be better finding out after the event.

8

Toni couldn't believe she'd agreed to be the one to tell their mother about Liv's pregnancy and decision to give up the baby. But, as much as she was regretting it at this moment, she planned to keep her word. She put the final touches on the table set for three as the doorbell rang.

Joel placed his hands on her shoulders as she let out a deep breath. 'Ready?'

She nodded. They'd invited her mother for dinner and seemed to have spent hours discussing the best way to handle her with regards to the baby situation. 'She'll go one of two ways,' Toni had said. 'She'll either be thrilled that we're taking the baby on as ours and convince us to not tell the baby that she was adopted, or she'll be horrified and do everything possible to convince Liv to keep it.'

'We'd have to tell the baby she's adopted,' Joel said. 'Not until she's old enough, but she would still need to know.'

'I doubt it will be relevant,' Toni said. 'My guess is Mum will go down *the horrified and convince Liv to keep her* route.'

An hour later, her assumption was proven right. Her mother arrived with a stunning bunch of lilies. Her hair had been recently styled and she had a healthy glow about her.

'You're looking good, Mum,' Toni said, hugging her and gratefully accepting the flowers.

'I'm feeling good,' Sara said. 'I'm not sure if I should say that, with your dad gone and all, but I am. I owe Liv, I really do.'

'We all do,' Joel said but stopped when Toni shot him a look.

'She seems to be enjoying having Mandy,' Toni said. 'I'm impressed. I wouldn't have survived three nights, let alone three months. Now, come through to the kitchen, and we'll pour some drinks.'

'I think we also need to thank Liv's neighbour,' Sara said. 'Barb spends so much time with Mandy. I don't think the trip would have been as much of a success without her.'

'Is this the old lady who needed company?' Joel asked, taking a bottle of Moët from the fridge.

Sara nodded, her eyes widening. 'Moët? What's the occasion?' She turned to Toni, a glimmer of hope in her eyes.

'I'm not pregnant,' Toni said, watching her mother's face fall. 'But the reason we're celebrating is baby-related.'

'Oh?'

'Let's take our drinks into the lounge. Joel lit the fire earlier. It's cold today. So much for spring weather.'

Sara laughed. 'This is Melbourne. This is spring weather. Rain, hail, drought, flood, heatwave. Any of that constitutes spring or any other season in Melbourne. You know that.'

Toni laughed and led her mother through to the comfortable chairs by the fire. The laughter took the edge off her nerves. She was excited, on the one hand, to be telling her mother the news, but dreading her reaction on another.

'Okay,' Toni said, glancing at Joel as he came and sat beside her. 'We do have some baby news.'

'But you're not having a baby?'

'No. Getting one is a better description,' Toni said. She held up her hand when her mother's mouth dropped open, wanting to explain before questions were asked. 'Someone I'm close to is pregnant and – as she is unable to keep the baby – she's offered it to us.'

Sara put her champagne on the small table next to her, her eyes wide. 'What? Why would she do that?'

'She's never wanted a baby, and this one is unplanned. She found out too late to terminate.' Liv had never actually said this, but Toni assumed it was the case. 'If we don't take the baby, then it will be put up for adoption.'

Sara stared at Toni, and Toni could only imagine what was going through her mind. Her mother's demons were no doubt emerging.

'We'd give the baby an amazing home, Sara,' Joel said. 'You know how much we want this. He or she will be loved as if they were biologically ours.'

Sara cleared her throat. 'I know. I'm trying to get my head around it, that's all. Toni's always said she wouldn't foster or adopt.'

'That was when there was still some hope we'd have one of our own,' Toni said. 'But that's not going to happen, and we're not doing any more IVF, so this is a chance to have a newborn. The baby would be ours from the moment it was delivered. We'll be at the birth.'

Sara nodded. 'That's an amazing gift.'

'We know,' Joel said. 'We can't believe it, to be honest.'

'What about your friend? What if she changes her mind? She might when the baby's born.'

'She might, and we've had that discussion. In fact, we've agreed that if she changes her mind during the first month, then we'll be giving the baby back.'

Sara's face clouded over. 'That would be heart-breaking. To go through all of that and never see the baby again. Are you sure you'd be strong enough?'

Toni shook her head. 'Probably not. But I'd still be part of the baby's life if that did happen. We all would.'

'I doubt your friend will be so generous if she takes the baby back,' Sara said.

Toni cleared her throat. 'It's not exactly a friend, Mum.'

'But you said—'

Toni cut her off. 'It's not a friend. It's Liv.'

She was greeted by silence.

'Mum?'

Sara's face drained of colour. 'You're telling me your sister, my daughter, is pregnant and giving you her baby?'

'Yes. Liv offered the baby to Joel and me first. If we say no, she's going to put it up for adoption.'

Sara closed her eyes, shaking her head to and fro. She opened them and did her best to smile. 'Toni, the moment the baby's born, she'll change her mind.' She stood up.

'Where are you going?'

'I need to speak to Liv. I want to make sure that she understands what she's doing.'

Joel also stood and took Sara's arm. 'She knows. We've made sure of that. She's set in her intention to give the baby up. The safeguard she has is that if she changes her mind, then we'll give the baby back. If she goes through official channels to have the baby adopted elsewhere that won't be an option.'

'She's made up her mind, Mum,' Toni added. 'She doesn't need you getting involved.'

'You mean, *you* don't need me getting involved and changing her mind. I'm sorry, Toni. I know that you're desperate for a baby, but I'm not sure taking your sister's is a good idea.'

'You'd rather she goes to strangers?'

Sara sucked in a breath. 'I'd rather she stays with Liv. If possible, a child should remain with their biological parents. Do we know who the father is?'

'No,' Toni said. 'A backpacker on New Year's Eve. She doesn't have any way to contact him.'

'That's good, at least.'

Toni gave a strangled laugh. 'How's that good?'

'There will be no man demanding custody or his parental rights. Liv can move back to Melbourne, and we'll just help her raise the baby without a man interfering.'

A wave of despair washed over Toni. Her mother was an organiser and a doer and would probably make this happen exactly as she'd described.

'I'd hoped you'd be supportive, not try to change the arrangement.'

'I need Liv to know that there are options for her to keep the baby. You can understand where I'm coming from, can't you? As an adoptee myself.'

Toni nodded. She'd expected her mother's circumstances to play a large part in her reaction.

'The hardest thing for me has been not knowing who my biological mother is. I have no idea where I came from or the types of people who made up my DNA. I don't want that for Liv's baby.'

'It's hardly the same. The baby will be with biological family, and when she's old enough, she'll be told where she came from.'

Tears filled Sara's eyes.

'Oh, Mum, we didn't mean to upset you,' Toni said.

'I'm sorry. It's all so unexpected, that's all.'

'Are you going to try and talk Liv out of it?'

'I'd like to talk to her,' Sara admitted. 'To make sure she realises how huge this is.'

'Of course, she does,' Toni said. Although the way Liv joked around, it was hard to tell at times if she really did realise the enormity of what she was offering. Toni wasn't going to tell her mother this, though.

'Then you shouldn't be worried about anything I have to say to her. If she knows how huge it is and still wants to go ahead, then you've got nothing to be concerned about.'

An uneasy feeling crept over Toni. As sensible as her mother's words sounded, why did she automatically assume that Liv would have one conversation with her and change her mind?

'Why don't you call her now?' Joel suggested.

'What?' Toni and Sara spoke in unison.

'Toni's not going to be able to sleep tonight until she knows what's going on, and to be frank, we've been through enough disappointment when it comes to babies. If there's going to be more, then I'd like to get it over with quickly.'

'He's right,' Toni said. 'Use the office if you like. You can use the computer to FaceTime or use the phone.'

Sara stood. 'Okay. I'll try and FaceTime with her. I want to look her in the eye and really see that she's at peace with this decision.'

* * *

'Olivia, what is going on?'

Liv hesitated. She'd accepted the call from Toni and hadn't anticipated her mother being on the other end. 'Are you at Toni's?'

'Yes, I came for what I thought would be a nice dinner and instead have been ambushed with this baby problem.'

Liv swallowed. She'd been expecting this call, but the reality of it had her bracing herself. She took a deep breath. 'There's no problem. I'm pregnant with a baby I'm not keeping, and Toni and Joel are desperate to be parents. It's a win-win situation.'

'Until you have the baby and realise you could never give it up.'

'Mum, you know I don't want children. I never have, and I never will.'

'You wait until you see that little baby, and you hold it in your arms. You'll change your mind instantly. You can't have any idea of what it's like until you go through it.'

Liv sighed. 'When I go through it, we can compare notes and see if you're right. Toni has agreed that if I change my mind, she'll give the baby back. But I won't. And anyway, I thought you'd be glad that you'll be able to be part of your grandchild's life. Being with Toni, he or she will be in Melbourne, not Sydney.'

'Why don't you wait and make the decision after the baby's born?' Sara said. 'Why rush into it now? When you were born, I was overcome with the most intense feeling of love and protection. There's no way I could have given you away to anyone.'

'That's where we're different then. I don't feel anything for the baby now, and I'm sure I never will. Other than it will be nice to spoil her as an aunt would, and it will be wonderful to see Toni happy.'

Her mother was silent for a moment.

'Are you doing this out of guilt? Because you owe Toni?'

Trust her mother to point this out.

'Because,' Sara continued, 'giving up a baby isn't the right way to repay a gift like the one Toni gave you.'

'What if my kidney gives out?' Liv said. 'Have you thought about that? I've had it for fifteen years already. A kidney from a living donor typically lasts twenty to twenty-five years. I don't want to have a baby and be worrying that I might not get another one or have a young child watching me go through dialysis and eventually die. That's no life for a little kid.'

Sara's face softened. 'Oh, Liv. Is there an issue with your kidney?'

'No, but it's quite possible during the next five to ten years there might be. Who knows? I don't have a crystal ball.'

'You could always make Toni and Joel guardians so that the child would go to them if the worst did happen. Then the child would know that you wanted it, and they wanted it too. It would never be left feeling rejected.'

The hurt in her mother's voice caused Liv's heart to contract. 'Oh, Mum, this isn't about you. I know you've had a tough time, but that's not enough to make me do something I have no interest in doing. I don't want a child for a few reasons. I know you'll hate me for saying this, but it was hard growing up with Mandy taking up so much of everyone's time. It made me realise I don't want to have someone dependent on me like Mandy is on you. Even if the baby is healthy, it's a lot of years of life being about them. And yes, I know that sounds terribly selfish, but it's how I feel.'

'It's a lot of years of enjoying life with them,' her mother said. 'Yes, it's a big change and responsibility but there's so much joy and love that comes with it, Liv. I'm worried that you'll regret missing out.'

'Do you think your biological parents feel like that? That they missed out by giving you up?'

'I hope they do,' her mother admitted, 'but I'll never know. I just know that I could never have given any of you up. You really need to think about it.'

'I thought about it for months before I called Toni. The main reason for that was so as not to disappoint her if something went wrong, but it was also to make sure I was making a decision I'd never regret, and I have. I really don't want a baby. I know that's hard for you to hear with your situation, but it's the truth. This child will be raised by parents who really want it, and it will have blood ties to Toni. Any other kind of adoption won't have any blood ties.'

Sara sighed. 'I'm worried you're making a decision that's going to destroy our family.'

'What? How would it do that?'

'Because Toni will be devastated if you change your mind and want the baby back. Every mother who gives birth practically drowns with love for their new baby. You need to have a baby to understand that.'

'Have you heard of post-natal depression? Not every woman *drowns in love* for their new baby. Many of them drown in other ways. Look, I get that you'd like to believe that's true, but we both know it's not. Let's move on, can we? Toni will be a wonderful mother, and while I wish I wasn't dealing with a pregnancy, the upside is I can do this for Toni.'

'But—'

'No buts. Look, I have to go. I promised I'd take Mandy and Barb out to dinner tonight. But before I go, is Toni there?'

Her mother turned around and called out to Toni, who appeared instantly. Liv imagined she'd been listening to every word, her heart in her throat. She smiled as Toni approached the screen. 'Don't worry. Nothing's changed. Mum will have to get used to the idea.' Toni visibly relaxed. 'Be happy for Toni, Mum, and for yourself that you'll finally be a grandmother. Love you.'

Liv didn't give her mother or Toni the chance to respond but instead clicked on the end button. She hoped she'd said enough to convince her she was doing the right thing and her mother wouldn't make a trip to Sydney to try and change her mind in person. While she was doing her best to hold it together and continue with her plan, facing her mother in real life would likely be her undoing.

* * *

The next morning, Liv had to curb her smile as she opened the door of the apartment. From the doula's name and information provided on her website, she knew she was going to be a little alternative, and first impressions of the woman confirmed that she was. Her bold, printed, flowing maxi dress was covered by a denim jacket that had fringes on the sleeves and pockets. Her outfit was accessorised with a chunky, hand-carved, wooden necklace with a large pendant and a few beads. But it was her dazzling smile that captured Liv's attention. She felt instantly at ease in the doula's presence and knew she'd made the right choice to opt for a home birth rather than at a hospital.

'Your sister tells me you like to be called Hon,' Petal Blossom said, looking from her notes to Mandy when they were all seated around Liv's kitchen table enjoying a cup of herbal tea. 'Is that right?'

Mandy shrugged. 'That's what she usually calls me, so I guess it's fine if you call me that too. But, why are you called Petal Blossom? Are you a hippy? My friend, Izzy, told me all about hippies and how they dress funny and smoke weird cigarettes. Izzy lives in Melbourne, which is where I normally live.'

Petal laughed. 'No, I wouldn't say that, but my parents were. Perhaps not the cigarette bit. They were also keen gardeners and argued as to whether they'd call me Petal or Rose. In the end, they decided Petal went better with Blossom which is my surname. And do you want to know a coincidence?'

Mandy nodded.

'I'm from Melbourne too, and my parents and sister still live there. I'm going to visit them in a couple of months.'

'That's nice.' Mandy frowned, dismissing Petal's coincidence. 'But, if you're not a hippy, why do you dress like that and have funny hair?'

'Hey,' Liv said, 'enough with the questions. Petal's here to chat about the baby and ask us questions, not the other way around.'

Petal smiled kindly as Mandy scowled at Liv. 'It's fine. These are questions I'm sure a lot of people would like to ask but don't have the courage to.' She turned her attention back to Mandy. 'It's refreshing. I like my clothes and I like my dreadlocks. I follow a lot of eastern spiritual practices and like to believe that every human being is divine in their own right. Life is a miracle and I live a life that embraces and celebrates that. I guess my hair and my clothes are part of that celebration.'

'Is that why you deliver babies?' Mandy asked.

Petal nodded. 'Speaking of which. I have some information to share with you both. Are you happy if we talk about that?'

Liv couldn't help but smile as Mandy nodded eagerly. Regardless of why Petal had come to visit, for someone to put Mandy at ease so quickly was all Liv needed to know she'd made the right decision about a home birth and engaging

Petal's services. She was, however, torn. She liked this woman and felt that she could trust her. But that wasn't enough to feel that she could ask Petal the one question she really wanted to. She could tell that the doula was a good person and knew it was unlikely she'd agree to doing anything outside legal channels. As much as she wanted to confide in her and ask for her help, the animated expression on Petal's face as she described the home birth process confirmed for Liv that the doula, if asked to make a slight tweak on the birth certificate, would say no. It was best, Liv decided, to not mention her plan to anyone. She paused as she had this thought. She'd told Mandy part of the plan. She'd had to in order to make sure her sister didn't question her in front of Petal, but would she need to tell her everything? Liv sighed. Mandy was great at keeping secrets, but this was next level. She could only hope, for Toni's sake, she could pull it off.

9

With Petal's information and instructions, Liv prepared as best she could for the baby's arrival. What she hadn't prepared herself for was the sense of guilt that seemed to grow each day. It was ridiculous. She knew what she had to do and she knew she couldn't ask for the doula's help. For a start, it wouldn't be fair and secondly, if Petal said no, what would there be to stop her telling the authorities?

When the labour pains began, she'd assumed they were a false alarm. She wasn't ready for this. But they weren't, and six hours after labour started, the baby was born. She was grateful that Petal had arrived before the birth, as she certainly made the experience less daunting. They'd ended up being a good team, her, Mandy and Petal, and experiencing the birth of Baby – as Mandy insisted they call her until Toni and Joel announced her name – was something she'd treasure for the rest of her life.

As much as she had wanted to avoid the hospital, she had to admit the free-birth plan had left her quite anxious. But there'd been no tearing and the pain, whilst horrendous during the birth, was quickly forgotten. She was grateful that nothing had gone wrong. It had been her biggest fear that she would be punished for what she was doing. Now, four hours after the birth, she found herself staring at a gorgeous little bundle with a mass of black hair, sleeping peacefully in the bassinet beside the bed.

Petal had left, making Liv promise she'd call her if they needed anything or experienced any problems. The fact that Baby would be bottle-fed eliminated any breastfeeding issues, but Petal did mention that if they needed help settling her, she'd be happy to come back and would certainly call the next day to check up on them. She reminded Liv that they should be taking the baby for a check-up at the hospital within twenty-four hours of her birth, but having chosen a free birth to avoid hospital intervention, that was completely up to Liv.

'We did good,' Mandy said, gently stroking the baby's head.

'We sure did, Hon,' Liv replied.

'Toni will be angry she missed the birth. She'll blame me.'

'You?' Liv couldn't help but laugh. 'Why would she blame you?'

'She blames me for everything. She'll say I should have called her when the labour started. "If the baby comes early and Liv can't call me, then you have to, Mandy. We'll fly straight up." That's what she told me on FaceTime.'

Liv cleared her throat. 'The baby came early and quickly. There's nothing we could do about it. I think she'll be so excited to meet this gorgeous little girl that she won't give it a second thought. No one could predict she'd be born three weeks early. Mum said we were all late, so it certainly wasn't genetic. And if she is mad, it'll be me, not you, that she's upset with.' Liv uncrossed her fingers as the lies rolled off her tongue. The baby was three days early, not three weeks by her calculations, but no one else needed to know that. She'd deliberately misled Toni with regard to the due date. She instinctively knew that Toni being at the birth would have been a huge mistake. Everything she'd planned would have unravelled, and what if something had gone wrong? Could she really have put her sister through that?

'When will she arrive?' Mandy asked.

'Tomorrow. She and Joel are flying up.'

Mandy frowned. 'I thought she would have come today. She said she would come straight away.'

Liv didn't respond. She chose not to tell Mandy that she hadn't told Toni yet. She knew she'd jump straight on a plane and she wanted Baby to be with her and Mandy for one night. After all that they'd been through, they deserved a little bit of time before she was taken away. She was going to ring at nine when it would be too late to get the last flight and they'd have to wait until the following day.

'Does that mean Barb can meet her?' Mandy said. 'She thought she was going to miss out. Do you think I should call her?'

Liv nodded. 'Yes, invite her over. But, Mandy, when Toni and Joel arrive, I don't want Barb here, okay?'

'Why not?'

'It will be a special moment for Toni, that's all. Private and special. Family only.'

'Will Mum come too?'

Liv shook her head. 'No, Toni and Joel will take Baby back to Melbourne on Friday and she can meet her then.'

'Oh, Baby,' Mandy said sadly. 'Only two more days with you and then you'll be gone.'

Liv put an arm around her sister. 'But you'll be going back to Melbourne soon too. Then you'll be able to see as much of her as you like. Show her who the best aunt is.'

Mandy's brow furrowed. 'You might be the better aunt.'

Liv laughed. 'I doubt it. I'm not cut out for babies or kids.'

'Which is why Baby will go to Toni,' Mandy said. 'Liv, bad mother. Toni, good mother.'

A lump rose in Liv's throat. Mandy had nailed it there. She was definitely a bad person. She hoped that every time she looked at Baby down the track, she wouldn't be reminded of this.

* * *

It was as if the energy in Liv's apartment shifted overnight to accommodate the new life. It was lucky that Baby had taken to the bottle and formula as no milk had arrived. Liv knew that was a blessing in disguise. In addition to not having to deal with the discomfort Petal had warned her would occur as the milk dried up, there would be no leaking breasts or any other signs that would remind Toni that she hadn't been the one to give birth. Liv had expected to be up all night with Baby, but she'd gone to bed at eleven after

Baby's feed and woke at six. She'd jumped up, her heart racing that she hadn't heard the baby. She checked the bassinet, and it was empty. She hurried from the room and stopped as she reached the lounge. Mandy was sitting on the couch, singing softly with the little girl sleeping peacefully in her arms.

Liv went in search of her portrait camera. She slipped back into the room and took some photos before Mandy noticed her.

'Have you had her for long?' Liv asked after she'd put her equipment away.

Mandy nodded. 'All night.'

'What? Why didn't you wake me?'

Mandy shrugged. 'No need. Baby loves me. I fed her at two and at five. I changed her nappy, and I sang to her. I don't think I forgot anything.'

'Have you had any sleep?'

Mandy shook her head. 'That's okay. I can sleep when Baby's gone.' Her smile wavered, and a tear ran down her cheek. 'Maybe you should keep her, Liv. I can help you look after her. I think you'll be a good mum.'

'Oh Hon, I can't. I'm sorry. Toni will be a much better mum for her. And as I said yesterday, you'll be able to spend time with Baby when you go back to Melbourne.'

'What if Toni says no?'

'She won't, I promise.' Liv crossed her fingers behind her back once again as she made this promise on Toni's behalf. 'How about I make you some breakfast to cheer you up? Pancakes with strawberries?'

Mandy nodded; her eyes fixed on the baby. 'And for Baby too.'

'Hon, Baby's too little to eat. You know that.'

Mandy looked up, smiled, and pointed to the doll that was propped up on a chair opposite her. 'No, *she's* not, and she wants a big one. This baby will have her bottle, though.'

Liv smiled as relief settled over her. If Mandy wanted two pancakes and would use her doll to secure the second, then she was all for that. If she'd been up all night, she was probably starving.

Her phone pinged with a text as she made her way to the kitchen and opened the fridge. It was her mother.

How are you, darling? It's not too late to stop Toni from coming up if you've fallen in love. As much as it might hurt, it's better to do it early if you're going to break her heart. I hope you've had a lovely first night with your little girl. I can't wait to meet her.

Liv shook her head. Manipulative or what? She wouldn't be changing any of the plans. She couldn't do that to Toni. She glanced across to Mandy, who was gazing at the baby with such adoration that Liv's heart shattered a little. It was unfair that her sister would never know the joy of being a mother. Even she would have made a much better mother than Liv, that much she knew. She could only imagine her mother's face if she let on that she'd enjoyed an uninterrupted seven-hour sleep while Mandy stayed up all night with the baby. She probably should tell her. It would help get her off her case about changing her mind.

* * *

After eating her pancakes, Liv convinced Mandy to put the baby down in the bassinet they'd borrowed from a friend of Barb's long enough to have a shower before Toni and Joel arrived. Now, as she looked down at the sleeping bundle, her heart contracted at the sheer beauty of the little girl. While she'd done everything possible to fight it, her mother was right that she'd find it hard not to fall in love with the baby. She closed her eyes momentarily. She knew how lucky she was to be alive. Not everyone needing a kidney transplant was fortunate enough to get one, but it didn't stop a sense of grief from settling over her. It was unlikely she would see old age, and she'd tried to live a life of gratitude for what she had. But knowing she could never raise a child stung. She was telling the truth when she'd told Toni that it wouldn't be fair to a child to start raising it, knowing the odds were high that she'd put it through the heartbreak and grief of losing a parent at a young age. A tear rolled down her cheek.

'Livvy?'

Liv flinched as Mandy entered the room.

'Are you okay?'

Liv nodded. 'Feeling sorry for myself, that's all. I know I wouldn't be any good at being a mum, which is why the baby must go to Toni, but it's a hard decision to make.'

'I think you'd be a good mum. I wish you'd keep Baby.'

Liv took Mandy's hand and squeezed it. 'I know you do, Hon, but it's not the right decision. I have health issues because of my kidney, and it wouldn't be fair to the baby to have to grow up not knowing how long I'd be around for.'

Mandy's eyes widened. 'Are you going to die?'

'Hopefully not soon,' Liv said, 'but in the next few years, I might need a new kidney, and there's no guarantee I'll get one.'

'And that's why you can't be Baby's mummy?'

Liv nodded.

'And I can't be her mummy because I'm stupid.' Tears filled Mandy's eyes.

'Oh Hon, you're not stupid. You're smart and kind and lovely.'

'But I still can't be a mummy because of my challenges. The bad people would take the baby away.'

'Not bad people. But child services are unlikely to allow you to raise a baby on your own. You'd need a lot of help.'

'Mum would help. And maybe Toni too,' Mandy said. 'I think Baby would prefer to be with me. She loves me already.'

Liv forced a smile, her own self-pity pushed aside as she saw the hope on Mandy's face. Her sister would never be a mother. It was a sad but simple fact and it was hard to be the one to tell her this. 'She does love you, Hon. But she needs a home with a mummy and daddy who don't have health problems or intellectual challenges. You and I can settle for being the best aunties in the world.'

Mandy peered into the crib and stroked the baby's cheek. 'Aunty Mandy. It sounds okay. Mummy would sound better.'

Liv wiped a stray tear from her cheek. She'd done the right thing. She knew that. And as much as she was beginning to think that she too would like to be called Mummy, they had to put the baby's needs first.

She reached across for Mandy's hand. 'Toni and Joel will be here soon. They're going to be upset that they missed the birth but excited that their baby is here.'

'*Their baby,*' Mandy repeated. 'It doesn't sound right, Liv. Will they love her? Like I do?'

Liv pulled Mandy to her and hugged her. 'There's no doubt about that. Toni's wanted this more than any of us ever have. This baby is going to be the luckiest baby ever born.'

10

The taxi pulled to a stop in front of the harbour-side apartment block, and Joel squeezed Toni's hand.

'Ready?'

Toni stared out of the window and silently shook her head.

'Me neither,' Joel said. He paid the taxi driver, and they climbed out of the car while the driver retrieved their bags from the boot.

Toni took a deep breath as the taxi drove away. She was about to meet Liv's baby. Her baby? Whose baby was it at this stage? She closed her eyes. She'd been driving herself mad with this question circling around in her mind for the entire plane trip. She opened her eyes and turned to Joel. 'Do you think we're going to be able to handle this? A baby is a big responsibility.'

Joel smiled. 'Would you be asking that question if you'd given birth? No. You'd accept that you had a baby and take it home with you. And that's what we're about to do.'

'What if Liv's changed her mind?'

Joel put his bag down and stepped towards Toni, pulling her towards him. 'She didn't sound like she had when she rang last night, but if she has, then we'll deal with it. Okay?'

Toni nodded. Joel was right. The main emotion that Liv had conveyed during their phone call the previous night was guilt. 'I feel awful,' she'd said. 'I didn't pick up the signs that the labour was coming on quickly and early. If I had, I would have rung you. I'm gutted you missed the birth.'

Toni had insisted it didn't matter. That all that mattered was the baby was safe, and Liv was alright. She couldn't believe her sister had opted for a home birth. 'Are you mad?' she'd said when Liv explained they were at home, not at the hospital. 'Surely you're high risk with your kidney?'

'I'm fine,' Liv assured her. 'I didn't tell you earlier because I knew you'd freak out, but I checked with the transplant doctors, and they consulted with my GP who ran all sorts of tests and declared me to be in perfect health. One of the transplant team spoke with Petal Blossom, the doula, and there was a detailed plan in place in case something went wrong. It didn't, it was all perfect.'

'But what if something had happened?' Toni shuddered as she had the thought. Losing Liv was not something she could even contemplate.

'It didn't,' Liv's voice was gentle. The voice she used when she knew Toni was worried about her. 'Don't worry, I'll be around to annoy you for decades to come.'

'Make sure you are,' Toni said, a little more gruffly than she intended. She softened her tone. 'Are you sure you don't need to be checked out by a doctor? Or have the baby checked?'

'No. Petal knew her stuff. She's given us both a thorough examination. I have all the notes here for you which you can take with you for the baby's medical history. I'm confident we'll be fine, and the thought of sitting in a waiting room for hours after what we've just been through holds no appeal. And anyway, everyone knows hospitals are full of sick people. We don't want the baby exposed to that. Of course, if anything changes, I'll call an ambulance or go straight to the hospital.'

Toni knew she should be reassured by Liv's confidence, but the fact that her doula was called Petal Blossom raised more alarm bells than she cared to admit. What kind of hippy had helped deliver her baby? *Her baby*. She couldn't help but smile at the thought. Liv had suggested they do a video call so they could see the baby, but Toni had said no. She wanted their first meeting to be in person.

'Now,' Joel said, his voice gentle. 'I know that you're scared, and I am too, but I'm dying to meet our daughter. Come on.'

Toni took his hand and allowed him to lead her up the path and into the foyer of the apartments. A quick trip in the lift, and they were standing outside Liv's door only moments later.

'Listen,' Joel said, putting his finger to his lips.

Toni expected to hear a baby crying, but instead, what she heard brought a lump to her throat. A sweet voice, filled with love, was singing 'Twinkle-Twinkle'.

'Is that Liv?' Concern flashed in Joel's eyes.

Toni shook her head. 'No, it's Mandy. She has a beautiful singing voice.'

Relief replaced the concern in Joel's eyes. 'That's good because if that was Liv, I'd be worried that she'd fallen in love with the baby and the likelihood of us taking her home tomorrow was slim.'

'That's still a possibility,' Toni said, all her fears rushing back over her. 'Mum was on the phone to me earlier, making me promise that if Liv has changed her mind, that I wouldn't pressure her into giving us the baby.'

'Hello.'

The voice of an older lady caused Toni and Joel to swivel to face her.

A woman in her late eighties stood across from them. 'Isn't Liv answering?'

'We haven't knocked yet,' Joel said.

The woman smiled. 'A few nerves, I bet. I'll leave you to it. My exciting outing for the day is to go and check my mailbox. Enjoy meeting your little girl.'

'You know who we are?' Toni said.

She nodded. 'I'm Barb. Liv's neighbour. I hope you don't mind, but Mandy insisted I have a quick visit yesterday. She was proud to introduce me to your little girl.'

'Yesterday?' Toni said. 'It must have been a late visit.'

'Not too late,' Barb said. 'In time for afternoon tea. I know Mandy's hoping you'll allow her to be involved in taking care of her.'

Toni frowned. It had been around nine o'clock the previous night when Liv had phoned with the news that the baby had arrived unexpectedly only a few hours earlier. It certainly wouldn't have been in time for afternoon tea. Was the older woman confused? It was highly possible. Rather than question her, she smiled. 'I think Mandy will have enough on her plate taking care of herself once she moves out of home. But she'll be welcome to visit.'

'Good,' Barb said. 'Now, you must be dying to meet *your* baby. Enjoy these first few moments. They're very special.'

Joel knocked on the front door as the older lady gave them a little wave and continued down the corridor towards the lifts.

The door flew open and Liv greeted them.

Toni's mouth dropped open, causing Liv to grin.

'Hey, new mum.' Liv opened her arms and pulled Toni into a hug.

'How do you look like that?' Toni asked. 'You had a baby, and you look completely relaxed and refreshed. You're not even fat. Aren't you still supposed to look fat until all the fluid goes?'

Liv pulled out of the hug and laughed. 'Don't underestimate the power of a baggy sweatshirt. As for the birth, it was unexpectedly quick, and I had a full night's sleep.'

'How did you manage that?' Joel asked, hugging Liv.

'Mandy,' Liv said. 'She's been amazing. I didn't even hear Baby last night. She got up to her and then cuddled her all night when she wasn't feeding her. I highly recommend you invite her over regularly once you get home.'

'Baby?' Toni asked.

'It's what Mandy named her once she found out I was pregnant,' Liv said. 'The same as her doll. She's needed a name since she was born, so I went with Mandy's choice. I expect that's about to change?'

Toni nodded, wishing she'd been there for the birth and that the baby had been handed to her the moment she'd been born. Instead, Mandy had enjoyed the first hours and night of her life. *Bloody Mandy*. She did her best to shake the irritation and resentment she harboured for her sister.

'Can we meet her?' Joel asked.

'Of course,' Liv said. 'Put your bags in that room.' She pointed to an open door leading off the short passageway. 'And meet me in the living room – where Mandy has her right now.'

'Hold on a sec,' Toni said. 'We met your neighbour in the hallway. She said she met the baby yesterday in time for afternoon tea.'

Liv frowned. 'Barb came over at about nine-thirty last night, after I called you. The baby wasn't even born at four. Sorry that she met her before you did. Mandy kind of insisted, and I was too overwhelmed to stop her.'

'Barb must have mixed up the times,' Toni said.

Liv nodded. 'She brought over a cake we had as a late supper. Maybe she mistook that for afternoon tea. Her grandson's worried she's got a touch of dementia. We invited her for dinner last week, and she turned up for breakfast, insisting that's what I'd said. As I rarely eat breakfast, I'm not going to be inviting someone over at that time of day.' She grinned. 'Or I've got baby brain and I did do all of that. I read somewhere that a large section of your brain is attached to the placenta and tends to fall out when the placenta is delivered. Who's to say? Now come and get settled and meet your baby. I'm dying to hear what you're going to call her. Oh, and make sure you wash your hands, Mandy's being very strict about hygiene.'

Toni, slightly overwhelmed by Liv's stream of chatter, deposited her bag with Joel's into the spare room and, a few moments later, after they'd both washed their hands, followed the passageway to the living room.

'Hi, Mandy,' Toni called out as she saw her sister sitting on the couch. Mandy turned her head, her eyes tired, but her cheeks were glowing.

'Come and meet Baby,' Mandy said, turning the rest of her body so that Toni could see the small bundle wrapped in a yellow blanket.

Toni's eyes filled with tears, and her lip quivered. She was about to meet her baby. She glanced at Liv.

'I haven't changed my mind,' her sister said gently.

Toni nodded, took a deep breath, and stepped towards Mandy.

'Sit next to me,' Mandy instructed. Toni sat next to her, getting her first glimpse of the baby's perfect, porcelain skin. She had thick, dark hair and her eyes were firmly shut. Her tiny fingers were clasped around one of Mandy's.

'She's beautiful,' Joel said. He'd moved closer to get his first look at his daughter. He looked up at Liv. 'She's got your hair.'

'And mine,' Mandy said. 'Not Toni's brown hair.'

'Mandy,' Liv prompted. 'Let Toni hold the baby.'

Mandy looked up at Liv. 'She might be scared.'

'She'll be fine.'

Mandy nodded and gently turned so she could put the baby in Toni's arms. The first thing that registered with Toni was how small she was. How fragile. She was going to have to be careful not to break her. She shook herself. *That* was her first thought?

'Oh my. She's perfect,' Joel said, his voice barely a whisper. He'd moved around to sit beside Toni and was stroking the baby's head. His eyes filled with tears as he looked from Toni to Liv. 'I don't know what to say. This is an unbelievable gift.'

Liv smiled. 'How about Mandy and I leave you alone and you can get to know your daughter? You'll have to let us know if you've named her.'

'Her name is Baby,' Mandy said, causing Toni to flinch.

'That was her temporary name, remember, Hon?' Liv said. 'She'll get her proper name when Toni and Joel are ready.' Liv held out her hand. 'Come on. I said we'd go and visit Barb. She was going to make some hot chocolate for us.'

Mandy looked at the baby and then back to Liv.

'You'll be able to hold her again when you come back,' Toni promised. It was obvious that Mandy was already attached to the baby. 'And Mands, I'm glad you love the baby, as I'm sure we'll need your help when you come back to Melbourne.' It almost killed Toni to say that, but this was an important moment, and she didn't want anything to spoil it.

Mandy's eyes filled with tears, but Toni was grateful when she nodded and stood.

'I've put a bottle in warm water in the kitchen,' Liv said. 'She'll probably be hungry soon. If you have any problems, we'll be straight across the hall at Barb's. Just come and get us.'

'Okay,' Toni said as Liv put an arm around Mandy's shoulders and led her from the room.

'She's gorgeous,' Joel said, his finger lightly stroking the baby's head. 'And I think the name fits her perfectly.'

Toni stared at the baby, whose eyes fluttered open. 'Hello, baby girl,' she said, hoping that her feeling of fear would be replaced any second with one of deep love for this tiny creature.

'Our little Ruby,' Joel added.

Ruby scrunched up her face, opened her mouth and wailed.

Toni froze.

Joel laughed. 'You should see your face.' He held out his arms, and Toni was quick to pass Ruby to him. He popped his little finger in her mouth, and the baby stopped crying and started sucking on it. 'She's going to work out pretty quickly that there's no milk coming out of that,' Joel said. 'Let's get the bottle from the kitchen and see if she'll take it.'

Toni stared in disbelief at her husband. 'How did you know how to do that?'

'I've read a lot of books in the past few weeks,' he said. 'I skipped the bit about what to expect when you're expecting and moved straight into the "how to cope from day one" style of books. I figured they were more relevant.'

'I'm not sure I'm cut out for this.'

Joel smiled. 'Babe, no one's expecting us to have any clue what to do. We'll need Liv to show us the basics, and then we'll figure out the rest. Relax and try and enjoy this. Don't forget Ruby has no idea how to be a human either. It'll be trial and error for all of us.' He looked down at the baby, his face flooding with happiness. 'We have a baby. A real live baby. We're going to be a family.'

A lump so large it started to ache rose in Toni's throat as she watched her husband. He'd fallen in love with Ruby on sight, whereas she was wracked with fear. She needed to push away her concern about Liv taking the baby back, which no doubt was the cause of her anxiety. She needed to relax when it came to working out what Ruby wanted, and most of all, she needed to relish this moment. They'd just met their daughter. Ruby Sara Montgomery. She forced a smile. She'd planned for years for this day – the happiest day of her life – she just hoped it lived up to her expectations.

11

Liv waited until everyone was asleep that night before going to the bassinet and checking on Ruby. It was a beautiful name and suited her perfectly. Toni and Joel would be taking her back to Melbourne in the morning. It was hard to believe only a few months ago she'd worked out that the thickening waist and weight gain was a pregnancy, not the result of comfort eating, and now, here they were. A new baby to celebrate. She bent down, picked up the sleeping bundle and carried her into the lounge. Mandy had been so possessive of her since the birth, she'd hardly had an opportunity to hold her. Her mother would have said it was a good thing, that it stopped her from getting attached, but it wasn't. Liv needed to hold her. To transfer as much love to her as possible and to make sure she apologised.

'I really am sorry,' she said to the baby, stroking the thick strands of hair on her tiny head as they settled onto the couch. 'If I could have thought up a way for this to work, I would have. I know what I've done is unforgivable, but please know I've done it for you. I know how much Mum struggled learning she was adopted and then discovering her mother hadn't wanted her. It isn't a case of you not being wanted either. If circumstances were different, then I'd take the risk and hope things would work out for the best, but they're not, and I can't risk your future. That's why I know that Toni is the best mother for you. She's wanted a baby for such a long time.'

Tears filled Liv's eyes as she thought of her sister's struggle and that now, with Ruby in her life, that struggle would be over. She cuddled the baby close to her, breathing in her baby smell. 'I love you, little darling, and I'll always be there for you. I think Mandy intends to fill the role of favourite aunt, but hopefully, I'll be a close second.'

The little girl snuggled against her, her eyes shut, her breathing deep. Liv closed her eyes. Her mother was right. Holding Ruby was stirring feelings in her she never expected to experience. Not that she'd admit that to her mother or to Toni, and not that she planned to act on them. She would be the baby's aunt, as would Mandy, and tomorrow, Toni and Joel would get to take their daughter home.

* * *

Mandy was startled awake at 5 a.m. At 10 p.m. the previous night, she'd planned to sleep for thirty minutes to get enough energy to stay awake all night with Baby, but exhaustion had got the better of her, and she'd fallen into a deep sleep.

She threw the covers off. If Baby had woken during the night, she hadn't heard her. She hurried into the living room where the crib had been left and discovered it empty. Toni and Joel must have Baby.

Mandy crept along the hallway to their bedroom and opened the door quietly. They were fast asleep with no sign of Ruby. She *knew* Toni would be a terrible mother, and she'd proven it already. Baby would have needed them in the night, and they hadn't woken to her cries. Liv must have.

She continued along the hallway to Liv's bedroom to discover Liv asleep in the chair beside her bed and Baby lying across her chest, sleeping. Why couldn't Liv keep Baby and be her mummy? It wasn't fair. She would be much kinder and more fun than Toni, and more importantly, she'd let Mandy be involved. Liv had promised her that Toni would let her help with Baby, and as much as Mandy wanted to believe her, she couldn't. Toni hated her. She always had. Sometimes, she was a little bit nice, but if there was no one else around, she wasn't. Mandy knew she was an embarrassment to Toni. Would Toni let an embarrassment be involved with her baby? Of course not.

A tear slid down Mandy's cheek as she reached across and gently took Baby from Liv's chest. Toni might not let her be involved, but for right now, she would be Baby's mummy. She would feed her and rock her back to sleep, and when Toni and Joel woke up, they'd see what a wonderful job she was doing and invite her to help when she returned to Melbourne.

* * *

After saying goodbye to Toni and Joel and giving Ruby a final cuddle, Liv walked back into the apartment, exhaustion enveloping her. Physically, she was a wreck, and mentally and emotionally, even worse. She knew everything about the birth, and handing Ruby over was going to be difficult, but she'd never expected it to be this draining. In an ideal world, she'd like to climb under the covers and sleep for days, but the muffled sobs coming from Mandy's room were a reminder that she was going to have to put her sister first.

Liv pushed open the door to the spare bedroom, her heart contracting as the sobs increased in volume. It was to be expected. Mandy had fallen in love with Ruby, and she was going to miss her. She'd always had a fascination with babies, and to have experienced the birth, and those magical first minutes and hours, made it hard to say goodbye.

Liv walked over and sat on the edge of the bed. She patted the blanket, feeling Mandy squirm as she did. 'It's completely normal to miss Ruby,' she said. 'We both fell in love with her, but Toni will do a much better job of looking after her than I ever will.'

'I could have looked after her.' Mandy's words were muffled.

Liv sighed. 'Oh Hon, as much as I would have loved that, I don't think you could have. Maybe while she was a tiny baby, but as she gets older and needs help with more things, I think you'd struggle.'

'You could have helped me.'

'It's not realistic. I love having you here for a holiday, but I don't want to share my apartment permanently and as horrible as this sounds, I don't want a baby here.' Liv closed her eyes briefly as the words left her mouth. She wasn't going to admit to Mandy that she missed Ruby too. She was such a precious little bundle. The last two days had passed in a blur with the newborn in the house. It was as if the world had stood still for a brief second in time.

Mandy's tear-stained face appeared from under the covers. She sat up and cuddled her doll to her. 'If you didn't want her, I could have taken her back to Melbourne and been her mummy. I would be much better than Toni. Mum would have helped me, and Izzy would have too. Izzy's two years older than me and much more mature. She's got a proper job and everything.'

'I'm sorry, Hon, but that was never an option. Mum's too old to raise another baby, and while I'm sure your friend, Izzy, is nice, she has her own life. She can't give up her job to suddenly look after a baby. The good thing about Toni being Ruby's mummy is that you can visit Ruby when you get back to Melbourne.'

'Did Toni actually say I could?'

Liv hadn't had a chance to talk to Toni properly about Mandy but hoped her sister would mellow now she had the baby she'd always dreamed of. Having promised she would talk to her, she wasn't going to admit this now. She crossed her fingers and slid them under a fold in the blanket. 'She said she'd love you to be involved.'

Mandy wiped her eyes. 'Really?'

Liv nodded silently, praying that Toni would allow Mandy to visit. 'I imagine Toni and Joel might ask Mum to babysit sometimes, too, so you could be there then to help out.'

Mandy nodded slowly. 'I think Baby would like that.' She cuddled her doll to her, and Liv wasn't sure whether she was referring to her doll or Ruby, but either way, she seemed a bit happier.

'Now,' Liv said, 'I'm going to have a shower and then I thought we could go out somewhere nice for lunch.'

'Where to?'

'Anywhere you choose. We can invite Barb if you like.'

Mandy nodded. 'She'll be upset that Baby has gone with Toni too. She might need cheering up.'

Liv smiled. She doubted their neighbour had strong feelings about the Ruby situation, but if Mandy wanted to believe that, then she'd let her.

* * *

Barb said yes immediately when Liv invited her to join them for lunch. They'd chosen Cruize, a café only a short walk from the apartments perched on the edge of Smiggin's Park, overlooking the harbour.

The three women were shown to a table out on the café's famous Harbour Deck. There was a slight chill in the air, and Liv asked that the patio heaters be moved closer for Barb's benefit. No sooner than they were seated, Mandy stood. 'I need the bathroom.'

'Did you want me to take you?' Liv asked, doing her best to contain a smile as Mandy rolled her eyes.

'I am thirty, Olivia. I am a woman, and I can do this myself.'

'Okay.'

Mandy looked from side to side and hesitated.

Liv lifted her hand and pointed in the direction of the toilets.

She and Barb exchanged a smile as Mandy turned and walked away from the table.

'It's been a difficult few days,' Barb said. 'How are you coping?' Sympathy flooded the older woman's eyes as she reached across the table and squeezed Liv's hand. 'None of this can have been easy. You look exhausted, love.'

'You're right that it hasn't been easy, and yes, I'm tired.' Dizzy too, but Liv didn't let on that she was experiencing some concerning symptoms.

'Do you still think you did the right thing?'

Liv withdrew her hand from Barb's and wiped away a tear that escaped from the corner of her eye. 'I hope so. I'm not sure I'll ever know completely. It seemed like the right thing during the pregnancy, and Toni and Joel will love Ruby to bits, but I'll probably go to hell for what I've done.'

Barb nodded, her face solemn, and Liv couldn't help but laugh. 'Contradicting me at this point would be a lot kinder than agreeing.'

Barb managed a tight-lipped smile. 'I'm not agreeing with you, but you've created difficult circumstances for yourself. It could all unravel. You do realise that, don't you?'

'I haven't lodged the paperwork yet,' Liv admitted. She'd ended up confiding in Barb her plans for the birth certificate. And while the older woman had thought it a terrible idea, she had promised to support Liv in whatever decision she made.

'Oh? Are you having second thoughts?'

Liv hesitated for a split second.

'You are.'

Liv shook her head. 'Maybe, but I know it's the right thing to do. I do feel bad, though, on many levels but particularly for deceiving Petal. She was lovely and lying to her was low. But she's a reputable doula, and there should be no reason for births, deaths and marriages to contact her to follow up. My mind is made up, and I'd prefer not to talk about it.'

'Understood,' Barb said. 'Now, how much longer is Mandy staying for?'

'She's itching to get back to Melbourne as soon as possible,' Liv said. 'If I'd let her, she probably would have gone back with Toni and Joel so she could help with Ruby. But her room at Wattle House will be ready in two weeks. I'm going to tell her she has to stay until then. It will give Toni and Joel some time with Ruby on their own before they're fending off offers of help.'

'Mandy told me she's worried Toni might not let her help with Ruby. That she's never liked Mandy, so can't imagine her allowing her to help.'

Liv sighed. 'She's not wrong, unfortunately. Toni struggled as we grew up with Mandy. I know she's not proud of her behaviour or how she feels, but she can't help it. Mandy took a lot of time and attention from Toni and me and a lot of financial resources. Mum and Dad were always forking out for specialists and special programs, and there were times that we had to miss out. Toni was really upset when she was about fourteen and was offered a partial scholarship to MLC. It's a private school in Melbourne, and now as an adult, I realise we couldn't afford the remainder of the fees, but at the time, Mum and Dad told Toni that Mandy had to come first, and she should be grateful for what we had. Toni had achieved this amazing thing to be offered the scholarship and it was a slap in the face to be told not to be selfish. I don't think she ever forgave Mandy for that.'

'But she forgave your parents?' Barb asked. 'After all, they were the ones making the financial decisions.'

'I'm not sure she forgave them, but she had no choice in the matter. It's a shame they didn't explain the financial situation better, but in all honesty, it might not have changed Toni's feelings on the situation. At the end of the day, Mandy's expenses meant there wasn't any money for private school, even with a partial scholarship.'

'I'm sure Mandy would have been entitled to government assistance?'

Liv nodded. 'She was, but there were gaps, and Mum always seemed to come up with some new plan to help her that would involve a different specialist or a class or something. It always added up. To be fair, I'm not sure they could have afforded the school fees regardless of Mandy's extra expenses, but Toni never accepted Mandy and still blames her to this day.'

'That's sad,' Barb said, 'for them both. As difficult as I'm sure it was growing up with Mandy, I'm sure she taught you a lot too. About patience, kindness and gratitude for all the things you were able to do that she couldn't. Perhaps having a child of her own will help Toni see some of this and appreciate that she's now been given an opportunity that Mandy never will be.' She gave a small smile. 'I do hope your sister lets her be part of Ruby's life. It would be incredibly unkind not to, and I think she has a lot to offer if she's allowed.'

'If who's allowed?' Mandy asked, flopping into the chair next to Liv.

'You,' Liv said. 'We were saying how much you have to offer Toni and Joel and I also believe your new housemates are going to appreciate having someone like you around.'

Mandy considered this for a moment. 'What if I don't like them?'

'There aren't many people in the world that we really don't like,' Barb said. 'It's often a case that you haven't got to know them properly. The main thing is to give everyone a chance. Even if you're not sure at first, don't assume you don't like them. You never know what friendships you might find.'

Mandy nodded.

'You're very wise,' Liv said. 'I'm often too quick to judge and make up my mind about people.' She nudged Mandy. 'That might be good advice for both of us.'

'And Toni too,' Mandy said. 'She needs to unmake up her mind about me and be a good sister. Izzy thinks that too.' She giggled. 'Izzy offered to whack her over the head to wake her up, if I think that's a good idea.'

Liv laughed. 'I hope you said no.'

Mandy shrugged. 'Maybe.'

'I'm sure when you spend time with Toni and Ruby, she'll see what a good sister you are, and Izzy won't need to whack her over the head.' A smile played on Liv's lips. She was glad Mandy had a friend outside the family she could joke with.

'Good sister and good aunt,' Mandy added. 'I'll be the best aunt to Ruby. Better than any of her other aunts.'

'Better than me, you mean?'

'Yes, and her other aunt.'

'Toni's not an aunt,' Liv reminded her. 'She's her mummy now. You need to remember that, Mandy.'

Mandy opened her mouth as if to object, then closed it again. 'Okay, Livvy.' She picked up the menu and looked at it while Barb raised a questioning eyebrow at Liv.

Liv shrugged. As much as she loved Mandy, she wasn't sure she'd ever fully understand how her mind worked, and the one thing she'd learnt since Mandy had come to stay with her was that it was best not to try.

* * *

As the days passed after Toni and Joel returned to Melbourne with Ruby, Liv set about trying to get life back to normal. She'd been fighting fatigue since before Ruby's birth and assumed that exhaustion through the entire birth ordeal and handing Ruby over to Toni and Joel had caused the fatigue to remain. She wondered if the lethargy and exhaustion were mental, rather than physical; that the secrets she'd been harbouring and the decisions she'd been making were causing her angst. She had one final job to complete before being able to put the baby saga behind her. Her preparation around the birth of Ruby had been meticulous and, amazingly, had gone to plan. While legally, it could be argued that she'd done the wrong thing, everything in her heart told her she'd done the right thing. The right thing for Toni and for Ruby.

Liv stared at the paperwork she'd completed. She was a terrible person without a moral fibre in her body. No, that wasn't true, and that was the problem. While she was doing her best to convince herself that there would be no consequences, her churning gut and recently broken-out skin told her otherwise. She did her best to push away her doubts, sealed the envelope and placed it on the stand in the entrance hall ready to post the next day. There was no reason anyone would question it. She'd forged both Toni and Joel's signatures as the birth parents and Petal had signed it as an independent witness, unaware that she'd been provided with false names from the day Liv had first contacted her. Petal had no reason to question Liv's story that the baby's father didn't want to be involved other than to be recognised as the father on the birth certificate. She'd promised to have him sign the paperwork, and she would forward it to Petal once he had. It made it easier that Toni had retained her maiden name so listing the parents as Antonia Montgomery and Joel Drayson didn't lead to further questions about their married state.

Now Ruby's birth would officially be registered with births, deaths and marriages with Toni and Joel as Ruby's biological parents. There would never be any reason for Ruby to know she was adopted or who her biological parents were. Liv thought of her sister's concerns that she'd want Ruby back and smiled. If anything was going to prove to Toni that this was not the case, the birth certificate would. Once it was issued, there would be no turning back for any of them. Ruby would officially belong to Toni and Joel, and Liv had done a fantastic job convincing herself that she couldn't be happier.

12

Ruby's cries increased in volume as Toni shut the infant's bedroom door and hurried down the hallway to the master bedroom. Her heart thumped as the cries rose to a wail. They'd been home from Sydney for six weeks, and Ruby's cry still caused adrenaline to shoot through her.

She moved across the room to her bedside table, where she'd left her earbuds and snatched them up, pushing an earpiece into each ear. Within seconds, music filled her head, and Ruby's screams disappeared. Relief flooded through her as she sank down onto the blue and white checked duvet. What would Liv say if she could see her now? She'd given her the ultimate gift, and this was how she was coping? Or not coping, more to the point. She shuddered. How could this be her life? She was an award-winning advertising executive. In the corporate world she could achieve anything, yet here she was the poster child for failing motherhood. If it wasn't so awful, she'd appreciate the irony. A woman desperate to have a baby gets what she wants. Or does she?

Her thoughts flicked to Joel. He'd been back at work for the past week, and the wheels had completely fallen off. Deep down, she'd known after her first few days of motherhood that they would. She'd only just been holding it together before he went back to work, and that was with him around full time and her mother helping a lot. Neither of them had seen through the facade that she wasn't coping. Being on her own with Ruby had confirmed every fear that Toni had ever had about motherhood. She was not cut out for it and was beginning to believe that the reason she'd been unable to carry a pregnancy to term was the universe protecting an unborn child from her pathetic attempts at mothering.

A tear rolled down her cheek as the music continued to block out Ruby's screams. Her life wasn't recognisable. No longer the high-flying executive, she'd traded in her suits and heels for prison garb. Day in, day out enclosed in a prison cell. She sighed, knowing she was being overly dramatic. She was sure few people would refer to their modern South Yarra apartment as a prison. But that's how it felt to her. At least Joel would be home on Friday, and she had a night out planned with Belinda, Rachael and three of their colleagues from Entice. A night out being recognised as Toni, the advertising executive, rather than Ruby's failing mother, might be what she needed to perk her up.

Toni lifted her head off the pillow, removed her earbuds and opened her eyes. She rose wearily from the bed, the cries from the nursery no longer muffled by the headphones. It amazed her that someone so tiny could produce so much noise for such a long time. As she did her best to ignore Ruby and instead focus on the luxury of having a shower, her phone rang. She frowned when she saw the caller was Mandy. How many more times was she going to call? Surely, she'd get the hint at some stage that Toni not answering her calls meant she didn't want to speak to her? She'd avoided Liv's calls since they'd returned from Sydney, too. At first, her reluctance to talk to her was in case Liv had decided she wanted Ruby back. But now, with the way Toni was feeling, she'd almost welcome that request. She tossed the phone onto the bed when a knock on the front door caused her to flinch.

She dashed into Ruby's room and scooped the baby up from the cot. Her cries stopped instantly, and Toni hurried to the front door as a second round of knocking began. She opened it to find Vera McKay on the other side.

'I'm sorry, Vera. I'm having a lot of trouble settling her.'

'You have to do something,' her neighbour said. 'I'm working night shifts and trying to sleep during the day is impossible. Have the child health nurses been to visit you?'

'Who?'

Vera shook her head. 'You're kidding me? They should have told you all of this when you left the hospital.'

Toni opened her mouth about to correct her neighbour when she realised it was quite possible that Vera thought she'd given birth to Ruby. She hadn't seen her neighbour in months, so it was unlikely that Vera had seen that she wasn't pregnant.

'You should call the council and find out. Or the hospital. They should come around and visit in the first few weeks to make sure you're not having any trouble with sleep issues, excessive crying and all the usual kind of stuff.'

'Thanks, I'll call them today,' Toni said. 'And again, I am sorry. I've tried everything.' She blinked rapidly, willing the tears away. She knew she was a failure in the motherhood department, but having the neighbours point it out was humiliating and upsetting. Why she'd pushed for IVF was beyond her. She'd assumed she'd be a great mum, a natural. The reality was far from that. While she had no intention of calling the health nurses, her second statement – that she'd tried everything – was true. Well, sort of true. She had given up the last few days when nothing had worked to settle Ruby, but up until then, she had picked her up each time she'd cried and done her best to settle her. As it hadn't worked, she'd decided to adopt the cry it out approach. That wasn't working either, and it was disturbing the neighbours, but tuning Ruby out with headphones was definitely working for Toni.

Vera's face softened. 'It's not easy, I get that, but anything you can do would be appreciated.' She turned to leave but stopped and turned back to face Toni. 'And congratulations. I haven't seen you in ages. I didn't even realise you were expecting.'

Toni smiled her thanks before shutting the door as Vera retreated down the hall to her apartment.

She took Ruby straight through to her bouncy chair that she'd left in the lounge room. The baby wailed as soon as she placed her in the chair, causing Toni's adrenaline to race. Would Vera be back knocking any minute? 'Hush, Ruby,' she said, forcing her tone to be calm and gentle. How was it that the sound of that wail made her want to scream at the baby to be quiet? She gave herself a mental shake and walked through to the kitchen to prepare a bottle. The upside was that she hadn't screamed at Ruby – yet.

13

Six weeks after Ruby's birth, life finally returned to normal. Mandy had moved back to Melbourne three weeks earlier, and while Liv had to admit she missed her vibrant energy, she was pleased to regain her privacy and the peace and serenity her apartment offered. She smiled as she stood out on the balcony watering the herb planters that Mandy had insisted on growing during her stay. Liv looked out to the harbour, the water glistening from the mid-morning sun, and reflected on how lucky she was. She lived in a beautiful part of the world, had a loving family and had her health. She frowned as this thought crossed her mind. The exhaustion she'd experienced following Ruby's birth and the emotional upheaval of giving her to Toni hadn't lifted. She probably needed to see a naturopath and get a plan for a healthier lifestyle. No doubt her iron levels were low as that often was the case when she felt exhausted.

Her ringtone echoed through the apartment, distracting her. Both her phone and computer were ringing, confirming it was a FaceTime call. She switched off the hose and hurried to the small office nook where she kept her computer and accepted the call. Her sister's beaming smile greeted her.

'Hey, Mands, how are you?'

Mandy clapped her hands together and squealed with delight when she saw Liv. 'I'm going to give you a tour of my new home,' she said, flipping the camera on her iPad so Liv could see the bedroom she was standing in. 'This is my room,' she said as she opened cupboards and drawers.

'It looks lovely, Hon,' Liv said. And it did. 'Is it brand new?'

Mandy flipped the camera back to be on her. 'No, but only two years old. Come with me, and I'll show you the kitchen and the lounge room.' She giggled. 'The television takes up most of the wall. It's huge.'

'Perfect for watching *Titanic*,' Liv said. 'Have your housemates seen it?'

'Six times since I've lived here,' Mandy said.

'Really? But you've only been there three weeks.'

'They love it as much as I do.' Mandy said.

'And you're okay with cooking and cleaning up and everything else we practised?'

Mandy nodded. 'Izzy's going to teach me how to cook pad thai. She thinks my housemates will like it.'

'Izzy? You know, I still haven't met your friend, Mands. Tell me about her. All I know is she's older than you and works at the animal shelter.'

'She's a lot of fun,' Mandy said, 'like my friend, Sam, was. I'm lucky I still have her. And she's so clever. She knows everything about being a kennel technician and has taught me how to look after the animals and even give some of them their medication.'

'It's great you have a friend like that,' Liv said. 'Is she coming over to teach you to make pad thai today?'

'Not today,' Mandy said. 'I'm doing something special today. Look at this.' She walked into the kitchen and angled the camera to point sideways at a delicious looking chocolate cake. 'Rose helped me make this. She's my favourite housemate. I'm going to surprise Mum with it and visit her today.'

'That's wonderful, Hon; she'll love that. I wish I was there too as I'd love a slice. You've become really independent.'

Mandy put the camera up to her face, pride reflected in her smile. 'I am. Barb calls me most days too. I have lots of friends now.'

Barb had mentioned to Liv her daily chats with Mandy. It surprised Liv what a strong connection Barb and Mandy had formed, and she could see that the older woman had been quite lonely since Mandy had returned to Melbourne.

'I'm happy for you,' Liv said. 'Have you seen Toni and Ruby lately?'

'I saw Toni and Baby at Mum's a few days ago,' Mandy said. She frowned. 'Too many days ago. But Toni never returns my calls. I only see them if they are with Mum, and Toni doesn't know I'll be there.'

Anger swirled in Liv's gut. Toni should be making an effort. She'd been given an incredible gift, and it wouldn't kill her to try and be more accepting of their sister. She would talk to Toni and see if she could convince her to include Mandy. No doubt it was annoying Toni if Mandy was calling Ruby, Baby. 'You're still calling her Baby?'

Mandy nodded. 'Not in front of Toni, if I remember. Mum told me it makes her mad. I try and call her Ruby then, although that seems wrong to me.'

'How is Ruby doing?'

Mandy stared down the screen at her. 'Toni said that if you rang wanting to know about Baby, I had to tell her straight away. She said that it meant you wanted her back, and she had to prepare herself for her heart breaking.'

A tiny piece of Liv's heart broke hearing Toni's concerns. 'You don't have to tell her. I will. I'll call her and assure her that I want to be Ruby's aunt and nothing more.'

Mandy nodded. 'Okay. I'd better go, Livvy. I have to get ready to see Mum, and I need to clean up the kitchen first. That's a rule here. If you make a mess, you clean it up.'

She ended the call before Liv had a chance to say goodbye. What a turnaround from a few months earlier when Liv had walked in on the disaster zone at her mother's house. A clean kitchen back then was the last thing Mandy was concerned about. Liv could imagine the immense pride her father would experience if he could see Mandy now. And Toni too. Tears filled her eyes as she thought of her father and all that he was missing. His first grandchild, and he never got to hold her.

Liv thought back to Mandy's comment that Toni wanted to know if she was enquiring after Ruby. She took her phone from her pocket and started writing a text message. The last thing she wanted was her sister worrying unnecessarily.

* * *

Ninety minutes after closing the door on Vera, Toni pulled into her mother's driveway and embraced the sense of calm that enveloped her. Getting out of the apartment was the only way she could guarantee quiet for her neighbours. As she undid her seatbelt, a text arrived.

> Just spoke to Mandy and asked about Ruby. She said she had to report back to you as me showing an interest meant I wanted Ruby back. Don't worry. It doesn't. I wanted to know how my niece was doing and my big sis. Hope all's going well. Chat soon. X

Toni didn't respond. Liv not wanting Ruby back was a good thing, in theory. The reality, however, was very different. She knew she should be providing Liv with updates on how their mother was doing, but as she'd been avoiding her, it made that difficult. Dropping in to see her mother was under the guise of checking up on her. A flicker of guilt settled over her as she considered her real reason for visiting today. She knew the moment she walked through the front door her mother would claim ownership of Ruby and refuse to let Toni do anything, wanting to spend every moment of Ruby's awake time with her. Before Ruby's birth, Toni would have described bliss as many things. Having a break from your baby for a few hours wasn't one she ever thought she'd need to add to the list.

'Toni!' The front door flew open, and her mother hurried down the path towards her. As much as Ruby had turned Toni's life into an unrecognisable disaster, the one thing she had to admit was that Ruby had helped her mother deal with her grief. 'She brings me so much pleasure,' Sara had said. 'A reason to get up on the days that I'm seeing you both.' Toni had been tempted to admit how much she was struggling and ask her mother for help, thinking it could be good for them both, but her pride got the better of her. Sara had been so against Toni raising Liv's baby that admitting she wasn't coping would play right into her judgement of it all.

Now her mother opened her arms and drew her to her. Toni fell into the embrace and closed her eyes. Part of her wished she was young again, coming home from school and her mother was there waiting to hug her. If she could turn back twenty years, knowing then what she knew now, she'd approach life differently.

'And where's my gorgeous girl?' Sara asked, pulling back, and peering in through the back window. 'Is she awake?'

'No, she fell asleep after we left home. I'll bring her in in the car seat, and she can continue her nap.'

Disappointment filled Sara's eyes.

Toni laughed. 'She'll wake up in an hour or so, and unless you have plans, we don't have anything on today. I can stay as long as you like.'

'Really?'

Toni nodded. She had absolutely no desire to return to the apartment and the judgemental stares and words of the neighbours. She opened the car door and set about unclipping the car seat from its cradle. Sara collected the nappy bag, and once Toni had the baby seat in hand, they made their way up the path and in through the front door.

'Pop Ruby wherever you like,' Sara said, 'and I'll make us some coffee.'

'Perfect,' Toni said. And it was. A sleeping baby, someone else making her coffee, and adult company. She took a deep breath. Imagine if she could do this every day. It would be much easier than the long days at home, where she seemed to achieve nothing other than failing to keep Ruby happy. She took the car seat into the lounge room and pulled the curtain across the front window. Keeping Ruby asleep for as long as possible was a priority.

She turned and walked along the passageway to the back of the house, where the kitchen and open-plan living area were. As she passed the door to what had been her father's home office, the door opened. Toni froze. What was she doing here?

'Toni!' Mandy threw her arms out and pulled Toni to her. 'I'm excited to see you. Where's Baby?'

The reference to Ruby as Baby immediately got Toni's defences up. Her only role in Ruby's birth was naming her. Why couldn't Mandy call her by her name rather than constantly trying to reinforce her disapproval of it by calling her something else?

Toni pulled out of the embrace. 'I didn't realise you'd be here. I thought you were still settling into Wattle House.'

Mandy giggled. 'I'm all settled, but I like to visit Mum. I surprised her. I caught a tram and then a bus here all by myself.'

'Really?' Toni was unable to hide her surprise. She couldn't recall Mandy catching public transport on her own before.

'I'm a grown-up now, Toni. I can do a lot of things.'

Sara glanced at Toni. 'I should have sent her to live with Liv years ago if I'd known this would be the outcome. Mandy's come back a lot wiser than when she left here.'

Mandy giggled. 'It's not Liv; it's Barb. My best old friend,' she clarified. 'She taught me a lot of things. How to catch trains, buses and ferries and book restaurants. She showed me how to use the GPS on my phone to give me directions. I was her *chief navigator* when I lived in Sydney.'

Sara's mouth dropped open. 'What? Liv had no idea?'

'I thought you stayed in her apartment all day and watched *Titanic*,' Toni said.

Mandy giggled louder. 'That's what we told Liv in case she wouldn't let us go out. Barb and I took trips every day and ate at lots of restaurants and visited all the sights. I learnt lots from Barb then and lots now from Izzy. She's my best young friend, and I see her all the time. She lives in Balwyn near me.' She looked around. 'Where's Baby? Did you leave her in the car? Because that's bad for babies and for dogs! They can die quickly.'

'She's in the lounge, Mandy, but she's asleep so let's leave her until she wakes up.'

'You can come and show Toni the cake you made for our morning tea.' As they followed Sara into the kitchen, a small cry came from the lounge.

'I'll go,' Mandy volunteered.

'No,' Toni said. 'Let's give her a minute and see if she settles herself.'

They all waited. Silence fell momentarily before a piercing wail erupted. Mandy hurried towards the lounge room before Toni or Sara moved. Toni went to follow, but her mother placed a hand on her arm. 'Let her go. She talks about Ruby nonstop. It's such a bonus for her that you've dropped in.'

Toni hesitated before allowing her mother to guide her into the kitchen, where a mouth-watering chocolate cake was on a cake stand in the middle of the island counter.

'Can you believe she made this?' Sara asked. 'One of the girls, Rose, helped her, but I'm still amazed. The girl who I thought wasn't ready for independent living makes me a cake and then catches a tram and then a bus to get here and surprise me.' Sara indicated for Toni to sit while she started fiddling with the coffee machine.

Toni hesitantly sat on a stool. Ruby's cries had stopped, so she should be grateful to Mandy, but she wasn't. If anything, she resented her even more for showing that she could placate the baby when Toni couldn't.

'Now, enough about Mandy for the moment. How are you? It feels like an age since I saw you.'

Toni covered her unease with a laugh. 'You saw me exactly four days ago.'

Toni was interrupted by her phone pinging with a text. She slipped it from her bag and read the message.

'That looks like a welcome message,' her mother said.

Toni looked up from her phone.

'From that lovely smile, I'm guessing it's Joel?'

Toni shook her head and slipped the phone back into her bag. 'No, it's from Belinda. She's organised a girls' night with some of the women I work with and wants to check I'm still going. I haven't been out since Ruby was born and I think I'm ready for some time to myself.'

Sara nodded. 'You know, I'd be happy to look after Ruby for you anytime. Especially when Joel's away. It's a lot to cope with on your own.'

Toni looked away as her mother's eyes seemed to bore into hers. Did she suspect Toni wasn't coping? She swallowed. This was an opportunity to talk to her mother about what she was going through and ask for help. She opened her mouth, then closed it again. She wasn't ready to admit she was failing. She turned and glanced back in the direction of the lounge room. 'I should probably check on them. It's very quiet.'

She was about to slip off the stool when Mandy appeared in the doorway with Ruby cuddled against her. The baby's eyes were open, and she looked happy and content.

'Can I keep holding her, Toni? She's happy with me, and it will help to socialise her.'

'Socialise?' Toni looked to her mother, who shrugged.

'To ensure she's not dependent on you when she's ready to go into the world on her own. I read about it.'

'She's only six weeks old. I'm not sure we need to start that early. But yes, you can hold her if you like. She might need a nappy change soon or a feed so you can hand her back when it's time for that.'

Mandy shook her head. 'No, Liv said that I should be helpful with Ruby. That way, you might like me better and not stop me from seeing her.'

A niggle of guilt started in the pit of Toni's stomach and started to spread. 'Liv said that?'

Mandy nodded. 'I will try hard, Toni. Then you can trust me with Ruby and hopefully even invite me to your house one day to play with her.'

Toni found herself nodding but was unable to speak.

Sara reached across and squeezed her knee. 'You can't fault her for trying.'

No, Toni thought as she did her best to blink back tears. She couldn't fault Mandy, but she could fault herself. Had she really convinced herself that Mandy's intellectual issues extended to her not picking up on the animosity she held for her? She was an adult, not a kid, and she should know better. Was it possible that Ruby was picking up on her feelings towards her too? If Toni was holding her now, she'd most likely be crying. But then Toni wouldn't be singing to her in the sweet tone that Mandy was. More likely, she would have put her in her bouncy chair and hoped she'd entertain herself.

She sipped her coffee. She needed to change her attitude towards Mandy and the way she dealt with Ruby. If she could be more like Mandy, maybe Ruby would respond. She shuddered. *Did I really have that thought? That I should be more like Mandy?* She could only imagine one scenario where a thought like that would surface: pure exhaustion had driven her insane. But regardless of her insanity, the one thing she knew was she needed to change her approach with Ruby and then she'd hopefully see a change in her baby's response to her.

14

Three days of plying Ruby with attention, learning songs suitable for babies and doing her best to be the perfect mother left Toni exhausted and more irritable than she had been prior to making a renewed effort. On day one, Ruby responded when Toni began to sing. She nuzzled into her as Toni had seen her do with Mandy. But after a few minutes, she started to fuss. Toni changed her, offered her a bottle and then continued to hold her and sing. Ruby looked at her as if she was mad, opened her mouth and screamed until she wore herself out and fell asleep.

Toni's next efforts met similar results. Ruby would wake and cry to be picked up. She'd settle momentarily but, after a minute or two, she'd cry, demanding something Toni didn't seem to be able to give her. By the second afternoon, her attempts at a sweet singing voice had deteriorated into forcing words through gritted teeth. If she hadn't seen Ruby content with Mandy for such a long period at her mother's, she would assume there was something wrong with the baby. That she was colicky or whatever other ailments could afflict a young baby.

It was Friday, and Toni couldn't wait for Joel to return. He would be back by four which would give her plenty of time to have a shower and get dressed, ready for her night out with the girls from work. It was the one thing, possibly the only thing, that had kept her going since seeing her mother on Tuesday. Finally, a chance to let her hair down with adult conversation. She already knew her work colleagues wouldn't have any interest in talking about babies, which was a relief.

She put Ruby down for a mid-morning nap and whipped around the apartment in record time, cleaning the surfaces and bathrooms. It was amazing that most days, she could hardly be bothered lifting her head off the pillow, yet today, when she had the combination of Joel returning and a night out to look forward to, she was suddenly full of energy. She ignored the cries from the bedroom, put on her headphones and started vacuuming. She had an online grocery delivery arriving in thirty minutes, and then she'd need to take some clothes from the drier and fold them, and she'd have everything done. She paused momentarily. Her to-do list used to be about client meetings and ensuring her team met their monthly sales targets, in addition to making weekend plans for her and Joel and catching up with friends. Now she was feeling elated because she was ticking the boxes of a good housewife. A lump rose in her throat, which she did her best to squash. This was not the time to analyse anything. She needed to get this done and hopefully quieten Ruby down before Joel got home to ensure she looked like she was on top of everything.

Fifteen minutes later, having finished in the bedrooms, she removed her headphones, bracing herself for the screams which miraculously had stopped.

She put the vacuum away in the storage cupboard, walked back into the kitchen, deciding a coffee would be her reward, and froze. Shopping bags were sitting on the kitchen counter. The delivery had arrived early, but they couldn't let themselves in. Had she left the door unlocked?

Toni hurried to the front door, discovering it locked from the inside, and pulled it open. She looked both ways down the hallway, but there was no one around. She closed the door, locked it, and walked back into the apartment. This was not on. She'd ring Woolworths and complain as soon as she'd put away the perishables. Reaching the kitchen she froze once more. Mandy's soft singing voice travelled from the nursery. She had to be kidding.

She marched to the nursery and flung open the door. 'What the hell are you doing?'

Mandy started at Toni's harsh words, and Ruby's mouth opened, emitting a loud scream.

'You can't let yourself into my house whenever you please.'

Mandy's lower lip trembled. 'I'm sorry. Very sorry. I called you last night and this morning, and you didn't call me back.'

'That doesn't mean you can just turn up.'

'But I was worried that you might be hurt or dead, and no one would be here for Ruby.'

'Dead?'

Mandy nodded. 'Like Sam. No one thought he'd be dead, and bang, suddenly, he was.'

Toni hesitated. Her mother had mentioned a friend of Mandy's dying, but she hadn't elaborated on the details.

Mandy stood and started swaying from foot to foot. Ruby settled down and nuzzled into her again, her eyes fluttering with tiredness.

'I'm sorry about your friend. I didn't realise it was unexpected.'

'It was. His brain blew up, and I thought that might have happened to you too. It was an anu-raisin.'

'Aneurism,' Toni said. 'That's very sad.' She sighed. 'But how did you get in, and did you let the Woolworths man in?'

Mandy nodded. 'He was down where you get the lift trying to call you, but you didn't pick up your phone. I told him you might be dead, and I was coming to check. He was worried, too. He came up with me. I knocked, but you didn't answer, so I used Mum's key. I knew I might need it if you were dead.'

'Does Mum know you're here?'

Mandy shook her head. 'She's out somewhere and her phone was switched off. I caught the tram and bus to her house and collected the spare key you gave her and then I walked to the station and caught the train here.'

'You did all that because you were worried about me?' Tears unexpectedly filled Toni's eyes.

'I worry about you. Babies are hard work, and I thought it was better I check. When we heard the vacuum cleaner, the Woolworths man left the shopping, and I went to settle Ruby. She was upset.'

Heat flooded Toni's cheeks. 'I couldn't hear her over the vacuum.'

'That's okay,' Mandy said and smiled, a brilliant smile at Toni. 'I was here, and I helped.'

'Thank you, I guess. But Mandy, if you thought I was dead, shouldn't you have called someone to come with you?'

'Mum wasn't home and she's still so sad about Dad. I didn't want her to be sad about you too until I knew for sure.'

Toni closed her eyes, briefly imagining her mother's heartache. She'd been so caught up in her own misery, she hadn't given her mum the time or attention she should have. She reopened her eyes and managed a smile for Mandy's sake. 'That was thoughtful of you.'

Mandy smiled again. 'I'm kicking points today.'

Toni was about to correct her but changed her mind. Points or goals, what was the difference? Mandy was definitely owed some credit. Not only for checking on her but because Ruby was fast asleep in her arms.

'Come into the living area and sit in the comfy chair,' Toni said. 'If you want to keep holding Ruby, that is?'

'I do,' Mandy said. 'I think Baby likes me.'

Toni allowed the reference to Baby to grate on her without mentioning it. If anything, Mandy was right. Ruby did like her.

'I was about to make a coffee,' Toni said. 'Can I get you something?'

'Do you have Coke?'

Toni nodded. 'There might be some. Joel likes it with his bourbon.'

'Then a Coke, please. But no bourbon. That doesn't sound nice.'

Mandy sat in the blue wingback chair that looked out over Toorak Road as Toni walked over to the fridge to get the soft drink. 'Would you like it in the can or with ice in a glass?'

'Can, please.' Mandy giggled, and Toni glanced over at her.

'What's funny?'

Mandy seemed to consider whether she'd answer. 'I'm not allowed Coke. Mum says it rots your teeth and is only good for cleaning driveways.'

'Oh.' Toni hesitated but then took the can across to her sister. 'Mum's probably right, but if you only have it every now and then as a treat, your teeth will probably survive.'

'Now I live at Wattle House, I could have it every day if I wanted. Couldn't I? I'm allowed to shop for my own food.'

Toni nodded slowly. 'Yes, but I think you need to be healthy too. You should work out an eating plan that gives you some treats. Like Coke every now and then, but overall, you eat healthy, and you stay fit. If you get unhealthy, then you won't be able to keep up with Ruby once she's walking and running. You need to stay fit and look after yourself.'

Mandy's eyes lit up. 'Will you let me play with Ruby when she's walking and running?'

'Of course,' Toni said. She wondered how Ruby would respond to Mandy as she grew older. She'd have to make sure she taught her to be inclusive and she wasn't unkind in the ways Toni had been as they grew up. Heat flushed her cheeks as she had this thought. It wasn't only as they grew up. If she was honest, her attitude towards Mandy had never changed.

Mandy held out the can to her. 'No Coke. Water, please.'

Toni returned to the kitchen. They'd probably be able to get Mandy to do anything by using Ruby as an incentive.

Her phone vibrated on the kitchen bench as she went to fetch a glass of water for Mandy. She picked it up. It was Joel.

'Hey, babe.' Weariness travelled down the line.

'You're back early,' Toni said.

'I wish. I'm stuck in the airport lounge in Perth.'

'Perth? I thought it was a direct flight from Dubai to Melbourne.'

'It would have been, but a technical malfunction forced us to land. They're working on it, but it's unlikely to be fixed for a few hours. I've reached my flying limit, too. The best case is I'll be flown as a passenger later today, and worst-case scenario, I'll be on the red-eye tomorrow morning.'

Toni's heart sank. She'd been looking forward to a night with the girls since Belinda made the arrangements a few days ago. 'When will you know?'

'Probably in the next hour or two. If I can get home today, it will be late, so don't wait up.'

'I was supposed to go out tonight.'

There was silence at the other end of the line.

'Joel?'

'Shit. I'm sorry, you did mention it the other day and I completely forgot. Can you ask your mum to look after Ruby? Or see if the girls can change to another night?'

'I'll ask Mum,' Toni said. 'Call me later when you know when you'll be back, okay?'

'Okay, love you.'

'You too.'

Joel ended the call and Toni threw her phone down on the counter. 'Shit!'

Mandy giggled. 'Toni swore.'

Toni looked across at her sister. She used to say that when they were teenagers, doing her best to get Toni into trouble. That's why Toni had assumed she'd said it. Looking at her now, it appeared she just found it funny.

She picked up her phone again and called her mother. She explained what had happened and asked whether Sara could look after Ruby for the night.

'Sorry love, I'm going to the ballet with Susan. We've had tickets for months. It's a matinee followed by dinner. I could be back by nine, but I assume you want to go earlier than that. Is there someone else you could ask? Joel's parents?'

'They're away.' Toni looked across to where Mandy was now singing to Ruby. 'By the way, Mandy's here, Mum. She let herself in with your key because she thought I might be dead.'

'What? How did she get the key?'

'She caught the tram and bus to your house and then a train back here, and I assume walked to the apartment from the station. I didn't know she knew the way.'

Sara was silent for a moment, digesting this information. 'Why did she think you were dead?'

'Because I didn't return her calls. She said her friend, Sam, died unexpectedly, and I guess so did Dad. It was sweet of her to be worried.'

'There's no need to be sarcastic.'

'I'm not! Why would you think that?'

'Because you never say anything nice about Mandy.'

Toni's throat squeezed shut. As much as she hated to hear the words, she knew her mother was right. She didn't. She took a deep breath. 'I guess I need to start trying to be nicer. She's good with Ruby. Do you think...' Toni let the words peter out. Mandy was good with Ruby, but would she really consider leaving her with her for a few hours?

'I think she'd be fine. She's much more capable than we've been giving her credit for. If you leave her with your number and mine and make sure she knows to ring about anything at all, she should be alright. Worse case, you come home to an upset baby and an upset Mandy. I can come to your place and be with her once my night's finished if you'd like?'

'Would you?'

'I'd love to. Now, I'd better go. Tell Mandy what the plans are, and you'll need to leave her some formula and instructions for Ruby. I'll see you later. Have a good time with your friends.'

'Thanks, Mum.'

Toni ended the call and fixed Mandy's water and a coffee for herself. She took them over to where Mandy continued to sing softly to Ruby. Would she really consider leaving Ruby in Mandy's care? Her mother had always said she was like a twelve-year-old. Would a twelve-year-old be old enough to babysit?

15

No baby deserves what you've done. Your lies and manipulation are unforgivable. You have two options. Prepare $15K payment to ensure your secret remains safe or do nothing and your sister and the authorities will be contacted. Await further instructions.

Liv turned her phone off and threw it across the room. Luckily, it landed on her favourite faded blue couch, not that she cared right at this minute. She'd like to destroy the thing if it would also get rid of the message she'd just received and the sender of it.

She dropped her head into her hands. She should have known she wouldn't get away with it. That not doing everything above board when it came to Ruby's birth would come back to bite her. But this quickly and for this much money?

She raised her head. There was only one person who could be responsible for this. Petal Blossom. She was sure she'd fooled the doula, but it appeared she hadn't. So much for the hippy, flower child she'd presented herself as. She was now demanding fifteen thousand dollars payment in return for keeping quiet.

Liv groaned. She had the money but if she paid it, what would stop the doula coming after more? And what if she didn't pay it? Would Toni finding out the truth really be that big a deal? Liv's stomach heaved as she had the thought, answering the question for her. She rushed to the toilet while wondering exactly how she would deliver the money to the doula.

* * *

It was close to 2 a.m. by the time Toni collapsed into a taxi and gave the driver directions to the South Yarra apartment. She'd had such a good night. As she'd predicted, other than some polite questions at the start of the night about Ruby, babies were not a discussion topic the women were interested in pursuing. They were all career-driven, all big drinkers and they loved to dance. A perfect combination for lively dinner discussion and a lot of fun on the dance floor.

She'd done her best to ignore the feelings of guilt and self-loathing that she hadn't rung home, but she'd checked her phone, and there were no messages, so she assumed Mandy had everything under control. She did her best to let herself into the apartment quietly, but as she was wobbly on her feet, it was hard to achieve.

'Toni?'

She followed her mother's voice to the kitchen.

'Why are you still awake? There are two beds in the spare room, and the couch pulls out.'

Sara nodded. 'I know, but I'm wide awake. Susan and I enjoyed an espresso martini after dinner and the caffeine must have been too much. Also, I haven't been sleeping the best. Thoughts of your father. It's been difficult.' She stood and picked up her bag from the bench. 'But I might go home now that you're here. Could you drive Mandy home tomorrow? No hurry, whenever you wake up and know you'll be under the limit again.'

Toni groaned. 'I'll be up in a few hours with Ruby. I can definitely take her back to Wattle House.'

'She's done an amazing job with Ruby tonight,' Sara said. 'She had her bathed and in bed before I even arrived. We've underestimated how capable she is.'

'I'll make sure I thank her tomorrow,' Toni said. 'But right now, I think I need to lie down.'

Her mother gave her a quick hug and let herself out of the apartment.

Toni turned on the tap, filled a large glass with water and stumbled into the bedroom. She kicked off her shoes and slipped under the covers, still fully dressed. The room began to spin, and she wished she'd said no to the last, okay, being truthful, the last four glasses of champagne. She'd hardly drunk in the last few years with staying as healthy as possible for the IVF treatments and trying to conceive. She'd made up for it tonight.

She closed her eyes, hoped with every fibre that Ruby would do the unthinkable and sleep through the 5 a.m. feed, and passed out.

* * *

Toni woke to a thumping headache, dry mouth, and aching body. She opened one eye, then the other, realising she was aching partly due to sleeping in her clothes which seemed to be strangling her. She couldn't help but smile. As much as she was going to regret her indulgence and late night, it was worth it. Worth it to be Toni again for a night. Not a stay-at-home mum, housewife or whatever her unglamorous titles now were. She glanced at the clock on the bedside table. Twelve-thirty? They must have had a power outage as there was no way it was that late.

She sat up us a deep laugh reverberated from the living room. Joel? No, he would have called her if he was on his way home. She picked her phone up from the bedside table. Two missed calls and a text message.

Should be home by nine. Arrived in Sydney late last night. Catching an early morning flight to Melbourne. Can't wait to see my girls.

Nine. He'd been home for over three hours and hadn't woken her? She pulled herself out of bed, regret matching the pain in her head, and went into the ensuite. She looked terrible. She knew that without even looking in the mirror. She splashed water on her face, brushed her teeth and quickly stripped off and had a shower. She couldn't walk out in last night's clothes.

Ten minutes later, she appeared, hopefully looking fresh and not hungover, with a smile plastered on her lips. Joel was sitting on the couch next to Mandy, and Ruby was on her rug on the floor, lying on her tummy, her little arms and legs stretched out.

'Tummy time,' Mandy said, looking up at Toni.

Joel jumped to his feet and came over to her. For someone who'd been travelling half the night, he looked amazingly fresh and gorgeous in his white t-shirt and jeans. He took her in his arms and kissed her fiercely on the lips.

'You look a little worse for wear,' he said as they pulled apart. 'Mandy said she looked after Ruby last night?'

The questioning tone he'd spoken in suggested he wasn't happy about that arrangement.

Toni pulled away from him and walked into the kitchen towards the coffee machine. She was going to need a lot of coffee today. 'Mum was here. She went home when I got back. It was late, and Mandy was already asleep. We didn't disturb her.'

The frown on Joel's face softened. 'Oh, that's okay then. I wasn't sure that leaving Mandy on her own with Ruby was a good idea.'

'Joel!'

'What?'

Toni glanced across at Mandy. 'Mandy's not deaf, and she's done an amazing job with Ruby. She helped me during the day yesterday when she thought I was dead.'

Joel's eyes widened. 'Dead? Are you okay? What happened?'

'I'm okay, and it's a long story, but you owe her an apology.'

Joel turned to Mandy. 'Sorry, Mands. I'm sure you were great with Ruby, but sometimes, I think it's a good idea to have more than one person here in case there's an accident.'

'Toni looks after Ruby by herself.'

'That's different,' Joel said. 'Toni's her mother, and she knows what she needs. Anyway, thank you for helping. It was kind of you.'

Mandy stood, glancing from Ruby to Toni, looking torn. Finally, she spoke. 'You should take me home now.'

It wasn't hard to see that Joel had upset her.

'I'll take you,' Joel said, pulling his keys from his pocket. 'I can check if Sara needs anything while I'm there.'

Mandy shook her head. 'Home is Wattle House. You should know that. I want Toni to take me.' She folded her arms like a stubborn child. 'Don't want you.'

Toni put her hand up to stop Joel from telling Mandy not to be silly, which was what he was likely to say. Mandy had been a huge help to her in the past twenty-four hours, and she owed her this, at least.

'Let me make a coffee to take with me, and then we'll go.'

Mandy nodded before getting down to her knees and kissing Ruby on the head. 'Bye, Baby. I love you.'

* * *

'I do love Baby,' Mandy reiterated as Toni drove along Toorak Road on the way to Wattle House.

'I know you do, Mandy. And she loves you too.'

'She loves me better than she loves you.'

Toni's grip on the steering wheel tightened. She was doing her best to make an effort with Mandy, but she knew how to push her buttons.

'I'm not mean to her. Are you going to tell Joel how you put earphones in and let her scream?'

'She wasn't screaming when I started cleaning,' Toni lied. 'And anyway, it's not your business. I'm doing my best.'

Mandy folded her arms across her chest before turning to face Toni. 'Your best isn't good enough. Dad would tell you that. He'd say, "Lift your game, Toni. Baby's counting on you".'

Toni swallowed as tears filled her eyes. Mandy was right. That was exactly what their father would say. She did need to lift her game, but right at this point, she wasn't sure she had it in her. She wiped her eyes with the back of her sleeve. She was hungover, and Mandy had hit a raw nerve. She needed to get home to Joel and be reminded that she was part of a team. With his support and help, it might not seem as overwhelming as it had the past week with him away for work. She needed to remind herself that Ruby was only six weeks old. She'd had no experience with babies before, and she, like many mothers, was struggling. She needed to trust the books and online articles that promised it would get easier. Toni did her best to inject as much confidence into her thoughts as possible while simultaneously not believing a word of them.

Mandy slammed her hand down on the dashboard, causing Toni to flinch. She thought her sister had said her piece, but it turned out she'd just started.

'You don't deserve to have a baby. You don't deserve to be a mother. You're a terrible mother, and I'm going to tell Liv. She would be a much better mother for Baby.'

'Her name is Ruby, Mandy, and I don't care what you tell Liv. She didn't want Ruby, and now I'm stuck with her.' The words were out of Toni's mouth before she could stop herself. She was glad that Mandy was the only one who'd heard. She could only imagine Joel's face if he heard her speak like that about their daughter. *Their daughter*. That was part of the problem. She didn't *feel* like Toni's daughter.

'Stuck?' Confusion filled Mandy's face. 'I thought you *wanted* a baby? I thought you'd do anything for one?'

'Yes, it turns out sometimes we don't know what we want, and when we get it, we wish we hadn't.'

Mandy sucked in a breath. 'You don't want Baby?'

Toni stopped. She hadn't shared her inner thoughts with anyone, and Mandy, with her big mouth, was certainly not the person to start with.

'I want Ruby,' she said, forcing herself to be calmer. 'But I want to work too. I need to find an arrangement where I can do both. I think I'll be better with Ruby when she's older, and we can do things together, but right now, I find it a bit boring. All I do all day is cater to her needs.'

'That's what mums do,' Mandy said. 'Life is about the baby. Mum did it for us, and now you do it for Ruby. When she's older, you can go back to work, like Mum did.'

She sounded like Joel. Didn't anyone realise that maybe Toni didn't want to give up her identity and everything she'd worked for? That she didn't want to disappear into the hole of being everyone else's servant? When she and Joel were both working, they shared the cooking and house-work, but now he seemed to expect she would do everything. She was a living cliché. Even as she had the thoughts, she knew they weren't the real problem. The problem was that around Ruby she felt like a complete failure.

'I need something that's mine. You wouldn't understand,' Toni said.

Mandy picked up her doll and held it in front of Toni. 'I understand. Baby is the only thing that is mine. Everything else is always taken off me. The sharp knives are too dangerous. Mum doesn't think I'm capable of driving or getting a proper job. If I didn't have Baby, I'd be lost. There'd be no point to my life.'

Toni nodded slowly, feeling like she understood a little bit more about her sister. 'I'm sorry that decisions are made for you.' It helped explain why she had the doll always glued to her.

'You want more when you already have more,' Mandy said. 'You have everything you always wanted, and now you want your job too.'

Toni nodded. 'I have everything I *thought* I always wanted but now realise I didn't know what I was thinking. I do want to work, but I don't think Joel will want me to. I said I'd stay home with Ruby for the first year.' She sank back against the car seat. 'You might have to come and check on me during that time that I'm not dead because I might get so fed up that that's what I do.'

Mandy's eyes widened. 'You'll kill yourself?'

Tears filled Toni's eyes. 'No. But some days, I wish this wasn't my life.' A tear rolled down her cheek. 'I wanted a baby desperately and thought I'd be such a good mother, but you're right. I'm a terrible mother, and I don't deserve Ruby.' Toni wasn't sure why she was telling Mandy this.

'You need to tell Mum or Liv,' Mandy said, breaking into her thoughts. 'They can help. I can help.'

Toni shook her head, immediately regretting her words. 'No, I'll be fine. I'll get used to it. Don't tell Mum or Liv, please, Mandy. They'll both be upset with me, and I don't want Liv to think she's a bad person for giving Ruby up.'

'She is a bad person,' Mandy said, her face clouding over. 'She should never have given Baby away. Barb thinks that too.'

'Barb?'

'My friend who lives across from Liv. She said Baby should never have been given to you and that babies should be raised by their mothers no matter what the circumstances are.'

Toni was about to object that a stranger had no right to voice her opinion, but the reality was Barb had a point. 'She might be right,' Toni said. 'Look at how being adopted affected Mum.'

'But Ruby will never know she was adopted,' Mandy said.

Toni frowned. 'She will when she's older.'

Mandy shook her head. 'She'll never know.' She lowered her voice. 'I'm good at secrets, Toni. Very good. I'll never tell anyone what Liv did. Petal Blossom won't tell either.'

'The doula?' Toni was confused. 'Why would Petal Blossom tell Ruby she was adopted? I don't think we'll ever see her again.'

'Secrets, Toni, lots of secrets. I know the truth. Liv knows the truth. Barb might know, but Petal Blossom doesn't know the truth.'

'Truth? Mandy, you're confusing me. Liv gave Ruby to Joel and me and we plan to officially adopt her. Liv's been talking to a lawyer about the legal side of doing that. I don't think it's something the doula would have any say in.' As the words left her mouth, Toni realised she hadn't followed Liv up to find out what the lawyer had advised. The reality was, she wasn't sure if she was ready to make everything official. She pushed the thought away and turned her attention back to Mandy.

Her sister gave a sly smile. 'No lawyers. A lot of secrets. I'm good at secrets. I won't tell anyone that you're a bad mummy on one condition.'

'What's that?'

'That you try better with Ruby, and you let me help. I'm good with babies, and you're not.'

Toni's mouth dropped open, and she had to stifle a laugh. Mandy's appraisal of the situation, while blunt, was accurate. She was good with Ruby, and Toni wasn't. She had no idea what she was talking about with regards to the secrets. She'd ask Liv when they next spoke but, for now, assumed it was Mandy and her love of being secretive and included.

Mandy held out her hand. 'Deal?'

Toni took it and shook it. 'Deal, Mandy. You keep what I've said to yourself, and I'll try harder to be better with Ruby.'

16

Twenty-four hours after receiving the text message, Liv's stomach churned as she stared at the computer screen. Her once-healthy bank account was dwindling to the point of scary due to a combination of the withdrawal she'd made the previous day and the fact she'd been feeling run down and wasn't actively pursuing work. In fact, she'd turned down two large jobs the previous week as she didn't have the energy for them and over the past six weeks, at least another six or seven. Of course, with what had unfolded this week, she regretted not working. She'd thought she'd always have her savings to fall back on, but now she didn't.

She continued staring at the screen, wishing the withdrawal would disappear, but instead, it stared back at her, big and bold. The fifteen thousand wasn't gone as such. It was currently stashed in a cheap black bag at the bottom of her walk-in robe, where it would stay until she received further advice on where it needed to be delivered. She'd be struggling to pay the mortgage this month, let alone her car payment or basic expenses. Her stomach knotted as the word *karma* floated into her head. Punishment for deciding Ruby's fate? Punishment in the form of bankruptcy and a possible jail term? She shook her head, picturing Toni rolling her eyes and muttering, *Melodramatic or what?*

She'd called Petal but her voicemail message stated she was overseas and had not confirmed a return date. The midwifery website Liv had originally discovered her services on said her profile was currently on hold and they were unable to confirm when she'd be contactable. She'd disappeared and for what, fifteen thousand dollars? It didn't make sense. Liv would be lying if she didn't admit that she was appalled that the seemingly spiritual, hippy doula was willing to blackmail her, but she guessed that her own actions had put the doula's job at risk if anyone was to discover her deceit. But she still couldn't work out how Petal knew what she'd done. She hadn't told her and Mandy swore she hadn't either.

Her phone chimed with a new text.

Bring the money to Sydney Domestic arrivals at 10 a.m. today. Leave it in a Smarte Carte locker and text the locker location and code to this number. Then take a train to Martin Place. Take a selfie with the Fullerton clock in the background at exactly 1 p.m. Text it to this number. Any stuff-ups, and I speak to 'Toni' and the police. Get it right, and you'll never hear from me again. You can consider our transaction complete.

She re-read the text multiple times. Was she really going to do this? Would a one-off payment be enough, or would Petal come back and ask for more? Liv sighed as an image of Toni and Ruby entered her mind. Any sane person would admit to her sister what she'd done and take away the blackmailer's power. But she couldn't do that to Toni, and if she was honest with herself, her actions of the past few months had proven that she was anything but sane. She'd dug herself into a hole and at this stage, intended to keep digging. She owed Toni her life, and if fifteen grand was what it was going to take to repay that, then who was she to argue?

* * *

Later that afternoon, a knock on the door snapped Liv out of her misery. She didn't have a date for the night, she hadn't spoken to any of her friends in weeks, and her family were over eight hundred kilometres away in Melbourne. She wasn't expecting anyone.

The rapping came again. She was tempted to ignore it. She was exhausted as a result of the adrenaline rush from delivering the money and following the blackmailer's instructions. She'd done as requested and assumed the money had been collected.

'Liv, are you home?'

Ah, Barb. It was five o'clock: wine time. That might be the lift she needed. Liv jumped to her feet and hurried from the kitchen along the short passageway of the apartment to the front door and flung it open, making a conscious effort to be enthusiastic.

'Babs, is everything okay?'

Barb frowned, clutching a bottle of wine to her chest. 'Enough with the Babs. I'll answer to Barbara or Barb.'

Liv pushed all thoughts of the day from her mind and grinned, nodding towards the wine bottle. 'You never mind after a glass or two.'

Barb shook her head and, failing to hide a faint smile, stepped inside Liv's apartment. 'I'll come up with a horrible nickname for you if you're not careful,' she said as they made their way down the hallway to the open-plan kitchen and living room. She passed the wine to Liv before moving over to the tall, floor to ceiling window. 'The keelboats are out training for the regatta. I've been watching them all afternoon. It's such a stunning day. I thought you might be down there enjoying it.'

Liv put the bottle on the kitchen counter and took two glasses from a shelf above the stovetop. 'No, I'm here, having serious doubts about how much longer I can afford this wonderful harbour view.'

Barb turned to face her, concern flooding her features. 'What's happened? I thought your business was a success?'

Liv opened the wine and poured glasses for them both. She passed one to Barb. 'Let's take them out onto the balcony.'

Barb took her glass and followed Liv outside.

'You see,' Liv said once they were seated, gulls screeching and the occasional traffic noise interrupting the otherwise tranquil setting, 'in addition to not working much for the past couple of months, I've done something a bit silly, and now it's come back to bite me.' *A bit silly. Did that cover off illegal and immoral?*

'Does this have anything to do with your sister and the baby situation?'

Liv nodded. 'The birth certificate.'

'I told you I didn't think it was a good idea.'

'You did and I should have listened. But I didn't and now I'm paying the price. It wasn't just the birth certificate.'

Barb raised an eyebrow, causing Liv to look away.

Liv's phone pinged with a text as she considered what she would tell Barb. She slipped the phone from her pocket and glanced at the screen, her hand trembling as she read the message.

Money received. A pleasure doing business with you. Next time, don't lie. Give that precious baby a kiss from me. I may be back in touch.

'Liv? You're as white as a ghost. Are you okay?'

Liv placed her phone on the table and, with a trembling hand, picked up her wine glass and took a sip. No, she wasn't okay. She'd stupidly hoped that the payment would be a one-off. She should have known better. This could go on forever if she let it. 'I think I need a lawyer.' As the words came out of her mouth, she knew that was what she needed. And should have contacted one before parting with fifteen thousand dollars. 'A lawyer who's not allowed to tell anyone what I did.'

'What you did? You're worrying me.' Barb lowered her voice. 'The birth certificate was bad but doesn't warrant this kind of reaction. Did you kill someone?'

Liv stared at the older lady. That was what she immediately thought? That Liv was a murderer? 'Of course not.'

Barb let out a breath. 'Thank goodness.' She gave Liv a wry smile. 'I have a few rules that I live by, and one is that I don't socialise with murderers, which would have been disappointing as your harbour view is nicer than mine, and I'm quite fond of you.' She picked her phone up off the table and pressed the call button.

'Hold on,' Liv said. 'Who are you calling?'

'My grandson, Gus. He's a lawyer. I'll arrange an appointment. He won't charge as he knows you've been looking after me, and he'll be discreet. He won't even tell me what's going on.'

'He'd better—'

Barb raised her hand. 'Hello, love,' she said. 'I've got a new client for you. A pro bonus.'

'Oh,' Barb said, listening to her grandson. '*Pro bono*, okay. I thought it was a bonus. Whatever it is, she's a bonus, and you'll love her.'

Liv couldn't hear everything Gus said, but it definitely started with something like 'Oh, Gran'.

'Don't be silly,' Barb said. 'It's my lovely neighbour, Liv. You know, the one who looks out for me. The one who does my shopping and keeps me company when my only living relative is too busy to drop by.' She winked at Liv before injecting as much old-lady guilt and sadness into her voice. 'It's not that I expect you to be around to see me every day or even every week, but I do need your help with this. Liv's got herself into a situation that requires confidential legal advice. If the pro bonus bit is an issue, then I'll pay her fees. There's that investment fund I can always break into. It doesn't really matter if you have the money as payment now or inherit it in a few years when I'm gone.'

Liv sipped her drink and pushed down the desire to laugh as she listened to Barb manipulating her grandson. She shook her head. How could she even consider laughing at a time like this? What she'd done had dire consequences for her family and now for her bank balance too. In fact, if they found out, her mother would most likely disown her. This was criminal behaviour. And no one wanted a criminal in the family, no matter how good their intentions were. Liv shuddered as her mother's face, a picture of disappointment, filled her mind.

17

Toni had enjoyed a blissful three days with Joel home and could only wish that he didn't have to return to work – ever. She couldn't believe that her definition of bliss had now become a case of being at home in a house with a contented baby. You'd think Ruby was a different child when Joel was around. He had the same calming effect Mandy had on Ruby. But right now, that blissful feeling had been thrown out of the window. Joel had waited three days to drop his bombshell. She wasn't sure whether to be grateful he'd waited and allowed her to enjoy a few days or be furious that he'd kept this from her.

Now, as they sat at the kitchen counter, she stared at her husband. Was he serious? She'd struggled enough with him away the last week. She'd hoped being together would show her that they were a team. It turned out they most definitely were not.

'Come with me,' Joel said. 'It would only be for twelve weeks. I know I'd be away flying part of the time, but I'd be home as well. Whereas if I go without you, it will feel like forever.'

'You want me and Ruby to sit around in an apartment where we don't know anyone for three months and be happy when you appear for a few days at a time?' Toni knew she sounded bitchy, but it was bad enough being in Melbourne by herself with Ruby and at least here she had friends and family nearby. Another country was out of the question.

Joel sighed. 'It's an opportunity to fly for Emirates and see what life in Dubai would be like.'

Toni's mouth dropped open. 'Emirates? What? Hold on. You want to move to Dubai?'

'Possibly. We always said we'd give living somewhere else a go, and if we're going to do it, it would be best to get settled somewhere before Ruby needs to be enrolled in school.'

Toni stared at her husband. They'd had discussions from time to time about possibly moving overseas but had always agreed that it wouldn't work for her job. 'But Emirates? What's happened with your current job?'

Joel's hesitation stretched just long enough for a twinge of anxiety to prick at Toni. 'Joel?'

'Look, I didn't want to say anything, but the airline's in trouble. They're talking about massive cuts, and even though I've flown for them for fifteen years, my job isn't guaranteed. The Emirates opportunity is only a trial, but it's a good opportunity to see whether I like the airline and the culture of the organisation and, of course, whether I'd be prepared to move. If I do get laid off, it will give us an option.'

Toni was doing her best to get her head around Joel's news. Southern Air had, like all airlines, taken a hit during Covid, but Joel had been lucky to remain employed during the pandemic when many others had been laid off. Once the Australian borders opened towards the end of 2021, Toni had thought the airline had slowly recovered. It appeared she was wrong.

'What about other Australian airlines? You've been approached by Qantas before.'

'I have, but if massive layoffs happen, every pilot at Southern Air will be queuing up at Qantas. I want us to have options.'

She nodded – everything he was saying, as horrible as it sounded, made sense, but there was something that just didn't sit right and that was his comment about whether he'd be prepared to move.

'Do you mean whether *you'd* be prepared to move, or *we'd* be prepared?'

Joel reached for her hand. '*We'd*. Look, it's nothing definite, and I'm not really expecting we would move, but I'd like to at least give it a go. If you don't want to come for the twelve weeks, you and Ruby could come and visit me while I'm there. As soon as I know my schedule, we can work out when I'll be on the ground the longest.'

Toni nodded, trying to absorb all of this. Moving to another country, one she'd never visited or even particularly desired to visit, didn't sound like a good idea. And flying with Ruby? The thought of being trapped in a plane with her for fourteen hours was enough to make her hyperventilate. But twelve weeks?

'Look, babe, I'm not asking you to move or do anything crazy. I'm asking you for the opportunity to let me explore something new and give us a safety net. I really wish you'd come with me, but if you don't want to come, let me find out if I love it and think we should move, then I'll ask you to come over and try it out. If you hate it, we won't even consider it.'

'You're really going, aren't you? When?'

Joel evaded her eyes. 'That's why I was scared to tell you. They want me there Wednesday of next week.'

Toni's mouth dropped open. 'But you'll miss my birthday. Mum was going to look after Ruby so we could go away for the weekend.'

'I know, and I'm sorry, but the dates aren't flexible, and if I don't go, I'll regret it. My work's a huge part of me. You know that.'

'I thought I was too.'

Joel took her hand. 'Don't be like that. I'll make it up to you. We'll talk to your mum and see if she can look after Ruby for a day before I go. I'll arrange something special as an early birthday present.'

Tears pricked the back of Toni's eyes. This was a nightmare. She could hardly cope with Ruby for a few days on her own, let alone twelve weeks, and what about her career? Moving to Dubai would have serious repercussions for her. 'You know, my work is a huge part of me too. I wouldn't be able to work in Dubai.'

Joel frowned. 'Hold on, you said you wanted to be a stay-at-home mum until Ruby's old enough for school and by then, hopefully we'd be back in Australia. Working in Dubai wouldn't be relevant. If we did go, I imagine it would only be for a few years.'

Toni swallowed. *A few years?* 'I never said I'd be a full-time stay-at-home mum. After my maternity leave ends, I plan to work part time. We agreed on that.' They'd more than agreed. When they'd originally discussed the changes taking on a new baby would bring, Toni had suggested to Joel that she might want to go back to work within the first six months. He'd been horrified. *Absolutely no way. She needs that first year with you.* She'd ended up having to promise Joel that she would give Ruby the year.

'Yes, sorry, I forgot. I think when we'd originally talked about having kids you'd always said you wanted to be a full-time mum. But you're right, we did agree, and if that's what you want to do, that's fine. You haven't mentioned work at all since Ruby was born. I assumed you weren't giving it much thought. I guess it has only been six or seven weeks. Even after you caught up with the girls the other night, you didn't talk much about work.'

'That was a night of drinking and dancing,' Toni said. 'The work talk was more gossip about people than what was going on with the company. I was hoping you'd be okay with me going out again this Friday night. Belinda sent me a text this morning inviting me to go out with her and Rachael for a quieter night. I imagine I'll hear more about Entice then. I'd like to go, assuming you're okay to look after Ruby.'

'Go. It will be good for you to get out with your friends while I'm still here.' He gave a little laugh. 'No getting ideas about going back to work early, though. That really wouldn't work with Dubai.'

A cold shudder ran through Toni. He was really going to Dubai. Just like that. Decision made. She took a calming breath and decided to change the subject. 'We should speak to Mum about looking after Ruby so we can spend some time together. Let's ask her this afternoon when we go over to help fix the washing machine. Maybe we should plan a night away, not a day out.'

Joel frowned. 'I'm not sure about a whole night. Don't forget, when I go to Dubai, I'm going to miss out on twelve weeks of Ruby's life. I should be making the most of the days before I go.'

Toni finally understood the saying *blood boiling*. She was on the verge of exploding. 'You're kidding, I hope? You're going to be away from me for twelve weeks and can't even give me one night?'

Joel pushed his hand through his hair. 'It's not that I don't want to, it's just Ruby's brand new and I'm going to miss out on so much. And, before you say it, I know it's my choice, but the opportunity with Emirates is too good to say no to. Don't think I haven't tossed and turned over this. If the airline wasn't talking about making cuts, I'd do everything I could to postpone this, but they are, and I feel like we might need a backup plan if the worst happens. If I can spend as much time as possible with Ruby now, hopefully, I won't feel so guilty when I'm in Dubai.'

Although Toni could see the logic in needing a backup plan if Joel's job was threatened, she was still finding it hard to get her head around the Dubai decision. How could he take off when their baby was this young? She'd love to, but that was different; she wasn't coping, and Joel was. Wasn't he? She stared at her husband. Had she imagined how easily he'd take to parenthood, and he was actually struggling and running away from it? It was possible. She'd keep a close eye on him over the next few days and see if there were any cracks in his perfect parenting.

'Is Mandy going to be there this afternoon?' Joel asked. 'I owe her an apology for what I said the other day.'

'You do. I'd like to say no, she won't be there, but Mum's already told her we're coming. I'm guessing she'll be there already, counting down to two o'clock. I'm tempted to turn up at three to annoy her.'

'You really struggle with her, don't you?'

Toni nodded, guilt stabbing at her. She sighed. 'I vowed to make more of an effort with her. She's excellent with Ruby and has been trying hard with me. She's my sister. But I'm not sure if I'll ever truly connect with her.'

Joel moved closer to her and took her in his arms. 'That means you're human. Some people are harder to deal with than others. Mandy falls into that category for you. I get it. She can be incredibly annoying.'

'She can, but I look at what Liv did for her. Taking her to Sydney for months, teaching her to be independent and keeping in touch almost daily now. Dad would expect us to be looking after Mandy for him, and I've failed terribly.' Toni thought back to Mandy's words. That their father would be expecting her to lift her game. He'd be expecting her to lift her game with Mandy *and* Ruby.

'You can always turn that around. Make more of an effort and be more accepting of her,' Joel said.

Toni nodded. In theory, she could, and she should. In reality, it was a hurdle she might never overcome.

* * *

A little after two, Joel pulled the silver Jeep into Sara's driveway. Toni wasn't sure whether to laugh or be annoyed when Mandy was standing beside her door before she'd had a chance to unfasten her seatbelt. It was one of Mandy's traits that had driven her mad as a teenager. Everything had to be done on her schedule and generally straight away.

Joel reached across and squeezed her knee. 'Don't let her get to you. It'll take me an hour tops to fix the machine, and then we'll leave.'

Toni smiled, appreciating that he hadn't pushed the issue of her being more understanding or inclusive as a *nice* person would. He accepted that she had issues with her sister, and therefore he supported her. It was one of the many things she loved about him. Her smile dropped as Mandy knocked on her window.

'Toni. Are you getting out?'

No, I'm going to sit here until Joel fixes the washing machine and not get out and talk to you or Mum or let either of you see Ruby. She shook her head. It was as if some unseen force took control of her thoughts and words whenever she interacted with her sister. She needed to *lift her game*, and right now was the perfect time to start.

She pushed open her door and plastered a smile on her face. 'Hi Mands, how are you?'

'Excited,' Mandy said and flung her arms around Toni. 'Thank you for coming today.'

Toni hugged her back, surprised at the display of affection. Mandy, while affectionate with most people, was generally more reserved with Toni.

Mandy pulled away and peered into the back window. 'Is Baby sleeping?'

Toni grimaced at the reference to Baby and responded by opening the car's back door. Ruby stared out at her and Mandy.

Mandy clapped her hands together. 'She's smiling.'

'I think it's wind,' Toni said and started to unclip the baby from the car seat.

'No,' Mandy said, shaking her head. 'Definitely smiling for Aunty Mandy.'

Toni didn't correct her. Ruby hadn't smiled yet, so it was unlikely.

Joel took the nappy bag and his toolbox from the back of the Jeep, and Mandy led the way into their mother's house.

Sara greeted them with her arms open, and Toni happily deposited Ruby into them.

'Oh, she's gorgeous, Toni,' Sara said, smiling with delight at her grand-daughter. 'Come through to the lounge, and we can chat.'

Joel handed Toni the nappy bag. 'I'll go straight to the laundry and start on the washing machine. I might have to disconnect the taps. Hope that's okay?'

'Anything you need to do,' Sara said. 'I really appreciate you doing this for me. I'm sure you have better things to do on your days off.'

'Can I hold her next?' Mandy asked Toni as they sat down on the couches. Toni could see her sister was dying to hold Ruby and was being uncharacteristically restrained in the way she was asking. She softened a little. Mandy's face was full of love for Ruby. 'Sure. In fact, she's due a bottle if you'd like to feed her too?'

Sara handed Ruby to Mandy, and the baby was given Mandy's full attention, her sweet singing voice eliciting a gurgle.

'Looks like those two are sorted,' Sara said. 'Why don't you come through to the kitchen and help me organise some tea? Mandy brought another cake that Rose helped her make. She's becoming quite the baker.'

Toni took the bottle from the nappy bag and placed it on the side table next to Mandy. 'If she starts to get grizzly, then she'll be ready for this.'

Mandy nodded and continued singing. Toni was about to turn and follow her mother when Ruby's mouth turned up at the edges into what looked much like a genuine smile. She stared at her. 'Did she smile?'

Mandy paused her singing and nodded. 'Like she did in the car.' Then she continued singing, stroking the baby's cheek as she did.

Toni turned and walked towards the kitchen. She stopped at the laundry and poked her head in. Joel was pulling the machine out from the wall, a wrench in one hand. 'I think Ruby might have smiled.'

He looked up. 'Really?'

'Go and check for yourself.'

Joel put the wrench down and hurried from the laundry.

'Now,' her mother said as she reached the kitchen. 'We can have tea, or we can have wine.' She glanced at the clock. 'Far too early here for wine. It's not even three, but the wine does come from New Zealand, and if we were in NZ, it would be almost five, which is quite acceptable.'

'I vote NZ,' Toni said. 'We've got a milestone to celebrate if Ruby's smiling.'

'You'd better get a photo,' Sara said. 'Mandy will be thrilled if she's the recipient of the first smile.' She pulled open the fridge door and took out a bottle of pinot gris. 'Thanks for coming over today. I know Mandy tests your patience, but she does want to spend time with Ruby and to be fair she's grown in leaps and bounds in the past few weeks. Moving into Wattle House was the best thing she could have done. She's become more independent and less demanding.'

'And she's brilliant with Ruby,' Joel added, coming back into the kitchen. He grinned. 'She smiled at me too. They say it happens around six weeks. She's certainly doing everything by the book.' He held up his phone. 'I got some photos, but you might want to get some more. I'll get back to the washing machine.'

After taking plenty of photos to capture Ruby's first smiles, Toni found herself relaxing and enjoying the visit with her mother as her wine glass was topped up. Mandy was still holding Ruby and seemed as enchanted with her now as she was two hours earlier when they arrived.

'Now,' Sara said as she, Toni and Joel enjoyed their wine at the outdoor setting. 'Are you free at the weekend? I want to do something special for Liv coming down. Sunday lunch, perhaps?'

Joel glanced at Toni, a panicked look in his eyes. She reached for his hand, knowing what was concerning him. 'Liv has hardly shown an interest in Ruby,' she said. 'I don't think we have anything to worry about.'

'But she's coming down to visit. Maybe she wants to see how she feels about her now.'

'Liv doesn't want Baby,' Mandy said, carrying Ruby out to where they were all seated. 'She told me she never wants babies and says that me and her will be the aunties and Toni will be the mummy. Now, can I take Baby for a walk in the pram? I'll be careful. Just around the block, no crossing roads.'

'Sure,' Toni said, surprising herself more than anyone as the word left her lips. She was interested that Liv had been so frank with Mandy. 'Mandy, when did Liv tell you she never wants babies? Was it before or after Ruby was born?'

'Both,' Mandy said. 'It was why she couldn't keep Baby.' She quickly looked around as if someone might be listening and lowered her voice. 'Sorry. I'm not allowed to talk about that. But she also told me last night.'

'You spoke to her last night?'

'I speak to Liv every day,' Mandy said. 'And Barb too. They are my Sydney sisters. Even though Barb is old and could be my grandma, she says she's my Sydney sister. Now, I'd better go for that walk.' She looked at Joel expectantly.

He turned to Toni. 'You're sure you're comfortable with this?'

'I think Mandy will be fine,' Toni said, smiling at her sister. 'She's kept Ruby quiet since we arrived, and if she'd like to take her for a walk, then she should be allowed.'

'Would you like me to come with you?' Joel asked Mandy.

'No, thank you, but could you get the pram, please?'

Joel hesitated but got to his feet and walked around to the side gate to access the driveway and the Jeep.

Sara lowered her voice. 'You sure?'

Toni shrugged. 'I think I need to lighten up a bit when it comes to Mandy. She's amazing with Ruby.' The truth was, Mandy was a lot better with Ruby than she herself was. And Mandy taking charge minimised the need for Toni to do anything or to be shown up as incompetent if Ruby started screaming and she was unable to calm her. As much as she should be asking for help, she couldn't bear the thought of her family knowing how badly she was failing. On top of that, she could only imagine her mother's words if she admitted to not being cut out for motherhood. *You should never have taken Liv's baby, Toni. I knew it was a mistake from the very start.*

'Thank you, Toni,' Mandy said, her face serious. 'I will never let you down when it comes to Baby. I will be like her second mummy.'

Toni smiled and took a long sip of wine as Mandy followed Joel out to the Jeep. Right at this point, with the wine relaxing her and someone else looking after her baby, she could honestly say that for the first time in weeks she was happy.

18

Liv looked out over the harbour from the meeting table in Gus's thirty-seventh-floor office in Sydney's CBD.

'I'm guessing you don't do a lot of pro-bono work,' Liv said, admiring the expensive furnishings and Gus's beautifully cut suit.

'No, and this isn't pro bono. From what Gran told me, you need some advice from a friend who happens to be a lawyer. And while we've just met, the fact you've been good to Gran makes us friends.' He smiled. Liv had to admit, with his dimples, sandy blond hair and dark-brown eyes, he was gorgeous.

'And because you're not a client and you're a friend, that gives me the ability to say something to you that I would never say to a client.'

Liv stared at him. Was he going to ask her out? She hadn't dated in over a year, and with the whole Mandy and Ruby situation, she'd been relieved she wasn't in a relationship and had to either hide or explain the situation to someone else. He was cute, had a good job and was related to Barb, who she loved. It was a possibility, she guessed, that they might have a good time if they did go out.

'Liv,' he said, 'what you've done is completely messed up. It's not great that you're being blackmailed, but you've given this person the perfect opportunity.' He shook his head. 'I can see the headlines. You'd be crucified by the media and the court.'

Okay, she might have misread this one. 'I realise the circumstances aren't ideal,' she began and stopped as Gus started to laugh.

'Ideal? They are far from ideal. Did you give any thought to the penalties if you were caught out with this?'

'Honestly? No. I wanted to help Toni, and I thought no one would ever have to know.'

'And you couldn't have done it legally, where your sister Toni simply adopted the baby?'

Liv sighed. 'It's a long story.'

Gus held up his hand and pressed a button on a speaker on the table between them. 'Marianne, could you bring in some coffee and advise my next appointment that I'm running late. It's Jack Coleman. When he asks, tell him yes, I'm happy to meet him at O'Reilly's instead of here.'

He turned back to Liv. 'Okay, the long story, please. I need to understand your motivations so that hopefully I can agree with my gran that you're a wonderful person rather than the lying criminal I've been presented with so far.'

Liv was about to object when she saw the corner of his mouth twitch. He was enjoying this, and strangely, she wanted him to agree with his gran's assessment of her.

* * *

The next morning, Liv found herself smiling into the iPad screen at a delighted Mandy. She loved that since her sister returned to Melbourne, she and Mandy were not only spending time together, but they were doing practical things, like baking the same recipe at the same time. 'This cake is amazing, Hon,' she said looking down at the freshly iced frosted cake. 'I can't believe you know how to do this kind of thing.' She shook her head. 'Honestly, I don't think I've ever made a cake that looked this good before.'

Mandy giggled, her face far too close to the iPad, but Liv didn't have the heart to tell her to move back.

'Are you going to share it with Barb? She loves cake. I would share mine if I was still in Sydney. Instead, I'll take it to the animal shelter. I'm volunteering later today, and Izzy's working too. She's picking me up soon.' Her smile widened. 'Izzy is like Sam was: she loves sweet things. She'll probably eat three huge slices.'

Liv could hear noise in the background and her sister turned away from the iPad screen and spoke to someone. She turned back again. 'I have to go, Livvy; Izzy's already out the front.'

The FaceTime call was ended before Liv had time to say goodbye. She picked up the plate with the cake and headed straight for the door of the apartment. Mandy was right, Barb loved cake.

The older woman was quick to open her apartment door, her eyes lighting up. 'That looks amazing. I was about to take my cuppa out on the balcony. Let's make you one and cut up that cake. Did you make it?'

'Yes. With Mandy's help.'

Barb's smile widened. 'Mandy's here?'

Liv shook her head. 'No, we did it over FaceTime. She made one at her end, and I made one here. It's taken us hours. Mandy's still quite slow in the kitchen, but she's a perfectionist. Where I throw in a rough cup of this or that, she's levelling the cup with a knife.'

Liv couldn't help but notice Barb's smile falter.

'You okay?'

'I think I fell in love with your sister,' Barb admitted. 'I'm really missing her. She provided a lovely distraction from my regular boredom, and spending time with Mandy was soothing. It's hard to explain.'

'No, it's not,' Liv said. 'While she acts like an annoying whirlwind part of the time, there's a peacefulness about her. It's why I loved having her to stay. It surprised me, actually. While I've always been closer with Toni, there's no way I could stand her staying with me for as long as Mandy did.'

They moved into Barb's kitchen, and Barb flicked the kettle on for Liv's tea. 'Mandy calls me most days,' she said. 'She seems happy on the days she sees Ruby, but otherwise, she seems as miserable as I am.' She sighed. 'Don't get old, Liv. It's not much fun.'

'Is there any reason to sit around here by yourself all day?' Liv asked.

'I don't sit around every day. Today, for instance, Gus was going to take me to the theatre.'

'Going to?'

'He had to cancel because of a work thing.'

'That's a shame,' Liv said. 'The cake was partly to thank you. Gus was helpful when I spoke to him yesterday.' She blushed. 'You also never mentioned how good-looking he is.'

Barb laughed. 'Didn't I? In that case, sorry to be the bearer of bad news, but he bats for the other team.'

'No way!' Liv said. 'I was sure he was flirting with me.'

Barb laughed harder. 'It's quite likely he was. I think he's a professional flirt. Male or female.'

'He's bisexual?'

Barb frowned. 'I don't think so. I think he uses his charm at work on everyone, but I'm pretty sure he's only into men in his personal life. Although, he's never officially come out to me. His father was homophobic,' Barb added as if that explained everything.

Liv nodded and turned the conversation back to Barb. 'Have you thought about joining some groups? I'm sure we could find some things to interest you.'

'Maybe.' She took two plates from the cupboard and some forks. 'Let's take the cake out onto the balcony. What about you, Liv? You've lived across the hall from me for five years and you're always on your own. There's been no one in your life since well before the baby, right?'

'I'm not good at dating,' Liv admitted. 'The guys you meet in bars these days are only looking for one thing, and online dating is just as bad.'

'You've tried online dating?'

Liv nodded. 'You can't date currently without it. My main problem is I assume everyone on the apps are nutcases or just after sex and end up cancelling half the dates before they even begin. Now, what's this theatre you're missing out on today?'

'An outdoor production of *West Side Story*. We'd planned to have a bite to eat at Rolling Tide first. It's such a waste of the tickets. I'd go alone, but...' Her words died as she looked at Liv. 'Would you like to go with me?'

Liv swallowed her mouthful of cake. 'I'd love to. What time does it start?'

'We'd booked an early dinner at six thirty, and the production starts at eight.'

'I'll pick you up at ten to six then,' Liv said, 'and we can be each other's dates tonight and continue our discussions about men. But rather than talking about me, we should be looking at hooking you up with someone.'

Barb laughed. 'If my understanding of hooking up with someone is correct, then I think we'll forget that idea altogether.'

* * *

Liv and Barb were seated at Rolling Tide a little after six thirty. The sun had set, and lights danced and twinkled on the harbour. A cruise ship was docking at Circular Quay, and ferries were blasting their horns as they came to and fro. There was an electric energy in the air which reminded Liv of why she loved Sydney. Not only was the harbour stunningly beautiful, but the city had a vibe to it that was impossible to replicate elsewhere.

'Here's to a perfect evening,' Barb said, raising her champagne flute once their drinks had been delivered. 'And thank you for coming. I haven't seen live theatre in ages and was so looking forward to seeing this.'

'Thank you for inviting me,' Liv said, clinking glasses with Barb.

Barb took a sip, frowned, and put her glass down. 'Are you okay? You're very pale. Are you having trouble sleeping after everything with Ruby? It's understandable if you are.'

Liv shook her head. 'No, it's not that. I think the last few months have caught up with me, and the legal situation I talked to Gus about has added some extra stress. I'm sure I'll be okay once I catch up on some sleep.'

'Okay, but if you need anything, you let me know. And in the meantime, I was thinking more about our quest to find you a man,' Barb said. 'I think we need to put our heads together and come up with a plan.'

Liv spluttered on her champagne. 'I thought that was a joke.'

Surprise registered on Barb's face. 'No, it wasn't. But if you're not interested, that's fine. I don't want to push you into anything. Especially not after your last relationship.' She reached across the table and squeezed Liv's hand. 'Sorry love, Mandy did like to tell me things.'

'She told you about Justin?'

Barb nodded. 'She said he was a "bad boyfriend", and because of him, you no longer dated. You had one-night stands.'

Liv's cheeks filled with heat, causing Barb to laugh. 'No need to be embarrassed. You never know where a one-night stand will lead. But it might be better to look for men who are after a bit more than one night if you want a relationship, that is. I just hope this Justin didn't put you off men. He didn't hurt you, did he?'

Liv shook her head. 'No, he cheated on me. Multiple times, I eventually found out and of course he lied about it. I'm not sure if the betrayal or the humiliation was the worst part to be honest.' Or perhaps the mortifying trip to the doctor to check she hadn't contracted any diseases. But, even with that experience, Liv did want a relationship. It had been two years now since she'd had anything serious. The past few months, with the pregnancy and the baby, had made it difficult to think about anyone new. They'd hardly have been attracted to her situation and, in all fairness, probably wouldn't have wanted to know her if they'd learned what she'd done with Ruby.

Liv was about to explain this to Barb when she noticed the older woman's face drain of colour. She placed her champagne flute on the table. 'Barb?'

Barb nodded in the direction of the bar.

Liv turned to where Barb was looking. Two men were sitting chatting. The one facing Liv and Barb had thrown his head back and was laughing at something the other man said. Liv couldn't see the other man's face. She turned back to Barb. 'Do you know him?'

'Not him, the one with his back to us. It's Gus.'

Liv turned back to look again. From her angle, he could have been anyone, but when he turned side on, she saw it was indeed Gus. The man opposite Gus leaned forward, his hand resting on Gus's knee as he spoke. Liv drew in a breath as he moved closer and kissed Gus on the lips. She turned back to Barb. 'Are you okay?'

She nodded. 'He lied to me. He cancelled on me to go out on a date. When I told him I would be staying in tonight, he must have thought the coast would be clear to come to the same restaurant. He's probably going to the performance too. The pig.'

Liv stared at Gus. So much for him flirting with her the previous day. 'Do you want me to go and say something?'

Barb pushed her chair back from the table. 'No, I will.'

Liv followed closely behind Barb as they crossed the floor of the restaurant to the bar. The other man raised an eyebrow as they neared, and Gus turned as Barb reached to touch him on the shoulder. He whipped his hand away from his friend's knee, his face paling. 'Gran, what are you doing here?'

'Using our dinner reservation,' Barb answered, anger rising in her voice. 'But you, Gus. Is this your work meeting?' She took a step back and folded her arms.

'Mrs Jenkins,' the other man said, holding out his hand. 'It's a pleasure to meet you. Gus talks about you all the time. I'm Freddie, a...' He hesitated, glancing at Gus. 'A friend of Gus's.'

Barb accepted the man's hand and shook it. 'Nice to meet you, Freddie. I'd like to say Gus has told me about you, but he hasn't.' She dropped his hand and turned to her grandson. 'Now, how about you start being honest with me?'

Liv couldn't help but feel a twinge of sympathy for Gus as he stared at his grandmother, seemingly unable to talk. He closed his eyes momentarily before opening them again. 'I'm sorry, Gran, really I am. Work got cancelled at the last minute, and I thought it was too late to call you about tonight.'

Freddie shook his head and stood. 'It's been lovely to meet you, Mrs Jenkins. I'm sorry, I didn't know anything about your plans tonight, or I certainly wouldn't be here.'

'Don't go on my behalf,' Barb said. 'Liv and I are about to enjoy a lovely dinner before seeing the production. I won't be doing either with Gus. The fact he's this dishonest horrifies me.'

'We have that in common,' Freddie said. 'Call me when you've sorted yourself out,' he said to Gus before walking towards the restaurant's exit.

'Shit,' Gus murmured under his breath.

'Shit, alright,' Barb said. 'You know, your father might have been homophobic, but he raised you to be a man. Go after Freddie and apologise and both of you are to come around to my house for dinner tomorrow night. Okay?'

Gus's mouth dropped open. 'But—'

'No buts. I've been talking to Liv about relationships and how lovely it is when you find someone compatible. If that's Freddie for you, then don't let him walk away. Be proud of who you are and who he is.'

'But—' Gus tried again, but his grandmother cut him off.

'I've known since you were twelve, Gus. I've only ever been proud of you, and if you were worried I'd be disappointed or upset, I can tell you right now that the only disappointment I have in you is that you didn't trust me enough to come out to me and that you lied to me tonight, and I imagine many other times. Now, Liv and I are going to enjoy our dinner. I'll see you and Freddie tomorrow night.'

She turned, and Liv followed her back to their table.

Liv's eyes followed Gus as he hurried from the bar. 'That was something.'

Barb smiled. 'It was. That Freddie is a bit of alright, isn't he?'

Liv laughed. Gus's date *was* more than a bit of alright. He was tall, dark-haired, and gorgeous.

Barb lifted her glass in a toast. 'Here's to my grandson finally coming out to me, even if I had to force the issue.'

19

Toni put the finishing touches on her make-up, stood back and checked her reflection in the mirror perched atop the polished wooden dresser. She smiled as Joel came into the bedroom.

He let out a long wolf whistle. 'Wow.'

Toni smiled. The black midi skirt with the off-the-shoulder turquoise top was one of her favourite outfits. Adding her black ankle boots completed the look. 'An upgrade from my usual vomit-stained outfits. Are you sure you're okay with me going out? It seems a bit crazy when you're only here for a few more days.'

'We've got Monday to look forward to, and it gives me a night to myself with Ruby.'

Sara had offered to take Ruby for the day on Monday to give Joel and Toni time to themselves before he left for Dubai on Wednesday. He slipped his arms around her waist and pulled her to him. 'You really do look amazing.' He kissed her and then pulled away. 'If I start that, I'm not going to stop and then all of your preparations for the night will be wasted.'

Toni raised an eyebrow. 'Not wasted at all. I can be talked into staying.'

Joel groaned. 'No, you deserve a night out. Take advantage of it while I'm here. But, be prepared when you get home that I might be waiting up.'

Toni laughed.

'Where are you going anyway?'

'To Interlude. Dinner and too many drinks, knowing those girls.' She picked up the black Louis Vuitton bag she'd put out on the bed, and took her credit cards and some cash from her wallet and put them in it. Ruby's cry echoed through the apartment as she added her lipstick, mascara and phone. *Not now.* The last thing she needed was having to change a nappy or risk being vomited on. Her face must have conveyed her thoughts as Joel flapped his hands, shooing her towards the door.

'Go. You are officially off the clock. As much as I know you love Ruby, avoiding projectile vomit with that outfit on would be recommended.'

Toni grinned. 'Thank you.' She hurried out of the apartment and into the lifts before he could change his mind.

* * *

Belinda and Rachael were sitting at an outside table, surrounded by patio heaters, when Toni arrived at the modern tapas bar. Music, laughter and chatter spilled from inside, reminding Toni of how alive South Yarra was on a Friday night. Adrenaline buzzed through her as she breathed in the atmosphere. The women squealed and stood to hug her when she joined them at the table.

'You look fabulous,' Belinda said. 'I didn't get a chance to say it the other night, but aren't you supposed to have bags under your eyes and be a walking zombie?'

Toni laughed. 'You should have seen me a few weeks ago. I was a wreck. Having Joel home means I've had some sleep this week, which is a bonus.'

'This calls for champagne,' Belinda said. 'Toni's back in the land of the living. Permanently, we hope.'

'At least until sprog number two,' Rachael added.

Toni shook her head. 'Never happening. One's enough.' She raised her hand and signalled to a waiter that they were ready to order drinks.

Rachael's eyes were wide when Toni looked back to face her.

'Really?' she said. 'This is what you've always wanted. Has it been that bad?'

Heat rose up the back of Toni's neck and crept onto her face. She didn't want them thinking she didn't love Ruby, even if she wasn't sure that she did. They ordered a bottle of champagne, and once the waiter left, she turned to Rachael. 'Of course not,' she said. 'I've finally got my head above water and can get back out and do things. I'm in no hurry to put life on hold again.' And this is why the human race continues, she thought, as she lied through her teeth. Everyone omitting how hard parenting was. No doubt humanity would have died out years ago if people told the truth.

'Does that mean you're coming back to work early?' Belinda asked. 'That would be fantastic.'

Toni smiled. 'Other than Joel killing me if I go back before my maternity leave is up, I don't think Zalia Watts would be too impressed if I walked in and tried to take over. She was ecstatic to get my maternity leave contract.'

'I heard she's leaving,' Rachael said. 'I'm not entirely sure that it is her choice either. She's stuffed up the Zoltron account.'

Toni's mouth dropped open. 'No, not Zoltron! What did she do?' Toni thought of the hours and hours she'd put into securing the real estate giant. It had been her most exciting acquisition in the twelve years she'd been at Entice.

'Told Pete Miller he was an arrogant idiot.' Rachael raised an eyebrow and nodded her thanks to the waiter, who poured three glasses of champagne before depositing the bottle into an ice bucket next to the table.

Toni was stunned into silence. You did not tell a client whose contract was worth several million to the agency that they were arrogant or an idiot, even if both descriptions were true.

'Apparently, keeping the account is pretty much conditional on her not working on it.'

'Wow,' was all Toni could manage.

'It wasn't only Zoltron,' Belinda added.

'She's created dramas internally with Ferguson's and Yambles, and I believe she lost us any chance of getting the hardware chain, Dixsons, as a client.'

Toni's face creased in confusion. 'How on earth did she get the job to start with?'

'She was leaving Hunters and Rob convinced her to spend twelve months with us.'

Toni was silent for a moment, a thought crossing her mind 'How did Rob find out she was leaving?'

'I think she contacted him,' Belinda said.

Toni rolled her eyes. 'She rang up Rob and said, "I'm leaving your biggest competitor. Can you give me a job?" And being a completely naïve idiot, Rob said yes.'

Belinda and Rachael looked at each other and then back to Toni. 'What are you suggesting?'

'I'm suggesting that she's set Entice up. She's come in and tried to lose our biggest accounts. I imagine Hunters are already wining and dining them and securing their clients.'

Belinda let out a whistle. 'You're probably right.' She pulled out her phone and started tapping at the screen.

'What are you doing?' Toni asked.

'Messaging Rob. He needs a heads up to switch into damage-control mode.'

Toni and Rachael sipped their drinks while Belinda sent the message. She put her phone down once the job was done and picked up her glass. 'We should have told you about this a few weeks ago. Could have saved Entice a fortune and our reputation.'

'Okay, let's talk about something else,' Rachael suggested. 'We came to have fun, not to get worried about work. Toni probably hasn't heard that Lucy and Fiona have been having an affair for two years.'

'You're kidding? I didn't even realise they were lesbians.'

'No one did,' Rachael said.

'And Lindsay's boyfriend, you know, the gorgeous Paul?' Belinda said. 'He's cheating on her with Jemima in marketing.'

'And no one's game to tell her,' Rachael added. 'I wouldn't want to be either of them when she finds out.'

'How on earth has all this happened in a matter of weeks? It's not like I've been gone for months,' Toni said. 'It was never this interesting when I was there.'

Rachael laughed. 'Imagine if this is seven weeks' worth of news, what six or twelve months will be like with you on maternity leave. The company will probably have gone under by then.'

Toni laughed, but as the waiter came back to take their orders, she couldn't shake off the niggle of concern that Rachael's comment planted. She'd put twelve years of hard work into Entice and couldn't bear the thought of it all being for nothing.

The three women continued discussing the staff and the fallout of their affairs and bad behaviour. As their main courses were delivered, Belinda's phone pinged.

'It's Rob,' she said, scanning the message. She looked up at Toni. 'He said to tell you a huge thank you and that he doesn't know how we function without you, and can you start back on Monday?'

Toni dropped her fork onto the table with a clatter. 'Is he joking?'

Belinda glanced at the message. 'He doesn't use emojis, so it's hard to tell.'

'But Monday? I'm not due back for months.'

'And?' Belinda said. 'What's the difference? You're not breastfeeding, which means anyone can look after Ruby, and from a few things you said earlier, it sounds like full-time parenting isn't all it's cracked up to be. Give it some thought.'

Her phone pinged again. Belinda laughed. 'He sent another message saying he needs your answer now.'

'Now what are you doing?' she asked as Belinda started texting again.

Belinda looked up at Toni and winked. 'Telling him you'll come in on Monday to discuss options and that you may not be available full time but might be able to provide some advice. How does that sound?'

Toni froze, unsure of how to respond. She couldn't go back to work. Ruby was only seven weeks old and Joel was about to be away for twelve weeks. She could hardly leave her in day care or with a nanny. Could she?

Her excitement built. What if she did consider it? It might be what she needed to give a better balance with Ruby. Her excitement died as quickly as it had risen. Joel would kill her. He'd been adamant about the importance of Ruby having a full-time parent for at least the first twelve months.

But then again, he'd hardly put his hand up to do it, and now he was taking off to Dubai. She sipped her drink and pushed the image of her husband out of her head. Nothing had been promised, only that she was happy to offer Rob some advice. That was hardly going to cause problems.

'Sounds good. Tell him I'll be there at ten.'

* * *

Toni tentatively opened one eye and then the other. She slowly sat up, expecting her head to explode at any minute, but it didn't. The other side of the bed was empty. Joel must have got up with Ruby. She glanced at the clock. Nine already.

She lay her head back against the pillows, stretched her arms out in front of her and smiled. If she ever wrote one of those stupid baby books, she'd have in the first chapter. *You must go out and get smashed with your closest girlfriends, ideally ones without children.* Toni's thoughts shifted back to work and the Monday-morning meeting with Rob. Joel would still be home, so that would be no problem as far as Ruby went, but she did experience a stab of guilt at even having to have the conversation this morning with Joel about the possibility of going back to work early. She was pretty sure he wouldn't be happy.

Two heads poked around the door. Toni sat up and smiled.

'Hey,' Joel said. 'You up for visitors?'

Toni laughed. 'I'm hardly sick.'

Joel smiled. 'Thought you might be feeling a little worse for wear after the state you came home in.'

Toni had vague memories of Joel telling her to quieten down as she'd started a noisy rendition of 'Say a Little Prayer' as she'd arrived home the previous night. She'd then thrown herself at him, which he'd been quite happy about. She must have passed out shortly after they'd had sex as she didn't remember a whole lot else.

'Bizarrely, I'm fine.'

Joel crossed over to the bed and sat Ruby down, his hands supporting her. Toni did her best to push the stabs of guilt that were trying to dampen her joy as she thought of the possibility of going back to work early. She reached out and picked Ruby up. She could do this. She could be a loving and devoted mother – if she knew there was an end in sight. 'Hello, sweet thing, how are you this morning?'

Ruby scowled at Toni, annoyed at being taken from Joel's hands. She opened her mouth, ready to let out a howl, but Joel took her from Toni before the sound erupted.

'None of that, little Miss,' he said. 'Your mummy is enjoying the post-glow sensation of her night out and,' he winked, 'the brilliant performance she arrived home to.' Toni smiled. 'Not that I think she probably remembers that brilliant performance.'

'Oh, I do.'

Joel's voice soothed Ruby, and she snuggled into him.

'Why don't you have a shower or relax, and Ruby and I will go and get some coffee started.'

'Did I ever tell you you're the perfect husband?'

Joel grinned. 'No, but I could have let you in on that secret years ago.' He waved Ruby's hand at Toni as they left the bedroom.

Toni sank back into the pillows. *Perfect in this moment*, she should have clarified. He would hit the roof when she broached the subject of going back to work. But if life was broken down to isolated moments, then in this moment, he was perfect.

* * *

Toni enjoyed a long, hot shower before getting dressed and walking through to the kitchen. Ruby was in her vibrating baby bouncer in the living area, her eyes drooping as if she was only moments away from nodding off.

Her phone rang as she sat down on one of the stools at the island bench and gratefully accepted the cup of steaming coffee Joel pushed across to her. She glanced at the screen. It was her mother.

'She left a message on the home phone earlier,' Joel said, 'something about tomorrow and Liv's visit.' He held her eyes for a moment, and his concern was obvious. Liv coming to Melbourne could mean she wanted Ruby back.

Toni accepted the call. 'Hey, Mum, everything okay?'

'It's fine, just disappointing,' Sara said. 'Liv's had to cancel.'

Toni looked at Joel and mouthed *she's cancelled*. 'Is she okay?'

'I think so. She said she was too busy with work. I'm wondering if it's to do with Ruby, though. That she's struggling knowing she'll see her.'

'Possibly, although I've hardly heard from her since we got back from Sydney. If she was that interested in Ruby, I'm sure we'd be getting Face-Time requests regularly, and she'd have come down weeks ago.'

Sara sighed. 'Hopefully. I hate to admit it, but this situation leaves me with a bad feeling. I can't put my finger on it exactly, but it's like I keep waiting for something to happen. Something we're not going to like.'

Toni fell silent. Her mother's words implied she thought Liv still intended to ask for Ruby back.

'I'd better go,' Sara said. 'Mandy's upset that Liv's cancelled. I might pop over and see her. I assume you and Joel would prefer to spend the day together rather than coming here, as he hasn't got many days left at home.'

'Thanks, Mum, that sounds good.'

'Okay, I'll see you Monday then when I look after Ruby.' Sara ended the call before Toni had a chance to change that plan. She placed her phone down on the kitchen counter and sipped her coffee.

'I know it's silly,' Joel said, 'but I'm glad Liv cancelled. I still worry every day that she's going to take Ruby from us.'

Toni raised an eyebrow. 'I think Mum thinks the same.'

Alarm flashed in Joel's eyes. 'Why, what did she say?'

'That the whole situation gives her a bad feeling. Not exactly subtle.'

'You aren't worried?'

'It's been weeks.' *A lifetime, actually.* 'Liv's hardly shown any interest in Ruby. I don't think she's in Sydney pining away for her. Her hormones after giving birth would have driven her crazy if she was suffering from post-natal depression or grieving for her baby. Liv's not the sort to walk away from something she really wants.'

'Even though she knows we'd be devastated?'

'I don't think we need worry,' Toni said. 'And if we do, we deal with it then.'

'Ruby's changed you,' Joel said. 'Before we had her, you were paranoid that Liv would take her back and now, when that situation is quite likely, you seem relaxed about it.'

Toni smiled. 'Yes, motherhood has relaxed me.' She would have laughed out loud except she knew how much it would disappoint Joel if she admitted how tense motherhood made her, and that perhaps she'd welcome Liv's arrival if she really did want to take Ruby back. 'But let's forget about Liv for the moment,' Toni said. 'There's something I need to talk to you about.'

Joel looked up from the coffee machine where he was preparing his cup. 'Sounds serious.'

'Not really. But you might not be too happy.'

Joel added milk to his coffee and sat on the stool next to her.

'The thing is, I've been asked to go in for a meeting at Entice on Monday morning. The person who took over my job has been fired. Turns out she was working for another agency and trying to sabotage clients. There's some damage control to be done, and Rob wants my advice on how to handle it.'

'What can you do?' Joel asked. 'Surely Rob or someone at the highest level should be dealing with it?'

'It's because the main client involved is Zoltron. You know that it took me absolutely ages to secure them, and I spent a lot of time with them once they came on board. I imagine Rob wants some ideas as to how to win them back or keep them if they haven't gone yet. Don't forget, it's only been a matter of weeks since I went on leave, not months.'

Joel pushed a hand through his hair. 'That's all they want? One meeting to pick your brains?'

Toni hesitated. Rob would want her back. She knew that without meeting with him. But as it hadn't been confirmed, there was no need to worry Joel. And if she was honest, she wasn't completely sure how she felt about it. In an ideal world, she'd love to be a doting mother, completely in love with her baby and who would hate the thought of leaving the house without her. The reality, however, was very different. If Toni did go back to work early, it might be better for Ruby to have someone looking after her who did shower her with the love Toni seemed unable to. 'That's my understanding. But I'm not completely sure. I guess going in on Monday will fill me in.'

'You've only just started maternity leave. You're seven weeks into fifty-two. Why not let them deal with it, and you can worry about it when you go back?'

'Joel, if they lose all their clients, then there will be nothing to go back to. Getting involved now at least means I have a say in trying to help save the company. Also, I feel like I owe them. They've been so good about the maternity leave. Most employers would be demanding the adoption papers and Liv's still waiting on advice from the lawyer.' Toni experienced a small stab of guilt at the reminder that she still hadn't followed Liv up about making the adoption official.

'You've worked there for twelve years, babe, and they know what we've been through with IVF and the failed pregnancies. I agree, they're being great about it, but I kind of feel like they should be. You've given them so much during the time you've been there and certainly more unpaid over-time hours than the maternity leave is going to cover. You know, it wouldn't be the end of the world if you didn't go back. You might decide you want to try living in Dubai and imagine all the time you'd get to spend with Ruby. A lot of people would kill for the chance to be a full-time mum.'

Toni shook her head. 'Would you want to be a full-time parent?'

Joel stared at her for a moment. 'Definitely.'

'Okay, why don't you then?'

'Because it wouldn't make any sense. My salary covers a lot of our expenses and, also, if I stop flying, then going back to it is going to be difficult down the track, not having kept up my hours and all that.'

Toni put her hands on her hips. 'I'm sorry, but I don't believe for one second that you'd be a full-time parent, and I think you're only saying you would because you know it isn't an option. Going to Dubai for twelve weeks hardly suggests you're a devoted father.'

Joel's mouth dropped open. 'Is that what you think? That I'm not devoted to Ruby? I'm completely devoted. The Dubai opportunity is bad timing. But if I say no this time, it won't be offered again, and with the rumours circulating at Southern Air, I don't think we can risk that. It's not a decision I've made lightly. I went over it again and again before I brought it up with you. But, if you're going to say I'm not devoted, then I'll pull out of going and start putting my feelers out with other Australian airlines.'

'It's not about Dubai. It's more than that. Suppose I earned more than you. I can't see you staying home full time. I think you enjoy the time you have to yourself and then the time you have here. It's a great balance.' *Exactly what I need.*

Joel thought for a moment, then sighed. 'You're probably right. I would prefer to be able to do both, and at least when I'm home, I'm like a full-time parent. You know what I mean. I'm not distracted by having to prepare for meetings the next day or put presentations together. I can be fully present when I'm here.'

Toni nodded. That was true, at least. 'Let's not get worked up about it,' she said. 'It's a meeting to help them out, nothing more.'

'Promise me you won't go back early.'

'It's probably not even relevant. It's one meeting.'

'Promise me.'

Toni squirmed in her seat.

Joel banged his coffee cup on the counter. 'A few minutes ago, you said you had no idea as to what Rob wanted, yet not being able to make that promise suggests you know he'll ask you to go back early.'

Toni sighed. 'Let's not argue about it when we don't know for sure whether there is anything to argue about.'

'What about our day out? I leave on Wednesday, and your mum was going to look after Ruby on Monday. You'll prioritise a meeting you really don't need to be at over us?'

Toni did her best to remain calm. It was a bit rich for Joel to lay on the guilt. He was prioritising his work over *them*. Though she was smart enough to know that pointing this out would not be helpful. 'The meeting's at ten. I'd be home by twelve at the latest. Mum will have her all day if we want her to. It would still give us plenty of time.' She ran her toes down the inside of his leg and licked her lips suggestively. 'We don't even have to go out if you don't want to.'

Joel groaned. 'I can't believe I'm going to allow you to manipulate me. But okay, fine. I'll drop Ruby at your mum's, and we can start our day the minute your meeting ends. But, Toni, please don't agree to going back to work without discussing it with me first?'

20

Don't agree to going back to work without discussing it with me first played on Toni's mind as she pulled into an empty parking space in the executive section of Entice's underground parking. She took a deep breath, doing her best to push all thoughts of Joel from her mind. She picked up her bag and shut the door of her Lexus. She strode across the car park to the lifts, her heels click-clacking. Even the sound of her heels brought a smile to her face. She'd been slopping around in Ugg boots the last few weeks. Nikes had been dressing up as they signified her leaving the house. To be in a suit, heels and make-up, even for a few hours, was a great feeling.

Toni rode the lift to level six and stepped out into the reception area. Lindsay looked up from behind the front desk and smiled. 'Toni, how wonderful to see you. Back from maternity leave already?'

Toni smiled. 'I wish!' The words escaped Toni's mouth before she could stop them. She coughed. 'How are you?'

Lindsay raised an eyebrow. 'You wish? I thought we'd never see you again the way you'd been talking about babies and motherhood.'

Toni gave a self-conscious laugh. 'Honestly, so did I. Ruby's gorgeous and wonderful but I'm so used to the hectic pace in here, I'd be lying if I said I didn't miss it. Now, how's that gorgeous man of yours?'

'He's great. We're moving in together.'

'Congratulations,' Toni said, wondering at what stage Lindsay would discover he was cheating on her. 'I'd better go and see Rob. No need to let him know I'm here. He'll work that out soon enough.' She flashed another smile and made her way down the corridor to Rob's office.

* * *

'Toni!' Rob got up from his desk, crossed the room and opened his arms to give her a big hug. Toni grinned. He was desperate for her to come back. Rob was not a hugger.

She awkwardly hugged him back, then placed her bag on the floor next to the chair and took a seat.

'What's been going on?' Toni asked.

'How much has Belinda told you?' Rob asked.

'A bit. From what she shared with me, it seems that Zalia was sent over by Hunters to steal clients, and from the sounds of it, she's done a good job.'

Rob nodded. 'Yep. We've lost Balmain Industries already, and unless someone weaves some magic, we're going to lose Zoltron.'

'Shit.'

'Yep, *shit* exactly. Look, at the end of the day, the best hope we have of getting Zoltron to reconsider and stay with us is if you were able to meet with them. Show them that we can look after them even better than we have in the past. If we lose them, then I'm worried it will have a domino effect. We've gained several clients because of that contract. They follow Zoltron to whichever agency Zoltron use.'

'What am I supposed to be offering them that will make the difference? And why didn't you offer it to start with?'

'You,' Rob said. 'That's what you need to offer.'

'Me?' Toni was expecting him to say discounts and extra staff working on their account, not her.

Rob nodded. 'Yep. That's what it comes down to. They want you. Pete Miller said clearly that the service and vision they'd received from you was exceptional, beyond anything he'd received at any other agency. He basically told me that the only hope in hell we had of retaining them was if you were heading up their account.'

'But I'm not back for another ten months.'

'Any flexibility on that?'

Toni stared at him. She swallowed. She was being offered what she wanted. An opportunity to escape full-time motherhood. But there was Joel. What was he going to say? She pushed that thought to the back of her mind. She already knew what he would say. He'd have a fit.

'I don't think it's realistic for me to come back full time right now,' Toni said. 'Joel would kill me.'

'Do you have anyone who could look after Ruby? Your mum or Joel's? I'm happy to employ a nanny that the company pays for if relatives aren't an option. Daley – in design – uses one and swears by her. Even part time, Toni, exclusively managing Zoltron?'

Toni gave thought to the offer. If someone close to them was looking after Ruby, perhaps Joel would be more flexible. Her mother might be an option or a nanny if she wasn't. At least if it was the same person every day looking after Ruby, she could be in her own home. One of Joel's biggest reservations about her returning to work was putting Ruby in day care. A nanny would bypass that.

'How would it work? Part time is fine in theory, but in this industry, if a client needs something, they need it that day. They're not going to wait if it's Tuesday and I'm not here until Thursday.'

'How about you have a chat with Pete and see what would work? You only need to be available for any dealings that are direct with him, which, let's face it, aren't all that often. His marketing director will be the main contact, and some of that work can be handed down internally here.'

Toni thought about it. Rob was overly positive in thinking the marketing director would work with someone more junior on Entice's staff. But there may be ways around it.

'If I could work from home part of the time, then as far as the client is concerned, I would be available every day. They wouldn't need to know I wasn't in the office or what my hours were.'

Rob grinned. 'You're giving it some thought.'

Toni smiled. 'I was giving it thought before I got here this morning. I've just got to find a way to make it work that means I don't end up divorced.'

Rob glanced at the clock. 'Miller will be here at ten forty-five.'

'What? Now?' Toni wasn't expecting to be put in front of the client this quickly.

'We're in damage-control mode. If we don't get this sorted today, Miller's walking.'

'What if I'd said I wasn't available? Would you still be meeting with him this morning?'

Rob grinned. 'The fact you agreed on a Friday night to come in today meant I could count on the fact you were interested. And yes, I'd still have to meet with him this morning to be professional and work out what information we needed to hand over to Hunters for him if he doesn't stay with us.'

The phone on Rob's desk buzzed. He picked it up. 'Okay, thanks, Lindsay. Show him into the boardroom. Toni and I will be there in a minute. Bring in coffee and the pastries we discussed.' Rob placed the phone back in its cradle and stood. 'Come on, time to save the company.'

Toni rose to her feet, feeling dazed. In the last few weeks, her challenges had been limited to trying to have a shower each day and stopping Ruby from crying. Both of which she'd failed to achieve most of the time. Now she had to come up with a grand plan as to why a multi-million-dollar client should stay with the agency. And an even grander plan to prevent her husband from hating her.

* * *

Pete Miller was sitting in the boardroom drumming his fingers on the oak tabletop when Rob and Toni entered the room. He stood and smiled. 'Finally, someone who knows what they're doing is in the room.'

Toni forced a laugh, throwing a sympathetic look Rob's way as she noticed the colour his face had turned.

'How's the baby doing? Boy or girl? To be honest, I didn't even know you were pregnant. You hid that well.'

'Girl,' Toni answered, deciding not to go into an explanation about how she acquired Ruby. 'She's doing fine, thanks.'

'Fine enough for you to come back and start running this sorry excuse for an agency properly?'

Rob cleared his throat. Toni could only imagine what was going through his head. Surely the agency couldn't have gone that far downhill in a few weeks? She wasn't the only employee who worked hard. It was a shame that one unhappy client held so much influence and power.

'Sounds like it might be the only way to keep you in line,' Toni joked. 'I don't think the answer is sending Zoltron off to some other agency. They'll disappoint you, especially when they don't know what to order when we head out to lunch. The wrong vintage of champagne is one of those things they should know, but I'm betting you they won't.'

Pete laughed, a great, booming laugh. 'See, Rob, this is what's been missing. Someone to put me in my place. You and the rest of the staff kiss my arse, and it pisses me off. Treat me with some respect and as a regular person.'

'As for the campaign the agency has presented you since I've been away, I can see room for improvement,' Toni continued, not missing a beat.

Rob raised an eyebrow.

She ignored him. Rob knew she hadn't looked at any of the work, but there was no reason Pete had to know this.

'Look, the creative team were deliberately given the wrong direction for the campaign. Zalia's strategy backfired, producing the quality of ads she did. At least if she'd presented amazing work and then told you she was moving back to Hunters, you'd have a good reason to leave. The fact that they were mediocre gives you a heads up for the sort of work Hunters would produce under her direction once they secured you as a client.'

Pete nodded. 'Good point. Very good point.' He laughed again. 'Rob, this is the sort of stuff you could have said yourself, and I would never have considered moving. Yep, you guys got played by Zalia and Hunters. That's all I needed to know and that you were going to put someone better on the job for me.' He sighed. 'But now that's not even a concern. Toni's back to look after us.' He pushed his chair back from the table. 'Come on. Forget the coffee. I'm taking us all out to celebrate. Lunch at the Lounge Room on me.' He stopped and looked at Rob. 'I guess you can come too.' He laughed as if this was the funniest joke ever and winked at Toni. 'Let's celebrate your first day back on the job. A bottle of Crystal will do the trick. We can start talking campaigns tomorrow.'

Toni managed to keep a smile plastered on her face as she looked at Rob for help. She could not go out for lunch. She'd promised Joel.

'Pete, we'll meet you in reception,' Rob said. 'I need to have a quick word with Toni.'

'No worries. But don't keep me waiting. A drink would go down nicely right about now.'

It wasn't even twelve o'clock and he wanted a drink. Toni would have laughed if this lunch didn't have the potential to ruin her.

She turned to Rob the moment Pete was out of earshot. 'Joel will kill me. Can you get me out of this? Mum's looking after Ruby. We were going to spend the day together, and he leaves for Dubai for twelve weeks on Wednesday.'

'Shit,' Rob said. 'This lunch is crucial. You know that.'

'Let me have a word with Pete. I'll see if I can get out of it without ruffling his feathers.'

Rob nodded.

They made their way into reception, where Pete was looking out at the view over the Yarra River. He turned as Toni cleared her throat, and smiled. 'Fabulous, let's go.'

'Actually, Pete,' Toni lay an arm on his. 'I have a slight problem. I came in this morning to work out when I'd be needed back and to meet with you, but unfortunately haven't organised childcare arrangements beyond twelve today. I'll be in tomorrow, but the rest of the day isn't possible.'

Pete moved his arm away from Toni's touch and shook his head. 'Honestly, Toni, you're the most resourceful person around here. Calling a babysitting service isn't that hard.' He frowned. 'What's going to happen when we have a deadline and your baby's sick? Does that mean you won't be here?' He ran a hand through his hair. 'Maybe this isn't going to work after all. Don't get me wrong. I do understand that this is how the world works, that parents get days off when their kids are sick. But it's not what I want to hear on the day Entice is trying to win my business back.'

Toni had to bite her tongue to avoid pointing out to Pete on how many levels what he'd just said was wrong and probably illegal. She looked to Rob, who shook his head. His face filled with a mixture of compassion and hope. 'It's your call.'

She took a deep breath and then smiled. She couldn't be responsible for Entice potentially being ruined, and, if she was honest with herself, Pete was forcing the issue in a direction that she wanted anyway. 'Give me a couple of minutes. You're right, I'll organise a babysitter, and we should be good to go. Alternatively, I can meet you at the restaurant?'

Pete clapped Rob on the back. 'Now that sounds more like it. Come on. We can get a head start on a bottle of Crystal. Meet us there when you're ready, Toni.'

Toni kept the smile glued to her face while she waited for Pete and Rob to get into the lift. 'I'll see you shortly.' She waited until the lift doors closed before turning and marching back to Rob's office to call Joel.

21

Liv struggled to get out of bed on Sunday and by Monday morning, her head was pounding, and fatigue was making it difficult to function. She drew her cardigan around her as she stood, coffee in hand, out on the balcony surveying the harbour. The sky was grey, and dark clouds threatened on the horizon. She imagined the regular harbour activity would be minimal today with a storm brewing.

Exhaustion overwhelmed her as she steadied herself on one of the balcony chairs. Had the Ruby situation and the blackmail caused this extreme fatigue? It was strange. Liv didn't remember her health ever suffering due to external happenings. She was the type of person who got a cold or flu and would be sick for a few days but wasn't generally affected physically by mental or emotional stress. Although she had to admit, during the last few months she'd brought an enormous amount of stress on herself.

She put her coffee down on the table and sat on one of the chairs. A knocking on her front door caused her to groan. At this time of the morning, it would be Barb. But she wasn't sure she had the energy to pull herself up out of the chair. She slipped her phone from her pocket and called the older lady. She could hear a phone ringing out in the hallway.

'Liv? What a coincidence. I was knocking on your door.'

'I know. I'm here, but I'm sick and wasn't up to answering. You can come in if you want, but you'll need to use the spare key I gave you. I could be contagious, though. I don't know what's wrong with me.'

Barb ended the call without responding. Minutes later, Liv heard the key in the lock.

'Liv?'

'Out here,' she called.

Concern was etched in every line of Barb's sun-aged face as she appeared at the door leading onto the balcony. 'Are you okay?'

Tears filled Liv's eyes. She wiped at them. 'Sorry, I don't know what's happened. I've been exhausted all weekend, and now I just want to cry.'

'Oh love, the baby situation was going to catch up with you at some stage. I'm sorry if it's now.'

Liv shook her head. 'I don't think it's that. But how are you? I haven't even heard how your evening with Gus and Freddie went.'

'Are you sure you want to talk about that? I think we need to get you to a doctor.'

'No, I'll be fine. Distract me with your news.'

Barb hesitated and then smiled. 'It went well. Freddie's lovely and they're perfectly suited. Gus and I had a good conversation before he arrived, and he explained why he hadn't come out to me. I knew already, but I'm glad he could put it into words. It was all about his dad, my son, and how homophobic he was. Anyway, it seems we're past all of that, and the best news is they're moving in together. I think he really is the one for Gus. And Freddie's been through a difficult time lately. He lost his sister, and it sounds like Gus has been there for him which has brought them a lot closer.'

'That's wonderful news,' Liv said. 'Not about his sister, but about their relationship.' She bent forward. 'Sorry, I think I'm going to be sick.'

Barb hurried back inside and returned with a bucket from the laundry. She handed it to Liv just in time.

Barb rubbed her back as she emptied the contents of her stomach. 'Sorry,' Liv said when she'd finished. 'You should go in case I'm contagious. I think I'll go back to bed.'

Barb nodded; the concern still evident on her face. 'Exhaustion and nausea. Anything else?'

Liv lifted a leg and pointed at her ankle. 'Hideous swelling. Other than that, I'm fine.'

As she stared at her ankle, a discussion she'd had with her doctor came back to her. *Fatigue and fluid retention can be one of the first signs of problems with the kidney. Come and see us straight away if you suffer any of these symptoms.*

'You've gone white as a sheet,' Barb said. 'What can I do?'

Liv looked up at her. 'Come with me to the specialist.'

'Specialist?'

Liv nodded. 'My kidney. This could be symptoms of kidney failure.'

Barb stared at her. 'No, you're far too young. Why would you think it's that?'

Liv took a deep breath. 'I've had a donor kidney for fifteen years. Twenty to twenty-five years is the most I can expect from it, and then I'll have to hope there's another kidney available from the transplant list. Toni gave me her kidney, Barb. She never hesitated the moment she found out I needed one. Didn't give her own health a second thought. In fact, I think she would have given me both kidneys if I'd needed them.'

'Ah,' Barb said, 'that explains a lot.'

Liv raised an eyebrow. 'What does that mean?'

'I've always had the impression that you felt like you owed Toni something, that's all. Just a few comments here and there made me wonder what it was about her, or if she was holding something over you. Then, of course, there was Ruby.'

Liv shook her head. 'She wasn't holding anything over me. She's an amazing sister. I was in a car accident, which is what caused the damage, and she acted like I was more important than her. It was at a time when I was really scared that I might die, but the way Toni acted was as if giving me her kidney was a completely normal thing to do. Even after the operation she never let on to being in any pain, and I'm sure she was. I've never been made to feel so loved or special in my life.'

'Would you have done the same for her?'

'I'd like to think so, but I don't know if I'd have been able to put on such a brave face. Surely the whole thing must have scared the pants off her. And what if something goes wrong with her kidney now? She gave away the spare. It was a beautiful, selfless act.'

'Which is why you wanted her to have Ruby?'

Liv nodded. 'Being able to help her have a baby was a way to repay her. Ruby would have been adopted by someone else if Toni and Joel had said no.'

There was a long pause as Barb digested this information. 'Do you have an appointment?'

Liv pushed her phone towards Barb. 'I need to lie down. Could you ring them? The number's in there under Doctor McCardle. They'll probably bring me straight in if you tell them what's happening.' She hauled herself to her feet and did her best to ignore Barb's devastated face. She'd had no reason to mention her kidney transplant to her neighbour before and certainly hadn't wanted to worry her now. But with her mother in Melbourne, Barb was the closest thing she had to family and right now, family was what she needed around her.

22

It was after four when Toni finally put the key in the lock of the South Yarra apartment. She hesitated before pushing open the door. Joel would be furious, and she didn't blame him. As much as she knew she needed to get away from the lunch as soon as possible, another part of her was glad for the delay. Dealing with the fallout from today would be bad enough. Discussing the fact she needed to be in the office the next morning was going to be even worse.

Toni's head was pounding after listening to Pete's booming voice, which got louder with each glass of wine he drank. Rob continually filled his glass, winking at Toni with each refill. Both he and Toni only had a couple of glasses each. They'd eventually pushed Pete into a taxi a little after three, promising to see him early in the morning for strategy discussions.

Rob had turned to Toni anxiously when the taxi departed. 'You're sure you can come back?'

'Don't think I have much choice now, do you?'

Rob relaxed and returned her smile. 'Pete was pretty insistent on getting you to commit.'

At one stage, Pete had drawn up a contract on a napkin and asked Toni to sign it. 'You could say that. Look, it will be fine as long as you're happy to work around me having flexibility. I can't guarantee I'll be in the office five days a week. In fact, I can guarantee I won't be. I can probably get Joel to agree to two, maybe three days in the office, and I can work from home on the other days.'

'Pete's likely to call meetings at random times and days,' Rob said, concern flooding his face. 'What happens if you can't make it?'

Toni took his arm as a second taxi stopped beside them. 'Before we met with Pete, you were the one saying I'd only need to deal with him and not the rest of his team and it wouldn't be that often.'

'Yes, well he gave me a different impression at lunch,' Rob said.

'Don't stress. Pete can think he's running the show for the next week or two, but then I'll make it clear that he's not my only client. If he thinks I'm at his beck and call, he won't value me as much.' Toni held up her hand when Rob looked like he was about to object. 'Trust me. I know what I'm doing. I'll see you tomorrow.' She opened the door of the taxi and climbed inside. She'd retrieve her car the next day.

Twenty minutes later, she pushed open the front door and could hear the faint sounds of music drifting from the lounge room. Joel was speaking softly, and from the squeal of delight that responded to his words, Toni knew he either hadn't taken Ruby to her mother's or had collected her already. While she knew that Joel wouldn't be happy at the thought of her returning to work, deep down, she knew that it wasn't just for her. Ruby would be better off being looked after by someone who adored spending time with her. Toni wasn't stupid. She knew the little girl was suffering with her negative energy and disastrous parenting and hopefully changing the routine would not only give Toni a break from motherhood, but Ruby a break from her too.

'I'm sorry.' They were the first words to leave her mouth as she entered the lounge room. 'I didn't plan for today to turn out like it did but saving the Zoltron account quite possibly saved Entice too.'

Joel sighed. 'Look, part of me wants to kill you. We finally had a day and a night to ourselves, and you chose work over us.'

Toni closed her eyes momentarily. The temptation to point out what he was doing with his work was hard to swallow.

She opened her eyes and managed a tight smile.

'I hoped we could salvage what's left of it and take Ruby for a walk,' Joel said. 'There's that new bar, The Corner, where we could have a glass of wine. When you rang to say you were delayed, I did some shopping. We have the ingredients for a stir-fry. If we can get Ruby off to sleep, there's still some possibility of a night for us.'

Joel's affability was the last thing Toni had expected to walk in on. She crossed the room to him and kissed him firmly on the lips. 'You're a great guy. Have I told you that lately?'

Joel pulled Toni to him and kissed her again. 'No, but have I told you that suit makes you look damn hot.'

Toni grinned. 'I was going to change before we go for a walk, but perhaps I shouldn't.'

Joel laughed. 'Get changed. You'll be a bit overdressed for walking beside a pram. I'll cement a picture of you in my mind for while I'm away.'

Toni blushed. Joel's compliments had been rather sparse since Ruby arrived. He'd been completely smitten with the baby. Was he seeing her as a woman again and not the mother of his baby? A lightness settled over her as she left the room to get changed. The day was turning out much better than she'd possibly imagined.

* * *

It was over a glass of Cab Sav that Toni's good mood evaporated. She was working up the courage to tell Joel that not only had she taken her old job back, albeit part time and with more flexibility but she needed to start the next day.

'There's something I need to talk to you about,' she said as the sun sank over the Yarra River. The Corner had popped up a few weeks earlier on one of the bends of the Yarra. Toni couldn't believe their luck when the trendy little wine bar had opened, giving them a spot to walk to in the evenings. Ruby was propped up in her pram, looking exceptionally cute in a purple jacket and matching hat.

'Me too,' Joel grinned. 'A surprise, actually.'

Toni raised an eyebrow. 'Really?' Is that why he'd been in a better mood than she'd expected. 'What kind of surprise?'

'You go first. You're going to love mine, so in case I don't love yours as much, let's leave it until last.'

Toni swallowed and took a deep breath. 'It's about work. Today's meeting went well, but the reality is Entice will lose the Zoltron account unless I go back. The knock-on effect from that could be devastating.'

Joel's smile turned to a frown. 'Now?'

Toni nodded. 'They're likely to go under if they lose Zoltron. Pete Miller made it clear today that without me, he's moving.'

'He's blackmailing you?'

Toni fingered the stem of her wine glass. 'No, he's not blackmailing me.' She took Joel's hand across the table and looked him in the eye. 'I want to go back, Joel. I need adult stimulation, and I need to do my job. I love it. You know that.'

Joel pulled his hand back from Toni's and pushed back his chair. 'Come on, let's go home.'

Toni looked at their half-full glasses. 'Can we at least finish our wine?'

Joel reached for Ruby's pram. 'You can, but we're going.' He didn't wait for Toni's response but instead pushed the pram away from the table and back down the street towards home.

Toni sat frozen for a moment. She sighed. She hadn't expected it to go particularly well but had hoped he'd at least discuss it. She picked up her wine glass and took a final sip before pushing back from the table and following Joel. Hopefully, he'd have calmed down by the time they got home, and they could discuss the situation rationally.

* * *

It was close to eight by the time Ruby had been bathed and put to bed. Joel had refused to look at Toni, let alone talk to her. Toni opened the fridge and pulled out the ingredients Joel had bought earlier for a stir-fry. Even after the large lunch she'd had, she was starving. She hadn't told Joel yet that she was starting work the next morning and ideally needed to spend some time tonight researching.

He came into the kitchen as she added the chicken to the garlic and spices already frying off in the pan. He picked up the bottle of wine from the bench, poured himself a glass and sat down at the island counter. 'Okay,' he said. 'I get it. Looking after a baby can get tiring.' He put his hands up as Toni was about to object. 'I understand that day in, day out, especially when I'm away, it isn't easy. With me going for twelve weeks, it will be even harder on you. What are you proposing with work, and how do you see it working with Ruby?'

A lightness settled over Toni. *He was willing to discuss it.* She lowered the heat on the pan and came and sat next to him. 'I'm thinking part time. Two to three days a week in the office with flexibility to work from home when I need to.' She wasn't planning to mention that the part time was part time in the office, but she really planned to work full-time hours if possible.

Joel nodded. 'And Ruby?'

'I'll ask Mum first, but if she's not available, then Rob's said that Entice will pay for a nanny. No day care, which I know is one of your concerns.'

'I don't mind day care when she's older, but when she can't even crawl or walk, I don't see any benefit of it. She'll probably catch a million illnesses.'

'It will build her immunity,' Toni said, although she did agree. The reality was the minute Ruby went into day care or kinder, she probably would catch all kinds of things, and it would build her immunity, but having to deal with colds, coughs and gastro meant that Toni would have to take time off work, which wouldn't be ideal.

'If it's what you want to do, then I'm not going to stop you,' Joel said. 'But you'll only get this opportunity once with Ruby.' He ran his fingers through his hair and shook his head. 'I don't get it. You pushed and pushed when it came to IVF and doing everything to have the baby you supposedly needed to complete your life. Now you have that, and you're choosing work over her. She'll grow up quickly, and you might regret missing out.'

'Are you regretting missing out?'

Joel nodded. 'I am, but as I'm choosing the Emirates opportunity over being here, I can hardly stop you from making your own choices. But Toni, I still don't get it. Ruby's the best thing that's ever happened to us. Isn't she?'

Toni bit the inside of her cheek. She wanted to tell Joel the truth about how she was struggling, but she couldn't. He'd be devastated. 'She is, but she can't become everything. I don't want to be one of those mums who puts everything into their child, and the day she goes off to school she turns around and realises she's going to struggle to find a job because she hasn't kept up with the market. Ruby's a huge part of my life now, but she can't become my whole life. There needs to be a balance for me, like there is for you.'

'Is it because she's not biologically ours? Do you think you'd feel different if she was?'

Toni sighed. It was a question she'd been asking herself over and over but hadn't wanted to share her fears with Joel. 'I guess we'll never know the answer to that. Probably not. As much as I wanted a baby, I didn't realise what that looked like day in, day out. It's relentless, Joel. My whole day revolves around someone else's needs. That wears a bit thin when it's seven days a week for the rest of my life.'

'It's hardly for the rest of your life. It'll get easier as she gets older and becomes more independent. This is the hardest bit. All the baby books say that.'

'I know, but right now, independence is a long way away.'

'Okay, you do what you need to do. But please promise me you won't agree to full-time work for a few years at least and without talking to me first.'

Toni smiled at him. 'Promise. And thank you. I really need to do this, and I'm grateful you're being supportive about it.'

Joel took a swig of his drink. 'I'm not sure I had all that much choice. I hope your mum can look after Ruby. That would be better than using a nanny. Keeping it in the family. We can ask her tomorrow when we drop Ruby off.'

'Drop her off?' Toni's heart began to thud.

'Yes, that was my news. The news I never got to tell you at The Corner. When I rang her to cancel today, your mum offered to have Ruby tomorrow so we could still have our day out. She said, with me leaving on Wednesday, she knew how important it would be for us and suggested we stay for a glass of wine when we go to pick Ruby up in the evening. That way, she can say goodbye to me too.' He took her hand and squeezed it. 'I've booked lunch at The Cellar Door on the Mornington Peninsula. After lunch, we could go down to one of the beaches or even right down to Point Nepean and do a walk if we think we'd have time. What do you think?'

Toni expected she might vomit there and then. It was as if she was dealing Joel one blow after the other. There was no way she could avoid going into work tomorrow.

'Toni?'

Toni looked over at Joel, who had concern written all over his face.

'What's the matter?'

'I'm dreading what I have to say next.'

'Oh?'

Toni took a deep breath. 'The thing is, I agreed to go back to work, and to keep the Zoltron account, my first meeting is with them at nine tomorrow morning.'

Joel stood up, his head shaking furiously from side to side. 'Jesus, Toni, I'm trying to be supportive, but you're making this too hard.'

Toni stood up and moved towards him. 'I know, and I'm sorry. Entice is in crisis mode, and I want to smooth things over.'

Joel glared at her. 'I fly out on Wednesday, or have you conveniently forgotten that? For close to three months. The longest we've ever been apart. Surely someone else can deal with Zoltron or you can delay it by one day?'

Toni shook her head. 'It has to be me.'

'I can tell you right now,' Joel said. 'You should be more worried about us being in crisis mode than that stupid company you're prioritising.'

He turned and pounded out of the room, leaving Toni staring after him.

23

Liv was conscious of Barb grabbing the arms of the chair she was seated in
to steady herself as Doctor McCardle delivered the news she'd been dreading. 'You okay?' she asked the older woman.

Barb nodded. 'I just wasn't expecting this news.' She reached across and
squeezed Liv's hand. 'Sorry, love, I'm making this all about me.'

'Don't be sorry,' Doctor McCardle said. 'It's lovely for Liv to see how
much you care about her. Now, this isn't the end by any means. Dialysis will
be necessary. We can arrange everything here, but I wanted to check if
you'd like to meet with the Melbourne team who did your kidney transplant? I think their advice as to whether you'd be suitable for peritoneal
dialysis which can be done at home would be quite beneficial. It's a more
convenient option than in-centre haemodialysis treatment. If you aren't
keen to travel, we can arrange a Zoom call and do the examinations here.'

Liv stared at the doctor. She could hear the words, but it all felt surreal.
She'd, of course, known this was a possible outcome of this appointment
but had done her best to convince herself that it wouldn't be the case.

'I can come with you,' Barb said, breaking into her thoughts.

Liv shook her head. 'No, I'll be fine. I think I would prefer to speak to
the team in person, rather than via Zoom. How quickly do I need to go?'

'Ideally, within the next three weeks,' Doctor McCardle said. 'If you're a suitable candidate for peritoneal dialysis, we'll need to schedule surgery to insert a catheter into your abdomen. Treatment can start about two weeks after that's done.'

Liv nodded. It was all going to happen quickly.

'Liv, I know this will take some getting used to,' Doctor McCardle said, 'but you're young and otherwise healthy and a great candidate for another transplant. There's nothing to say you won't live a long, relatively healthy life.'

Relatively healthy. Three hours later, Liv played the words over in her head as she scooped the last spoonful of soup from the bowl Barb had prepared for her. She wondered what 'relatively healthy' looked like compared to regular healthy? In the time since she and Barb had arrived home, it was as if she was operating in a fog. A fog of disbelief.

'I think you should ring your mother,' Barb said as she took the empty soup bowl from the table beside Liv. 'She'd want to know what's happening.'

'She'd just worry,' Liv said. 'There's nothing she can do. You heard what the doctor said today. The kidney's failing at a rapid rate, and I'll need to start dialysis.' She spoke calmly now, as if this was a normal day in her life, but the news had been devastating to hear. She'd always known it was a possibility but had hoped she'd be one of the miracle stories who lived for fifty years or more with a donor kidney. Instead, she was falling into the majority statistics. 'I don't want Toni to know,' Liv said. 'She's got enough on her plate with Ruby, and I know she'll blame herself.'

'What? Why?'

'Because it was her kidney. She'll run through everything she should have done differently to ensure it was healthy. Not that it would have made any difference. It's my body rejecting it, not hers.'

'You can have my kidney,' Barb said. 'I mean it. It's no use to me.'

'And I appreciate it, but you heard what the doctor said when you offered earlier. It's generally better if a younger person has a younger kidney. It's a lot to recover from at your age. They do use kidneys from older people, but they're usually deceased.'

'It's a three-year wait,' Barb said, 'unless you can get one donated.'

'I know,' Liv said, and while she dreaded the idea of having to start dialysis three times a week, she knew it was what could buy her enough time to make it through the three years. 'It's okay, Barb. I'll deal with it for now. I'll tell my family when I'm ready and when I know what's happening. None of them are suitable kidney donors. Everyone was tested when I had my accident, and Toni was the only one who was compatible.'

'What about your mother's family?' Barb asked. 'She's adopted, isn't she?'

'She is, and we don't know who her biological parents are. And even if we did, I'd hardly expect a total stranger to give up a kidney.'

'They gave up a baby,' Barb said with a wink, 'so they're used to the concept of giving things up.'

Liv smiled. 'Whatever you do, don't make that joke in front of Mum.'

Barb regained her serious face. 'You're a good person, Liv Montgomery. You have a good heart, and while I'd suggest at times your actions are questionable, you're selfless and lovely. Don't worry, leave it with me. I'll find you a kidney, and while we wait, I'd be happy to accompany you to your dialysis sessions if you have to have them in the hospital.'

'It takes hours,' Liv said. 'You'd be bored out of your mind.'

Barb shook her head. 'We'll take the Scrabble with us or sit quietly together. I'm not taking no for an answer. Since Mandy left, I don't have much of a purpose in life. This will give me one.'

Liv was about to object when she realised Barb was speaking the truth. She'd known she was lonely but was beginning to see how much. Instead, she nodded. 'Thank you. I'd love that. Hopefully, it won't be necessary and – if I have to have dialysis – I can do the home-based one. I guess the trip to Melbourne will confirm all of that.'

Barb nodded. 'I guess it will.'

24

The atmosphere in the car was so icy that Toni contemplated turning the
heater on as she turned the Lexus off the Tullamarine freeway in the direction of Melbourne Airport's international terminal. On the one hand, she
wanted to cry. Joel not talking to her since Monday night had been awful,
but on the other, she was feeling angry that he wouldn't discuss her work
opportunity. Her mixture of emotions left her excited in the knowledge that
once she arrived home, she could respond to the emails she knew were
piling up in her inbox.

Ruby sighed, content in sleep from the back seat, seemingly oblivious to
the tension in the vehicle.

Toni glanced sideways at Joel, his jaw set in a firm line. He was going to
be gone for close to three months. She should at least make one more
attempt to get through to him.

'Joel?'

He flinched but didn't respond.

'You're going to be gone for twelve weeks. Leaving like this is awful. Can
I do anything to get things back on track?'

He turned and stared at her, the coldness in his eyes making her
relieved she could turn away and concentrate on the road ahead.

'You had Monday and Tuesday to get things back on track, and you chose not to.'

Toni sighed. She didn't choose not to. She'd been put in an awful position. She had gone into work on Tuesday morning, but she'd ensured she was home by two. That would have given them the entire afternoon and evening together if Joel hadn't been so angry. Instead, she'd arrived home to find he'd taken Ruby out. When she'd rung him, he'd said he was at his parents' and would be back after dinner. She'd stared at the phone as she hung up, hardly believing that he'd do that. But he had. He and Ruby had arrived back at nine, in time to put Ruby straight to bed. He'd refused to talk to Toni, had spent an hour packing for Dubai, and then slept in the spare room.

'We could have spent time together yesterday,' Toni said. She wasn't going to let him get away with putting everything on her. 'You chose to take Ruby to your parents and not be available. I told you I'd get home as soon as possible. We could still have had Ruby babysat and spent time together.'

'You promised the same on Monday too and look how that turned out.'

Toni shook her head. He wasn't going to budge. 'Okay. I'm sorry. I would have loved to have spent the time with you, but work did come first. I'm excited to be going back. I need something that's more than Ruby, that gives me an identity and a purpose. I assumed you'd be able to understand that, considering how important that is to you.'

Toni noticed Joel was clenching his fists, his knuckles white from the strain. She turned into the short-term cark park.

'Drop me off. You don't need to park.'

'No, I don't want you leaving when things are like this between us. We need to talk.'

He shook his head. 'No, we don't. You've made it clear that Ruby and I aren't enough for you, and you need more in your life. You've gone out and got that at huge expense to our marriage, and now I'm leaving for twelve weeks. You should be relieved that you can do whatever you want without me being involved.'

Toni found an empty parking space on the ground level of the parking tower. She switched off the engine and looked at Joel. She took a deep breath. 'I've really struggled since Ruby was born. I've been a complete failure from day one. To be honest, that hasn't changed. But work's something I'm good at and can be in control of. I need something for me.'

'For Christ's sake. We spent eight years trying to get pregnant. When it didn't happen, we spent a fortune on IVF, all because *you would be incomplete without a child*. I was happy to have a baby, but it wasn't the end of the world for me. I didn't need to do IVF. I would have been happy to keep trying naturally, and if we got pregnant, great, but if we didn't, I would have accepted that. IVF failed, which should have told you it wasn't meant to be, but then Liv comes up with this brilliant plan, and you get the baby you've supposedly always wanted.'

Tears filled Toni's eyes. 'But it's not what I expected. It's exhausting and unrewarding, and I'm no good at it.'

'It's been eight weeks, Toni. Everyone says the first twelve weeks until the baby settles into its own routine are challenging. It's early days.'

'Maybe, but I know in my gut I'm failing, and I know that Ruby must be sensing it. She prefers to be in anyone's arms except mine.'

'Like I said, it's been eight weeks. Give it some more time.'

'I can't believe you're not listening to me.' Tears rolled down Toni's cheeks. 'I can't do the baby thing on my own. If you had a regular job, it might have been different, but being away for a week to ten days at a time has been horrible. Now, for you to disappear for twelve weeks is unthinkable. I don't think I'll get through it without something else to focus on.'

Joel hesitated momentarily, concern replacing the anger in his eyes. 'You've really struggled that much?'

Toni nodded. 'I've absolutely hated it.'

'You hate Ruby?' Joel's words were filled with wonder rather than accusation.

She flinched as if physically wounded by the accusation. 'Of course I don't hate her. I'm talking about the overall experience. At times, Ruby will do something, and I'll experience a little surge of something I guess is love. But I haven't fallen head over heels with her, as all the books say you will. She takes too much from me for me to really appreciate what she gives back.'

'She's a baby, totally dependent on us. That will change, and things will become easier with different stages. Most people find parenting a challenge. You must know that?'

'I do now. And if you're such a fountain of knowledge, why do you think it's okay to go away for twelve weeks? Why should I be the only one having to deal with the challenge?'

'You shouldn't. I wish this had happened before Ruby came into our lives, but it didn't. I've talked about working for Emirates since I became a pilot and with the situation at Southern Air, we'd be crazy to say no to it. This is a once-in-a-career opportunity. Yes, the timing sucks, and I'll miss Ruby terribly, but that's how it is. This could lead to all sorts of opportunities, and I know I'd always regret it if I said no.'

'And I'd regret not helping Entice keep their accounts now if, in ten months' time when I was supposed to go back to work, they'd closed their doors. And to be honest, it's what will get me through the next twelve weeks.'

Joel sighed. 'Fine, let's agree to disagree, okay? It's just that I was so proud of you for dedicating twelve months to staying home with Ruby. I know it's a huge ask, but her having one main caregiver was going to give her a great start as far as bonding and security are concerned. But, I'm not willing or able to do it, so it's unfair of me to expect you to.'

Guilt gnawed at Toni. When she saw the situation from Joel's point of view, she did get why he was upset.

'If I'd had any idea how it would be, then I wouldn't have pushed for IVF, and I certainly wouldn't have agreed to be a stay-at-home mum. In an ideal world it would be good to give Ruby the start you're talking about, but I'd worry she'll pick up on – if she hasn't already – how much I resent her at times. I'm hoping by doing something for me, I'll be happier and better when it comes to her.'

Joel was silent for a moment. 'Maybe I shouldn't go. I didn't realise you weren't coping and I'm going to worry about you both the whole time I'm away.'

Toni felt an unexpected warmth spread through her as his words settled in; maybe he really did care enough not to leave her alone. But, as much as part of her wanted to push him to make the decision to stay, in the long term, he'd just resent her.

'No,' she said, 'you need to go. You need to see if the experience lives up to your dream. And I need to work out a routine that works for me.'

Joel nodded. 'It'll be finding the right balance where neither of you suffers, I guess. You said the role would be part time, two to three days a week?'

Toni nodded. He didn't need to know exactly how many hours she worked.

'If you can give Ruby the other four or five days a week, then hopefully, it won't do too much damage.'

Toni had to bite her tongue. He was coming around, but he was throwing in a bit of arsehole with it. She would let it go for now as, whilst it was a small victory, it was a victory, nonetheless.

Joel leaned across the centre console and kissed her. He then turned to the back seat and smiled at Ruby, who was still sleeping.

'No need to walk me in. I'm going straight through to the lounge anyway. It'll save waking Ruby.'

Toni nodded, opening her car door. She'd at least get out and say goodbye properly.

Joel opened the rear door and kissed Ruby lightly on the forehead, careful not to wake her. 'Bye Princess,' he whispered in Ruby's ear, before taking Toni in his arms. 'Promise me you'll still put Ruby first in your decision-making where you can. Okay? No day care, for instance, and no male nannies.'

Toni raised an eyebrow. 'You're worried about me and a male nanny?'

The corner of Joel's lips turned upwards. 'Geez, no, I wasn't until you said that. But that's a good point to add to my argument. I was worried that Ruby would mistake them for her dad. I don't want some stranger being called Dada before me.'

'Okay, that's easy. We have a deal.'

Joel smiled, his face full of genuine warmth and love. 'I'll miss you.'

'Me too.'

He leaned forward and kissed her deeply on the lips before pulling away and retrieving his luggage from the boot.

'I'll call you when we land in Dubai.'

Toni nodded.

'And we'll FaceTime every day if possible so I can see both you and Ruby, okay?'

Toni smiled and nodded as Joel walked towards the pathway leading to the international terminal. He stopped halfway across the car park and turned back to face Toni. 'I love you.' He blew her a kiss, grinned and continued.

* * *

A weight lifted as Toni drove back to South Yarra. A week ago, she'd been dreading Joel leaving for twelve weeks, and now she was excited. The increasing volume of Ruby's cries from the back seat weren't going to dampen her mood. Soon she wouldn't be the one dealing with them.

Toni took a deep breath. She needed to think ahead when it came to Ruby. Some of the meltdowns could be avoided then. She was hungry. Something that could easily have been fixed if Toni had thought to pack a bottle before they left for the airport.

'We'll be home in a few minutes, Ruby, then you can have your bottle.' Toni turned on the radio and increased the volume, which diluted the wails from the back seat.

She switched into work mode as she turned into Toorak Road. Ideally, she wanted to work in the office on Thursday and Friday of this week. To make that happen, she needed to get childcare sorted out today. She considered her mother but decided it was too much to ask. She wasn't sure she wanted Sara knowing exactly how many hours a week she'd be absent from Ruby and that information filtering back to Joel. She remembered Rob's comment when asking her to come back that Daley on the design team used a nanny. She wondered where she got her from. She picked up her phone. It was easy enough to find out.

She was about to call but decided to wait until she had Ruby settled.

Forty minutes later, Ruby lay on the sheepskin rug in the living area, nappy changed and belly fully of formula. Toni picked up the phone and called the office. Lindsay answered and put her straight through to Daley.

'Toni?'

'Hey, Daley, I'm ringing to pick your brain.'

She went on to explain the work situation and that she needed a nanny for Ruby.

'Mine's brilliant,' Daley said. 'My sister-in-law uses one too. Ooh, actually, she might be finishing up at my brother's place soon. They're moving to Perth for Simon's work, and Jaya was really upset that they'd be losing their nanny. Let me give her a call and see what's happening. I'll call you straight back.'

Ten minutes later, Daley was back on the phone. 'You might be in luck. The nanny, Rebecca, finishes with them on Friday, and while she's been offered work through the agency she works for, she hasn't accepted anything yet. Jaya said she's brilliant and absolutely loves babies. It would be worth contacting her straight away as she's probably in high demand.'

Toni would call, but it didn't sound like she'd be free to start tomorrow. That had probably been unrealistic to even consider.

'You there?'

'Sorry, I was thinking. Thank you. I'll contact her as soon as we end the call. I was thinking through what I'll do for tomorrow and Friday.'

'Bring her with you,' Daley said. 'We can pass her around among the staff. It'd be lovely to see the high-flying Toni Montgomery in her role as a mum.'

Toni gave an uneasy laugh. That would be the quickest way to lose respect from her staff. 'I'm not sure Rob would be too happy if I started that trend. No, it's okay. I'll work something out. Thanks for Rebecca's info. I'll get in touch with her.'

They ended the call, and Toni rang her mother. Sara was delighted at the prospect of having Ruby for two days. 'I'll invite Mandy over to help.'

Toni bit her bottom lip, about to say *no, don't do that.* But she changed her mind. Mandy had proven how good she was with Ruby, so why was it she'd still prefer her sister wasn't involved with her baby? Was she jealous? Guilt flooded through her. Her intellectually challenged sister was better with her baby than she was. That could have something to do with it. Instead of saying no, she thanked her mother and arranged to drop Ruby off at seven thirty the next morning. Then she called Rebecca.

25

Liv's flights to Melbourne were booked but she'd hesitated to tell her family she was coming. She didn't want to have to explain herself and had no intention of sharing the truth. She'd sworn Barb to secrecy and other than taking it easier than usual, life had continued relatively normally since her doctor's appointment. She'd regained some of her energy and wasn't feeling quite as bad as she had been, but she knew it was only a temporary reprieve before she went downhill again.

'Knock, knock.'

At the sound of Barb's voice, Liv looked up from the bed where she had her clothes out, deciding what to pack. Barb had been checking on her daily since the visit to Doctor McCardle, sometimes three or four times. Liv had given her a key and told her there was no need to knock, just come in. Barb, however, did insist on announcing herself.

'I'm in the bedroom,' Liv called. She lifted her small suitcase onto the bed and started adding clothes to it.

'I've made us a lasagne for dinner,' Barb said, entering the room. 'And I got a lovely bottle of that Cab Sav you like. It'll go very nicely with it. Even though I still think you shouldn't be drinking.'

'Oh Barb, you didn't need to do that, but thank you. You've cooked me dinner nearly every night since we saw the doctor and the doctor did say alcohol was okay, as long as it was only a small glass every now and then.' She grinned. 'It's not like this kidney is going to get any worse.'

Barb sat down on the end of the bed. 'No, but you still need to look after it, and there's no need to thank me. You're giving me a purpose. Since Mandy left, I've been at a loose end, you know that. Now I have a reason to get up each morning. I have to find a recipe, go shopping and then put up with you in the evening.'

Liv laughed. 'Not for the next week or so.'

Barb's face fell. 'Are you sure you don't want me to come with you?'

Liv walked into the ensuite to collect her make-up bag. 'Not this time, but I appreciate the offer. Mum would be suspicious if we both turn up.'

'You should have told her. This is a big deal.'

Liv returned to the bedroom shaking her head. 'No way. With Dad passing, and now Ruby on the scene, Mum's got enough to deal with. She doesn't need to worry about me, and she doesn't need to deal with Toni, who'll be devastated and blame herself. It's just not worth the angst. If anything goes wrong or I get worse, I'll tell them then, but not before.' She threw her make-up bag into the suitcase and flipped the lid shut. 'Okay, I'm all yours. Let's go eat.'

Forty minutes later, Liv leaned back against the cushion of Barb's comfy balcony chair. The lights were twinkling on the water below and there were plenty of people milling around the harbour walking tracks. Liv patted her stomach. 'That was amazing.'

Barb smiled. 'It was pretty good, wasn't it? It's actually one of Mandy's recipes. One of the girls she lives with spends hours on YouTube learning how to cook and now she's teaching Mandy. We FaceTimed earlier and made the same recipe together.'

Liv smiled. 'She's come a long way, hasn't she?'

Barb nodded as Liv's phone pinged with a text. She stood and retrieved the phone from the kitchen bench and glanced at the screen. She froze as the phone slipped from her hand and clattered onto the bench.

'Liv?'

Liv shook her head, unable to make her tongue work. There was no way she could tell Barb what the message said. It was one thing that Barb knew what she'd done with the birth certificate, but if she knew the full extent of what she'd done, Barb would never speak to her again.

* * *

Toni sank down in the chair, a glass of wine in one hand, and waited for the familiar ringing of the FaceTime call. Two weeks had passed since Joel left for Dubai, and so far, they'd managed to navigate the six-hour time difference and Joel's flight schedule to FaceTime every second day. Rebecca had been employed and had proven to be a godsend, not that Toni had admitted to Joel that she'd taken her on full time. A sense of relief had accompanied Rebecca's employment. Toni knew she was failing at motherhood but had been too proud to ask for help. At least now Ruby had someone in her day-to-day life that adored her and showered her with love. While sceptical, Toni hoped that one day she'd wake up and magically have acquired the skills of a loving mother, but until then, at least Ruby's emotional needs were being met to a degree.

She clicked on *accept* as the call came through and smiled. Joel was wearing his pilot's jacket, his captain's wings glimmering above the breast pocket.

'Hey, sexy.'

Toni laughed. 'I take it you're not in the cockpit, then.'

'No, about to leave the apartment. A car will be waiting for me in a few minutes. Sorry, I wanted to call earlier, but I've had Mum on the phone for the last half hour.'

'Really? Is everything okay?'

'She and Dad are talking about coming over for a few days. They wanted to know whether they should invite you too. That way, they could share looking after Ruby on the plane.'

Toni's mouth dropped open. 'Really? Your mum said she'd help?' Joel's parents had shown little interest in Ruby since Toni and Joel had brought her home. Toni wasn't close with them, so it didn't concern her, but it had upset Joel, who'd confronted his mother. 'We're excited to see Ruby,' his mother, Dawn, had said, 'but we have our own lives too, Joel. And to be honest, babies were never my thing. I'm sure as she gets older, we'll see more of her.'

Toni had been horrified by this admission at first, but as the days had passed and she'd become aware of how challenging caring for a newborn could be, she understood Dawn's comment that *babies were never my thing*. If she wasn't too proud as to admit her own feelings towards motherhood, she and Dawn would finally have something to bond over.

Joel laughed. 'Yes, she did. What do you think? I know you're working a few days a week, but you said that was flexible.'

'It is, but even with your mum's help, I'm not sure I want to fly all that way with Ruby. If your mum and dad are there, we're not exactly going to have time for ourselves.' Toni found herself rambling. She could not disappear now for four or five days. She was only getting on top of a new campaign for Zoltron, and the last thing she wanted was to have to walk away. Also, she had Rebecca employed five days a week. What was she supposed to tell her?

'It'd be nice for me to see you and Ruby. It probably wouldn't be for another couple of weeks which would break up the twelve weeks perfectly. I have to confirm my flight schedule to see when I get the biggest break, and then I'll have some dates. I'll know that in the next few days.'

That would at least buy her some time. 'Okay, sounds good. I'll think about it.'

'It would be great if you could come over, babe. I know I've only been here a couple of weeks, but I love it. The airline is amazing to work for, and flying the different routes is much more interesting. It sounds like there's an opportunity for me to stay here longer, after the twelve-week trial, too. I'd like for us to consider it, but we can only do that if you've had a chance to visit first.'

Toni was silent. She should have known this would happen. He'd want to take a position if it was offered, but she was not moving from her job. It meant too much to her, and for the first time since Ruby was born, she resembled her old self. Happy, confident, with a purpose. If she was sitting in an apartment in Dubai where she knew nobody, wasn't working and only had Ruby for company, she hated to imagine what would happen.

'Think about it, okay? Now I'm going to have to run. I've looked at my schedule, and I should be able to FaceTime at lunchtime, your time, tomorrow. I'm dying to see Ruby. Can we lock in twelve o'clock? You're not working tomorrow, are you? You've worked three days already this week. Unless you've got other plans, I'd love to see you both.'

Toni swallowed quickly, trying to think of other plans she might have that would make the call impossible. Telling him she would be at work was not an option. She decided the easiest thing would be to change a meeting she had at eleven and come home. 'Twelve will be great. I'll do my best to make sure Ruby's on her best behaviour.'

'Fantastic. Love you. I'll see you both tomorrow.'

'Love you too.' She smiled until his face disappeared from the screen, then lowered her head to her hands.

* * *

The next morning, Toni hurried down the passageway from the lifts and pushed her key into the lock of the apartment. It was two minutes to twelve and having changed her meeting and made an effort to be home, she needed to be ready to answer the FaceTime call.

Rebecca came to the door, concern on her face. 'Is everything okay?'

Toni smiled. 'Sorry, I forgot to tell you this morning that I'd be back to do a quick call with Ruby and Joel at twelve.'

'No problem.'

Toni could tell from the look on the nanny's face that she considered it was a little odd.

'I could have done it from work, but he wanted to see Ruby. She was asleep yesterday when he called.'

Rebecca smiled. 'That makes sense. She's in her bouncer. She's vomited up some of the milk and is a bit messy. Sorry, I was about to change her.'

'Could you clean her up for me? I'm going to get changed, and I'll be out to grab her in a minute.'

Toni hurried into her bedroom and slipped off her work jacket. She pulled on her favourite pale-blue hoodie and checked herself in the mirror. Her skin was flawless with the make-up job she'd done earlier. Should she scrub it off? Would Joel question why she was made up if she was home with Ruby?

She heard the FaceTime incoming call tone from the computer in the office nook. There was no time to worry about make-up. She hurried down the hallway, flashing Rebecca a grateful smile as the nanny handed her a freshly changed Ruby. 'Thanks.'

As soon as Toni sat down and Joel, dressed in his pilot's uniform, greeted them, Ruby pushed her hand against the monitor as if reaching for him.

'Hello, my gorgeous girls,' Joel said, the delight in his voice at seeing Ruby obvious.

'Where are you flying to today?' Toni asked, jiggling Ruby as a whimper left her lips.

'London. I'll be there overnight and fly back tomorrow. Just a quick trip.'

Ruby started to wriggle on Toni's lap.

'I think she's getting restless,' Toni said. 'Do you want me to put her down and come back and chat?'

Joel shook his head. 'No, she'll probably cry if you do that. Has she done anything new?'

Toni thought for a moment. Rebecca had said something yesterday about her cooing. 'She's making different noises,' Toni said. 'Like she's experimenting with sounds, and she's started holding her head up when she's lying on her tummy.'

Joel smiled, then looked crestfallen.

'You okay?'

'I hate that I'm missing these milestones, that's all. Did you video her?'

'Of course,' Toni said, making a mental note to video Ruby the next time she did these things. 'I'll upload it and you can see it a bit later.'

Joel's smile returned. 'You're amazing. Now, I'd better chat to Ruby.' He held a book up to the camera for Ruby to see. 'Look, Ruby. I bought a copy of *Hairy Maclary* so I could read to you from all the way over here. The man I sat next to on the plane said his baby loves it. Would you like to hear the story?'

Ruby stopped wriggling and again reached to touch the screen. The moment Joel's tone changed to the one reserved for her, she responded.

Joel grinned and started to read.

Toni kept a smile on her face but couldn't stop her mind from wandering. Joel reading to Ruby was something she normally enjoyed, but right now, her stress levels were increasing. She had so much to do that afternoon and coming home in the middle of the day wasn't ideal. Perhaps she should come clean with Joel, tell him that she was working more than she'd originally thought and that sometimes, she wouldn't be available during the day. She dismissed the thought as quickly as she had it. She was certain of what his reaction would be.

By the time Joel had finished reading, Ruby's eyes were drooping, and she was breathing heavily.

'You two look gorgeous,' Joel said. 'I can't believe she went to sleep.'

Neither could Toni. Ruby rarely slept in her arms.

'I should probably let you go so you can put her down and enjoy a break yourself. I do get it, you know. That it's hard doing what you're doing. I'm proud of you. Ruby's one lucky little girl.'

A knot twisted in Toni's gut. He wouldn't be proud if he knew the truth.

'I think it will be Saturday your time when I can next call. Will that be okay?'

Toni nodded. 'Now I'd better get her into the bassinet while she's still asleep. I love you. Fly safe.'

'Love you too.'

Toni kept smiling until Joel's face disappeared from the screen. The moment it did, she called out for Rebecca.

Rebecca appeared instantly.

Toni held Ruby out to her. 'I'm so sorry, but I have to rush back to the office. Can you take her? Put her to bed or bathe her. Whatever you were planning to do.'

Rebecca took Ruby from her and cuddled her close. 'Certainly.' Her eyes travelled down to Toni's suit pants. 'I think you might need to change before you go back.'

Toni looked down to see a patch of liquid on her grey pants. Ruby's nappy must have leaked. 'Shit!' The anger and volume of her voice woke

Ruby, and she began to cry. Toni's hand flew to her mouth as Rebecca gave a tight smile and carried Ruby towards the kitchen. Toni could hear her talking to Ruby softly.

She hurried to the bedroom and stopped when she reached the walk-in-robe. She took a deep breath and found herself sinking to the floor, burying her head in her hands. What was wrong with her? Joel would be so upset if he'd seen the way she'd spoken in front of Ruby and Rebecca. In fact, if anyone had told her that she'd be putting her needs before those of a defenceless baby, she wouldn't have known whether to laugh at them or be mortified. It was one thing to want to work as well as have a baby, but Ruby should still come first. She knew that. Why was she so bad at this? She needed to do better, for everyone's sake.

She took several deep breaths before pulling herself back up to her feet. Advertising Executive Toni Montgomery didn't have time to meltdown. She needed to focus her thoughts on work. She turned to the row of suits. Luckily, she had another grey pants suit which was only a slightly different shade to this one. She changed quickly, took the wet pants through to the laundry and then went in search of Rebecca. She could hear singing and splashing coming from the bathroom. She poked her head in. Ruby was all smiles, lying back in the water with Rebecca's hand supporting her. Rebecca stopped singing and smiled at Toni.

'I'll clean those pants for you after I put Ruby down. I'm sorry. It was a clean nappy, so I'm not sure how it leaked.'

'It's no big deal. And there's no excuse for how I reacted. I'm sorry about that, but I'd better run. I'm due in a meeting in fifteen minutes, and I'd say I'm going to be late. I'll see you around seven.'

'Sure.' Rebecca turned to Ruby. 'Say goodbye to Mummy, Ruby darling.'

Ruby continued to splash the water, making Toni laugh. 'Bye Ruby, see you tonight.'

Rebecca smiled apologetically. 'Not even mums can compete with splashing. Have a good afternoon.' Toni turned to leave the bathroom. 'Oh, Toni—' She stopped. 'I wasn't deliberately eavesdropping, I promise, but I did hear you say you'd filmed Ruby cooing and holding her head up.'

Heat rose in Toni's cheeks.

'It's no big deal,' Rebecca continued, 'but I did video it. I have a ton of videos and photos for you. Not just the one I send you each morning to let you know all's fine. I could airdrop them onto your phone tonight if you like?'

Toni stared at the nanny. She really was a lifesaver. 'That would be amazing. Thank you.'

'No problem. I knew you'd want to show Joel and see the first time she held up her head yourself.'

Toni swallowed the lump in her throat. What was missing in her make up that she hadn't been upset to discover she'd missed seeing these firsts? She was sad for both her and Ruby. Why couldn't she be a normal, doting mother? Would her feelings ever change? Would she be excited by the first tooth, the first steps, the first words? She guessed she wouldn't know until they happened. She didn't voice any of this out loud. Rebecca was more excited about Ruby's achievements than she was. She'd probably consider her a terrible person, which, if Toni allowed herself to consider how far she was going to deceive Joel, she would have to agree with her. Instead, she blinked back her tears, thanked her, made her way out of the apartment, and headed back to work.

26

Liv drew in a lungful of Melbourne's chilly air as she stepped down onto the tarmac. She hadn't been in Melbourne since she'd taken Mandy back to Sydney with her. That trip had sprung up unexpectedly, and in hindsight, she'd do everything differently if she could have a do-over. She certainly wouldn't have offered Toni the baby before it was born. It had been both devastating and a relief to discover her exhaustion and emotional state were a result of her kidney, rather than the stress of the birth and her decisions involving Ruby. But there was still part of Liv that wondered if feeling low had been a combination of both those things. And then, there was Petal Blossom demanding her payment. The text message Liv had received while having dinner with Barb had been eye-opening. So much for the first payment being all that she was going to be blackmailed for. That certainly hadn't helped Liv's stress levels.

Liv followed the line of passengers into the arrivals terminal and made her way to the baggage collection. On the last trip, she'd brought hand luggage only, but this time she had a suitcase full of presents. She'd been adding to a pile of gifts for Ruby every week since Toni and Joel had returned to Melbourne with her. She was a little confused as to whether it was her guilt or love that was driving her to want to spoil Ruby. What she did know was she couldn't wait to see the little girl. It was hard to imagine she was ten weeks old already. She'd be nothing like the newborn Liv had welcomed into the world in Sydney. A twinge of longing caused Liv to stop before she reached the baggage carousel. She was going to have to be careful around Toni. Her sister would be suspicious of her surprise visit to Melbourne, and the last thing she wanted was for her to find out the truth behind her trip – not until Liv had it clear in her mind, at least.

* * *

Toni read through the marketing strategy again, tweaking some of the finer points and ensuring the strategy for launching the voice app was easy to understand for Zoltron's management team. She glanced at the clock on her desk, wondering, as she often did, how it was late afternoon already.

Her phone rang, and she accepted the call.

'Toni, it's Mum.'

'Everything okay?'

'Everything's perfect. You'll never guess who turned up.'

Toni stopped breathing. Joel wouldn't turn up without telling her first, would he? She'd organised everything carefully to ensure that when he returned, she'd be able to walk away from her full-time role at Entice and continue with the part-time hours he'd been told she was doing. There was no reason for him to know that she had been working full time. He couldn't turn up now. It would ruin everything. She gave herself a shake. What reason would he have to see her mother before he saw her?

'You there, Toni?'

Toni cleared her throat. 'Who turned up?'

'Liv.'

'Oh.'

Sara laughed. 'I can tell you right now, she's a lot more excited to see you than it sounds like you are to see her. We're hoping you and Ruby can come for dinner.'

Toni stared at the report in front of her. She hadn't seen Liv in person since she and Joel returned from Sydney with Ruby. They'd caught up on FaceTime a few times and spoken on the phone, but something made her hesitate about seeing her in person. Initially, it was her fear of Liv wanting

Ruby back. But now, if Liv was to ask for her daughter, it would almost be a relief. She'd need to practice her devastated look, in case.

Toni quashed the thought. She couldn't think like that. But on the flip side, she didn't want Liv to see what an awful job she was doing with Ruby. Although, when she went to her mother's, usually Mandy was there, and she would take charge of Ruby, so Toni didn't have to do anything.

'We're home now,' Sara continued. 'You could come straight over.'

Toni glanced at her watch. It was only four, and she had a mass of work to get done. She'd told Rebecca she was unlikely to be home before seven.

'Or we can come to you and bring a meal with us if Ruby's unsettled or asleep?'

'No,' Toni said. She didn't want her mother to meet Rebecca and chat with her about Ruby's childcare arrangements. Sara, like Joel, thought Rebecca was just employed for a few hours a week. Not full-time hours. And while it was unlikely she would be speaking to Joel while he was in Dubai, Toni wasn't taking any risks. 'We'll come to you. I've got a few things to do first, but we'll be there by six. Will Mandy be there?'

'Would you mind if she was?'

Toni swallowed. *I really am a horrible person.* She'd gone from excluding Mandy and acting as if she didn't exist to using her when she wanted her help with Ruby. 'Of course not. I was going to suggest you invite her. I'm sure she'd love to see Liv and Ruby.'

'Really?'

'Of course.' Toni closed her eyes, relieved her mother couldn't see her face. She knew it would be filled with guilt. She wasn't sure when she'd become such a selfish person. Maybe it was how she'd always been, but it wasn't until now – until Ruby's appearance – that it had become prominent. If Ruby didn't exist, the reality was she wouldn't want Mandy coming to dinner at her mother's, but if she was able to look after Ruby, then she definitely wanted her there. Once again, she was grateful she didn't believe in God. That meant hell didn't exist either, which was a relief because if it did, there was no question as to where she'd be going.

'Wonderful. We'll have the whole family together. Well...' her mother's voice petered off, and Toni's heart squeezed for her. It wasn't the whole family without her dad, and it never would be again.

'What can I bring?' Toni asked, deftly changing the subject.

'Just yourself and Ruby,' Sara said. 'See you at six.'

Toni ended the call and sighed. She used to love Liv's flying visits, but right at this moment, it was the last thing she wanted. It meant that she would need to send off this report and leave the office. To get home, pack Ruby up and be at her mother's house within two hours was going to be a challenge.

* * *

It was close to six thirty by the time Toni pulled Joel's Jeep into her mother's driveway. She'd been using it since he was in Dubai as it was easier to take Ruby in and out of, and it guaranteed a vomit-free Lexus.

She got out of the car, surprised that Mandy hadn't appeared already. On most of her visits to her mother's, she hadn't even had to take Ruby from the car as Mandy had been quick to claim the job. She unclipped her car seat buckles and lifted the baby carefully from the seat.

'No crying, okay?' Toni spoke in the best sing-song voice she could muster. It was the way Rebecca spoke to Ruby, and it seemed to work for her. It was completely unnatural for Toni to speak in the ridiculous voice, but if it was going to stop Ruby from crying until they got into the house and she could hand her over to whoever wanted to hold her, then she would continue with it. She looked at the nappy bag next to the car seat and decided she would come back for it. She could manage Ruby on her own, but adding too much to the load was bound to raise Liv's alarm bells when she saw how awkward she looked.

Toni made her way up the path to the front door. 'I wonder where everyone is?' she said to Ruby. 'Hopefully, they're home to see you.'

The front door opened as she reached it. Toni stopped. She'd assumed it would be Mandy, but instead, Liv stood there, her lips curled into a huge grin and her eyes fixed on Ruby. 'Oh, Ton, she's grown so much. It's not as obvious on FaceTime as it is in person. Joel's going to be blown away when he returns. She must have doubled in size since he left.'

She held her hands out, and Toni handed the little girl over. 'It's unusual for Mandy not to meet me at the door when we arrive.'

Liv smiled. 'She was itching to, but Mum suggested it would be nice for me to greet you as I don't get to do that often.' She jiggled Ruby up and down and tweaked her gently on the nose, causing a giggle to erupt from the little girl. Liv laughed. 'She's precious.'

Toni forced a smile, willing it to come naturally. Surely the giggle should waken something in her? Rebecca had mentioned the giggle, but this was the first time she'd seen or heard it. She would have to try and get some video footage for Joel.

'Come in,' Liv said. 'Mum's in the kitchen, and I imagine Mandy's spying on us.'

'Not spying, Livvy,' Mandy's voice came from the formal lounge room situated by the front door. 'I'm waiting patiently. When it's my turn, I hope I might be able to cuddle Baby.'

Liv raised an eyebrow and lowered her voice. 'Baby? She still calls her that?'

'Most of the time. I guess she wasn't a fan of the name we picked. It annoyed me at first, but she's been really good with Ruby. It's not a big deal. It's just Mandy. You know what she's like.'

'"*Just Mandy*"?' Liv frowned, keeping her voice low. 'Mandy normally drives you crazy.'

Toni shrugged. 'Not as much these days. I guess I'm juggling new experiences and trying to be open-minded.' Toni hoped her relaxed act appeared natural and in no way reflected the jumble of guilt and nerves that were lurking under the surface.

'Wow. Motherhood really suits you if you've mellowed that much.'

Toni averted her eyes. Liv was staring at her like she was trying to analyse her. Trying to get her head around her uptight sister changing. Ironically, since the introduction of Ruby, the Mandy situation was the only thing Toni had lightened up on. In nearly every other situation, except for work, she'd say she was more uptight than ever.

They walked into the house, and Sara hurried down the hall to greet them. 'Toni, how are you?'

'Good, Mum. Sorry, we're late.'

'Don't apologise. Hello, poppet,' she added, gently stroking Ruby's cheek. 'We're glad you made it. I know what a hassle it can be trying to leave the house with a baby. There's a nappy change, getting the nappy bag ready, loading them into the car. It always takes a lot longer than you antici-pate. Now, a glass of wine?'

'I'd love one, thanks.' Toni wasn't about to let on that Rebecca had Ruby ready to go, and all she'd had to do was hurry inside, change out of her business suit, and throw on some jeans.

Her mother stared at her for a moment. 'You look lovely.'

Toni blushed. 'It's an old shirt and jeans.'

'No, I meant your hair and make-up. Did you have something special on today?'

Oops, she'd forgotten to clean off her face. 'Lunch earlier,' she lied. 'I met a few mums at a baby and mum's yoga class, and we got together.'

'That's wonderful,' her mother said. 'It makes a huge difference having friends going through the same experiences. I met Susan at a mother's group. Did I ever tell you that?'

'At least a hundred times,' Liv said.

Sara laughed. 'I'll get the drinks.'

'You take Ruby to yoga? I'm impressed,' Liv said. They moved into the front lounge room, where Mandy was sitting waiting for them. She remained seated on the couch, but it was obvious that she was dying to jump up and see Ruby. Liv carried Ruby over to where she was sitting and passed her to her. 'Your turn, Mands.' She turned back to Toni. 'What else do you do with her?'

Toni could have sworn that the way Liv was looking at her was more than someone showing an interest. Was her hesitation at the office when their mother rang with the dinner invitation valid? Was Liv here to check up on her? 'Um, I don't know. The usual stuff you do.' She racked her brain, trying to think of the activities Rebecca took Ruby to. 'There's a nice program at the library called "Giggle Time" that she enjoys.' Or was it Wriggle Time? Something like that. 'They sing songs and read a few books. And the park's within walking distance, so she goes there a lot. She likes to be propped up in the pram and watch everything. I guess when she can walk, she'll enjoy it even more. Now, I might leave you and Mandy to enjoy some time with Ruby and help Mum with that glass of wine. I think I could use one.'

Toni didn't wait for Liv to respond. There was something off about her. She was all smiles and compliments, but she had dark rings under her eyes, suggesting she wasn't sleeping. When Liv wasn't sleeping, it meant she was worried about something and trying to come up with a solution. On top of that, there was a look in her eye. A look that Toni had seen many times growing up. It clearly said that she had another agenda and whatever reason she'd given her mother for coming to Melbourne was unlikely to be the real one. Sara had implied a few weeks earlier that this was going to end badly. Was she right? Was Liv here to get her baby back? And if she was, would Toni even care?

* * *

Toni leaned back in the kitchen chair, enjoying the smooth, velvety merlot as her mother stirred the Alfredo sauce she was making to go with the pasta. 'Why's Liv here?'

Her mother looked up. 'What do you mean?'

'I wondered why the flying visit?'

'Ask her, but she has a meeting tomorrow that she's come down for.'

Toni nodded. That sounded unlikely. Liv's photography business was in Sydney. As far as Toni knew, she didn't have any clients in Melbourne.

Liv entered the kitchen and sat down across from Toni. She poured herself a glass of water from the jug Sara had left on the table. 'Mandy's got Ruby. I assume that's okay?'

'Definitely,' Toni said. 'She's good with her, and Ruby loves her.' *A lot more than she loves me,* she omitted.

Liv nodded thoughtfully before sipping her water.

'Everything okay?' Toni asked.

'What? Why do you ask that?'

'I don't know. You've got that look in your eye. The one you get when there's something going on.'

Liv laughed. 'I had no idea I looked suspicious.'

'You're sure you're okay? No offence, but you're pale and look tired.'

Liv nodded. 'All good. Just working too hard.'

Toni sipped her drink and studied her sister. Something was going on. 'Why are you in Melbourne?'

'I'm meeting with a client tomorrow.'

'Really? I thought you only worked in Sydney.'

'Usually, but one of my clients up there wants to include their Melbourne and Brisbane offices in a shoot for images for a new website.'

'Really? Wouldn't they use local photographers?'

'Not if they want uniformity in them. If I do all three locations, then the lighting and angles will be the same.'

'Who's the client?'

Liv frowned. 'Why all the questions?'

'I'm interested.'

'I'm interested in what's happening with you and Ruby,' Liv said. 'How has it really been without Joel around? A baby on your own must be a challenge.'

'Why would you assume that? Do you think I can't cope?'

Liv put her glass of water down. 'It's my turn to ask. Are you alright?'

'Me? I'm fine. You're the one acting strangely. Questioning whether I'm coping.'

'I wasn't questioning whether you're coping,' Liv said. 'I assumed it would be hard work without Joel sharing the load. That's all.'

'What's going on?' Sara demanded. It appeared their mother had tuned in to the tone of the conversation. She put her wooden spoon down and came over to the table.

'Toni's acting weird, and I was checking that everything's okay,' Liv said.

'Oh,' Sara said. Toni and Liv looked at their mother. 'Well, this is the first time you've been to Melbourne since Ruby was born,' Sara said. 'So, I'm not surprised Toni's acting weird.'

Liv allowed her mother's words to sink in before turning her attention to Toni. 'Is that the problem? You're worried I'm here to ask for Ruby back?'

'Baby's going to Sydney?' Mandy entered the kitchen carrying Ruby with her. 'Can I go too? I can help Liv with Baby, and I can visit Barb.' Mandy smiled. 'It would be perfect.'

Toni almost choked on her wine at how simple Mandy made it sound.

'Ruby's not going anywhere,' Sara said. 'She's Toni and Joel's baby, and she'll be staying with Toni. Right?' She looked from Toni to Liv.

'Of course,' Liv said. 'I didn't come to ask for Ruby back. Don't get me wrong. She's adorable, but nothing's changed in that department, and it never will.'

Toni knew she should be relieved, but instead was filled with shame at her immediate reaction: disappointment. 'You're sure?' She knew she should act as would be expected of her, even if internally, her thoughts were going in a different direction.

'I'm sure,' Liv said. She took Toni's hand and squeezed it. 'I'm sorry I turned up unannounced. It has nothing to do with you and Ruby, I promise. Next time, I'll give you advance warning.' Liv laughed. 'She's all yours whether you like it or not.'

Toni forced a smile. 'Okay, no more surprise visits then.'

'Does this mean I can't visit Barb?' Disappointment clouded Mandy's face.

'You can visit Barb and me,' Liv said. 'Why don't we book some dates for you to come and stay for a holiday? Barb would love to see you, and I'd love to have you. You could come for a long weekend or even a week.'

'And Baby can come?'

'No,' Liv said. 'She stays here with Toni.'

Mandy's eyes widened in horror. 'Why does Toni get Baby? She already has Ruby.'

Liv shook her head. 'Now I'm getting confused. Are you talking about your doll or about baby Ruby?'

'My doll.'

'Then, yes, Baby can come too.' Liv smiled. 'It would be a lot easier if you'd call Ruby by her name.'

'I try to remember when Toni's around,' Mandy admitted. 'So she doesn't get upset with me. But Baby, I mean Ruby, is a baby and doesn't mind what she's called. Mum calls her Poppet. I call her Baby because my Baby is the thing I love most in the world that's mine, and Ruby's not mine, but she's my favourite person in the world. I'll try and get better at calling her Ruby.'

'She's got a point,' Sara said. 'Joel was calling her Princess before he left for Dubai, so she's probably got an identity issue already. Does anyone ever call her Ruby?'

Toni considered the question. Rebecca tended to call her 'gorgeous' and 'darling'. She referred to her as Ruby when talking to Toni, but she wasn't sure she used her name when talking to her. She'd need to check. Toni used her name, but it was usually in the context of, *for God's sake, Ruby, would you shut up,* and Toni hoped, usually only in her mind or out of the little girl's hearing. 'Probably not enough,' she said now. 'I'll make sure I do so she knows who she is.' She made a mental note to remind Rebecca.

As their mother took bowls from the cupboard to serve the pasta, Toni couldn't help but watch Liv. Her sister had been watching Mandy place Ruby on her stomach on the rug by the television for some tummy time and had gone over to join them.

'She's lovely, isn't she?' Liv said to Mandy, the wonder in her voice clear to Toni. She'd assured them that she didn't want Ruby back, yet everything about her body language said otherwise. Toni knew her sister enough to know that something was off. While she'd said all of the right things tonight, there was one thing Toni could be sure of: Liv was lying.

27

Lying to her family left a bitter taste in Liv's mouth, but what option did she have? Her mother had been through the trauma of losing her husband, and Toni was dealing with motherhood. They didn't need to be worrying about her too. And anyway, it was quite likely the visit to the doctors in Melbourne would be a one off. Her treatment in Sydney was first class, even though Doctor McCardle believed the second opinion from the Melbourne team was important.

Liv left her mother's house early, hoping to avoid questions from Sara. She'd shown far too much interest in Ruby the previous night as both her mother and Toni seemed convinced that she wanted her back. She'd said it was the last thing she wanted, but from their reactions, she had been less convincing than she'd hoped. She had to admit that she'd found Toni's behaviour puzzling. However, she'd probably have been on edge herself if the circumstances were reversed. She wondered how they would have reacted if she'd told them the truth. She gave herself a mental shake as she opened the door of the rental car. She knew exactly how they would have reacted. Devastated. Toni would have been, for sure.

She sighed as she started the car and glanced at the clock on the dashboard. She had thirty minutes to get to her meeting. It wasn't with a client, but for now, neither Toni nor her mother needed to know who it was with.

* * *

'I'm sorry, Liv, really I am.'

Liv was taken back fifteen years when the same words came out of Doctor Curtis' mouth.

'As the team in Sydney has told you, another kidney is a possibility.'

'But?'

'No buts. Some people end up having three or four in their lifetime. The waiting period is the difficult part. Unless you have a relative willing to donate, you're looking at around four years wait time.'

Liv sucked in a breath. 'Four years? They told me three in Sydney.'

Doctor Curtis frowned. 'They might be right. Blood and tissue types mean that it could be a shorter period than that, but it could be longer.' The doctor flicked through her notes on Liv. 'We tested all of your family members the first time around. Except for your younger sister.' She looked up at Liv. 'Why was that?'

'She developed meningitis as a baby which left her with intellectual issues. My older sister, Toni, was a match, and there was no need to test her. Also, there'd be legal issues around consent even if she agreed to it and was compatible. Honestly, I don't think I want to go down that path. She's terrified of hospitals, and I think it would be too much for her to handle.'

The doctor leaned back in her chair. 'Unless you have close friends or further relatives come out of the woodwork and are willing to be tested, our best option is to move forward with the plan the Sydney team have put in place. The first step with that is to determine whether you're suitable for peritoneal dialysis and whether it's the route you'd like to take. There are pros and cons of both haemodialysis and peritoneal.' She typed something into her computer and waited. 'We need to schedule a meeting with you and our education team so they can go through everything with you. There's a good chance that you'll be eligible for peritoneal if you choose that option. The team will put you through some tests and then talk you through each step. The actual procedure requires a catheter to be inserted into your abdomen. It's a day procedure and can be done here or in Sydney depending on your preference.'

'Sydney,' Liv said, without needing to give it any thought. Her family wouldn't need to know anything about it and Barb could accompany her if she wanted to.

The doctor nodded. 'Okay, we'll book you in for tests in a few days and go from there. And if you are eligible for peritoneal, there are two different options as to how you do the treatment. Some people opt to do it during the day, which involves four exchanges of about thirty minutes, while others prefer to do an overnight option known as APD. The team in Sydney can go through the options and what's involved once you're at that stage. Hopefully, it will be a short-term solution, Liv. Just while we wait for a kidney.'

As she made her way back to her mother's house, the doctor's words played over in Liv's mind. *Just while we wait for a kidney.* Her gut churned as the reality of those words sank in. What Doctor Curtis was really saying was Liv had to wait for a compatible donor to die in order for her to live.

As Liv pulled up outside her mother's house, her phone pinged with a text. She turned off the car and slipped her phone from her bag.

Your time's up. You'd better have the 12K. Details of the drop-off to a Melbourne location will be sent tomorrow. No money, and your sister learns the truth.

Liv stared at the message. It was the third she'd received since enjoying the lasagne with Barb a couple of weeks earlier. Each time from a different phone number that was not in service when she tried to call it. She'd managed to delay the payment by saying she didn't have the money but would have it by the end of the month. She wasn't sure what was more concerning: the demand for money or that Petal knew she was in Melbourne.

Why do you think I'm in Melbourne? I can't pay any more. Can we meet to discuss?

Your movements are being tracked, and I suggest you work out a way to find another twelve thousand. This will be the last payment. And no, we can't meet.

I know who you are. I'm going to track you down through the midwifery association, and then we will meet. I know why you're doing this, but it needs to end. I'm going to tell Toni the truth today. You have nothing to hold over me.

The whole truth? Interesting. No money equals repercussions. Instructions will be sent tomorrow. PS: you have no idea who I am.

Liv shivered. *The whole truth?* They were talking about the birth certificate, weren't they? Unease washed over her. Had she been naïve in what she assumed Petal knew?

She tossed her phone into her bag and leaned back in the car seat. It had to be Petal. There was no one else who knew what she'd done or would think they could get away with this. She had planned to give Toni the birth certificate during this visit and hoped she'd be grateful for what Liv had done, but now she was wondering if she'd made a mistake. She sighed. *A mistake.* She'd made more than *a mistake.* One bad decision had led to another, which had led her to today. She couldn't pay another twelve thousand dollars, but if she didn't, could she risk the repercussions that had been threatened?

28

Toni ended the call, threw the phone down on her glass-topped desk, and, shock propelling her, made a mad dash to the office bathroom. She kicked open the door, only reaching the toilet bowl before her stomach heaved and emptied. Her carefully orchestrated existence was about to crash down around her. *She only had one week.* Joel had surprised her and announced he'd managed to get five days off, which gave him enough time to come home to see her and Ruby. 'Speak to Rob about having those days off,' Joel said. 'I know you're only working two days. Try and schedule them around my days home if you can.' *Schedule them around his days home.* Not only was she working full time, but the day Joel was arriving home was the launch of Zoltron's voice app. There was no way she could hand that over to anyone else. She'd already booked Rebecca to work longer hours for the full week. Toni wiped her mouth, flushed the toilet, and moved to the sink, where she splashed her face with water. She should be ecstatic – it was the longest she and Joel had been apart since they'd married – but she wasn't.

Dread? Yes. Ecstasy? No.

In the four weeks he'd been gone, she'd made things work. Ruby was thriving, she'd found a way to manage motherhood, and she was excelling at work. Joel would go ballistic when he found out she was working long, full-time hours and Ruby was being raised by Rebecca.

She pushed open the door to the ladies' room and wound her way through the buzzing open-plan area to the corner office. *Her* corner office. The office she'd earned through thousands of hours of overtime over the years. The office she'd dreamed of occupying and the role she'd clawed her way up through the company to secure. She sat down at her desk and dropped her head into her hand. She must be crazy. It was the only explanation. Motherhood had driven her beyond depression into a land of crazed decisions, irrational behaviour and a great big mess to deal with.

Toni closed her eyes. She was kidding herself that she'd made things work. She was lying to Joel and her family and putting herself first, rather than Ruby. She shook her head. How had she let working for someone else's business take priority over spending time with Ruby and trying to bond with her? She knew that her situation wasn't unique. That other women struggled with motherhood and with help and time, they would often come to love their new role and, of course, fall in love with their baby. She opened her eyes. She needed help. She couldn't turn to her mum or Liv on this occasion, but she could certainly seek professional help. She picked up her phone and scrolled through her contacts. She'd had multiple sessions over the years with Doctor Amelie Rogers, a psychologist specialising in grief counselling following miscarriage. She might not be the right person to talk to about depression, assuming that was what she was dealing with, but she'd be able to refer a colleague, for sure. A weight lifted from Toni's shoulders as she made the decision. She pressed the call button to connect with Doctor Rogers's practice.

As she waited for the call to be answered, a message appeared on her screen.

Toni, your 3 o'clock is here. Do you want me to show him to the boardroom?

Damn. She ended the call. She'd call back after her meeting. Toni stood and took a deep breath. In this moment, she needed to push all images of Joel and Ruby from her mind and concentrate on Mick Sabre of Columbus Industries. She had an opportunity to steal a huge client from Hunters, and nothing could impact her performance.

* * *

Toni was moving in for the kill. She had Mick eating out of her hand. He'd devoured the presentation she'd gone through with him and was asking about timelines for getting their first campaign up and running. If Toni played her hand right, he would be signing on with the agency before he left the room.

'Mick,' Toni began, 'what I see as the biggest asset we have compared to Hunters is—' They were interrupted as the door to the boardroom opened, and Lindsay appeared. Her face was flushed, and her lip trembled.

The frustration that swept over Toni was quickly replaced by concern. She'd asked for no interruptions but one look at Lindsay's face told her something was terribly wrong. 'What's happened? Are you okay?'

'There's an emergency. I'm sorry, but I need to speak to you.'

'It's no problem,' Mick said. 'I've got a few messages I need to reply to.'

Toni flashed him her brightest smile. 'Thanks, and sorry. I'm sure this will only take a minute.'

'Actually, it might take longer,' Lindsay said.

Toni swallowed the lump that had formed in her throat. Had something happened to Joel? Or her mother? She couldn't lose her so close to her father's passing. She took the receptionist by the elbow and guided her out of the boardroom. 'What's happened? Is it Joel?'

Lindsay shook her head. 'I'm so sorry, Toni, but your nanny needs to speak to you. She says Ruby's gone missing.'

Toni dropped Lindsay's elbow and took a step backward. 'Missing? What does that mean?'

'The nanny is on line four. I don't know any more than that.'

Toni continued to stare at Lindsay. How could a baby go missing? It wasn't like she could wander off. She wasn't even crawling yet. 'There must be a mistake. Are you sure she said she was missing?'

'Line four, Toni. Speak to her. She's very upset.'

Toni hurried to her office and picked up the phone. 'Rebecca?'

Rebecca's voice came through in choked sobs, making it difficult for Toni to grasp her words. 'I'm so sorry, Toni. Ruby's missing.' Her sobs intensified. 'I've called the police, and they'll be here any minute.'

'How is she missing? What happened?'

Toni heard Rebecca draw in a breath, doing her best to control her tears. 'I don't know. I brought her to the park like I do most mornings, and while she was asleep in the pram, I got a coffee from the coffee truck by the car park. I turned away from the pram for a really short time, long enough to add some sugar to my coffee and stir it, and when I turned back, she was gone.'

'How can she be gone? You would have heard someone taking her, or someone must have seen something?'

Another sob echoed down the line. 'She was asleep and other than a couple of people jogging that we passed on the way into the park, I didn't see anyone else, and I had my AirPods in, so I didn't hear anything. The guy in the coffee truck had gone into the back area to prepare some food. It was just me: me and whoever took Ruby.'

A cold shiver ran down Toni's back. This was happening. Ruby was missing. 'Where are you now?'

'By the coffee truck.'

'Okay, I'll be there in ten minutes. Let the police know I'm on my way and call me if she turns up.' Even as the words left her mouth, she knew how ridiculous they sounded. How was she going to turn up? You don't *accidentally* take a baby from a pram.

She ended the call and turned to Lindsay, her heart racing. 'I have to go. Ruby's been taken. Explain to Mick and reschedule the meeting.'

'Can I do anything to help?'

Toni shook her head and raced to her office to grab her bag and keys. An ache settled in her chest as she did her best to hold back tears. *Ruby has been taken*. The photo on her desk of her and Joel cradling Ruby between them on their first day with her glared back at her. A cry lodged in her throat. Her baby was missing. Joel would never forgive her, and she'd never forgive herself.

* * *

Toni's mind whirled as she sped through the streets of South Yarra towards Fawkner Park. Who would want to take Ruby? It had to be a random act, or had someone been watching Rebecca's movements? Was her baby in the hands of some kind of pervert or psycho? A suffocating sense of dread engulfed her. What if they'd hurt her, or even worse, killed her? A choked sob escaped her lips. This was her fault. She should have been looking after Ruby, not a nanny. How was she going to tell Joel that someone had their precious daughter?

Joel. A tear escaped the corner of her eye, and she wiped her face roughly with her sleeve. She'd call him as soon as she reached the park and knew what was going on. Hopefully, Ruby would have been returned by the time she got there, and there would be no need for Joel to ever know.

She pulled into the car park, flung open the door and hurried towards the coffee van. Rebecca was talking to two police officers. They turned as she reached them.

'Ms Montgomery?' the female officer asked.

Toni nodded.

'I'm Senior Sergeant Dwyer, and this is Constable Grady. We were called by your nanny regarding the disappearance of your daughter.'

She nodded, noticing how young Constable Grady looked. Had he literally just graduated?

'How do we find her?'

'There are procedures that will be put into place as soon as we've established some details regarding Ruby's disappearance.'

'But I thought when a child went missing, it was urgent. The first three hours were crucial to finding them. That an amber alert needed to be raised immediately. That's what it's called isn't it, when a child is abducted?'

Dwyer nodded. 'That's correct, and we'll be notifying the regional duty officer as soon as we've established a few details. She'll consult with the regional crime coordinator to decide the best steps forward. Now, are you aware of any reason someone would take Ruby?'

Toni shook her head, a sick feeling churning in her stomach.

'What about Ruby's father? Are the two of you together?'

'Yes. But Joel's in Dubai. He's a pilot.'

'What about other family members? Would anyone have a reason to take Ruby?'

'No.'

'Friends or anyone else you can think of?'

Toni hesitated for a split second. Liv? She'd assured Toni the previous night that she didn't want Ruby, but something had been off with her. Toni was sure she'd been lying.

'Ms Montgomery?'

The officer broke into Toni's thoughts, and she did her best to push an image of Liv from her mind. She'd speak to her before mentioning it as a possibility to the police. 'No, no one.'

'And can you confirm for me what Ruby was wearing this morning?'

Toni stared at her. 'No. She was asleep when I left for work. Rebecca dressed her.' She turned to the nanny, who was wiping her tear-stained cheeks.

'That's okay. We've already asked Miss Collins,' Dwyer said. 'I wanted confirmation.'

'I have a photo,' Rebecca said, pulling her phone from her jeans pocket. 'I usually send Toni a photo mid-morning to keep in touch and show her Ruby's happy.' She found the photo and handed the phone to Dwyer. 'You can see the yellow outfit I told you she was wearing.'

'Perfect,' Dwyer said. 'Okay. I need to contact my regional duty officer. Stay here with Grady, and I'll be back in a minute. Ms Montgomery, if there's anyone you think you should call to check if they might have Ruby, then please do that.' She hurried towards the patrol car.

'I'm so sorry, Toni,' Rebecca said. Her eyes were puffy and red. 'I don't know what else to say.'

'It wasn't your fault,' Toni said. She assumed it wasn't. Would Rebecca have arranged to take Ruby? Had she seen how terrible Toni was at parenting? How she put work first, and Ruby a late last? She stared at the nanny. 'This isn't your way of showing me how important Ruby is, is it?'

'What do you mean?'

Grady's eyes widened in interest.

Toni swallowed, heat rushing through her body. 'We both know I'm not the most maternal person and overall, I'm struggling a bit with Ruby. I want to check that you aren't behind this, trying to show me how important she is?'

Rebecca's mouth dropped open. 'I'd never do something like that and for the record, I never considered that you were *struggling*. You're not even home when I'm with Ruby. How would I know how you're doing?'

That was true. Just because Toni had judged herself didn't mean the nanny had too.

She took her phone from her bag and found Liv's details. 'I'm going to call my sister.' It was a reflex; since they were teenagers, the first person Toni turned to in times of trouble was Liv. Her parents were always so preoccupied with Mandy that she'd called the one person she knew would always be there for her.

Liv picked up after the first ring. 'Hey, Ton, what's up?'

'Ruby's been taken.'

There was a brief silence. 'What?'

Toni's lips began to quiver. 'Taken from her pram at the park.'

'Where are you? I'll come straight away.'

She gave Liv the details.

'Should I let Mum know?'

'Hold on.' She turned to Grady. 'Should my sister tell my mum and other family members what's going on?'

'Yes. Anyone who might have information will need to be contacted, and you'll probably want them around you for support. I'd suggest you contact your husband too.'

Toni squeezed her eyes shut. How was she going to tell Joel?

'Toni?'

Her eyes flicked open. Liv was still waiting. 'They said you can tell Mum, but let's wait a bit longer in case Ruby's found quickly. Mum doesn't need this right now. I'll call you back in a minute.' Dwyer was walking briskly towards them, and Toni ended the call.

'Okay,' Dwyer said. 'My superior is meeting with the regional crime coordinator, and they'll determine whether an amber alert is to be implemented. They'll make that decision quickly, and assuming it is approved, they'll contact the Media and Public Affairs Group to broadcast it. For now, we need you both to come to Prahran Police Station where we can ensure all the details have been established and you can be provided with information as to how things will proceed.'

'I should stay here,' Toni said. 'It's where she last was and whoever has her might bring her back.'

'We'll have officers here searching the area,' Dwyer said. 'You'll be of more use to us at the station.'

Toni swallowed, then nodded. She needed to believe the police knew what they were doing and follow their instructions.

Two patrol cars pulled into the car park beside Toni's car as Dwyer finished speaking.

'Our team are here. They'll be speaking with the owner of the coffee business and searching the park. Let me quickly brief them, and then we can get you to the station.'

* * *

Time seemed to be moving in slow motion when five minutes later, Toni found herself following the patrol car along Commercial Road towards Prahran. Rebecca sat beside her in the passenger seat, rigid as a stone. She was pale and, like Toni, stunned. If Toni had any emotional or mental capacity available, she'd probably try her best to comfort her, but right at this moment, her own levels were in deficit.

She instructed the car's hand's free system to call Joel's phone. She doubted she'd be able to get any words out, but, as much as she'd like to avoid this, he had a right to know. She was relieved when the call clicked through to voicemail. She didn't leave a message; he was probably in the air and would see the missed call. She'd try again from the police station.

Tears clouded her eyes as she slowed to a stop behind the patrol car at a red light.

Ruby was gone.

What if they hurt her? What if she was already dead? Toni couldn't bear to imagine what her little girl might have been put through. An over-whelming sense of guilt settled over her. *Her little girl.* She'd let Ruby down every day since they'd brought her home. She'd put herself first. She'd lied to Joel. She'd lied to her family. She was a terrible mum and a terrible person, and now she was being punished. She deserved it, but Ruby didn't.

The little girl had been punished enough by having Toni as her mother. She'd do anything right now to turn back time and do everything differently. To ensure Ruby knew she loved her and wanted her. What if she never got the chance?

Tears streamed down her cheeks as she accelerated through the intersection. She'd called Liv again as they left the park and asked her to meet them at the police station. Only a few months ago, it had been Liv who'd asked Toni to meet with her on FaceTime. That call had changed Toni's life. She wiped her eyes with the back of her hand, once again thinking of Liv's unusual behaviour the previous evening. First, she'd arrived in Melbourne with no pre-warning. Said she was here to visit a client but had seemed jittery and un-Liv-like. A feeling of unease curled its way into a knot in Toni's stomach.

'I'm sorry,' Rebecca said again, breaking into Toni's thoughts.

'It's not your fault.' Toni's words solicited a sob from Rebecca.

The nanny wiped her eyes. 'I can't believe this has happened. Someone must have been watching me.'

Toni nodded. 'I'd say that's the most likely case.'

Rebecca stared at her. 'Most likely? You say that like there's some other scenario.'

Toni sighed. 'There's a lot I haven't told you about Ruby. Including that she's not my biological daughter.'

'Really?'

'She's my sister, Liv's baby. She was unexpectedly pregnant and offered the baby to Joel and me. We've struggled with IVF unsuccessfully for years, so we said yes. My sister lives in Sydney, but she came down to Melbourne without any warning yesterday and was acting strangely last night. She said her behaviour had nothing to do with Ruby but that's hard to believe right now. My biggest fear in agreeing to raise Ruby was that one day Liv might want her back.'

'You think your sister took Ruby or arranged for her to be taken?'

Toni hesitated, realising if Liv had taken Ruby then she was the last person she should have called. But surely, Liv wouldn't do something like that, would she? 'I'd like to say no. But, I'm not sure. If Liv hadn't been acting weird at dinner, it probably wouldn't have even crossed my mind. She's meeting us at the police station, so we'll find out soon enough.'

The two women lapsed into silence as the traffic moved forward once again. Toni realised she could only hope that Liv had taken Ruby. At least then they'd know that the little girl hadn't been harmed.

29

Liv manoeuvred the car off the main road into a side street and stopped abruptly. Her hands shook so badly she didn't trust herself to drive any further. The sheer panic in Toni's voice when she'd rung to tell her that Ruby had been snatched had set her adrenaline racing. There were so many secrets. Too many secrets. What if they were to unravel now? Toni would never forgive her, and she could go to jail.

There was no reason anything would unravel. She did her best to convince herself that it was probably a simple case of someone picking up the wrong baby, and worked even harder to push away the thought of how unlikely that would be. She could only hope she'd arrive at the police station to find Ruby returned to Toni, and everything would go back to normal. No explanations would be required.

She shuddered. But what if it was real? What if the threats she'd been receiving were more than threats? The last one had said the truth would come out on Friday. Today was Friday.

An image of Mandy snuggling Ruby to her popped into Liv's mind. She shook her head. No, Mandy wouldn't be able to orchestrate something as sophisticated as an abduction. Although... she loved Ruby to the point of being obsessed and had been showing an independent side. Was it possible?

With trembling fingers, Liv took her phone from her pocket and called her sister.

'Livvy!'

Mandy's happy tone blasted Liv's ear. 'I was just telling Mum about the breakfast Barb made us that morning in Sydney. You know, the crêpes.'

'You were on the phone to Mum?'

'No, I'm at her house again.' Mandy giggled. 'I turned up at eight with all the ingredients to surprise you and her with the famous crêpes. But you'd already left for your meeting.'

'How did you get there?'

'Tram and bus and walking.'

'Can you put me on speaker?'

'Sure.'

'Mum, it's Liv. Has Mandy really been with you since eight this morning?'

'She has. Why?'

Liv could picture her mother screwing up her face, wondering why Liv was questioning Mandy's movements.

'Great, keep her with you until I call you back. Something's happened, but I need to go.' She ended the call before her mother had a chance to ask any questions. She wasn't ready to upset her just yet.

Mandy wasn't involved, which meant it quite likely was the threat against Liv being played out. Why couldn't they have waited a few hours? Liv had the money. It was supposed to be the final payment and the end of the threats. But *she'd* taken Ruby. Nausea churned in Liv's stomach. All of her careful planning was unravelling. She was going to have to tell Toni what she'd done.

She restarted the car and pulled away from the kerb, the nausea intensifying as she neared the police station. It was bad enough that someone had tried to take advantage of the situation, but abducting Ruby took everything to a whole new level.

* * *

Liv tapped her foot nervously on the path outside the Prahran Police Station. She'd already been inside and discovered Toni hadn't arrived yet. She opened her bag and checked that the envelope was still there. She'd planned to give it to Toni the previous day, but their mother or Mandy had been around them all evening, and she hadn't had the chance. She'd hoped her sister would be pleased with what she'd done, but now, with Ruby's disappearance, it seemed unlikely. She took a deep breath as Toni's Lexus pulled into a vacant spot outside the station. Liv was the reason Ruby had been abducted. Admitting this, however, was going to open a can of worms she'd planned to keep firmly shut. The police would need to be told, too, which Liv couldn't imagine would end well.

Liv held out her arms as Toni hurried from the car. Her sister's face was white. Toni fell into her embrace, tears streaming down her cheeks.

'She's gone, Liv. She's really gone.'

A woman in her twenties hung back from them.

Liv nudged her sister. 'Who's with you?'

Toni turned and looked at the woman. 'Sorry. Liv, this is Rebecca. Rebecca, Liv.'

Liv nodded at her. 'Are you a friend?'

'Nanny,' Rebecca said. 'I work for Toni.'

'We need to go inside,' Toni said. 'The police want to talk to us.' She turned towards the police station, stopping when Liv took her arm.

'Hold on a minute. There's something you need to know.'

Toni stared at her sister. 'It was you, wasn't it? You took Ruby. You decided you wanted her back. Why didn't you tell me? I asked you last night, and you assured me you didn't want her now or ever.'

Liv closed her eyes, horrified that Toni would think she would do something so awful. She reopened them and met her sister's gaze. 'I can't believe you think I'd do something like this.'

Toni's face instantly reddened. 'I don't know what to think. Last night, you were acting all weird, and then today, Ruby disappears. Mum keeps telling me that you'll want Ruby back one day and that no mother can give up her baby easily. Why else would you have come to Melbourne? You never work with clients here. That story didn't ring true.'

Liv sometimes forgot how accurately Toni could read her.

'Well?' Toni demanded. 'I'm right, aren't I? You're not here for work, are you? You lied to Mum and to me.'

Liv opened her eyes. 'Yes, I lied. But my reasons for being in Melbourne have nothing to do with Ruby.'

Toni crossed her arms. 'It's a bit too convenient that you're here lying to us, and this happens. Be honest with me.'

'Fine, but I'm only telling you this to prove to you that my reason for being in Melbourne has nothing to do with Ruby. I saw the specialist this morning as I've been really run down... I thought it might have been related to my kidney.'

'Hold on,' Toni said. 'You said your kidney was fine.'

'It is, turns out I'm just run down and need to look at my diet. There's nothing to worry about.' Liv's fingers were firmly crossed behind her back as the lie rolled off her tongue.

'You're sure?'

Liv nodded. 'And anyway, my health's not important right now. We need to focus on Ruby.' She took a deep breath. 'I wish I had taken Ruby because then we'd know where she was, and you could get her back.'

'Mandy!' Toni's eyes lit up. 'I can't believe I didn't think of her.'

'I did,' Liv said. 'I spoke to her. She's been with Mum since eight. She didn't take her.'

'Did you tell them Ruby was gone?'

'No, I wanted to get here first in case she'd been found. I told them something had happened, and I'd call back. They'll both be hysterical when we do tell them.'

'It must be a random abduction then,' Toni said. 'There's no one else that we know who'd have a reason to take her.'

'Maybe,' Liv forced the word out, her voice catching. She took a shaky breath. 'The thing is... while I didn't take her, it might be my fault she's gone.'

'Your fault?'

Liv nodded and pulled an envelope from her bag. She hesitated before passing it to Toni with trembling hands. 'You need to see this. I did something incredibly stupid, and I'm worried it could have something to do with Ruby's disappearance.'

Toni's brow furrowed as she opened the envelope and took out the document. She scanned it quickly, her puzzled expression remaining as she looked up at Liv. 'Ruby's birth certificate? I'd forgotten about it. You said you were going to forward it to us after she was born. Why are you giving it to me now? You could have posted it.'

Liv swallowed, thinking back to Ruby's birth. 'Because it needs an explanation. One that I hoped would come across better in person.'

Toni waited for Liv to continue. Liv took a deep breath, wishing with everything she could turn back time and not come up with such *good* ideas. She'd planned every last detail leading up to the birth to ensure that all went to plan with regard to the birth certificate, but she could never have anticipated this turn of events.

'Read the detail, Ton.'

* * *

'You didn't?' Toni's eyes flicked over the birth certificate, stopping at the top section that listed the parents' names.

Mother: Antonia Montgomery
Father: Joel Drayson

'Liv, you could go to jail. It's fraud.'

'I know that, and someone else does too.'

Toni stared at Liv. 'What does that mean?'

'It means that I'm being blackmailed. Someone knows that I did this and demanded money a few weeks after Ruby was born. They assured me it was a one-off payment, and I stupidly went along with it.'

'Why would you do that? I was going to see the birth certificate at some stage. I assume you weren't hiding this from me?'

'I was doing it *for* you,' Liv said. 'The problem is they could report this as fraud, and I'd be in huge trouble.'

'Okay, that makes sense. But if you paid them, why is it still an issue?'

'I received another message where they demanded more, and said there would be repercussions if I didn't pay.'

'Oh, Liv. You know that if they've asked for more, it will never end. You can't give it to them.'

'Toni, they've got Ruby. It must be them. Taking her *is* the repercussion.'

'Who do you think is blackmailing you?'

'The doula, Petal Blossom. She's the only person who might have found out about this. I have no idea how, but there's no one else. She was one of the witnesses when Ruby was born.'

'But she's in Sydney, isn't she?'

'No. According to the birthing service she works for, she's taken leave. She went overseas and then possibly returned to Melbourne. She mentioned when she first met with me that she had family in Melbourne and that she'd be visiting them in a couple of months. That must be now. She was there in Sydney when the first payment was demanded, so it makes sense that it had to be left in Sydney. This time she asked for the same scenario of leaving the money in a locker, but she wanted it left at Southern Cross Station in Melbourne.'

'And you're sure it's her?'

Liv nodded. 'I assume she found out that I tricked her and is angry. No one else knows or has a reason to blackmail me.'

'What do we do now?' Toni asked. 'We need to tell the police, but what will that mean for us and the birth certificate?'

Liv's face drained of colour. 'It's fraud, Toni. I imagine it won't mean anything good.'

Toni considered this. 'What if we play dumb? Say you weren't thinking about the biological parents when you wrote down the details. That you put down the people who would be Ruby's parents without thinking, and your witnesses signed off without reading it? Or you presumed this was the case, but you've now worked out that Petal Blossom had another agenda.'

'I doubt the police will buy that. And assuming they speak to Petal, they'll find out that I lied to her. She was led to believe that it was you giving birth.'

'You called yourself Toni?'

Liv hesitated, then nodded. 'It was the only scenario I could think of that made it seem real.'

'Didn't you have to prove your identity?'

'I got a fake one.'

Toni stared at her. 'Why would you do all of that? It doesn't make sense.'

'I was hoping Ruby would never have to know she was adopted. Look what it did to Mum. It really messed with her.'

'Really? Or was it because you didn't want Ruby to know you're her biological mother?'

Liv dropped her gaze from Toni's, confirming in Toni's mind that she was getting to the real answer behind Liv's actions.

'What you've done is really extreme, Liv, and while I'd like to think it's because you care about Joel and me, there must be something in it for you.'

Liv shook her head. 'That wasn't my reason, and for now, we need to do everything we can to help the police find Ruby. They need to speak to Petal.'

Toni watched her sister's facial expressions and body language. Something was off, but she was also right. They needed to move quickly, and this conversation was slowing things down. 'Do you know where this doula is?'

Liv shook her head. 'No. Like I said, I tried to contact her and got a message saying she was overseas and the birthing agency she's registered with said her profile was on hold until she returned. I'm guessing she's in Melbourne based on her saying she'd be visiting family. The police should be able to get all her details from the agency, which for privacy reasons they wouldn't give me, and track her down.' She turned towards the entrance of the police station. 'Let's get inside. The quicker I admit to this, the quicker they can find Ruby.'

'Hold on,' Toni said. 'Assuming you really did do this for Joel and my benefit, Liv, you did something amazing for us. Tell the police you made a mistake. Blame hormones and post-natal depression. Say you weren't thinking clearly and didn't realise the repercussions of what you'd done until you were blackmailed. After all, there's a lot of truth to that. You were trying to make something amazing happen for Joel and me, nothing more than that.'

Liv opened her mouth as if to say something but shut it again.

'There's nothing else, is there?'

It was impossible not to notice the split second of hesitation before Liv shook her head.

'Liv?'

'No, nothing.'

Toni knew her sister well enough to know that, even if there was something else, Liv wasn't going to tell her. 'Okay. Let's get inside.'

30

Liv wrung her hands as she sat next to Toni across the table from Senior Sergeant Dwyer. She'd spent so many hours planning the legalities around Ruby's birth that she could hardly believe it had unravelled this quickly. What Toni believed to be a generous gift was rapidly turning into a nightmare.

'Let me get this straight,' Dwyer said, 'you made a *mistake* on the birth certificate and listed your sister and her husband as the biological parents?'

Liv nodded. 'I read it as parents. It was when I had the first message demanding money that I knew I'd made a mistake.'

'Okay,' Dwyer said. 'You received a threatening message that alerted you to this mistake?'

Liv nodded again.

'And what did you do then?'

Liv's cheeks flamed. 'I made the payment.'

Dwyer stared at Liv. 'Why would you do that? If this really was a simple mistake, you could have contacted births, deaths, and marriages to correct it. Or engaged a lawyer to fix this for you.'

'I...' Liv hesitated.

'Are you going to contact Petal Blossom?' Toni interrupted. 'Isn't that what's important right now? Liv did something amazing for Joel and me, and this Petal Blossom woman's trying to take advantage of it. You've heard of women doing crazy things with pregnancy hormones running rampant and post-natal depression taking hold, haven't you? None of that matters right now. What matters is finding Ruby, and Petal Blossom has her. It's obvious.'

'We have an officer doing that as we speak,' Dwyer said. 'Our team have also issued an amber alert, and every available resource is being used to find your daughter. It's my job to work out what else you might not have told us or what other *mistakes* your sister made.' She turned to Liv. 'It's in your best interest and Ruby's to tell us everything you know. Your actions don't add up for someone who made a *mistake*.'

Liv stared at the officer. She couldn't tell her everything. Toni would be devastated. Liv could only hope that Ruby would be found with Petal before the full story needed to come out. Although Petal was likely to tell the police everything. Liv swallowed. It might be better that she told them everything now. She closed her eyes, briefly dismissing the idea. When she opened them, she spoke with confidence. 'I've told you everything. I've had difficulty coping since Ruby's birth and have done some questionable things. This situation is one of them.'

A police officer knocked on the door and stepped inside the room. 'A minute?' he said to Dwyer.

Dwyer excused herself and followed the officer out of the room.

Liv groaned. 'I'm sorry, Ton. She's right. I shouldn't have paid the money. I don't know what I was thinking. I hoped that one payment would make it all go away, and no one other than us would know what I'd done. I should have known better. I've really let you and Ruby down.'

Toni closed her eyes.

'Toni?'

Toni shook her head. 'I've let her down, not you. You went out of your way to give Ruby an amazing start in life, while I've rejected every possible opportunity to embrace motherhood.'

'Rejected?'

Toni nodded. 'I'm a terrible mother, Liv. I can't begin to tell you how terrible.'

* * *

Liv had no time to question Toni. She found her legs trembling as Grady announced that Petal had been found and was being brought in for questioning. 'I don't have to see her, do I?'

Grady eyed Liv with interest. 'Any reason you want to avoid her?'

'Because I'd want to slap her silly,' Liv said. 'You'd probably have me cuffed within seconds of her appearing.'

Grady nodded. 'Okay, that's fair enough. And no, there's no reason you'd need to see her. She'll be questioned, and we'll go from there. I can confirm that there were no signs of Ruby at the house she's been renting a room in. She's upset by the news of Ruby's disappearance and that you think she's been blackmailing you.'

'Think? I know she has. There's no one else who could possibly know what I did.'

Grady nodded. 'How did the blackmailer contact you to demand the payment?'

'Text messages. She used different phone numbers each time, and when I tried calling them, it said the numbers were out of service.' Liv pulled out her phone. 'I had to make the first payment in cash and leave the money in a bag in a locker at Sydney airport. You'll see that I sent the person, I assume Petal, the details for the locker and combination.'

Grady raised an eyebrow. 'You didn't wait around to see who was accessing the locker?'

'No, the instructions specified I had to send a selfie from Martin Place at 1 p.m. I assume they planned to access the locker knowing I wasn't there.'

'Even though you could have had someone there watching them?'

Liv blushed. 'I'm not the best at this. It did cross my mind, but that meant telling someone else, and I didn't want anyone else involved.'

Grady shook his head. 'I'll be back soon. I've got a few questions for Ms Blossom.'

Forty minutes later, Grady returned to the room Liv, Toni and Rebecca were waiting in.

'We don't believe she had anything to do with Ruby's disappearance or you being blackmailed,' he said to Liv. 'She's been overseas the past month and only landed in Melbourne a few days ago. She's visiting her sister before returning to Sydney on the weekend. Her movements check out. She would like to speak to you, and we think if she's lying, observing a conversation between the two of you will help confirm that.'

Liv stood. 'She's definitely lying. I'll speak with her now.'

Grady led Liv to a meeting room. She pushed open the door to find Petal sitting at the table, her face strained and tear-stained. 'Liv – if that's what your name actually is – what's going on?'

Liv hesitated before moving into the room and sitting down across from the doula. Grady shut the door behind them. Liv assumed the large mirror on one side of the room was two-way and they were being watched. 'You tell me. Where's Ruby?'

Petal wiped her eyes. 'I have no idea. I'm devastated by the news that she's been taken. But I still don't understand why you think I had anything to do with it. Or why you'd think I'd blackmail you.'

'Because you worked out that I put the wrong names on the birth certificate,' Liv said.

'How on earth would I work that out? The police explained to me today that you'd done that by *accident*,' Petal said. 'They seemed sceptical that it was an accident, and I certainly don't like to think you deliberately deceived me, but I'm still not sure how you think I knew you'd done that and why I'd think I was entitled to your money.' She lowered her voice. 'Although I'm gathering there's more you haven't told them about *your baby*, am I right?'

Petal's question sent a shiver through Liv and she chose not to answer the question, knowing the police were likely to be listening. 'You really had nothing to do with Ruby's disappearance?'

'I did not.' Petal pushed her chair away from the table and stood. 'Right now, all I can do is pray with every fibre that Ruby is safely returned and that you're never in the position to decide the fate of a child again.'

Liv watched as Petal left the room. She didn't have Ruby, and if anything, Liv should be thanking her. She could have told the police a lot more than she had, and for some reason, she hadn't. Liv dropped her head into her hands. Petal was right. Someone else knew what she'd done. And if that someone had harmed Ruby in any way, she'd never forgive herself.

* * *

Liv walked out of the meeting room with Petal, unnerved that someone was willing to take the blackmail game to this level. She stopped in the corridor of the police station before reaching the room Toni and Rebecca were waiting in. That was a huge assumption. It was quite possible this was a random abduction, and nothing Liv had done had caused this. If the blackmailer had Ruby, they hadn't contacted Liv or the police demanding monies be paid for her return. She needed to think before she did or said anything incriminating.

'It wasn't her,' she said as she walked into the room where Toni was waiting for her. 'She only knew about the birth certificate because the police told her. She didn't blackmail me.'

'Who did then?' Toni demanded. 'Who else did you tell?'

'My neighbour, Barb, knew, and her grandson, Gus, did too. I spoke to him for legal advice, but that was after I paid the first amount.'

'And what did he say?'

'That I should never have paid the money, and I shouldn't have tampered with the birth certificate.' And a lot more Liv decided was better kept to herself.

'Would he or Barb have told anyone else?'

Liv shook her head. 'No, and they only found out after I'd paid the first amount. And Barb wouldn't have anything to do with it. She adores Mandy and me. She'd never do anything to hurt us.'

'She could have told Mandy,' Rebecca suggested. 'If she's close to her.'

Toni looked at Liv. 'She's right. Barb might have told Mandy.'

'She didn't need to. Mandy knew what I did. I told her at the time.'

Toni's mouth dropped open. 'What? How could you trust her with something like that?'

'She's amazing at keeping secrets. You know that.'

'But still.' Toni shook her head. 'I know Mandy was with Mum this morning, but do you think she's involved?'

Liv frowned. 'I can't see how or why. She can't hide Ruby at Wattle House, and I can't imagine she had the ability to put together a blackmail plan, let alone pull off an abduction. As much as she loves Ruby, I can't see her doing something like this.'

'Neither can I,' Toni agreed. 'I need to try Joel again. Can you call Mum and tell her?'

Liv nodded. She could only imagine the reaction she was going to receive from her mother when she found out about the birth certificate.

Toni shook her head as she walked out of the room. 'He's going to kill me – and he should.'

* * *

Toni bumped into Dwyer as she exited the small room they'd been waiting in. 'I need to call my husband.'

'There's a private room you can use.' Dwyer ushered her along the corridor and into another small room with a table and three chairs. 'A media release has been issued,' Dwyer said, 'and I can assure you everything is being done to find your daughter. We're looking further into the blackmail situation with your sister too. Now, can I get you something to drink? Tea, coffee, water?'

Toni shook her head. 'No, but thanks.' Her lip trembled, and she did her best to blink away tears.

Compassion filled Dwyer's eyes. 'As a mother myself, I can only imagine what you're going through. And in your circumstances, with years of trying for a baby, this seems doubly cruel.'

The tears she'd tried to blink away cascaded down her cheeks.

'I'll leave you to make your call,' Dwyer said.

Doubly cruel. Doubly cruel to Ruby, perhaps. She had two mothers who hadn't wanted her. Her biological mother and then Toni. It was awful to think that she'd done this to an innocent baby. She'd half joked about karma coming back to get her, but now it really had. Ruby was gone. The thoughts she'd had about the little girl, wishing she'd never had her, prioritising work over motherhood and lying to everyone in the process, were unforgivable.

She waited until Dwyer disappeared back out of the doorway and took her phone from her bag. How would she even begin to explain to Joel what had happened? Her worst nightmare, times a million, was unfolding.

She brought the phone to her ear after selecting his number. Hopefully, he'd be in the air and not answering as it might buy her some time. If they found Ruby before she spoke to Joel, he might never find out.

'Hey, babe.'

Hope plummeted as his rich voice filled her ears.

'I wasn't expecting to hear from you until tonight. Don't you and Ruby have the mother's group catch-up?'

Toni swallowed again. The mother's group she'd fabricated to ensure at least twice a week Joel didn't call because he believed she was out with other mothers and babies.

'Ton? Are you okay? Is Ruby okay?'

The concern in his voice caused tears to roll down her cheeks.

'Ton?'

Toni cleared her throat. 'No. Someone snatched her from her pram at the park this morning.'

She was greeted by a momentary silence.

'What?'

'She's disappeared. I'm at the police station. They're organising an amber alert to get her details out to the public to see if anyone knows what's happened to her.' Toni's voice broke, and gigantic sobs erupted. 'I didn't know how to tell you.' She forced the words. 'I'm sorry, Joel.'

'Did you see someone run off with her?'

'No. No one saw anything. The police said there are CCTV cameras in the area. They're being searched. I'm so sorry.'

'Stop apologising,' Joel said. 'It's not your fault. I wish I was there with you. I'll get a flight as quickly as I can. Do the police have any idea of who took her?'

'Someone's blackmailing Liv. It might be them.'

'Blackmail? What? Why?'

'She forged Ruby's birth certificate. It has our names on it as Ruby's biological parents.'

'What? Why would she do that? It's fraud.'

'She wanted us to *really* be Ruby's parents. She did it for us, Joel, for no other reason.'

'What about the guy?' Joel said. 'Ruby's father. Maybe he found out about Ruby.'

Toni was silenced. This was a scenario she hadn't considered. 'I'm sure Liv would have said. Don't forget, she didn't have any contact details for him, and he didn't know she was pregnant.'

'Check with her,' Joel said. 'If he's been in touch, she needs to tell the police. Can I speak to whoever's in charge?'

'Hold on. I'm in a private room. I'll go and find one of the two detectives I've been dealing with.'

Toni found Detective Grady waiting outside the room.

'Joel's asked to speak to you,' she said, holding out the phone.

Grady took it. 'Mr Drayson, I'm Constable Grady. As I'm sure your wife has told you, we're investigating the disappearance of your daughter. She was last seen at Faulkner Park in the care of your nanny.'

He paused while Joel spoke. Toni closed her eyes. She'd told Joel the day before that she wasn't working today. He'd be wondering why Ruby was with Rebecca.

Grady gave Toni a questioning look as he listened to Joel.

'No, we're at the Prahran police station. Now, can you think of anyone who might take Ruby? Have you upset anyone or have any reason to believe you or Toni have any enemies?'

Grady listened for another minute or two before suggesting Joel get back as quickly as possible. He finished speaking and handed Toni the phone.

'Why was Ruby with Rebecca today?' Joel demanded. 'What's going on?'

'I needed to go into the office for a meeting this morning, so I asked Rebecca to do a few extra hours. It was no big deal. She's helped out before.' Toni didn't know why she was continuing with this charade. She was pretty sure it would all come crashing down when Joel returned.

'Do you do that often?'

While she knew she was in the wrong, anger welled inside Toni. 'Really? Our daughter's been kidnapped, and this is your concern. That I might have worked a few more hours than I'd planned? Whether Rebecca had her or I had her, she would have been snatched. I follow the same routine as Rebecca when I do go to the park. Arrive, get coffee, and walk around. Anyone watching knew that. Right now, all I care about is getting our little girl back.' Toni's voice broke as a large sob forced its way to the surface.

'Oh, Jesus. I'm sorry, babe. I don't know what I'm saying.' He let out a breath. 'Oh God, let her be okay.' Toni could picture Joel pushing his hand through his hair the way he did when he was upset or stressed. 'I'll get on the next flight home as soon as I get off the call. Are you okay?'

Tears ran down Toni's cheeks. She'd been lying to Joel for weeks and had now guilted him into changing the subject. The universe was making sure she knew what an awful person she was. How would she explain any of it to Joel when he returned? She could only hope Ruby was found before he touched down.

31

It was after four when Toni slipped her key in the lock and pushed open the front door of her apartment. Her mother and Liv would be arriving at any minute. They were dropping Mandy back to Wattle House first. She'd been questioned by the police and had become upset and agitated when she'd been asked about Ruby. No, she hadn't taken her, and she had no idea who had. She kept shaking her head as fat tears rolled down her cheeks.

Sara had appeared speechless when the blackmail situation had been explained. And Liv had reassured Toni that she didn't know how to contact Ruby's biological father, so him being involved was a highly unlikely scenario.

'Are you sure it's a good idea for Mandy to be staying at Wattle House?' Toni had asked Sara before leaving the police station. 'She's really distressed about Ruby. Maybe she should stay with you and Liv, or even come back to my place, as I assume that's where we'll all be going after we leave here?'

'I'll call Izzy,' Sara said. 'Mandy's friend. See if she'll come over and collect Mandy and take her back to her place. She can call us if Mandy gets upset and needs us.'

Mandy's eyes lit up with this suggestion, and Toni was relieved to know she'd be distracted and they wouldn't have to comfort Mandy on top of their own distress.

Now, as Toni's eyes travelled to the baby bouncer sitting empty in the middle of the lounge, she was relieved that Mandy hadn't come back to the apartment. She wasn't sure she could deal with Mandy's grief on top of her own. Tears rolled down her cheeks and she found she had to look away. She'd been given the most incredible gift, and until this moment, she hadn't appreciated it.

Toni made her way to the bedroom, a wave of exhaustion washing over her. If only she could climb into bed, sleep, and wake to find this was nothing but a bad dream.

She found herself drawn to the walk-in-robe, but she hesitated. She hadn't visited her heart box for months, not since Liv offered Ruby to her and Joel.

Entering the walk-in-robe, the familiar process of rummaging at the back of the small shelf she kept her scarves on took over. Her fingers connected with the cool metal she was searching for, and she pulled out a small silver box. She stared at it. She'd neglected more than just Ruby in the last few months. She'd neglected all her babies.

Lifting the lid, the first photo hit her, as it always did, with a force that took her breath away. Her broken-heart box was a better description, as it housed small pieces of her shattered heart. Toni slid to the floor, removing the six precious early ultrasound photos, taken between six and eight weeks from their IVF attempts. Six babies. Six joyous celebrations, five followed by trepidation after the first miscarriage, but all with a sliver of hope. Tears wet her cheeks as the pain she'd felt with each loss resurfaced. *How could I have felt so much love for these babies and not felt that for Ruby?* It didn't make sense to her. She hadn't carried any of the babies beyond the first trimester, each pregnancy ending between ten and eleven weeks, yet she'd grieved each one for months, and if she was honest, her grief had never left her.

She lay the six photos in front of her, each image distorted by the tears in her eyes and the image of Ruby taking over her thoughts. Ruby smiling. Ruby giggling. Toni wiped her eyes. She had been given the most precious gift ever, and she'd fallen apart. She'd not coped with Ruby and to avoid unpacking exactly why, she'd done everything she could to hide her failure from those around her and, if she was honest, herself.

Was it possible she hadn't allowed herself to get close to Ruby in case the unthinkable happened? That she was taken from them? Toni knew after the last miscarriage that she wasn't strong enough to lose another baby, so she'd agreed with Joel when he suggested they stop IVF. Had pushing Ruby away been easier than risking falling in love and then dealing with the grief if Liv had asked for her back? It was possible, Toni guessed, but certainly not something she'd done consciously.

She rose to her feet, crossed over to Joel's side of the bed, and lifted the photo frame from his nightstand. It was a photo of Ruby, snug in a purple onesie, her black hair poking out from a fluffy white beanie Joel had insisted she wear for the photo. Toni had glanced at the photo before but never had it impacted on her as it did at this moment. Tears continued to cascade down her cheeks, and she closed her eyes as waves of grief enveloped her. *What if she's dead? What if I've lost her for good? She mustn't be. I need to make it up to her. To let her know that I want her. That I love her.*

Toni held the photo close to her, sobs wracking her body as she considered the loss. She'd barely functioned after her miscarriages, but to lose Ruby, a living, breathing little girl, was something different again. She doubted she'd ever recover. She would be riddled with guilt, and the despair would be too much. She wasn't sure she'd be able to survive a loss this enormous.

The doorbell chimed, interrupting her misery. She replaced the photo and wiped her eyes. Falling apart wasn't going to help anyone. She needed to pull herself together and do what she could to find Ruby.

She hurried to the front door as the bell chimed again and pulled it open to find her mother and Liv waiting.

Liv took one look at Toni, stepped inside the apartment, and opened her arms wide.

Toni gratefully sank into them.

'It'll be okay,' Liv said. 'They'll find her.'

'How do you know that?'

'Gut feeling.'

Toni pulled back from Liv. 'There's not more to this blackmail, is there?'

Liv frowned. 'More? What does that mean?'

'More that you aren't telling the police. More that could help us find Ruby?'

Liv shook her head.

'And I'm going to ask again because I know what I told you last night could have triggered this.'

'Told me last night?'

Toni nodded. 'I mentioned that I'd been working longer hours than I told Joel I was and using Rebecca more than I probably should have been.'

'So?' Liv said. 'I didn't have a problem with that. In fact, I didn't get to say anything about it as Mandy interrupted us.'

'What do you mean using Rebecca more than you should have been?' their mother asked.

Toni's cheeks heated, and she refused to meet her mother's gaze. 'I've gone back to work full time.'

'What?'

The disbelief on Sara's face was the exact image Toni had imagined when she thought of her mother hearing this news. She was predictable, at least.

Toni walked through to the lounge room and sank down onto the couch. 'I'm not proud of it, but yes, I've been lying to everyone.'

'Why lie about that?' Liv asked. 'Is that a big deal if Ruby's being looked after? Or is it because Joel wants you to be a stay-at-home mum?'

'That's a big part of it,' Toni said. 'But there's more.'

'More?' Sara said, her eyes wide.

Toni nodded as tears ran down her cheeks 'I didn't want to admit that motherhood hasn't lived up to my expectations. I even lied last night when I pretended to be upset that Liv might have wanted Ruby back. I couldn't let you know this then, but I would have happily handed her over.'

'Really?' Liv said. 'You've hated motherhood that much?'

Toni nodded again, wiping her face with her sleeve. 'Enough to have given her back without a second glance. If you have got her, Liv, you can have her. Honestly, I'd give her back in a heartbeat if I can just know she's okay.'

'What are you saying?' Sara asked. 'That if we find Ruby, you want Liv to have her?'

Toni shook her head. 'No, that's not what I want, but I'd understand if it was what Liv wanted. Losing Ruby,' she pushed down a sob, 'has made me realise how much I do love her. I'd give anything to turn back the clock and start again from the day she was born.'

Liv pushed a hand through her hair and began pacing up and down. 'I don't have Ruby. But I can't believe you've been going through this and didn't tell anyone. Does Joel know?'

'Before he went to Dubai, I told him I was struggling, but I don't think he really heard what I was saying. I ignored his wishes about me working, employed Rebecca to look after Ruby and went back full time.'

'Toni, that's awful.' Her mother's horrified face gave her a good idea of how Joel was going to react when he got home.

'I understand from what you've said that you were struggling, but how could you do that to Ruby?' Sara asked. 'These first few months are crucial for bonding and making her feel safe and secure. You've done everything in your power to have a baby in the last eight or so years, including twisting your sister's arm to get her to give you hers, and this is how you show your gratitude.'

'Mum,' Liv said. 'This isn't helping. Toni didn't twist my arm. She didn't even know about the pregnancy when I made the offer to her. And post-natal depression is a real thing. It sounds like Toni's experienced an extreme case of it, and none of us picked up on it.'

Sara frowned. 'Post-natal depression is hormone-related. As Toni didn't give birth to Ruby, I'm not sure that's the issue.'

'Still not helping,' Liv said. 'And it's not just hormone-related. Post-adoption depression is a real thing. Petal Blossom gave me a bunch of brochures when she found out Toni and Joel would be raising Ruby and one of them talked about depression and other issues that could occur.' As she explained this to Sara, Liv realised she'd never given Toni the brochures. She pushed the thought from her mind; it was just another thing she'd done wrong. 'Now, let's move on and concentrate on what's important right now.'

Sara had the good grace to blush. 'I'm sorry. It's not something I ever imagined would be an issue for you.'

Toni remained silent. Ruby was missing, and Liv was right. None of this was helping. She'd be dealing with all kinds of questions and accusations from Joel when he arrived, and she didn't need a preliminary round now.

'We need to focus on Ruby and getting her back,' Liv continued.

Two red splotches appeared on Sara's cheeks. 'Sorry, I'm beside myself about Ruby. What if—'

She didn't finish her sentence, but Toni knew what she was thinking. A tear slid down her cheek. She was a complete failure, and Ruby had paid the ultimate price.

* * *

Toni managed a few hours of fitful sleep after Liv and Sara went home, promising to return in the morning. 'Not too early,' Toni had said. 'Joel's going to be distraught when he gets back, and probably quite angry when he learns the truth. We might need some space. I'll ring you when I think it's safe to appear.'

Now, she lay in bed, again going over who might want to take Ruby. She couldn't imagine anyone she knew being involved. Liv's blackmailer still seemed like the obvious person, but the police hadn't worked out who that was. They'd explained that while it might have been a calculated abduction, there was the possibility that someone saw a spur of the moment opportunity. She could only hope that whoever had her was looking after her.

There were times when she was going through IVF and miscarriages that Toni believed she would do anything for a baby, including stealing one. She'd find herself watching women at cafés with prams and daydreaming about casually pushing the pram away from the table and taking the baby home. She would never have acted on it, but she could imagine doing it. Part of her hoped, for Ruby's sake, that whoever had taken her was in a similar situation. That their circumstances of wanting a baby had driven them to do something crazy, but as a result, they were doting on Ruby rather than neglecting or hurting her.

They'd heard back from the police the previous evening to advise that everything was being done to find Ruby, and they would be in touch again this morning.

She dragged herself out of bed before six, having spent no time sleeping and too much time thinking of other cases of child abduction she knew of. William Tyrrell had been missing for nine years, and Madeleine McCann, taken at three, would now be in her twenties if she was alive, and then, of course, there was Daniel Morcombe. She couldn't imagine the strength his parents must have had to endure eight years of him missing to discover he was murdered within hours of being abducted. The thoughts had gone around and around in her mind all night long. She could only keep going back to the hope that whoever had taken Ruby had taken her because they were desperate for a baby.

Toni made her way into the kitchen, checking her phone. Nothing from Joel or the police. She needed to be out looking, but where should she look? She had no idea where she'd even start, and the police had suggested she stay close to home.

It was just after seven when she heard Joel's key in the front door. She braced herself. She couldn't begin to imagine how angry and upset he was going to be.

He dropped his bag in the doorway. 'Babe?' She stepped into view, and he rushed towards her and drew her to him, squeezing her so hard, she could barely breathe. 'I can't believe this has happened.'

'I'm so sorry, Joel, really I am.'

'It's not your fault.'

Toni pulled out of his arms. 'But that's the thing, it might be. It's karma.'

'Karma?'

She nodded. 'It might never have happened if I hadn't gone back to work and hired Rebecca.'

'Do you think she was part of it?' There was an incredulous edge to Joel's voice. 'That the nanny helped whoever took Ruby?'

'Definitely not. Rebecca loves Ruby to bits. The police questioned her endlessly about what happened, and they told me that she wasn't considered a suspect.'

'Then who would have taken her?'

Tears filled Toni's eyes. 'I don't know, but it's my fault.'

'Come and sit down,' Joel said, guiding her to the couch and living area. 'Blaming yourself won't help. Right now, all that's important is getting Ruby back.'

'It is, but I lied to you. About work.'

Joel sat next to her and took her hand. 'What do you mean you lied?'

Toni couldn't look him in the eye. 'I went back full time, not part time. Rebecca's been working full time looking after Ruby.'

Joel dropped her hand. 'What? How could you lie about that?'

'Because I didn't want to argue with you. I wasn't coping with Ruby, and I didn't want to look after her full time. That's why I think this is my fault. After wanting a baby for years, the reality of it was nothing like what I imagined, and I couldn't cope. Work made me happy again, and Ruby... didn't. I know she picked up on my feelings towards her. I resented her, Joel, and I'm sure she could sense that.' She buried her head in her hands. 'We're being punished because of me.'

They sat in silence for a moment before Toni lifted her head. Her voice soft, the disbelief evident. 'Our child has been abducted.'

'She has.' The anger in Joel's tone faded. 'And right now, that's what we need to focus on. Not you going back to work or telling lies, unless you can think of anyone who knew who might have had a problem with what you were doing. Did your mum know or anyone at work?'

'No one at work knew that I'd gone back to work against your wishes or that I was struggling with Ruby,' Toni said. 'And Mum didn't know until last night. I couldn't even bring myself to tell *her* I wasn't coping. I knew I'd get a lecture on how I should never have taken Liv's baby. I was down enough on myself. I didn't need her confirming it. I didn't love her enough, Joel.' Tears flowed down her cheeks. 'She was an amazing gift, and I didn't bond with her, and I resented her.'

'I know you were struggling,' Joel said, 'but I'm sure you didn't resent her.' He ran a hand through his hair. 'I would have noticed, Ton.'

'You didn't. I tried to tell you how I was feeling, but I didn't give you the full picture. I was ashamed and I guess I mastered hiding it. Ruby changed our lives, and for me, it wasn't for the better. I suddenly had everything I've ever wished for, and it wasn't what I wanted at all. I wanted my old life back. My job, my social nights. I didn't want to be a slave to a screaming baby.'

Joel flinched at her words, and she didn't blame him. Even to her ears, it sounded awful.

'I woke up most mornings not wanting to get out of bed. It was okay when you were here, but during the weeks you were flying, I couldn't cope. I'd lie in bed most of the day, and she'd scream and scream, and I'd put my AirPods in to block her out.'

'You're kidding?'

Joel's horrified expression was mortifying, but Toni knew that as much as she sounded like she was rambling, she needed to continue. If she didn't tell him everything now, she might lose the courage. 'As soon as you went back to work, everything fell apart. Work was the thing that saved me.'

Toni's phone pinged with a text. She picked it up off the coffee table and saw Liv's name.

32

Liv's head was pounding by the time they'd pulled into her mother's driveway the previous afternoon, and even though it was still early, she'd gone straight to bed.

She'd managed a few hours of fitful sleep, but before daybreak, found herself too restless to lie in bed any longer and went in search of a cup of tea.

'There's something I need to talk to you about,' Sara said, startling Liv as she entered the kitchen. Her mother was still wearing the same clothes as yesterday.

'Have you been to bed?'

Sara shook her head as Liv switched the kettle on. 'I can't stop thinking about Ruby. There's been no news overnight.'

'Tea?' Liv asked.

'No, I've had too much already. Now, like I said, there's something I need to talk to you about. I didn't want to bring it up around Toni yesterday, but you and I need to discuss it.'

'I'm not sure I have the capacity to discuss anything right now,' Liv said, putting a tea bag into a cup.

'Well, you don't have a choice. You've brought all of this on us, and you're going to need to find the capacity.' Her mother took a deep breath. 'How could you turn up here and not tell me the real reason?'

Liv froze. They were no longer talking about Toni or Ruby.

'Liv?'

'Mum, let's not get into this right now,' she said slipping into a chair across from her mother. 'There's more important things to worry about.'

'There's a lot to worry about, including you. I appreciate you trying to protect us, but at some stage, we were going to find out. What, were you going to go back to Sydney and start dialysis without telling us?'

Liv fixed her gaze on the steam rising from her drink, not meeting her mother's eyes.

'You can't deal with this on your own. I spoke with your doctor, and she says a second transplant is quite feasible.'

Liv's head jerked up. 'Hold on, why would you talk to Doctor McCardle?'

'Barb called,' Sara said. 'She couldn't get on to Mandy, so she called me instead. She asked how your appointments had gone and whether there was anything she could do to help.'

Anger surged through Liv. 'She had no right. I told her about my situation in confidence. I'm going to kill her.'

'Don't be silly,' Sara said. 'She was worried. And she assumed you'd told me.'

'You're telling me that you then rang Doctor McCardle, and she provided you with all that confidential information?'

Sara nodded. 'Doctor McCardle was a friend of your father's. You know that. I rang her and said I wanted to thank her for everything she's doing for you, and she then assured me that it would be a positive outcome. She assumed I knew what was going on.'

Liv shook her head. 'I don't believe this. So much for patient confidentiality, and Barb knew I didn't want to worry you with everything you've just been through with Dad.'

Sara rested a hand on Liv's forearm. 'There's nothing more important to me than you, Toni and Mandy. You're my daughters, my proudest achievement, and you've all taught me a love I never knew existed before becoming a mother. Whether we're going through tough times or celebrating good ones, I always want to know what's going on. I feel like I've let you down in that you felt you couldn't tell me. Sure, I'm devastated that your dad's gone, we all are, but that doesn't change my role as your mum. I worry about all three of you all the time and I need you to know I'm here for you. With your kidney, I'll do anything you need.'

As her mother continued speaking, Liv felt a lump forming in her throat. She opened her mouth to respond, but the words caught.

'If you want to move back to Melbourne and live here,' Sara continued, 'that's fine with me. Depending on how things turn out with Toni and Ruby, she might appreciate having you closer too.' She shuddered. 'If Ruby's not found, I don't know if she'll recover.'

'I don't know if any of us will,' Liv said, blinking to stop the tears that threatened. 'But thanks, Mum. I should have told you earlier.' She sighed. 'If I'm honest, I was hoping the whole thing would conveniently go away. None of us need to go through this again.'

'Unfortunately, life doesn't usually allow us to choose,' Sara said, 'but we can choose how we deal with the situation, and as a family, that means dealing with it together. You know your dad would be going crazy that you hadn't told us, don't you?'

Liv smiled at the thought. 'How can I fix it if you don't tell me the problem?' She recited one of her father's sayings. 'Speaking of problems, did you tell Barb about Ruby going missing?'

Sara nodded. 'I assumed she knew. She was horrified. Said to send you her love and for you to let her know if there was anything she could do. She suggested you get in touch with her grandson, Gus.' Sara frowned. 'Not that I can see how he can help.'

Liv sighed. 'He might be able to. It's a good idea, actually.' She glanced at the clock on the microwave. It wasn't seven yet. She should probably give him a little longer. 'I'll finish my tea and then call him.' She didn't wait for Sara's response, but instead made her way to the spare room and closed the door.

She sank down on the bed and picked up her phone from the bedside table. She waited until the clock finally clicked over to seven, took a deep breath and found Gus's number. It clicked straight through to his voicemail, and she left a brief message. She lay back against the pillow. She'd created a huge, ugly mess that she wasn't sure could be fixed. Finding Ruby was obviously the most important thing right now, but once she was found – *if she was found* – how would things work? Would Toni be allowed to keep Ruby? And what about her? She was going to need treatment for her kidney, but what if she went to jail? She could hardly imagine she'd be on top of the priority list for treatment then.

Her phone buzzed as she had this thought. She glanced at the screen. It was Barb. Anger surged through her. As much as she appreciated her mother's words just now about loving her and wanting to support her, Barb had still betrayed her. She knew that Liv was keeping her medical appointments from her family and believed it was a bad idea, but it was not her position to tell them. Liv was tempted to rip through her but instead pressed the decline call button. She was angry at Barb, but she knew deep down that the person she was really angry at was herself. She'd created the situation with Toni and Ruby, and going off at Barb wasn't going to help anyone.

Liv had been tempted to turn her phone off when Barb called for the fifth time in a fifteen-minute period, but she couldn't risk missing a call from Toni with an update on Ruby. She'd sighed and picked it up. 'I'm beyond mad with you. It was my decision to tell my family, not yours.'

'When did you last speak to Mandy?' Panic laced Barb's words as she ignored Liv's outburst.

'What?'

'I said, when did you last speak to Mandy?'

'Yesterday, why?'

'Because she just sent me a bunch of photos of her with Ruby, or Baby as she calls her.'

'What?'

'She said they were from before Ruby was abducted, but I don't think they were. Hold on. I'll forward them to your phone.'

Liv put her phone on speaker and a few seconds later, a text message appeared from Barb. She clicked on the photos and slowly looked through them. Mandy was holding Ruby and beaming in each of them. She continued to flick through. 'Why do you think these are current?'

'I don't think they all are, but the last one might be. Keep going. There's one with Mandy and her friend, Izzy. She told me in her message that one of the girls at Wattle House, Rose I think, is learning how to be a hairdresser and cut Mandy's hair yesterday. She has a new hairstyle in that photo.'

'Shit!' Liv reached the photo Barb was talking about. 'This was definitely taken yesterday. She's wearing the same clothes she had on, but you're right about the hair. It's so much shorter. Izzy was coming to collect her after we dropped her back at Wattle House.' She shook her head. Mandy had been so convincing. 'Izzy must have helped her do this.'

'That would make more sense than the doula stealing her,' Barb said.

'Why would her friend take Ruby?'

'Liv, you know Izzy is more than just Mandy's friend.'

'What do you mean?'

'I mean, she's Sam's sister.'

Liv froze. 'What?'

'How did you not know that? Mandy talked about Izzy all the time and how Izzy arranged for both her and Sam to volunteer at the animal shelter.'

'She never mentioned the bit about her being Sam's sister.'

'She did to me. And she's also said many times that Izzy would do anything for her, just as Sam would. I'd hate to think she'd be as silly as to help Mandy take Ruby, but that photo suggests perhaps she was.'

'Oh my God. I have to call Toni. If Mandy and Izzy have Ruby, at least we can assume she's safe.'

'Call me later and let me know if you find her,' Barb said.

Liv ended the call and, not wanting to explain the situation over the phone, sent Toni a text.

I think I know where Ruby is. Pick you up in twenty minutes.

She grabbed her bag from the table, called for Sara to join her and hurried to the door. A surge of adrenaline was quickly followed by a surge of hope. Right now, she'd do anything to find Ruby alive, including voluntarily walking into the nearest police station and confessing to every stupid thing she'd done.

* * *

'Where is she?' Toni opened the passenger door to Liv's car and, without being asked, Sara got out and slipped into the back seat with Joel. Toni and Joel had rushed down to Toorak Road to wait as soon as they'd received Liv's text. Toni froze as she stared at Liv. It was impossible to miss the grey pallor of her complexion. 'Jesus, you look awful.'

Liv shook her head. 'I'm fine, and if I'm right, you don't need to worry. She's perfectly safe.' Liv manoeuvred the car out from the kerb and back into the traffic, a noticeable tremble in her hands as she turned the steering wheel.

'Jesus, Liv, are you for real? My baby's been taken, and you tell me I don't need to worry. Are you insane? Where is she?' An overwhelming sense of protectiveness settled on Toni's shoulders. She'd do anything at this moment to get Ruby back.

'Okay, let's all settle down,' Joel said from the back seat. 'We need to hear Liv out, and if she's right, we need to call the police.'

'Maybe,' Liv said. 'If I am right, we might want to approach it a different way. Shit...'

Toni stared at her sister, noting the grey tinge of her skin turning green. 'Shit, what? Liv, are you okay? You're scaring me.'

Liv pulled the car to a stop, unclipped her seat belt and pushed open the car door. They were opposite a small park and Toni scrambled to follow Liv as her sister rushed across the grassed area to a small group of trees, bent double and threw up.

'What's happening?' Toni was the first to reach Liv as Joel and Sara hurried after her. 'Are you okay?'

Liv shook her head.

'Is this about you or Ruby?' Sara asked, confusing Toni even further. *About Liv?*

'Ruby.' Liv closed her eyes. When she opened them, she took a deep breath before meeting Toni's gaze. 'Toni, she's with her mother. Ruby is with her mother.'

* * *

Toni took a step backward. 'What? You're her mother.' Realisation settled over Toni. The fear she'd had from the day Liv offered her the baby was unfolding in front of her. Her throat tightened, making it difficult to speak. 'You're saying you've taken her? You've had someone help you take her and now you feel guilty and are going to let us see her?'

Liv didn't respond or meet her eyes.

Toni kicked at the ground. 'I don't believe this. If you wanted Ruby back, why did you deny it all day yesterday and now you're admitting it? You didn't need to go through all this pretence that she'd been abducted. Jesus, Liv, the police are involved. We could have kept this within the family if you'd been honest. Now you'll probably be charged. Where is she?'

Liv lifted her head to meet Toni's eyes. 'As I said, she's with her mother.'

Toni looked to Joel. 'Am I going insane? She keeps saying Ruby's with her. I don't see a baby. Do you?'

Joel's face was ashen, and he was staring at Liv. Had he interpreted her words differently?

'Who is Ruby's mother, Liv?' There was a tremble in Joel's voice.

Toni turned to Liv, bile rising in her throat as the meaning of his words registered.

'Toni,' Liv's voice was gentle. 'I'm not Ruby's biological mother.'

Sara gasped, and her hand flew to her mouth. 'Oh, Liv.'

Toni shook her head in disbelief. 'Don't be ridiculous. You were pregnant. I saw your bump. She was born in your apartment. I know that from all the bloody towels we threw out.'

'Yes, she was born in my apartment, but I didn't give birth to her. My bump was a cushion stuffed under my shirt to make you believe I was pregnant.'

'You lied to us?' Joel's voice had the cold edge to it that he adopted before he exploded.

Liv nodded. 'I wanted to give you a baby, and I knew someone who couldn't raise a baby. It was a win-win.'

'A win-win? For you and me perhaps, but not the mother. How could you? And, if Ruby was born in your apartment, both Mandy and Barb know who the mother is.' Toni shook her head. 'You all lied about this? I can't believe you risked Mandy knowing.'

'She's good with secrets,' Liv said. 'And she's with Ruby now.'

'Mandy is?'

Liv nodded. 'She sent Barb a photo this morning of her and Ruby. She's with her friend, Izzy.'

Toni stared at Liv. 'Izzy?'

Liv nodded again. 'Sam's sister. Remember, Sam was Mandy's friend who died.'

'And Mandy helped Izzy take Ruby?' Toni's mind whirred, trying to connect the pieces. 'So, Izzy is Ruby's mother and Mandy helped her abduct her?'

Liv opened her mouth to respond but Toni spoke over her.

'Oh my God, Liv, if Izzy's the real mother and she's gone to the extreme of snatching her and you've lied on all the paperwork, we'll never get Ruby back.' At the realisation that even if Ruby was found, she could lose her baby, Toni was hit with an intense pain that made it difficult to breathe. She lowered her head into her hands. 'I can't believe you did this.'

'I was trying to do the right thing,' Liv said. 'I owed you for what you did for me. You saved my life.'

Toni raised her head. 'You didn't owe me anything. You would have done the same if the situation was reversed and I'd needed a kidney. Stealing someone's baby wasn't the answer.' She turned in the direction of the car. 'Come on, let's go. We need to check that Ruby's okay. If she's with Mandy then I want to see her, and I need to talk to Izzy. How do we make it up to her, you stealing her baby?'

'Wait.' Liv hurried after her sister. 'Stop for a minute. Let me explain. I didn't steal Ruby.'

Toni hesitated before turning to face Liv. 'You're saying she consented to you taking her baby and me raising it?'

'At the time, *Ruby's mother* did, so yes. But I think she's now changed her mind and decided she wants her.'

'I can't see how we'll be able to stop her if she wants her back,' Toni said. 'There was no paperwork for adoption. Nothing at all that legally gives Joel and me the right to have her.'

'I think we can talk to her and convince her to give her back,' Liv said. 'She can't raise a baby.'

'Why not?'

Liv averted her eyes from Toni's. 'Because it's not Izzy. It's Mandy. Mandy is Ruby's biological mother.'

33

Time stood still as Liv's words registered with Toni. This had to be a joke, but Liv didn't look like she was joking. Toni staggered towards a nearby picnic table and slumped onto a seat. 'No. She can't be. Mandy cannot be Ruby's mother.'

'I'm sorry,' Liv said, sitting across from Toni. 'But she is.'

'No. Please tell us this is a sick joke,' Sara said, putting an arm around Toni. 'I would have known if Mandy was pregnant.'

'I wouldn't play a joke this cruel on any of you.'

Joel remained standing, his arms folded tightly across his chest. 'You had better start talking, Liv, and explain how this happened. Honestly, I think we would all like to kill you right now. All I can say is this had better be good.'

'No,' Toni said, shrugging Sara's arm off her and pulling herself to her feet. 'Not here. We need to get to Mandy and check that Ruby really is safe. Tell us on the way.'

* * *

Liv gripped the edge of the front passenger seat as Joel floored the accelerator and the car lurched into the road. She took a deep breath. She should have known better than putting Toni and Joel, or Mandy, in this position. 'It was the weekend I came down to help after Dad died. You know, when you rang to tell me that Mum was in bed and the place was a pigsty. I'd planned to take Mandy out for a few hours to tell her that I'd be taking her back to Sydney with me to give Mum a break, but when I went into her room to tell her to have a shower and get dressed, ready to go out, I got the shock of my life.'

When Liv had told Mandy she was going to take her to St Kilda for lunch, but she had to shower and dress first, Mandy had rushed to pull off her pyjamas and get into the shower. Even at thirty, she wasn't shy in showing off her body. Liv had found herself staring. She'd noticed when she'd hugged Mandy the previous day that she'd gained weight, but now she was seeing how much. She'd always been a little bit chubby, but this was different. Her breasts were enormous, and her stomach had a small, yet defined, round bump. Liv frowned. Her mother would have said something if... No, she was being ridiculous. But then again, her mother hadn't surfaced for the past three weeks, and if Liv's suspicion was correct, Mandy might have only just started showing.

'Mands, have you got a boyfriend?'

Mandy looked over at Liv, tears filling her eyes as she shook her head. 'Sam died.'

'Sam was a boy?' Her mother had mentioned a friend of Mandy's passing away unexpectedly a few months ago. She'd assumed Sam was short for Samantha.

'My boy. He loved me.'

'He was your boyfriend?'

Mandy nodded.

'And where did you meet Sam?'

'At the animal shelter. We both volunteered and would work together cleaning the kennels.'

And a lot more than that, Liv was beginning to think. 'And did you see Sam outside the animal shelter?'

Mandy shook her head. 'He wasn't allowed to have a girlfriend. His gran said I wasn't good enough for him and he should stick to dinosaurs.'

'Dinosaurs?'

'He loved them almost as much as he loved me.'

'I'm sorry he died,' Liv said. 'Mum told me your friend had passed away, but I didn't know he was someone important to you.'

'Sam was like me,' Mandy said. 'He was special too. Together, we were extra special, but his gran didn't see that.'

Liv took a deep breath. 'Mandy. Did you and Sam love each other enough to do the things boyfriends and girlfriends do?'

Mandy put her hands on her hips and stared at Liv. 'Boyfriends and girlfriends?' She gave a sly smile. 'Sex. Yes, we had loads of sex in the stables at the riding school next door to the animal shelter.' She stopped smiling. 'Don't tell his gran if she's still alive. He lived with her because his mum's dead and he doesn't know who his father is. She'd be angry. He wasn't allowed to have sex until he got married. But he wasn't allowed to marry me, so it made a problem.'

'You know that sex can create a baby, don't you, Mandy?'

The smile returned to Mandy's lips. She nodded, patted her stomach, then turned her back on Liv and walked in the direction of the bathroom.

As the shower turned on, Liv sank down on Mandy's bed, her head spinning. *Mandy's pregnant.* She lay back and closed her eyes. There was no way Mandy would be able to raise a child, and it was unlikely that child services would let her. Her mother might offer to help, but she was grieving and really should be moving on and enjoying her retirement. The baby would most likely be taken from her. She wondered if Mandy realised this. And how was Toni going to take this news? That their little sister, who couldn't raise a child, had fallen pregnant when Toni herself couldn't have the child of her dreams? Toni already resented Mandy, and she imagined this news would push her over the edge.

Liv opened her eyes as a sweet rendition of 'Frère Jacques' drifted from the shower. She'd forgotten what a lovely singing voice Mandy had. Was she practising for the baby? A baby she would give birth to and possibly never see again. Despair was quickly replaced by hope. Liv sat up as an idea formed. The solution was obvious. A smile spread across her face. It was perfect. Mandy would be able to be a part of her baby's life, and Toni's dream would be fulfilled. Her smile slipped as she thought of Toni and her feelings towards Mandy. She'd like to think her sister would rise above those feelings in this circumstance, but she wasn't entirely sure Toni would be able to. It was a good plan, but she would have to work out how to convince her sisters to go along with it.

'Joel!' Toni's screech from the back seat alerted Liv to the fact he'd just accelerated through a red light. 'You don't need to get us all killed. Slow down.'

'Sorry,' he muttered, his eyes focused intently on the road ahead.

'Next left,' Liv said.

He glanced at her, his eyes dark with fury. 'Leave the driving to me and the nav system. It knows where we're going. But how about you explain why it didn't cross your mind to talk to us about your concerns rather than lie?'

'Toni would have said no,' Liv said. 'There's no way she would have taken on a baby knowing it was Mandy's.'

Toni's sharp intake of breath was enough to suggest Liv's words were right.

'But that was our decision to make, not yours,' Joel said. 'You had no right.'

'And how did you convince Mandy to go along with this?' Sara asked. 'She obviously loves Ruby, and I can't imagine giving her up was easy.'

Liv shook her head. 'She knew she wouldn't be able to raise the baby herself, but if Toni and Joel raised her, she'd still be in the baby's life.'

It had been a relief to Liv that Mandy had admitted she'd kept her pregnancy a secret because she knew the baby would be taken from her if anyone knew.

'But surely you could have told Mum,' Liv had said as she'd sat across from Mandy at Charred, a popular burger place on the St Kilda foreshore.

'She would make me give Baby away or maybe even terminate her.'

'And you want to keep the baby?'

Tears had filled Mandy's eyes. 'Yes, but I think Mum would say I'm not ready.'

'Do you think you're ready?' Liv's voice was gentle, and she'd reached across the table and taken Mandy's hand.

'I would need a lot of help. I don't have a job and would need Mum to help me. She's too sad to do that.'

Liv nodded. It was bigger than her mother being sad. She couldn't imagine at sixty that her mother was going to want to raise a child, even if it was her grandchild.

'Can you help me, Liv?'

Liv nodded. 'Right now, I'm not sure what the best way to deal with all of this is. Will you trust me, Mandy?'

Mandy nodded.

'Okay. Then, for now, I want you to keep your secret, okay? Have you told anyone?'

'No, not even Izzy.' Mandy wrapped her arms around her stomach. 'I wanted Baby to be all mine and no one else's. While she's inside me, no one can take her away.' She frowned. 'Can they?'

'No, they can't. Now, I think it would be best if you come back to Sydney with me, and we work out a plan for you and for the baby. That will buy us some time. We don't have to tell Mum or anyone until we've worked out what to do.'

Mandy's eyes lit up. 'I can come and live with you?'

'For a holiday,' Liv clarified. 'I want to think through what the best situation would be for you and for the baby. I love you, Mandy, and I need you to trust that I'll do the best for both of you.' She squeezed her hand. 'I want to be honest with you. It might mean having to give the baby up for adoption or to someone who will look after her and love her. I do need you to understand that.'

A giant tear rolled down Mandy's cheek. 'That's why I didn't tell anyone. If you can think up any way that Baby can stay, I'll love you forever, Liv. Forever.'

* * *

'And this is what you came up with?' Toni said. 'A way to manipulate all of us?'

'I wasn't trying to manipulate any of you,' Liv insisted. 'I wanted to find a way to make it work for everyone. It took me ten weeks after we got back to Sydney to decide it was the right thing to do. It wasn't an easy decision at all. Mandy talked to me about her challenges and her concerns that she wouldn't be able to raise a baby. She also knew that I didn't want to and Mum wouldn't be up to it. The only way to keep Ruby in the family, and in a position where Mandy would get to be part of her life, was to offer her to you and Joel.'

'But you didn't do that,' Joel said. 'You said the baby was yours.'

Liv sighed. 'Because both Mandy and I knew that Toni would say no if she was aware that it was Mandy's baby and not mine.'

'Okay,' Toni practically spat the word. 'You manipulated Mandy, but how did it work with the doula? We already know you forged the birth certificate, but what, did you tell her that Mandy was me?'

Liv nodded. 'I knew Mandy couldn't go to a hospital for this to work, so I looked into a doula.'

Toni shook her head. 'What if something had gone wrong, Liv? I can't believe the risks you took.'

'Neither can I,' Sara said. 'I'm shocked, Olivia, and I know your father would be too. Manipulating Mandy, lying to the doula and then to all of us. I don't think I want to hear any more of this.'

'I do,' Joel said. 'Tell us how you convinced Petal Blossom, or whatever her name was. She would have had to see some identification, or was she that flaky she didn't ask?'

Liv's cheeks flamed with heat at Joel's question. 'I got a fake ID.'

'A fake ID?' Toni gave a yelp of disbelief. 'Surely the doula saw it was a fake?'

'It looked exactly like any other Proof of Age Card,' Liv said. 'She had no reason to question anything I told her, and honestly, showing it to her was a mere formality. She filled in the forms and that was about it. Her focus was on Mandy and the baby and their physical states.'

'But she called Mandy, Toni, throughout the birth?' Sara said. 'How awful for Mandy.'

'She called her Hon,' Liv said. 'I led her to believe that was Mandy's preferred nickname, so it wasn't as awful as you're thinking.' Actually, it was getting more and more awful with every word that came out of her mouth. If anything, she realised she'd be best to stop talking. She glanced at Toni, filled with regret at the pain and confusion etched in every line of her sister's face. She had been sure that she'd done the right thing, but she had a strong suspicion that no one else was going to agree with her.

'I've heard enough,' Toni said. 'I don't know what to say. That you could do something morally and legally reprehensible is beyond my comprehension. And poor Mandy. Ruby is her baby.' Tears rolled down Toni's cheeks as this sunk in. 'You took her baby from her. You allowed us all to think you'd done this wonderful thing while Mandy has been grieving for the loss of her baby. It's unforgivable.'

Liv hung her head. This wasn't playing out how she'd pictured it when she'd come up with the crazy idea. 'I never meant to hurt anyone. I thought this was a way of Mandy still having Ruby in her life.'

Toni shook her head. 'What, by giving her baby to the sister who's always resented her? If I hadn't struggled with motherhood, I probably wouldn't have allowed Mandy near Ruby. You know she went off at me one day. Told me what an awful mother I was and how I didn't deserve to have Ruby. I'm surprised she didn't flatten me. I think I would have if the situation was reversed.'

Liv closed her eyes. At this point, she couldn't see any way this was going to end with her family still talking to her.

34

The car squealed to a stop as Joel slammed the breaks on outside Izzy's house. Three other doors pushed open as Toni, Liv and Sara followed him onto the footpath.

The front door of the house flew open as they ran up the driveway, and a woman in her early thirties, who Toni assumed was Izzy.

'What do you want?'

'You're Izzy, right?' Toni said.

The woman nodded.

'We need to see Mandy,' Toni said.

'She's not here. She went out.'

'By herself?'

Izzy hesitated. 'Yes. I'll tell her to call you when she gets back.'

'No,' Liv said, walking towards Izzy. 'We'll wait. And in the meantime, I'd like a tour of your house.'

Izzy put her hands on her hips and blocked Liv's path to the front door. 'This is my house, and you have no right to be here. Go away, or I'll call the police.'

Liv stopped and stared at her.

'I know what you did, Liv,' Izzy continued. 'Stealing Mandy and Sam's baby. I'll be telling the police.'

Liv hesitated for a split second before an incredulous look spread across her face. 'It was you, wasn't it?'

'Me what?'

'Who blackmailed me and then helped Mandy abduct Ruby.'

'What? I did not. I've never even met Ruby before today.'

Toni had heard enough. 'Where's my baby?' she demanded.

Izzy smirked. 'That's a good one. *You* don't have a baby. You've been looking after stolen property, from what I understand. My brother and my best friend's property. You should be ashamed.'

Toni strode towards her, then pushed Izzy aside when she reached her.

'Hey,' Izzy said, stumbling. 'What do you think you're doing?'

Liv grabbed Izzy's arm as Toni opened the front door. 'Leave her. She needs to know Ruby's safe.'

Izzy tried to shake Liv off her. 'She's not here.'

Toni ignored Izzy, hurrying from room to room. A flicker of hope sparked as she saw an empty baby's bottle in the kitchen sink. She entered the main bedroom and found clothes strewn all over the floor. She shut it and moved along the narrow passageway to the next room. It was filled with boxes. She passed a small bathroom and stopped at an open bedroom door. The room was painted bright pink. Soft toys formed a border around the room and in the middle was a cot with a pink blanket draped across it and a mobile with small animals hanging above it. A single mattress was on the floor next to it with Mandy's doll, Baby, tucked in next to a teddy bear.

A tear ran down Toni's cheek. They'd found her. Mandy had taken her, which meant Ruby was safe. Her legs wobbled, and she sank to her knees as footsteps reached her.

'Babe?' Joel kneeled next to her as she used her hands to gesticulate around the room. 'Thank God.' He let out a deep breath.

Toni hoisted herself up on Joel's arm. 'We need to tell Liv and make sure Izzy doesn't contact Mandy. We don't want her disappearing on us.'

They hurried back to the front door where Liv was talking to Izzy.

'I didn't know Sam had a sister,' Liv was saying. 'I'm sorry, Izzy, I really am. But stealing Ruby wasn't the answer.'

Izzy snorted. 'You stole her first, from Mandy.'

'Mandy agreed to my solution,' Liv said. 'I didn't steal her.'

'Mandy has intellectual difficulties,' Izzy said. 'She isn't in a position to make a decision like that.'

'And neither are you,' Liv said. 'Let's go inside. I don't want Mandy to see us and get scared off.'

'She definitely has Ruby?' Toni asked.

Liv nodded before ushering them through the front door.

* * *

'There's a matter of fifteen thousand dollars to discuss,' Liv said as they followed Izzy inside. 'I can't believe you thought it was okay to blackmail me.'

Izzy's eyes shot daggers at Liv. 'I can't believe you thought it was okay to steal your sister's baby and pass it off as your own. And the money wasn't for me. It was for Mandy, to make sure she had money to care for Ruby. I was going to help her too, but I knew long term I wouldn't be able to afford it.'

Liv wasn't sure if she could take another layer of guilt to add on to the many that were accumulating. Izzy had blackmailed her and then helped abduct a baby, yet it was Liv that was the bad person, not Izzy.

'Why didn't you just get in touch and tell me that you were Sam's sister?' Liv asked. 'It could have saved a lot of trouble.'

'Mandy didn't tell me that Ruby was hers until recently,' Izzy said. 'I was away when your dad died, and then you took her to Sydney. I saw her on FaceTime when she was in Sydney and thought she was getting fat. She told me that she was eating a lot of cakes with her friend, Barb, and that you were pregnant. She went along with all the lies and secrets you made her agree to.'

'I didn't...'

'You did,' Izzy said, cutting her off. 'It wasn't your place to decide who Mandy's baby went to. And it wasn't your place to manipulate her into giving her to someone she hates.'

'She doesn't hate Toni.'

Izzy rolled her eyes as Toni walked back into the room and sat beside Joel.

'If you're talking about Mandy,' Toni said, 'I've given her a million reasons to hate me.'

'See,' Izzy said, 'even she agrees.'

'Okay,' Liv said, ignoring the comments about Toni. She wanted to find out more about what had happened. 'So, you decided to blackmail me, and then I assume you took Ruby?'

Izzy shrugged.

'I can't imagine it was Mandy's plan to abduct Ruby?'

Izzy didn't respond.

'After telling me what an awful person I am, you've manipulated her into being involved in something you wanted. Plus, you're basically a criminal. Blackmail is against the law, you know.'

Izzy snorted with a derisive laugh. 'Fine, we'll call the police, and they can sort it all out for us.'

Liv swallowed. While she couldn't imagine this ending in her favour, if there was any way around telling the police the full story, she'd like to find it.

'I haven't touched the money,' Izzy said, her face softening a little. 'The whole point was to get it for Mandy, for Ruby. If Mandy keeps Ruby, I'd like it to go to her, but I'll return it to you, and you can make that decision.'

'But you must have known that we'd find Ruby at some stage. There's no way Mandy could keep a secret this big, even if Ruby was living with you.'

Izzy's cheeks reddened, and Liv had the feeling she hadn't thought through this plan. 'She could have kept her for a few weeks,' Izzy said. 'Long enough to experience being Ruby's mother, and long enough to make you lot,' she looked from Liv to Toni and Sara, 'realise that you've done something awful to her.'

Liv stared at the woman across from her. 'You've made your point. Can I ask why you asked for the first lot of money to be deposited in Sydney and not Melbourne?'

'Mandy told me about Sydney being wonderful and that I had to go one day. I used it as the perfect excuse to make a trip. I spent one night looking around the harbour, collected the money and left the next day. I didn't imagine you'd connect me with it if the drop-off was in Sydney.'

As Liv hadn't been aware there was a connection between Izzy and Sam, it was unlikely she would have made a connection if the money had been dropped in Melbourne.

'You can't take Ruby from her again,' Izzy added. 'It's not your decision. My family have rights too.'

Liv nodded slowly. 'They do. Are you from a big family?'

Izzy shook her head. 'No, it's only me since Gran died. But I know she and Sam would want Ruby to know about them and our family. You can't decide we don't exist.'

'I never decided that,' Liv said. 'I've only ever known of you as Mandy's friend. She mentioned that you, Sam and she worked together at the animal shelter, but she never mentioned that you were Sam's sister.'

'And if she had when she was pregnant? What would you have done then?'

Liv sighed, exhaustion suddenly settling on her shoulders. 'I have no idea. All I can say is I hope I would have made different choices.'

'Which you should be doing now,' Joel said, getting to his feet. 'Sitting around here chatting isn't bringing Ruby back.' He turned to face Izzy. 'Where are they?'

Izzy folded her arms across her chest. 'Guess you'll need to work that out for yourself.'

35

'Look, my little love,' Mandy said as she pushed the pram under a large oak tree, 'the wind's blowing the leaves, and they're waving at you.'

Ruby gurgled from her vantage point in the pram. She was lying on her back, her arms and legs stretched upwards as if trying to reach the leaves.

Mandy sighed as she looked at the little girl. 'Baby will be jealous that I took you and not her. And I think she's upset that you kept her awake last night.' Mandy yawned. 'I don't know how Toni does this. One night without sleep was bad, but two was impossible. If only your daddy was here, then we could share the work.' She continued to push the pram as her mind shifted to Sam. She smiled, remembering his big, blue eyes and happy smile. He was easy to be around, and he loved her so much. He told her every day that he loved her and would marry her. And he would have, too, if his brain hadn't exploded.

'Poor Baby,' Mandy said. 'No daddy and a mummy like me. But I'm a better mummy than Toni. She doesn't want you, and I do. It'll be hard, but with Izzy's help, we'll get through.' She pushed away an image of her own mother and the one of Liv that entered her mind. What would they say if they knew she had Baby? Would they let her keep the little girl? No, they wouldn't. She already knew that. It wasn't fair. She smiled at Baby. 'No bad thoughts today. It's Mummy and Baby time, and we should enjoy our outing. We'll go back and see Aunty Izzy soon.'

She continued to push the pram, watching Ruby's reactions as they walked under more trees. The baby cooed and gurgled, and Mandy knew without a doubt that she was talking to the trees. She was a clever baby, thank goodness. She wasn't like Mandy. She was smart and beautiful, and no one would ever call her stupid.

* * *

'Okay, calm down,' Sara said. 'My guess is Mandy has taken Ruby for a walk. Is that right?' She looked at Izzy.

Izzy hesitated, then nodded. 'I got an old pram from the op shop that she's using.'

'I'm going to go and find her,' Joel said, heading towards the door.

'No, wait,' Sara said, causing Joel to stop. 'Let Mandy enjoy this time she has with Ruby. The plans she's made, and the dreams she has, are going to be destroyed the moment she walks back in here. We'll need to be kind when she returns.' Sara gave both Toni and Joel warning looks. 'As shocking as it is finding out that she's Ruby's mother, to go to this extreme shows us how she really feels about the arrangement that was made for Ruby.'

Liv's cheeks reddened at the comment, and as Joel came back to sit beside her, Toni experienced a pang of pity for her sister. Part of her loved Liv for what she'd done, but another part wanted to slap her. She'd put Mandy through this, and who knew where it would end. Didn't she realise that they couldn't deal with more disappointment? Who would end up with custody of Ruby? Possibly none of them if the authorities found out the type of family they were.

The front door opened.

'Run, Mandy,' Izzy screamed before anyone could stop her. 'They're going to take Ruby.'

Toni was on her feet a split second after Joel, and they reached the front door before Mandy had a chance to turn the pram around. Her face fell as she saw Toni.

'Oh, Mandy,' Toni said. 'I'm sorry.' She looked down into the pram. Ruby was fast asleep, a smile fluttering on her lips. Toni's breath was taken from her. She looked up at Mandy, fresh tears in her eyes. 'You've done such a good job. You're such a good mum to Ruby. Her real mum.'

Mandy looked from Toni to Liv, who nodded. 'She knows. They all do.'

Toni stepped towards Mandy, her arms open. 'I want you to know how sorry I am. If I'd known Ruby was your baby, I would have done things differently. I don't know how I'll ever make it up to you, but I want you to know how sorry I am.'

Mandy pushed away Toni's arms, her eyes darting from Toni to Joel and then to Liv and Sara, who stood behind them. 'Am I in trouble?'

'No,' Joel said. 'Definitely not. Come inside, and we'll all talk. We need to work out what's best for everyone.'

'It's best that Baby stays with me,' Mandy said. 'She's my baby, not yours.' She looked at Toni. 'And you're a bad mother and don't deserve her.'

A crippling pain ripped through Toni's chest.

'You okay?' Joel asked, steadying her as her legs shook.

She nodded, not wanting to admit how true Mandy's words were.

* * *

Toni was grateful that her mother took charge once they were all seated in the family room.

'We're a family,' she said. 'And Ruby is part of that family, and through Ruby, Izzy is too.' She smiled at Izzy as she spoke. 'And we need to band together and work out what is best for Ruby and for Mandy.'

'We need to call the police,' Izzy said. 'You might be her family, but from everything I've seen, you're a bunch of criminals. Lying, stealing, cheating.' Her eyes bored into Sara's. 'Please don't tell me you're proud of these people you call *family*.'

Sara cleared her throat. 'I happen to be proud of all of my daughters.'

'Even Liv?' Mandy asked.

'Even Liv,' Sara confirmed. 'I think we can all agree that Liv's intentions were good, but her execution wasn't the smartest. She was trying to protect Mandy's baby and ensure she stayed within the family, and she wanted to give Toni her dream of becoming a mother. On paper, it seems like a sensible idea. In reality, it wasn't.' She looked at Liv. 'You didn't take into account people's emotions or whether they'd cope. And I mean that both as far as Toni coping with motherhood and Mandy being able to cope with seeing her baby raised by someone else. As much as we all want Ruby to stay within the family, it might have been kinder to Mandy to allow an adoption to take place where she didn't have to watch Ruby grow up.'

A collective gasp was raised around the room. 'You can't be serious,' Liv said. 'If Mandy had come to you and said she was pregnant, you honestly would have suggested she give the baby up?'

'I don't know,' Sara said. 'I wasn't given the option to have any input in the decision.'

Liv shook her head. 'Look at how you reacted when I said I was going to give what you thought was my baby to Toni. You were hellbent on my keeping her. That the scars from being adopted had affected you so much that you wouldn't wish that on anyone.'

'And what?' Toni added. 'You would have stopped Joel and me from living our dream?'

'From what I gather, your dream has been a nightmare,' Sara said. 'Or did I get that wrong?'

Toni reluctantly shook her head. 'I've realised how lucky I've been and what an amazing opportunity Liv and Mandy gave me.' She turned to Mandy. 'Losing Ruby made me realise how much she means to me and how much I've taken for granted. I'm sorry, Mandy. If I'm given a second chance, I'll make it up to Ruby and to you.'

Joel's phone rang, interrupting Toni's speech. He glanced at the screen. 'It's Grady.'

'Don't answer it,' Toni said. 'We need to work out what to do.' She looked at Izzy. 'We need to get some legal advice. Ruby's your family too, but for now, would you allow us to look into what is best for everyone? In particular, Mandy and Ruby?'

Izzy looked at Mandy, then nodded. 'It's all I ever wanted for Mandy. For it to be fair. For people to know she's Ruby's mummy and that Sam was her dad.'

'Okay,' Joel said, 'as much as we need to have this discussion, I need to call Grady back, and we need to let the police know we've found Ruby.'

'Let me ring Gus first,' Liv said. 'He's my lawyer,' she added for Izzy's benefit. 'He'll know what to do.'

* * *

Ten minutes after moving into another room to make the call, Liv took a deep breath and returned to the family room. All eyes turned to her except Mandy's. She was cuddling Ruby, her eyes shut.

'What did he say?' Joel asked.

Liv sat down next to Mandy and put a hand on her sister's knee. 'I'd like you to listen, Mandy. What Gus suggested affects you, and I'd like to know what you think.'

Mandy opened her eyes, tears glistening. 'You're going to take Baby, aren't you?'

Liv shook her head. 'No, I'm going to tell you what Gus suggested and then we'll discuss our options.' She looked around at the group. 'See what everyone thinks. Can I ask you something first?'

Mandy nodded.

'You had Ruby with you for two nights and three days. Was it wonderful?'

Mandy nodded slowly. 'Most of it. Except for the parts when Baby wouldn't sleep, and I couldn't sleep either. It made me tired.'

'Do you think that, if you were Ruby's mum, you might need some help?'

Mandy nodded again. 'I wish Sam was alive. We could get married and be a family. He'd help me with Baby.'

'But sadly, he's not alive,' Liv said. 'Do you think without his help you'll be able to look after Ruby? She'll need to be driven places, go to school when she gets older and be given lots of advice.'

Tears rolled down Mandy's cheeks. She shook her head. 'I love Baby, but I think I can only look after her a few days a week. I'd be too tired to do it every day, and I can't drive her places.'

Toni moved over and sat on Mandy's other side. 'Mandy, I know I haven't done a good job with Ruby, but if you give me a second chance, I promise I'll be the best mummy to her.'

'I'm her best mummy.'

'You are,' Toni agreed, 'but I'd like to show you that I could be almost as good as you.'

'Will you quit your job?'

'No, but I'll only work part time. Two or three days a week.'

'Will you let me see Ruby?'

'Of course. In fact, on the days I work, you might want to come over and look after her. You could do it with Rebecca or on your own if you think you can handle it?'

Mandy hesitated. 'I like Rebecca. Maybe she could be there too, and we can see how it goes.'

'You should text her,' Joel said to Toni. 'Let her know Ruby is safe.'

'Hold on,' Izzy said, looking from Liv to Toni as Toni took her phone from her pocket. 'I have as much right to Ruby as either of you. I'm her aunt too and I should have a say in this.'

'You should,' Sara agreed. 'Regardless of what is decided for Ruby, you are Sam's sister and should have a say in her upbringing. What would you like, Izzy?'

Liv realised she was holding her breath waiting for the other woman to answer. She was Ruby's biological aunt and Sam's sister, and she was in a position to cause a lot of trouble for Liv if she chose to.

Izzy looked at Mandy. 'Sam would want me to look out for Mandy. He loved her so much and would want to make sure that she had what she wanted and what was fair. Mandy made him feel special and loved and it was the first time he'd ever had someone outside of the family show him such kindness. I would like to be part of Ruby's life, but my main aim in all of this is to support Mandy in whatever she wants for Ruby.'

'Sam did love me,' Mandy said, tears glistening in her eyes. 'I want Toni and Joel to raise Ruby, but Izzy, I want you to visit when I'm looking after Ruby and we'll tell her all about Sam and do things with her Sam would have wanted us to do.'

Izzy nodded, and the tension in the room lessened.

'What did Gus say?' Joel asked again. 'I imagine we need to contact the police as soon as possible.'

'We do,' Liv said. 'Are there security cameras in your building?'

Joel looked to Toni before he answered. 'In the foyer and lift. I'm not sure about the corridor that leads to our apartment.'

'Is there a stairwell or some other way someone could get to your floor where they wouldn't be caught on camera? A fire exit, maybe?'

'The fire exit?' Toni said. 'What are you suggesting?'

'Gus recommended we tell the police that Ruby was returned, and we have no idea who took her. If there aren't any cameras, then it could be that she was returned to your apartment. If that's too risky, then we say she was left on Mum's doorstep, which suggests whoever took Ruby knows where Mum lives.'

'Izzy took Ruby,' Mandy said. 'She was kind and offered to help me. She won't get in trouble if we tell the police that Ruby is my baby, and she was returning her.'

Toni looked at Liv in alarm. 'The thing is,' Liv said, her voice calm, 'for now, Gus suggested it's better the police don't know that Ruby's yours. He's going to investigate the legal repercussions of what I've done and see if he can sort it out for us. The police know I changed the birth certificate, but that's all they know. They don't need to know that I'm not Ruby's mother until Gus has worked out how we manage things. Does that make sense, Mandy?'

Mandy nodded. 'We say Baby was returned, and we don't know who had her and pretend Liv made a mistake on the birth certificate.'

Joel stood. 'I'm going to ring the police now.'

'No,' Liv said. 'If we're going to say that Ruby was returned to Mum's, which is probably the easiest solution, then let's go there now in case the police want to meet. It doesn't make any sense that we're here.'

'Toni,' Mandy said, 'could you get Baby's blanket from my room?'

Toni nodded and stood.

'Are you going to keep calling her Baby?' Izzy asked. 'Because... well, I have to say, I like Ruby and think it suits her better.'

Mandy stared at her for a long moment before slowly nodding. 'Okay.

I'll call my doll Baby still, though. Ruby,' she said, gazing at the baby. 'I guess it's an okay name. Can you hold her, Izzy? My arms are a bit sore.'

'It was my mum's name,' Izzy said, taking Ruby from Mandy.

'Sam's mum?' Mandy asked.

Izzy nodded.

Mandy smiled. 'I never knew that. Okay, I like Ruby's name better now. It's connected to Sam.'

'We should all go to Sara's,' Joel said. 'The police need to be contacted.'

'And what about you, Mands?' Liv asked. 'Will you stay here with Izzy or go back to Wattle House?'

'Or come and stay with us,' Toni said, returning to the room with a pink blanket and Mandy's doll. 'For a few days while we all get settled?'

Mandy took her doll from Toni, staring at her sister as she did. 'You'd let me stay with *you*?'

Toni nodded. 'We have a lot of making up to do, Mandy. We owe you a lot. You're wonderful with Ruby, and if you'd like to be more involved, then I would love that.'

A tear rolled down Mandy's cheek. She moved closer to Toni and threw an arm around her, as her doll remained securely under the other. 'I love you, Toni.' She hugged her for a long moment before pulling away. She looked from Toni to Ruby and back again. 'Can I come over tomorrow, though? I'm tired. I was up all night with Ruby and need a night of better sleep.'

Liv wondered if anyone else noticed Toni's shoulders sag with relief. Mandy admitting she was struggling was a good thing for Toni and Joel. It would be unlikely a court would allow Mandy to raise a child, but it seemed that might not be relevant.

'Definitely,' Toni said. 'It will be nice for Joel and me to have Ruby to ourselves this afternoon.'

'And I'll look after Baby,' Mandy said, clinging to her doll. She lowered her voice. 'She's a bit easier to manage. But if you need help today, I'm sure Liv will help you.'

Toni shook her head, her body tensing at the suggestion. 'No, Liv's done enough damage. She's not someone I want anywhere near Ruby.' She turned and looked directly at Liv. 'I mean it. What you've done is unforgivable. Regardless of how all of this turns out, I want you to know that I'll never forgive you.'

Liv swallowed a suffocating lump that had formed in her throat. The look on Toni's face was pure hatred, and she didn't blame her.

* * *

Joel pushed his hand through his hair as he paced in front of the floor-to-ceiling windows that overlooked Toorak Road.

'I've said I'm sorry,' Toni repeated. 'Ruby's home and the truth about everything's been revealed. I don't know what else to say.' Exhaustion overwhelmed Toni. They'd been home for four hours since Ruby had been found, and the police had been contacted. It had taken some time to explain the situation to the police, that Ruby had been returned anonymously, but for now, they'd allowed everyone to go home. Liv was seeking further advice from her lawyer friend as to what she needed to disclose to ensure Mandy and Izzy were protected and not charged for abducting Ruby.

Joel stopped pacing and glared at her. 'How am I supposed to trust you again? It's like you've been cheating on me the entire time I've been in Dubai.'

Toni took a deep breath. 'It's hardly the same as cheating.'

'You deliberately set out to deceive me. Hiring a full-time nanny. Pretending to be at home all day when I FaceTimed you but then clearly dashing straight back to work afterwards. Tell me how that isn't cheating me into thinking one thing when in fact, you're doing another?'

'There was no one else involved, which is what I'm getting at. I didn't cheat on you in the sense of having a relationship with someone else. I'm not sure what else I can say. I was in an awful place with Ruby, and I needed to have something of my own back. I did try to tell you, but you didn't listen, and there was no one else I could tell that I wasn't coping or enjoying motherhood. I would have sounded like a monster.'

'Instead, you acted like one.'

Toni bit down on her lip, holding back the response she wanted to fire back at him. Calling him a selfish prick wasn't going to help the situation. 'No, I did what I thought was best for Ruby and for me.'

'How do you figure that?'

Anger bubbled inside Toni. Yes, she'd done the wrong thing, but couldn't he see that there was a reason for it? That her unhappiness had driven her to extreme lengths? 'Ruby needed love and attention, and I was no good at giving it to her. I hired someone who was. I was doing a terrible job, Joel, and was worried I'd damage her permanently if I was her only caregiver. Yes, the job was partly for my sanity, but employing Rebecca was to give Ruby the best start I could.'

Joel snorted, causing Toni's anger to escalate.

'How dare you? Yes, I stuffed up, I know that. But you took off for twelve weeks when our baby was only a few weeks old. That's hardly supportive, and I didn't see you saying no to that opportunity to be here to help give Ruby the best start.'

Joel opened his mouth, then closed it again. He sighed and flopped down on the couch. 'You're right. I should have been here.' Toni waited for him to say something but instead was horrified when tears ran down his cheeks. 'It was a completely selfish move on my behalf, and I'm sorry. The timing wasn't right, and I should have said no. If I had said no, none of this would have happened. I should have been at home to share the load.'

Toni's eyes widened. He was apologising? She hadn't expected that.

'We've both messed this up, haven't we?'

Toni nodded. 'We have. But the main thing is Ruby is happy and healthy. She loves Mandy, and her abduction was hardly a traumatic experience.'

'Not for her,' Joel said. 'But for us, that's a different matter.' He wiped his tear-stained cheeks. 'What do we do now? Do you even want to be a mother?'

Toni nodded. 'More than ever. I want another chance to show Ruby how much I love her. I still want to work but find a better balance to make sure I'm doing both things to my best ability. I also think that we need to invite Mandy to be a bigger part of Ruby's life.'

Joel pushed his hand through his hair. 'She might want full custody.'

'I don't think she does,' Toni said. 'We can talk to her about it. But she might like to be involved in raising Ruby. I think she should be asked, at least. I'm not sure how it would work, but I'm beginning to understand why in other cultures, the entire village raises the child. It's hard work at times but joyful at others, and both of those times should be shared.'

Joel moved next to Toni on the couch and took her hand. 'As should our fears, frustrations, and thoughts on raising her. I want you to promise me you'll talk to me if you're struggling. I don't expect you to know what you're doing or to love every minute of it. But I do expect you to communicate with me. To not get us back into this situation again. If we need help, we ask for it. Okay?'

Tears filled Toni's eyes. Earlier that day, she thought she'd lost Ruby and her marriage. It was hard to believe that she was being given a second chance on both fronts.

36

Six weeks after Ruby was found, Toni found herself smiling as she slipped the key into the front door of the apartment. Her last meeting of the day had been cancelled, and she'd seized the opportunity to leave work early and hurry home. Prior to Ruby's abduction, she would have been looking for any excuse to stay at work later rather than be at home with her, and now she found herself not only being excited to come home but missing her baby during the day.

Her smile grew wide, and she heard a barrage of giggles coming from the bathroom amongst the splashing of water. She wasn't sure who was laughing the most.

'Hello,' she called out. 'How are my giggling girls?'

One laugh grew louder, and the splashing continued.

Toni dropped her bag by the front door, smiling at the feature wall of photos that greeted her. A week earlier, a parcel had arrived from Liv containing three beautiful frames with photos from when Ruby was born. At first, Toni wasn't interested in anything from Liv, but the more she looked at them, the more she knew they deserved to be displayed. It didn't change her anger towards Liv or her refusal to speak to her, but the photos were too lovely to hide away in a box. Although, if she was honest, she had begun to realise that a lot of her anger was really at herself and her own actions.

She pushed that thought away as she studied the photos. One was of Ruby with Toni and Joel when they first met her, the second was of Ruby minutes after her birth and the third was of Mandy and Ruby. A candid photo Liv had taken of the two of them on the couch the morning after she'd been born. Her eyes rested on the photo of Mandy and Ruby, once again admiring Liv's ability to capture the magic of the moment. Mandy's love for Ruby came across so strongly that it had taken Toni's breath away. To think she and Joel had walked in later that day and taken the baby from her. She shuddered now as she thought about how devastated Mandy must have been.

A squeal from the bathroom broke into her thoughts, and she hurried down the hallway.

'Hey, Mands,' she said as she entered the bathroom and smiled at her sister. 'How was your day?'

'Wonderful,' Mandy said. Toni couldn't help but notice the dark circles under her eyes.

'Are you sure? You look tired.'

Mandy returned her attention to splashing bubbles on Ruby. 'I dreamt about Sam last night, and when I woke up, it made me sad, and I couldn't get back to sleep.'

'Oh, I'm sorry. You must miss him terribly.'

Mandy nodded. She pointed to Ruby's nose. 'That's Sam's nose. Every day, Ruby looks more like him.'

'I can see it too,' Toni said. 'From the photos of Sam that you showed me, and the ones Izzy brought around last week when she came for dinner, of him as a baby. She looks like her daddy.'

'Do you mind?' Mandy asked. 'That she looks like someone you never met? And not like you or Joel.'

'I see a lot of you in her, too,' Toni said. 'Which means she does look like someone I've met. She has your sparkling eyes and your hair, and I think she has your cheekbones too, although Joel says he thinks she looks like him.' She laughed. 'I think he's joking.'

Mandy smiled. 'He is.'

'And there's nothing else bothering you?' Toni asked.

Mandy frowned. 'No, like what?'

'I guess I wanted to check you're happy with what was decided for Ruby, that's all.'

'That you and Joel are her mummy and daddy, but I'm still her biological mummy and get to help with her during the week?'

Toni nodded.

A week after Ruby had been found, Liv's lawyer friend, Gus, had contacted births, deaths, and marriages on behalf of the family and explained that there had been a mistake made on the birth certificate. It had been a fairly simple process to correct the original certificate, and Gus had made contact with Petal Blossom to arrange a statutory declaration from her that it was Mandy who had given birth. The documents were completed, and within three weeks, a new birth certificate arrived with the parents listed as Mandy Montgomery and Samuel Taylor.

Gus had also recommended that the family contact The Department of Families, Fairness and Housing and have an independent advisor talk to Mandy about her rights, and if she wanted to raise Ruby, then an assessment of her capabilities could be undertaken.

Sara had arranged for this meeting and taken Mandy with her. Gus had suggested that Toni and Joel stay in the background and allow Mandy's voice to be heard first before they got involved.

A week after Mandy's first meeting with the caseworker assigned to her, Toni and Joel were called into a meeting.

Toni had been a nervous wreck leading up to the appointment. Mandy and their mother had been waiting outside the building where the department's offices were located, and dread had settled over Toni with Mandy's first words.

'I'm sorry, Toni...'

She was going to keep Ruby was all that Toni could think of with those words. She broke out in a sweat at the thought of losing her little girl. Joel took her hand and squeezed it. She couldn't meet his eyes, knowing how much pain would be in them. She'd done her best to force a smile. Ruby was Mandy's baby, and as much as it was going to hurt, she had every right to her.

'...for calling you a bad mummy that day,' Mandy continued.

'What?' Toni looked from Mandy to her mother. What was she talking about?

'That I called you a bad mummy when you had your headphones on. I would never do that, but I understand now. Babies are hard.' She sighed. 'Very hard. I don't know how you work, too. I've only been helping Rebecca during the day with Ruby, and I'm exhausted, but I get to go home. You and Joel are with her all the time. I just wanted you to know that I'm sorry.'

Tears filled Toni's eyes at the sincerity of Mandy's apology. Babies were hard, and mothering was a challenge. One that Toni was grateful to be a part of with Ruby, even if it was only temporary. 'Thank you, Mandy. That means a lot to me. And whatever's decided now, know that Joel and I will be there to help you. If you are going to be a full-time mum to Ruby, then we'll be the best aunty and uncle we can be.'

It was an hour later that the family walked back out of the building, Ruby's future determined.

'Mandy has been very clear with what she would like for her daughter,' the case worker had said when introductions had been made and they were seated around a meeting table. 'She would like the legal guardianship of Ruby to be placed with you and Joel,' she'd said to Toni, 'which is most likely what the department would also be recommending if a formal assessment had been required.'

'But I'll still be Ruby's mummy?' Mandy asked.

'You will always be her biological mother,' the case worker said.

Mandy turned to Toni. 'And I can still help when you're at work?'

'Of course you can. I need you, Mandy, and so does Ruby. We won't be the most conventional family, but we'll be the best family possible for Ruby.'

The case worker had gone on to talk to them about the legalities around the decision and the process that would need to be undertaken for an official adoption to take place.

Now, as Toni waited for a reply as to whether something else was troubling Mandy, she briefly wondered what they'd do if Mandy had changed her mind. 'Mands?'

Mandy turned her attention to Ruby, who she was supporting in the bath water, and looked up at Toni. 'Do you think she'll be sad when she's bigger?'

'What do you mean?'

'That I'm one of her mummies? I have challenges, and I'm not smart. She might not like that.'

'Oh, Mands, she'll love you to bits. Those things aren't important. What's important is that she feels your love and kindness and knows you'd protect her no matter what. She loves you, and that will never change.'

'But kids can be mean. They were mean to me when I was growing up and might be mean to her when they know I'm one of her mummies.'

'Let's not worry about any of that now,' Toni said. 'It's still years until it's relevant, and for now, let's both enjoy being her mums.' Toni and Joel had decided the best way to include Mandy was to involve her for exactly who she was. Ruby's birth mum. Mandy had been ecstatic when they'd suggested it.

'She'd have two mummies?' Mandy asked.

Toni nodded. 'We're both raising her, so I think that's fair if you do. Joel will be her daddy, and when she gets older, we'll tell her about Sam, show her photos and tell her how special he was. She'll know that a lot of people love her.'

Mandy had smiled then, and she did again now. 'I'm happy, Toni.'

'Well, if how you feel ever changes, you talk to me, okay? Joel and I want to make sure you're always happy with the situation.'

The apartment's intercom rang, interrupting their conversation.

'I'll just see who that is,' Toni said. 'There are some nice fluffy towels in the cupboard under the sink if you want to wrap Ruby in one when you're finished.'

She left Mandy with Ruby and went to check the intercom. The video screen showed her mother standing outside the apartment block. It was unusual for Sara to turn up without messaging first. Although, with Rebecca having left early, it was possible she'd come over to keep Mandy company and help her look after Ruby.

Toni held the front door open, waiting as the lift opened and her mother stepped out. She couldn't help but be alarmed by the tight-lipped expression she wore. As Sara drew closer, her pale face and bloodshot eyes suggested several sleepless nights. Toni had thought her mother was doing so much better the past month in dealing with the grief of losing her husband, but maybe something had caused her to spiral down again.

'Mum? Are you okay?'

Sara stopped in front of Toni and shook her head.

'What is it?' Toni asked.

'Can I come in? We need to talk.'

'Of course,' Toni said, ushering her mother in. 'Mandy's in the bathroom with Ruby. Did you want to pop your head in and say hello?'

Sara hesitated. 'Mandy's here?'

Toni nodded. 'I assumed that was why you were stopping by.'

'No, it's not, and I don't want her to overhear what I need to talk to you about.'

Toni stared at her mother. Whatever was going on wasn't going to be good. 'You're scaring me.'

'Sorry,' Sara said. 'Let's go out onto your balcony.'

Toni led her mother out onto the small outdoor balcony before shutting the door firmly behind her. 'What is it?'

Sara crossed her arms across her chest, hugging them to herself. 'It's Liv.'

Toni shook her head and turned to walk back inside. 'Not interested.'

'Toni!' Her mother's voice was sharp. 'You need to listen to me for a minute, and then if you're still not interested, I'll leave.'

Toni turned back to face Sara. 'Fine, what?'

Sara took a deep breath. 'She's in the hospital. They're operating tomorrow. The kidney failed.'

Shock triggered a sudden expulsion of air from Toni's lungs. 'What? When did that happen?'

'Around the time Ruby was taken. She made me swear I wouldn't tell you, that she's put you through enough recently, but I decided there are some promises I can't keep, and this is one of them. Dialysis has been keeping her going more recently, but a kidney has been offered, and the transplant's happening tomorrow.' She avoided Toni's eyes. 'I'm sure it will all be fine, but if something happened, I don't want you to regret that you cut her out of your life.'

'Tomorrow? Where?'

'Here in Melbourne, at the Alfred. Some of the same team who did the last one.'

Toni nodded, trying to get her head around what her mother was saying. Her anger towards Liv evaporated and was replaced with an overwhelming feeling of sadness. What if something went wrong? 'Can you stay with Mandy? I need to go and see her.'

Relief flickered in Sara's eyes. 'Of course. I'll make us all some dinner for when you get back.'

'What about Mandy? Shouldn't we tell her? Give her a chance to speak to Liv?'

Sara shook her head. 'Liv called her today. She knows how much Mandy would worry if she knew about the operation, so she doesn't want to put her through that. She told her how much she loves her and said a few other things to make sure Mandy knows how important she is. She gave me a message for you if something does go wrong, but I'd much rather you speak to her directly.'

Toni's heart ached at the thought that Liv had gone through dialysis and now was about to have another transplant. It was unthinkable that she hadn't been there for her.

'Thanks for telling me,' she said. 'I'll go straight to the hospital.' She hurried back inside and collected her bag, before ducking her head into the bathroom. Mandy had Ruby snuggled in a white fluffy towel and was cuddling her. 'Mands, I have to go out for a couple of hours. Mum's here, and she'll make us all some dinner if you want to stay a bit later tonight. I can drop you home, or she will when I get back.'

Mandy nodded. 'I'd like to stay for dinner. Thank you.'

Toni leaned forward and kissed Mandy on the forehead and did the same to Ruby. She did her best to ignore the startled look on Mandy's face. They'd grown a lot closer the last few weeks, but a display of affection like that from Toni was still unusual. 'Back soon,' was all she said as she hurried from the apartment.

37

Liv lay back against the hard pillows of the hospital bed. The operation was scheduled for the next morning, but several tests and preparations had to be done beforehand, and she'd been admitted that afternoon.

'How are you holding up?' Barb asked.

Liv shrugged. 'I'm okay. I appreciate you coming with me, by the way. Mum needs someone with her. Last time she had Dad, but this time she's on her own.'

'Toni still doesn't know?'

Liv shook her head. 'No. I'm keeping my distance. She's angry and has every right to be.'

'I still think she would have liked to have known what was happening.'

'If we ever make up, I'll tell her down the track. For now, I'd rather she just enjoys Ruby and tries to forget about what happened. But like I said, Mum will be happy to have your company.'

'And Gus, too,' Barb said. 'He's a nervous wreck.'

'I'm not surprised. I'm more nervous for Freddie than I am for myself. I can't believe he's doing this.'

Two weeks after Ruby had been found and Liv had returned to Sydney, Barb had invited Liv in for afternoon tea, saying she had some news.

'So, what's the big news?' Liv said, declining a piece of Barb's famous strawberry shortcake. She hardly had an appetite these days, and as much as she used to love the shortcake, just the thought of anything sweet made her stomach turn.

'Kidney news,' Barb said. 'Freddie has been tested. It turns out he's a match.'

Liv's mouth dropped open. 'What? Why would he do that? He doesn't even know me.'

'No, but he loves Gus, and Gus would do anything for me,' Barb said. 'I told Gus how devastated I was about the whole situation, and he decided to get tested. Mind you, he didn't tell me, and neither did Freddie until last night. Gus wasn't a match; he was tested first, and then Freddie stepped in and asked to be tested.'

Liv shook her head. 'I don't understand. I don't think I'd do that for someone I hardly know.'

'Freddie's sister was a heart and double lung transplant recipient fifteen years ago,' Barb said. 'I only learned this when they came to dinner last night. Unfortunately, Tessa contracted the flu a few months ago and ended up in ICU where she developed pneumonia. Her lungs couldn't handle it, and sadly, her system shut down. Freddie was very close with her and, according to Gus, has struggled in the last few months without her. He didn't say much about being tested other than he wouldn't want your sisters going through what he's been through losing Tessa.'

Emotion overwhelmed Liv. That Freddie would do this as a tribute to his sister was incredible, but she couldn't ask someone she barely knew to donate an organ.

'You're not going to have a say in it, Liv,' Barb continued. 'He's made his mind up. I believe your doctors will be contacting you tomorrow. Freddie had a counselling session with them this morning to ensure he was given all the details, including the risks, and to confirm he still wants to proceed.'

'And he still does?'

Barb nodded. 'As heartbroken as he was to lose his sister, he made the comment that a donor gave Tessa another fifteen years through the generosity of organ donation. While he and his family were celebrating the miracle they'd been given, another family was grieving the loss of a loved one. He thought he wouldn't be able to repay this generosity until he died, and his organs were harvested, but this gives him an opportunity to do something sooner.'

A buzzer beeped across the hospital's hallway, interrupting Liv's thoughts.

'You know,' Barb said, 'I feel so lucky to have met you and your family. I love Mandy, as you already know, and I feel like I'm getting to know your mum too. You're a lovely lot, you Montgomerys.'

Unease uncurled in Liv's stomach. She felt lucky to have met Barb too, but wasn't looking forward to the news she had to share with her. She opened her mouth. Her plans had been coming together over the last few weeks, and it really was time she shared them with the older woman. She closed her mouth as footsteps entered the hospital room.

'You've got no idea how happy that makes me to see you waiting for my kidney,' Freddie said, stopping at the end of the bed, Gus beside him. He grinned. 'I offered to help for purely selfish reasons, nothing to do with you.'

Tears filled Liv's eyes. 'I still can't believe you're doing this.' She turned to Gus. 'Especially after the nightmare you had to help me climb out of with Ruby.'

Gus shrugged. 'All in the past. Now we just need to think about the future and enjoy a long and happy one.'

'He's right, Liv, that's what we all need to do.'

Liv's hand flew to her mouth as Toni stepped into the room.

Barb stood. 'Boys, we might leave these sisters to chat.'

'I'll drop back in later,' Freddie said, winking at Liv. 'I've got a few instructions for you around the care of my kidney. There are certain foods and drinks it likes.'

Liv managed a weak smile, not taking her eyes off Toni.

Toni approached the bed when Barb and the two men were gone. 'You should have told me.'

'Mum *shouldn't* have told you,' Liv said. 'I didn't want to worry you, not after everything. I've given you enough grief to last a lifetime.' She hesitated. 'I know I've said it before, but I am sorry, Ton. My intentions were never to hurt you or Mandy. You know, I originally thought if I was to turn back time, I'd do it all the same, but I've come to realise that I could have saved everyone a lot of heartache if I'd told Mum that Mandy was pregnant and left her to deal with it.'

Toni sighed and sat down on the edge of the bed. 'If she hadn't been grieving for Dad, you probably would have done exactly that. You know, as much as I've been angry with you, I've come to realise a few things since Ruby's disappearance. The first is that my anger at you was partly me deflecting the anger I'd bottled up at myself. I was such a terrible mother to Ruby before she was taken. Until we found out that Mandy had her, I assumed it was the universe's way of punishing me, which I deserved.'

'You were struggling,' Liv said. 'And none of us saw that. It's called post-natal depression for a reason. It leaves you feeling depressed and unable to cope. I just wish I'd given you the information Petal gave me before Mandy gave birth. It explained how it affects adoptive parents in the same way as biological parents. I'm sorry I didn't give it to you, but I do wish you'd said something.'

'I couldn't tell you,' Toni said. 'At first, I was worried that you'd take Ruby back because you'd be upset with me, and then there was part of me that prayed you would take her back, but I was too ashamed to let on that I was failing.'

'From what I hear from Mum and Mandy, you're not struggling now,' Liv said, 'and that's what's important. And, if you do have problems, you speak to Joel or Mum or me if you can bear the thought of that.'

'I've got a better balance now,' Toni said. 'Losing Ruby was horrific. And then waiting to hear whether she'd be raised by Mandy or Joel and me when I knew how much I wanted her was hard, too.'

Liv reached out and squeezed Toni's hand, relief settling over her when Toni didn't flinch or pull away. 'Mandy seems to have accepted the decision.'

'She has. And, for the first time in my life, I can honestly say I enjoy having Mandy as a sister. I wish Dad was still alive to see that we have a relationship. He was always at me about Mandy's strong points and being accepting. If only I'd listened.'

'Life unfolds as it's meant to,' Liv said. Her cheeks coloured as her father's famous phrase rolled off her lips. 'Unless I get to it and try to manipulate things, that is.'

Toni gave a wry smile. 'The other thing I've realised is that I need to forgive you, and I need to thank you.'

Liv's mouth dropped open. 'What? Why? The thank you bit, that is.'

'Because you were right from the start. I wouldn't have wanted Mandy's baby. She probably would have been evaluated before Ruby was born and deemed unfit to raise the baby. She would have been put up for adoption, and we would have lost her,' Toni said, her voice quiet. 'And I may or may not have understood what an opportunity I gave up.' Tears filled her eyes. 'As much grief as I've given you over everything you did, I need to thank you. I'm not sure there was any way you'd have been able to talk me into raising Ruby.'

Liv wiped her cheeks with the back of her hand. 'It's turned out for the best, even if it was a bumpy ride to get here.'

Toni nodded. 'And now, this,' she said, waving her hands around at the hospital room. 'You have to go through this again.'

Liv smiled. 'I'm grateful to be able to go through this again. Knowing my kidney was failing has had me thinking a lot more about what's important.'

'Oh?'

'Family's important, Ton. I'm thinking of moving back to Melbourne. I've been thinking about it for a while, but then, with everything that happened with Ruby, I thought it better that I stay far, far away. But if you've really forgiven me, I'd love to be closer to you, Joel and Ruby, and Mum and Mandy too. I want to be part of Ruby's life, not just some aunt she sees a couple of times a year.'

Toni's eyes lit up with genuine delight. 'That'd be great, Liv. So great. We'd love you to be a bigger part of her life.'

Liv couldn't help but laugh. 'Imagine if I'd told you a couple of months back that I was moving back to Melbourne to be closer to you. You probably would have moved, scared I'd be wanting Ruby back.'

Toni smiled. 'Maybe. Or who knows, it might have been the thing that made me admit to struggling, or perhaps to make me realise how lucky I was to have Ruby if I'd thought you were going to take her. But like you said earlier, life unfolds as it's meant to be.'

'It does. However, Barb might not share our sentiments on that one. As excited as I am at the idea of returning to Melbourne, I haven't told her, and I'm painfully aware she'll be devastated.'

EPILOGUE
SEVEN MONTHS LATER

Liv drew in a lungful of salty sea air, a broad smile appearing on her lips as she watched Mandy take Ruby from her car seat and clip her into the stroller. How could the little girl be almost one?

In many ways, the last few months had passed in a blur of hospital procedures, recovery, and if Liv was honest, pain. But she was on the other side of it now. Seven months had passed since she'd undergone her second kidney transplant. She'd dealt with a minor infection three weeks after the operation, but antibiotics had cleared it quickly, and the issues since then, mainly side effects from the immunosuppressants she was taking, were relatively minor. It had been a relief to hand back the dialysis equipment which she desperately hoped she'd never have to use again, or at least not for the next twenty years. She'd been relieved that Freddie had recovered quickly from his procedure and hadn't experienced any complications. She still wasn't sure how she could ever thank him, but he'd reassured her that she already had. 'You've given me a chance to repay a little of what my sister's donor did fifteen years ago. He or she gave us an extra fifteen years together. I'm not sure I can ever really do enough to pay that back, so this at least pays it forward a little.'

'Mandy's doing an amazing job,' Sara said, breaking into Liv's thoughts as she stepped out from the passenger seat onto the footpath. 'I can't ever thank you enough for taking her to Sydney when you did. What you taught her about being independent still blows me away. Your dad was right that she was much more capable than I ever allowed her to be.'

Liv smiled. 'You can thank Barb for a lot of that. The two of them took off on all sorts of adventures when I thought they were sitting in Barb's apartment watching *Titanic*.'

Sara laughed. 'She's been amazing for Mandy, as has Izzy. I just wish your father was here to see how far she's come.'

'Me too,' Liv said. She'd realised in the last few months what a big hole her father had left in her life. Following his death, she'd hardly had time to allow herself to grieve with Mandy coming to stay, the Ruby saga and then the transplant. But during her recovery, she'd missed him terribly. She knew how much he would have wanted to help her, and his absence hit her every day. Barb's insistence on being there almost around the clock had helped fill the void, but it still wasn't the same.

'Are you coming, Livvy?' Mandy called over to her.

'We're waiting for Toni and Barb,' Liv called back. 'We'll catch up to you. Find a nice spot on the sand where we can all sit.'

Mandy nodded and took off with Ruby and Izzy along the coastal path.

'She'll go to our usual spot,' Sara said. 'She's a creature of habit along with everything else.'

'There's Toni and Barb,' Liv said, pointing in the direction of the car parking area. 'It's so nice she came down to Melbourne for a visit. She was nowhere near as upset as I thought she would be when I told her I was moving back. I guess us being here gives her an excuse for a holiday. And it's been lovely of you to let her stay with you.'

Sara's smile seemed to morph into a smirk.

'What?' Liv demanded.

'Nothing. Now come on, let's go and watch Ruby on the beach. I know Mandy plans to bury her in the sand, which she used to love as a little girl herself.'

* * *

A wave of pleasure washed over Mandy as she pointed out the family's usual spot on the beach to Izzy. Her beach memories from when she was a little girl were always at this spot. With the coloured beach houses lining the sand, it was easily identifiable as the place their father had loved. They'd played hide-and-seek around the beach houses for years, a game she'd be introducing Ruby to when she was old enough.

'It's a beautiful spot, Mands,' Izzy said. 'Sam loved it here too.' She picked up the front of the stroller so they could carry it across the sand, and Mandy found herself deep in thought about her two favourite men. It was nice to have a place to visit where she felt close to them both. And she missed them both so much. She gave herself a shake. Today was a happy day. All of Ruby's aunts, mothers and grandmothers would be here. When they were little, Toni had told her that she'd pushed their family apart, but now she knew that she – through Ruby – had brought them together. She hoped her father would be proud of her. The only thing that would have made today perfect was Joel being there too. But Toni had explained that him being away was a good thing. He'd started his new job with Qantas and all thoughts of moving to Dubai had been forgotten. Ruby's disappearance had made one thing very clear to both Toni and Joel, and that was the importance of family.

Mandy unclipped the straps on Ruby's pram and lifted the little girl out. She planted a kiss on her forehead before placing her on her bottom on the sand and sitting down beside her. Ruby immediately gathered fistfuls of sand and threw them into the air, giggling as she did. Mandy smiled. 'You're not even one yet, and look at you, my little love. You're so clever.'

'She's amazing, Mands,' Izzy said. 'She's smart like you.'

Mandy frowned. 'I'm not smart.'

'Someone told you that, didn't they?'

'Lots of people. I'm "challenged",' Mandy said, her fingers rising in air quotes.

'You should ignore them. I think you could do anything you set your mind to. You shouldn't let challenges hold you back. Sam always told me you were smart.'

Ruby continued throwing sand and as Mandy watched her, she pushed herself to her knees and crawled at high speed towards the water. Mandy jumped up and hurried after her. Ruby loved the water as much as she loved the sand, but Mandy hadn't taken her pants off yet. 'Hold on, little miss,' Mandy called after her. 'I need your pants.' Izzy followed them to the water's edge. 'She's got swimmers on underneath,' Mandy said. 'I just didn't want her knees getting sore if she was crawling.'

Izzy smiled. 'I told you you're clever. I never would have thought of that.'

Ruby slowed down and pushed herself back to a seated position, allowing Mandy and Izzy to catch up. As Mandy reached her, she looked up at her. 'Mama.'

Mandy stopped and stared at her daughter.

'Mama,' Ruby said again, a wide grin lighting up her features as she waved her arms at Mandy.

Mandy turned around and looked behind her. Had Toni, Liv, Barb and her mother caught up already? Ruby had used the words *hi* and *da* so far. Joel believed *da* was Ruby saying Dad, but Mandy and Toni didn't think that was the case as Ruby said it all the time when Joel wasn't home. But she hadn't said Mama before, and Toni wasn't there, which meant the word was being used for Mandy.

'Mama.' Ruby held out her arms to be picked up.

Mandy swooped down and swept her up, tears filling her eyes.

'She called you Mama,' Izzy said, the wonder in her voice evident. 'I can't believe she did that.'

'Mama,' Ruby said again, pushing her head against Mandy's and giving her a kiss on the cheek as Mandy did to her all the time. Mandy kissed her back, her tears now running freely.

'You okay, Mands?'

Mandy wiped her eyes with the backs of her hands and looked up to find Liv, Toni, their mother and Barb standing in front of them. She nodded. 'Just happy.'

'Aren't you going to tell them why?' Izzy prompted.

Mandy looked from Ruby to Toni and gave a gentle shake of her head. Hearing Ruby call her Mama was the most magical moment of her life. She wanted Toni to have this moment too. She wouldn't spoil it by telling her that Ruby had called her Mama first.

'I think I need to sit down,' Barb said. 'Why don't you and Ruby join me?' she looked to Mandy and Izzy. 'We could bury Ruby's legs or make a sandcastle.'

Mandy cheered and put Ruby down on the sand. 'Or better still, you could bury me. Dad used to do that all the time. I love it.'

'How about Liv and I go and get us some coffee while you do that,' Toni suggested. 'There's a kiosk over there,' she added, pointing towards a small take-out venue.

'Sounds good to me,' Sara said. 'I'll come with you to help carry them back.'

Barb, Mandy, and Izzy watched as the three women walked away.

Mandy turned to Barb. 'Do you remember in Sydney when I told you I was good at secrets?'

Barb nodded. 'And you were good at secrets. I never knew that Liv had said the baby was hers until Ruby went missing. I assumed Toni and your mum knew it was your baby.'

'I have another secret,' Mandy said, lowering her voice. 'One you can never tell Toni.'

'I think you should,' Izzy said. 'Why should she think she's the first one if Ruby does it to her?'

Mandy shook her head. 'No, it's a secret.'

'Oh, Mandy,' Barb said, 'this was what started the trouble in the first place. You can't keep things from Toni. She's Ruby's other mother.'

Mandy grinned. 'Ruby, tell me what you said before.'

Ruby dropped the sand in her fists and looked up at Mandy. 'Mama,' she said. 'Mama, Mama.'

Barb's mouth dropped open. 'Oh my. I wasn't expecting that. But I'm confused. Why can't we tell Toni? That seems like a strange secret. Ruby talking is a good thing. It's exciting.'

Mandy shook her head. 'Because she might be sad. Ruby hasn't called her Mama yet, and she might be sad or angry and jealous.'

Barb nodded. 'That's kind of you. You're a good sister and a good mother.'

'And a good keeper of secrets.'

Barb laughed. 'That goes without saying. You are the best keeper of secrets I've ever met.' She leaned her head closer to Mandy. 'Do you think you can keep another secret? I haven't told Gus yet, or Liv. In fact, your mum's the only one who knows my secret.'

Mandy nodded eagerly.

'I'm not just here for a holiday. I'm going to move to Melbourne to be closer to you and Ruby. I was waiting for the sale of my apartment to settle before I told you. I'm not going back to Sydney, love. I'm here to stay.'

Mandy's eyes widened. She looked from Izzy to Barb and back again. 'Are you joking?'

'No, I'm not. And,' Barb shook her head in disbelief, 'I can hardly believe this, but your mum has asked me to live with her.'

'Did you say yes?' Mandy held her breath, waiting for Barb to answer. Imagine if her mother and Barb were in the same house. She could visit all the time and see both of them.

Barb nodded, and Mandy flung her arms around the older woman, causing Barb and Izzy to laugh.

'It's wonderful news,' Izzy said as Mandy released Barb, 'but what about Gus? Won't he be upset if you move?'

'Possibly,' Barb said. 'But he's busy with his life and Freddie. He can always come and visit if he wants to. Living with Sara will be lovely. We have shared connections which has brought us together. We share our love for Mandy and Liv.'

'And Toni?' Mandy added.

'Hopefully, Toni,' Barb said. 'Don't forget, I don't really know Toni yet. I've only spent a little bit of time with her. But I hope that changes. And you too, Izzy,' she said, smiling at Ruby's other aunt. 'I've got lots of new friends to make in Melbourne. A whole new life to start.'

'You can be Ruby's great-grandma,' Mandy said. 'Mum doesn't have a mum, and Ruby doesn't have a great-grandma. You could be that person in her life.'

'Great-grandma?' Toni said as she and Liv re-joined the group with a tray of coffees each.

'Oh no,' Barb said. 'It was an idea of Mandy's. Don't worry, I don't expect to be anything other than Barb.'

Toni shook her head, smiling at Mandy. 'No, I think it's a wonderful idea. The more people in Ruby's life, the better. And you've officially joined the family now, so you'll need a title that sounds right, and Great-Grandma sounds wonderful to me.' She turned to Ruby. 'Don't you agree, my little darling?'

'Mama,' Ruby said and held her arms out to Toni.

Toni's eyes widened as she looked from Ruby to Mandy. 'Oh, my goodness. Did she really say that?'

'Mama,' Ruby said again.

Tears filled Toni's eyes as she picked up her daughter. 'This is the happiest moment of my life,' she said and stopped. Her joy evaporated as she looked at Mandy. 'I'm sorry, Mands. I didn't expect her to say that.'

'It's okay,' Mandy said, sharing a secret smile with Barb. 'It's the happiest day of my life too. Barb is going to live with Mum, I have a daughter, and my sisters love me.'

'Barb's going to live with Mum?' Liv said, looking from Barb to Sara. 'Really?'

The two older women nodded.

'As soon as my apartment settles,' Barb said.

'See,' Mandy said, taking in the wide smiles of Liv, Toni, her mother, Izzy and Barb, 'it really is the happiest day of my life.'

'Mama,' Ruby said again, this time holding her arms out to Mandy.

'She knows,' Toni said through her tears and handed the little girl to Mandy. 'Oh, Mands, she knows we're her mamas. She's so clever.'

Mandy took the little girl in her arms and kissed the top of her head. Sam had always called her clever, but she'd never believed him.

Until now.

ACKNOWLEDGEMENTS

It's incredibly rewarding to see a story that started as a small question – *what if?* – come to life. There are several people who have helped bring My Sister's Baby to publication to whom I owe a very special thank you.

To my exceptional team of early readers: Judy, Maggie, Ray, Robyn and Tracy. Thank you for dedicating your time to reading and providing feedback on another of my stories. I'm very lucky to have you supporting my journey.

To Kirsty McManus and Christie Stratos; a HUGE thank you to you both for stepping in at a point where the manuscript needed fresh eyes. Your insights have helped bring the story to another level.

To Janine Kimberley, thank you for your continued support of my books, and particularly for sharing your experiences and personal insights around the topic of support housing.

To Marion Waba, I'd like to extend a heartfelt thank you for sharing your intimate experience with dialysis treatment. Your courage and resilience are inspiring, and your story added depth and authenticity to this narrative.

To Stacey Collins, your knowledge of midwifery and the role that a doula can play, were crucial in ensuring the realism of this storyline.

To Isobel Akenhead, thank you for not only offering me the opportunity to join the Boldwood stable of authors, but also for your invaluable editorial insights.

To the entire team at Boldwood Books. Thank you for making me feel so welcome and for your expertise and guidance with the publication of this story.

Lastly, to my readers, reviewers and the extraordinary circle of friends and family who tirelessly promote my books, thank you for your continuing support.

ABOUT THE AUTHOR

Louise Guy is a bestselling author of six novels, blends family and friendship themes with unique twists and intrigue. Her characters captivate readers, drawing them deeply into their compelling stories and struggles. My Sister's Baby is her first novel with Boldwood Books. She lives in Australia.

Sign up to Louise Guy's mailing list for news, competitions and update on future books.

Follow Louise on social media:

facebook.com/LouiseGuy

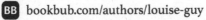
bookbub.com/authors/louise-guy

Boldw@@d

Boldwood Books is an award-winning fiction publishing company seeking out the best stories from around the world.

Find out more at www.boldwoodbooks.com

Join our reader community for brilliant books, competitions and offers!

Follow us
@BoldwoodBooks
@TheBoldBookClub

Sign up to our weekly deals newsletter

https://bit.ly/BoldwoodBNewsletter

Milton Keynes UK
Ingram Content Group UK Ltd.
UKHW040051310124
436962UK00002B/9

9 781835 331279